Milly Johnson is a half-Scots, half-Sassenach author who lives in Barnsley, South Yorkshire with her two sons, a squadron of cats and Teddy, her German Eurasier pup.

Her hobbies include salivating over handsome vampires, watching Nicolas Cage films, taking warm holidays on big ships and learning Italian.

She is also a very proud Patron of Haworthcatrescue.org and promoter of their £2 million appeal to build a cat re-homing centre. All donations gratefully received.

A Summer Fling is Milly's fourth novel.

Also by Milly Johnson

The Yorkshire Pudding Club
The Birds and the Bees
A Spring Affair

A
Summer Fling

Milly Johnson

POCKET
BOOKS

LONDON • SYDNEY • NEW YORK • TORONTO

First published in Great Britain by Pocket Books, 2010
An imprint of Simon & Schuster UK Ltd
A CBS COMPANY

3 5 7 9 10 8 6 4 2

Simon & Schuster UK Ltd
1st Floor
222 Gray's Inn Road
London WC1X 8HB

www.simonandschuster.co.uk

Simon & Schuster Australia
Sydney

A CIP catalogue record for this book is available
from the British Library

ISBN 978-1-84739-283-1

Typeset in Bembo by M Rules
Printed by CPI Cox & Wyman, Reading, Berkshire RG1 8EX

This book is dedicated to six fabulous women who inspired this book.

To Nancy Scrimshaw, Sheila Isherwood and Mary Sutcliffe, who taught me that age is no barrier to friend-ship, laughter or fun, especially when eating illegal mince pies in front of a Yorkshire range.

And to my SUN Sisters: Pam Oliver, Helen Clapham and Karen Baker. Life would not be the same if we didn't share our stories about work, men – and what some of us have done on a mountain.

'To love and be loved is to feel the Sun from both sides.'

DAVID VISCOTT

April

Chapter 1

After only three words of Malcolm's speech, Dawn tuned out. She didn't want to listen to his monotonous voice. Nor did she want to think about old people retiring from Bakery departments. Her head was too full of confetti and honeymoons and she was counting down the hours until tomorrow morning, when she would finally be choosing her wedding dress.

While Malcolm was still droning on about being at the end of an era and raising his thick polystyrene cup full of cheap white wine in Retiring-Brian's direction, she was calculating how long it was to her big day. *Eighty-four days, eighteen hours, eleven minutes and forty-three seconds, forty-two seconds, forty-one seconds.* Every tick of the clock brought her one tiny step closer to being Mrs Calum Crooke.

People were clapping now, so Dawn joined in to make it appear that she was part of the celebrations. Malcolm was smiling, she noticed. Crikey. Fourteen million more of those and he'd have a wrinkle. Probably wind, thought Dawn, watching Malcolm's face return to its normal 'pissed off with the world' cast. Mind you, he *was* very pissed off with the world at the moment. He had presumed, as Deputy Head of Bakery, that he would jump straight into the top slot when Brian retired. He wasn't best pleased to find out he was being shunted over to Cheese and the new Head of Bakery was going to be an unknown outsider that the MD, Mr McAskill, was bringing in.

That he was going to be 'Cheese Head' and no longer a deputy, didn't do much to take the edge off his disappointment. Bakery was growing and secure, Cheese was sinking. Rumour had it that Mr McAskill was in the process of phasing it out totally. And Cheese was an entirely male department, unlike Bakery, which would now be all female. There would be far less opportunity to look down blouses or sidle up closer to his co-workers than he should do by the photocopying machines. Dawn shuddered as she remembered feeling his hand on her bum on her first day in the department. He'd said 'whoops' and left it at that, but she'd known it was deliberate. She had kept herself out of his way as much as possible after that.

Raychel stood alone, swilling the awful wine around in her cup. She was a natural wallflower, most comfortable against the sidelines. She felt awkward in social situations like this, but also she felt obliged to stay behind after work with the others and wave Brian off. He was an affable enough man, and talking about spending the summer in a caravan with his wife, a new microwave and his Cairn Terrier, Lady, was probably the most animated she had seen him since she joined the department late last year.

When she heard that Brian was leaving, she'd presumed that Malcolm would take over as boss, seeing as he had been acting more or less as Head anyway. She had started looking at the noticeboard for any up-and-coming jobs within other departments then. She didn't like Malcolm one bit. He was too touchy-feely for her liking, using any excuse to have skin-to-skin contact and Raychel hated to be touched by anyone – except her husband Ben. She hadn't told Ben about Malcolm and his inability to understand the concept of 'personal space' because he would have been down at the office like a shot to sort the little squirt out. So she was delighted and as surprised as the other three women in the department to hear that Malcolm was being moved to Cheese, and that Grace – the oldest lady in the department – was being made Deputy. The big boss, James McAskill, was bringing in a woman from outside as Head of Bakery, which had got the tongues wagging.

Not that Raychel had discussed any of this with her co-workers. They had all been in the same department for ages now and hadn't progressed beyond the 'morning, nice day' or 'have a good weekend' stage – give or take a bit of work talk. They were nice enough women, all different ages though. And now there was going to be another woman amongst them. Raychel wondered how all these changes would affect the dynamics of the department, but it didn't really matter that much. Work was a place to get her head down and earn a crust, nothing else.

Anna gave Brian a big kiss on the cheek. As bosses went, he was a nice man who just couldn't be arsed any more, if the truth be told. His retirement had been long in his sights and he had let Malcolm take over most of the running of the department. Thank goodness that creep was leaving as well. He hadn't been at all happy about his move to Cheese though, that was obvious. Actually he was a miserable sod at the best of times. It was as if he had a row with his wife every morning and was intent on polluting the office air with a bad mood. He was always so rude to his underlings. 'Please' and 'Thank you's didn't feature in his vocabulary and he would bark 'tea' at any of them when he wanted a drink. Plus she hated the way his eyes flicked to her breasts when he was talking to her. She wondered what sort of woman found him attractive enough to marry him. But apparently he could sustain a relationship: he had been married for over fifteen years, which is more than she could say for herself.

Anna listened to Brian getting all excited about spending the summer in a caravan on the coast and she envied him that enthusiasm for something. She had not one single thing to look forward to this weekend or after. She couldn't get interested in the storylines of *Coronation Street*, didn't fancy anything particular to eat, had lost the ability to lose herself in a book and knock out the image of her fiancé bonking the nineteen-year-old hired help in his barber's shop. Life stretched before Anna – longer, greyer and wetter than the entire British coastline in February.

Grace picked up Malcolm's retirement present to look at it – a carriage clock which had a very loud tock. She could almost hear it saying 'slow death, slow death, slow death' to the beat.

'You next, with any luck!' said Brian in her ear hole.

'Wha . . . at?' said Grace, before quickly recovering. 'Oh yes, maybe.' *God forbid*. The thought of standing where Brian was now, admiring her own clock, being toasted in warm plonk, brought on a cold, clammy sweat at the back of her neck. She came over ever-so-slightly faint.

Slow death, slow death, slow death.

'I just can't understand why you'd want to up the ante when you'd got the chance to leave this place and live a life of leisure. Could have been your retirement do as well,' said Brian with a smile.

'Oh well, you know me, I like a challenge,' said Grace. She had worked with Brian for just over three years now and liked his merry ways, even though he was a man who was born old and was just happily growing into himself. He would *so* enjoy not having to set his alarm clock any more and spending his days pottering around busily doing nothing. Apart from his cheery disposition, he reminded her so much of her husband Gordon – too much for comfort, as he prattled on about the joys of retirement.

Grace's thoughts drifted off. Did Brian ever think when he was seventeen and in the dance halls that he would one day be standing here, getting excited about taking a new microwave to Skegness? Was that the zenith of his ambition? Or was Grace not normal in being the same age as him and panicking every time the word 'caravan' entered a conversation? She'd done the caravan thing when her three children were small and they had enjoyed it, even though she herself had found it far from relaxing as a choice of holiday. The children were adults now but she was still very close to them and didn't want to spend weeks and weeks away from them and her grandchildren with only Gordon for company.

She had always said that she would leave him when the children grew up. She wondered how many other women had resolved to do the same and were still there years after the kids had moved out because they simply weren't brave enough to go. Her son and two daughters had left a huge, gaping hole in her home when they left, as if they had taken its heart along with them.

Her eyes caught Malcolm refilling his cup with wine. He wasn't a happy man by any stretch. She could easily believe the rumours he was being moved to the much less prestigious department of Cheese because he wasn't efficient enough to handle the growing Bakery department. Malcolm Spatchcock was neither liked nor respected, although his ego was so big that he was oblivious to that fact.

Grace only hoped that she wouldn't be wishing Malcolm back after meeting her new boss. Still, *Mrs Christie Somers* would have to be really bad to knock Malcolm off the unpopularity stakes, ghastly little gnome. She had worked under his inefficient management for too long.

The wine and crisps were gone now and people were starting to pack up and drift off. Grace's weekend stretched out long and stark in front of her. Same old, same old. Babysitting her granddaughter tonight while Gordon went to the Legion and her daughter and son-in-law went out for some posh meal. Shopping, washing and cleaning tomorrow, then on Sunday morning she would make the lunch, clear up, iron and then sit down in front of *Heartbeat* – or really break out and watch *Frost* – before a hot bath and bed, ready for the week ahead.

She looked at the office youngsters from other departments filing out of the door, full of Friday night beans. She hadn't done that whole donning lippy and going out with friends thing for well over twenty-five years. She said goodnight to Brian and her three co-workers. They all seemed nice women, although they didn't really mix much. Still, the atmosphere at work was so much lighter than it was at home. Gordon's hair had gone grey in his thirties, but when did he get so grey in his head? Life would have been so much easier for Grace had she done the same.

Chapter 2

Calum was virtually sitting on the telephone but it would have rung forever had Dawn not come in from the kitchen and picked it up. She mouthed 'Idle beggar' at him, but he was too lazy even to look up.

'Hello, love,' said the cheery voice down the line.

'Hi, Muriel,' said Dawn. Calum exhaled loudly and waved his hands like an irate air-traffic controller. The message was clearly *I'm not here if she asks.*

'So, what time are you picking me up tomorrow, pet?' asked her future mother-in-law brightly.

'Half-past ten all right for you, Mu?'

'Well, I'll make sure I'm up, seeing as it's a special occasion,' said Muriel.

'I'm so excited, I bet I don't sleep much.'

'Knock yourself out with a few lagers. That's what I do when I can't sleep, lass!'

Dawn laughed. Muriel was ever so funny sometimes. She had laughed with Mu from the first time they met, over two years ago, in the miserable hairdressing salon where Dawn used to work. Dawn had given her a perm and Muriel had chattered on for two solid hours. She had been an absolute tonic that day with her rough, bawdy sense of humour. She had exploded into Dawn's life when she badly needed some laughs.

'Is our Calum back?'

'Yes, but you've just missed him.'

Calum stuck up a satisfied thumb.

'Aw well!' said Muriel with a deep sigh. 'Mind you, it is Friday and a bloke deserves a pint after a hard week at work.'

Dawn didn't know about the hard week. All he seemed to do was faff about on a fork-lift truck and have fag breaks.

'Anyway, when you see him, tell him Killer's brought him a box of DVDs.'

'I will.'

'See you tomorrow then, pet.'

'See you, Mu.'

Dawn clicked the phone off and Calum stood up and stretched like a lean, scraggy street cat.

'Killer has brought you some DVDs apparently,' Dawn delivered the message.

'Oh, cheers.'

'Not pirates, are they?' she asked suspiciously.

'Don't be daft, they're from house clearances.'

'And what do you do with them?'

'Questions, questions,' he sighed. 'Sell them on for him down the pub – for a cut.'

'OK,' said Dawn, temporarily satisfied by his answer. 'So, what do you want for your tea?' she asked.

'Thought we were having a Chinese?' he said.

'And I thought we were cutting back. I've got a wedding dress to buy tomorrow.'

Calum scratched his head, leaving his hair all sexily mussed up.

'We've got to live, Dawn! We've both been working all week. We need a bit of a treat.'

'OK then,' she reluctantly agreed. He could always talk her round. 'I'm hungry now; shall I ring up and order? I'll have chicken and mushroom with fried rice and *won tons*. Are we sharing? If we are, don't get that black bean thing.' She went to the drawer for the Chinese menu. It was at the top of a stack of takeaway menus all clipped neatly together. Her fastidious organizational skills were something Calum teased her about on a regular basis.

'I'll share if you want. But I thought I'd go out for a couple and then pick it up on the way back.'

'Aw! Don't go out!' Dawn tutted, disappointed.

Calum yawned. 'Just for a couple. Won't be any more than that, 'cos I'm shattered.'

'Now, where have I heard that before?'

Calum grinned his cheeky schoolboy smile that had got him into and out of all sorts of trouble ever since he was old enough to use it to its full advantage. It disarmed Dawn, as usual.

'I promise this time,' he said. 'No later than ten past nine. You have the plates warmed up for us.'

'Oh, anything else I should do?' asked Dawn with her hands on her hips.

'Funny you should ask. You couldn't lend me twenty quid, could you?'

Dawn opened her purse and handed over the money with a sigh, hating herself for being unable to say no. Especially as she knew that at ten o'clock she would, most likely, have given up waiting for Calum to come home early. She would go and make herself a cheese toastie. Calum would roll in after midnight, having forgotten the Chinese. She hoped one day he would break the pattern and surprise her, but so far he hadn't.

'Oh bloody hell, I've burned the garlic bread!' said Ben as the smoke alarm went off.

Raychel followed his mad dash into the kitchen and laughed.

'It's not funny, Ray, I was really looking forward to that,' said Ben, looking like a little kid who had just watched his ice-cream drop off his cornet and get eaten by a lucky passing mongrel.

Raychel grabbed the broom handle and poked up at the smoke alarm, but she was too small to reach it.

'Shift yourself, shorty,' said Ben, pushing her gently out of the way. He stretched up his long, muscular arm to depress the button with his big thumb. 'God, that's better; it was deafening me!'

'Look, it's not that bad, Ben,' said Raychel, inspecting the damage. 'It's only the top bit that's burned. I can cut it off.'

'Can you really do that? For me?' He sank to the floor and pretended to thank God.

Raychel slapped him playfully. 'You're so easily pleased.'

He grabbed her around the legs and pulled her to him as she squealed. He was almost as tall as her full height on his knees.

'I'm not actually. I'd say I was rather fussy myself.'

Raychel looked down into his lovely, sweet, smiling face. The stubble was growing back even though he'd had a good shave that morning. Dark and manly, his arms were tight around her. His body was hard with muscle and solid against her. She loved him so much.

'I'll get the pasta dished up then, shall I?'

'In a minute,' he said, savouring the feel of her, curling strands of her long, black hair around his finger, taking in her long-faded perfume. He could have breathed her in for hours.

'Am I enough for you?' she said, eventually. It was a question he had heard so many times and he answered it as always.

'Ray, you're all I could ever want.'

Chapter 3

Grace got up the next morning at five-thirty and watched the *Teletubbies*, *Bob the Builder* and *Thomas the Tank Engine* for a brain-numbing two and a half hours with four-year-old Sable. The combination of a young child's energy and an early morning following a restless night made her feel far older than her fifty-five years. Gordon was, of course, in bed. It was women's work getting up and seeing to the children. Or, at least, that was the regime she had always been used to – first at home with Mum and Dad, then when she married the widower with the four dependants: Laura aged six, Paul aged five, Sarah aged three and Rose aged fifty-four. It was funny to think she was older than her mother-in-law was when she died. Rose had seemed like an old, old woman.

Sarah arrived at eleven with her customary 'Sorry I'm late. Thanks for letting her stay the night. I know it was last minute.'

'It's all right, love,' said Gordon, up and dressed now in his gardening clothes, his thick, steel-grey hair still wet from a leisurely shower.

'Any chance you could look after her for another hour?' asked Sarah in her best wheedling little girl tone. 'Just so I can go to the supermarket?'

' 'Course she can stay here,' said Gordon, his voice drowning out anything Grace might have had to say on the subject.

He chucked Sable under the chin. 'She can come out and watch her grandad plant some seeds.'

'It's far too chilly for her to be outside,' said Sarah, wrapping her fur-trimmed maternity coat a little further around herself at the mere thought of it.

'Well, she can stay inside with her grandma then,' said Gordon. *Grandma.* The word grated on Grace's nerves like a fingernail scraping down a blackboard. She preferred Nana and Gordon knew that. It was as if he was using the word on purpose – a Chinese water torture slow drip, drip: 'you *will* be old'.

'I promise I won't be longer than two hours,' beamed Sarah, happy at having an extension to her freedom. 'Three at the most.'

She tried to ignore how tired her mother looked and concentrated on her father's expression of bonhomie instead. Gordon disappeared out to his allotment. Grace wrestled with trying to get the washing done, the beds stripped and entertaining a hyper Sable. She needed to go out shopping herself but she was exhausted. Gordon was so generous with other people's time.

Sarah came back after lunch, just as Sable had drifted off to sleep. And just as the postman arrived with two catalogues for caravan sites in Blegthorpe-on-Sea.

Calum's loud beer-snoring awoke Dawn. She went downstairs to try and sleep on the sofa but what she gained in peace levels, she lost in comfort. The sofa was old and past it; they really could do with another one but every spare penny was being put aside for the wedding. Well, every spare penny of hers, that was. At least Calum had a job at the moment, and one he was sticking at – not that it brought in mega-bucks. But where she was saving everything she could, Calum contributed what was left out of his 'social fund'. She would have to get a loan out at this rate for the honeymoon, but she was going to have the fairytale. If it took her the rest of her life to pay off her wedding day, she would have the frock, the flowers and the fancy cake. She knew it was the start to a marriage that her mum and dad would have wanted for her. Then, when the wedding debt had been paid off, they could start looking at something a bit better than Calum's dump of a house. Dawn had moved into it eight months ago and not managed to persuade Calum to do anything to it. There were still wires hanging down from the ceiling, bare plaster walls, furniture that looked as if it had been dragged out of a skip. He was five years younger than her. Dawn rationalized that as some sort of excuse for his student-like existence.

Calum was still in bed when she pulled up in front of her future mother-in-law's council house semi at the other end of town. She beeped the horn of her antique, but thankfully reliable Fiesta, and a minute later Muriel wobbled down the path in tired leggings, a grubby-looking fleece and flip-flops. Not that Dawn would ever have been ashamed to be seen with her. Muriel was Muriel, and Dawn loved her to bits, just as she was.

'Morning, lovely,' said Muriel with an excited little half-toothless grin. The Crookes were a rough family, but they had taken Dawn to their bosom. This was especially important to Dawn since her own parents had died in a car crash sixteen years ago and left a gaping hole in her heart. She missed them so much. She wished it was her mum sitting in the car beside her now, helping to pick out her wedding clothes. But Muriel Crooke was the next best thing.

Their first stop was 'Everything but the Bride' on the outskirts of town by the new Tesco. The tired display in the window was awful and was a perfect indication of what lay inside. A cracked, headless mannequin with no bust was wearing a white dress that was the colour of old greying knickers and would have better befitted a toilet roll doll of the 1970s. The accompanying bridesmaid mannequin did have a head, and a face that had been painted on by someone with a very shaky hand and no artistic talent: she wore the pained expression of a kid being given a wedgie. She looked uncomfortable in her lilac satin dress that had long faded in the sun. Yellowing confetti was sprinkled around their feet, resembling bird poo.

Dawn went in but knew instantly that she wouldn't find her dress in here. The buyer wanted a slap. There wasn't a lot of choice because the owner was obviously phasing the wedding dresses out and prom dresses in. Each one seemed the same as the rest but in a different colour. It was as if there was only one standard pattern for all the frocks – big wide skirt and puffy sleeves – with slight variations of neckline or ribbon/sequin detail. They weren't harassed by the sales assistant whose ear was stuck on the phone.

'. . . it can't be too short, you were there when we measured you. I asked you if that length felt comfortable and you said yes. Well, maybe you should have had on the shoes you'd be wearing for your wedding. If you come in here in flats to be measured up and you're wearing heels on the day, how can that be our fault?'

Dawn reckoned the gold stars for customer service might be thin on the ground in this place.

Muriel pulled a face at her, making Dawn chuckle. They slid out of the shop and Dawn took a big gulp of air.

'If that were me on the other end of that phone, I'd have slammed it down, got a taxi over here and smashed her cocky bleeding face in,' said Muriel.

Dawn was laughing so hard it took her four attempts to open her car door. She knew Muriel would tell the others how the day went, adding her funny embellishments. She hoped she would save it until Dawn was present to hear it.

They drove through Penistone and to stop number two, 'Love and Marriage', a far superior site on the Holmfirth Road. The window display was gorgeous: an ivory dress around a wire frame that represented an exaggerated hourglass figure. It was surrounded by handbags and shoes with expensive designer names. This was a pendulum swing to the other end of the market. A frighteningly big one if those names were anything to go by: Choo, Prada, Chloe, Louboutin . . .

They had barely stepped foot in the shop when an assistant bore down on them offering help.

'Just looking, thanks,' said Dawn.

'Are you searching for anything in particular?' pressed the assistant, giving Muriel a sneaky look up and down, which Muriel saw and her lip instinctively curled back over her teeth.

'I don't know,' said Dawn, wishing she could just wander around for a bit, unharassed.

'This is nice, Dawn,' said Muriel, picking out a long, cream dress. 'Can't find the price tag though.'

'Nine thousand,' said snotty assistant woman.

'Pounds?' gasped Muriel. 'You're having a laugh?'

'No, it's a Vladimir Darq. The reason it's so cheap is that it's second-hand.'

Muriel's jaw dropped. Cheap was the last word that came to her mind. She was speechless with amazement that someone would pay that amount of money for a *frock*.

'He's a famous designer,' said the assistant. 'You *have* heard of him, presumably?'

'Can't be that famous if I've never heard of him!' sniffed Muriel, enjoying that she was rankling the snotty cow.

'I have,' nodded Dawn. 'I didn't realize he was a wedding dress designer though.'

'He doesn't make bridal gowns any more,' said the assistant. 'This dress was from his very last collection of them – very much sought after.'

'Aye, by people with more money than sense.' Muriel clicked her tongue loudly.

'I'm not looking for anything that . . . fancy,' said Dawn. Of course the assistant knew she meant 'expensive' by 'fancy'. She'd taken one look at the pair of them and knew they'd be leaving empty-handed. The mother, she presumed, would have thought a Vera Wang was something that came with fried rice and prawn crackers.

'Our range starts at five thousand for this one,' said the assistant, presenting a plain white satin dress in a thick polythene cover.

'Oh,' said Dawn. She cooed over the dress to be polite, but all parties knew this was a no-go sale opportunity. Dawn made noises of 'maybe having to go home and look at some magazines first,' in order to leave the shop with some dignity intact. Two minutes later, she let loose a long breath of relief as she stepped outside.

'She thinks she's in Paris not bloody Barnsley!' Muriel laughed loudly on the doorstep. 'Twenty-two quid for a pair of tights? A pair of tights, did you see?'

It was as they were coming back to Barnsley, via the small, pretty village of Maltstone, that Dawn braked hard opposite the church, nearly sending Muriel through the windscreen.

'Didn't know there was a bridal shop here, did you, Mu?'

'I wouldn't know,' said Muriel with a sniff. 'I've no reason to come to Maltstone. There's nothing around here for me.' She wasn't a woman for garden centres and rural tea-shops.

Dawn reversed into a parking spot in front of a shop with a bay-window full of the prettiest display of bridalwear. Above the door hung a sign in romantic, swirly text, saying simply 'White Wedding'.

The doorbell tinkled daintily as Dawn and Muriel entered.

' 'King hell, it's a Tardis!' said Muriel over-loudly as the narrow shop seemed to go on forever in length. Racks of dresses lined the walls, and showcases of tiaras and shoes ran floor to the cottage-low ceiling. Dawn's mouth opened in a round O of delight. *This is more like it!*

A very slim and smart assistant greeted them with a big

smile. On her plain, black fitted dress she wore the name badge
'Freya'. She was probably the same age as Muriel, thought
Dawn, although with her coiffeured hair and unchewed nails,
she looked fifteen years younger.

'Can I help you?' Freya asked Dawn politely.

'I'm getting married and I er . . . need a dress,' replied Dawn
shyly.

'Well, do feel free to wander,' said Freya. 'I will say though,
don't judge the dress until you have tried it on. You'd be surprised how many brides go out looking for one particular style
only to find it doesn't suit them at all.'

'Thank you,' said Dawn, feeling very much at ease in this
shop. She and Muriel had a look around but Dawn realized she
might need some expert help after all.

'I don't know where to start, there's just so many,' she said.
She wanted to get it right because what if she found a dress,
bought it, then spotted another one that was nicer? That
thought had tortured her a few times.

'Well, let's start with colour,' said the assistant. She studied
Dawn's pale, heavily freckled skin and her shoulder-length
copper hair. 'May I recommend ivory rather than white? White
isn't always flattering, especially to people with pale skin like
yourself. Size 10, at a guess?'

'Spot on,' returned Dawn. Freya went to the rack of 10s as
Muriel was pulling size 24s off the hangers and holding them
up against herself.

'And are we going to be a summer bride or a winter one?'
asked Freya.

'June,' said Dawn.

'I might try on one myself,' said Muriel. 'Get Ronnie to
renew his vows, seeing as I'm a lot thinner than the first time
we went down the aisle.'

Freya's face never twitched, even though Muriel was twenty-
five stone plus now.

'We'll have a joint do,' laughed Dawn.

Freya pulled out a long, tapering gown, shaking out the creases.

'This is silk, ivory as you see, a bow on the back, beaded detail on the front bodice. Very flattering for the smaller-busted woman.'

'Not do me any good then,' snorted Muriel and laughed so hard that her enormous and flimsily restrained breasts jiggled like two giant blancmanges. The bra hadn't been built that could hold them in place without industrial strength scaffolding.

'It's lovely,' said Dawn, but she was shaking her head. 'It's not leaping out at me, though.'

'OK,' said Freya, and flicked the plastic protective case swiftly back over it. 'What about this?' She presented something swimming with ruffles.

'Oooh,' squealed Muriel.

'Too fancy,' said Dawn quietly. 'Sorry, it's not me at all!'

'Oh, don't apologize,' said Freya. 'Finding out what you don't want is the most effective way to lead us to what you do want. So, less frills . . . let me see.'

She pulled out a very unfussy number in satin.

'Ah, it's too plain. Heck, I'm not easy to please, am I?' Dawn half-expected Freya to sigh in that annoyed way that Calum's sister Demi was always doing.

'Don't worry,' said Freya, though. 'I've seen would-be brides come in here and reject forty dresses!'

'How much is this?' called Muriel, holding up a white satin gown. There was enough material in it to make a sail for a billionaire's yacht.

'That particular one is three thousand pounds,' said Freya.

'Chuffing hell, they aren't cheap, are they?' said Muriel and slid it back on the rail, none too straight either, although Freya didn't give a hint of disapproval.

'This one, perhaps?'

'Neck's too high.' Dawn shook her head. 'That's gorgeous though.' She pointed to a rather full-skirted confection in white. Freya didn't look convinced that Dawn and the frock were a good match, but hung it up in the changing room for her all the same. A couple of minutes later, Dawn emerged to show herself off.

'Bleeding hell, where's your sheep, Bo Peep?' asked Muriel with a snort.

The dress drowned Dawn and, true enough, the white material made her skin look like the colour of uncooked pastry. Freya nodded in an 'I told you so', but kindly, way. She was holding up a gown that made Dawn's eyes shine.

'It's from our vintage collection,' explained Freya. 'It's a very special dress.'

Long and flowing, it had a beautiful scooped neck with peach rosebud detail, a full skirt, three-quarter sleeves and was made of smooth, smooth ivory silk. Dawn's hands reached greedily for the hanger. She closed the dressing room curtain and when she opened it again and emerged in that dress, both Muriel and Freya gasped with delight.

'Gorgeous,' said Freya. The dress suited the tall, slim woman to a T. The ivory lent her pale skin some colour, her neck looked extended by inches and the fitted bodice gave the illusion of curves where there were few.

'Oh. My. God. This is the one, I just know it,' said Dawn. She was almost in tears imagining the skirt trailing behind her, brushing the aisle floor. 'Do you know anything about the original owner? Was she happy?' She didn't want a dress with negative vibes stored in the threads.

'Very,' Freya said, adding, 'Eventually.'

'Well, you would say that,' parried Muriel. But Dawn wanted to believe Freya anyway. She was hooked.

'It is lovely, mind,' said Muriel. 'How much is it though?'

'It's fifteen hundred pounds. Any alterations are free and you will most likely need them despite it being a near-perfect fit now. Most brides lose some weight and have to have their dresses nipped in nearer the date.'

'Fifteen hundred quid – for a second-hand frock!' Muriel gave a mirthless little laugh.

'It's very special,' said Freya again, smiling. 'It looks meant for you.'

Dawn gulped. It was over her budget, but she knew anything else would be second-best. She could cut back on something else, but not the dress. She would pray for a miracle pay rise or a big win. She would start putting an extra line on the lottery, starting this week.

'I don't care – I'll take it,' she heard herself say.

An hour later, Dawn had spent another two hundred and fifty pounds on shoes, a medium-length ivory veil, a tiara and some matching earrings. She hid the purchases on her Visa card and tried not to let worries about the expense spoil the excitement.

'Look at this one,' said Gordon. 'It's an eight berth.'

Grace dutifully left the sink, peered over his shoulder at the catalogue and then returned to scrubbing the Sunday dinner pans, which were infinitely more interesting.

'Plenty of room for our Sarah and Hugo and Sable and the baby when it arrives, and our Laura and Joe.'

And Paul too, Grace added to herself, but there wouldn't have been much point saying it aloud. Gordon was a master at ignoring what he didn't want to hear. Paul was as good as dead to his father.

'It's got central heating and a built-in washing machine and dishwasher.' He looked at Grace standing with the tea-towel. 'It's got more than we've got here, in fact. It would be just ideal for us when you retire. You're over ready for a long rest.'

'I'm only fifty-five, Gordon.'

'Only?' he snorted. 'You're getting older every day. You've got to be in the next batch of early retirements. I can't understand why you haven't been asked already. They've retired loads at your place!'

Grace shrugged, but didn't say any more. If Gordon had a magic wand, she was sure he would use it to age her and see her in a bathchair wrapped in a nice shawl.

'I don't know, anyone else at your age would be looking forward to winding down. Can't you imagine, long summers and walks by the sea? According to the brochure, there's even a social club on site and Skegness, Mablethorpe and Ingoldmells are only a short drive away.'

'Gordon, wouldn't you prefer to go on lots of fortnights abroad in the sun? Italy, Spain, France?'

'Oh, I can't do with all that travelling.'

'It's only two hours to Spain. It would take us not much less than that to get to Blegthorpe in the car.'

Gordon changed tack then. 'Oh, I can't be doing with all that heat.'

'We don't have to go in August!'

'Anyway, we couldn't take the grandkiddies abroad. Our Sarah wouldn't agree to that.'

Grace doubted that. Sarah was greedy as far as babysitting duties were concerned. It wasn't that Grace minded helping her daughter out, Sable was her granddaughter after all and she loved her dearly, but Sarah presumed that if her mother wasn't at work, she should be on hand 24/7 for her convenience. Grace also knew that Sarah was another one who was pressurizing her to retire early so she could take over as permanent child-minder and Sarah could escape back to work.

'We should go for a weekend and take a look at some of these in the flesh,' suggested Gordon, flicking through the pages of the 'Clark's Caravans' brochure.

'Gordon, we've talked about this before and I don't really want to,' said Grace, standing her corner for once. She couldn't remember how many times they'd had this interchange and as usual Gordon did not acknowledge her point of view.

'You don't know what you'd like until you try it,' he said, which was ironic seeing as he would have spontaneously combusted had he ever tried anything out of his very small comfort zone. 'It'll be lovely having our own caravan instead of renting someone else's, just you wait and see,' he said, because Gordon Beamish always knew best.

Chapter 4

Christie Somers studied herself in the huge hall mirror, smoothed the red suit down over her hips and then whisked around with a flourish.

'Niki, will I do? What do you think? Is this too bright?'

'When do you not dress in primary colours?' her brother said, shaking his head in mock exasperation. 'Don't tell me you're nervous and want to hide yourself inside a black suit?'

'I have no black clothes, so it's just as well that's a ridiculous observation,' said Christie with a good-humoured sniff. 'You know I don't do nerves.'

'Yes I do, and I also know that you must be the only woman in the world without black clothes.' Niki grinned at his little sister.

'Possibly,' said Christie. 'But my new department is full of women and I don't want to frighten them into thinking I'm a power-suited ogre.'

'Just because you always dress so beautifully it doesn't mean you're an ogre. Even though you are,' said Niki, bending to give her a kiss on the head. She was a totally different body shape to him, hourglass-figured and short, where he was tall and rangy, but their wide smiles, serious cheekbones and bright blue eyes made them instantly recognizable as siblings.

'It will be funny going back to work after so long a break,' said Christie, looking in the mirror again. Maybe scarlet was too aggressive a colour for a first meet.

'James knows what he's doing,' said Niki. 'He wouldn't have offered you this job had he thought you couldn't do it. He's a businessman first, soft touch second. You're up to speed, you'll be fine and it will do you good. You've been a long time in hibernation away from the world. I have every confidence in you and, more to the point, James has every confidence in you.'

'Thank you, Niki,' said Christie with a fond look at him.

'Pleasure, Sis,' said Niki, saluting her as he left by the front door.

'OK,' said Christie to her own reflection. She clapped her hands together and grabbed her minx-red handbag. 'Let's start as we mean to go on.'

Chapter 5

Grace arrived first into the department after the weekend. She found that the Maintenance fairies had been at work. A thick new carpet had been laid and a huge executive mahogany desk replaced the standard issue ones that Malcolm and Brian had been working from. There was a whiteboard now on the wall and boxes of stationery and what looked like promotional gift examples piled up in the corner. A rather arty iron coat-and-umbrella stand had arrived too. Mr McAskill wasn't a man renowned for splashing his cash on fripperies so the gossip machine would be well cranked up by this expenditure.

No sooner had Grace sat down and switched on her PC than Dawn came in.

'Hiya,' she said breezily. 'Car park's a bit full this morning, isn't it?'

'Yes it is,' said Grace. They were still at that polite nicey-nicey stage, having the sort of lightweight interchanges with each other that they'd have with a hairdresser. *Had a nice week-end? Lovely weather we're having!*

'This carpet new? It's like a bouncy castle, isn't it?' Dawn jumped up and down on it, enviously wishing the carpets in Calum's house were anything like as thick and fresh – and free from cig burns and spilled beer stains.

'Yes, it is,' said Grace, spotting an unfamiliar clock on the wall as well. 'So are quite a lot of things which seem to have appeared since Friday.'

'Morning, everyone,' said Raychel, shyly walking in, and just behind her chestnut-haired Anna arrived with an even quieter greeting, equally mesmerized by all the changes in the department. They all seemed a bit nervy that morning. They had hardly got to know each other and now there would be a mighty impact on even those flimsy dynamics. It felt as if it were the first day in a new class and they were all waiting for the teacher to come in and take control.

Over half an hour later, at nine o'clock precisely, a surge of excitement Mexican waved towards them. The exalted figure of James McAskill appeared at the far end of the office alongside a woman in a bright red suit, red shoes and coordinating bag. A personal appearance from him was unusual in itself, but the fact that he was smiling whilst he was talking to this woman – as one would with an old friend – was extraordinary. Immediately, the status of the new Bakery boss went up by a few notches. Grace noticed that Malcolm was looking over with great interest from his department further down the long open-plan office.

'Ladies,' said Mr McAskill, 'may I present Mrs Christie Somers. Christie, may I present the ladies of my Bakery department. This is Grace' – he gestured to them all one by one – 'Dawn, Anna and Raychel.'

'How do you do, girls,' said Christie in a confident, cigarette-smoky drawl. From her clothes to her voice, there was nothing quiet about this woman.

'I've just been giving Christie a guided tour and, can you believe it, I got lost,' said James McAskill with lips full of a beaming smile. Mr McAskill never smiled, despite being the multi-millionaire MD and majority shareholder of the chain of mini-supermarkets, White Rose Stores, which his grandfather had started and he had developed to an incredibly successful degree. Not only was WRS a national institution, but they had recently gone international too, putting stores in ex-pat-heavy areas in Europe with very encouraging results. More than one business newspaper columnist referred to James as 'McMidas'.

'I'm sure I'll find my way around in no time,' said Christie Somers. She reminded Grace of her old hockey teacher, with her assured delivery and fag-ravaged voice.

'I'll leave you to get settled in then, my dear,' said Mr McAskill. Had the others known each other better, they would have exchanged furtive glances at that point. *My dear?* They could see rubber-necks from personnel in other departments. Malcolm's neck was almost popping off his spine.

'So I get the posh desk, do I?' said Christie as James McAskill left her to settle herself in with her new team. 'This one?' She indicated the curved desk behind the privacy screen.

'Yes, that's yours,' said Grace with a kindly smile.

'That screen will have to go,' said Christie. 'Can't see what's going on behind that thing!'

Malcolm had insisted on the screen when he came. That way he could play games on the Internet and read crime thrillers without anyone seeing he was skiving.

'I'll call Maintenance for you, shall I?' asked Grace.

'No, just show me the way to the telephone directory and I'll do it myself,' said Christie. 'I've always been a believer in throwing myself in at the deep end!'

Lord, she was different from Malcolm, thought Grace, who would have let the girls wipe his bottom if he could have got away with asking.

'So, first things first. Let's all go for a coffee and bond,' said Christie. 'I think I can just about remember my way to the canteen.'

'What, now?' said Dawn.

'Yes.'

'All of us?'

'Yes.'

'What – and leave the phones?' said Grace. Cardinal sin. Malcolm would have had them all beheaded for less.

'I'm sure that voicemail can pick them up for half an hour. Come on. I need to meet you properly and for that we need coffee and biscuits,' said Christie and she marched off in the direction of the stairs, the others trailing behind her like little ducks behind their mam.

Twenty minutes later, the five women were halfway down their coffees in the canteen. Five women working together could be a disaster or a joy. Christie was determined it would not be the former and for that she needed to know the personalities involved.

James McAskill had told Christie that he thought he had the ideal mix in his department now. It hadn't been a deliberate ploy to exclude men, that's just the way it had worked out. But still, Christie thought, he couldn't have found a more varied selection of females if he'd tried. The older one, Grace, was fifty-five and very well named too, with her lovely white-blonde hair that fell in a delicate swoop of silver to her jawline. She had, apparently, been especially keen to take up the position, even turning down the chance of early retirement for it. She looked too regal to be working in an office, exuding all that quiet class, thought Christie. She seemed more suited to being the manager of an old-fashioned, exclusive dress shop than working behind a desk. Then there was Anna, thirty-nine, quiet and unsmiling, hiding behind her twin curtains of long chestnut hair with the odd silver root poking through. She twiddled constantly with a small, diamond-studded ring on her wedding finger and her eyes looked dull, as if she hadn't had a top quality sleep for a long time. Then there was Dawn, thirty-three, a young woman with an outward smile on her freckly face, but too many worries behind those large, toffee-coloured eyes. Last, but not least, the 'baby', Raychel, twenty-eight – a beautiful girl with gentle, grey eyes and gypsy-black curls, who, Christie suspected, hid her light well and truly under a bushel. She doubted she had them wrong, she rarely did. She shook her head at herself in exasperation. She'd inherited her psychologist father's genes and was constantly analyzing people. It could be an annoying habit.

'James has great plans for Bakery, were you aware?' smiled Christie, mainly to Grace, who was to be her second in command. 'He wants to launch his flagship Suggestion Scheme from here. We will be in charge of administrating all the ideas that come in from colleagues in the field about Bakery. If it works, he'll be rolling the scheme out to other departments.'

'That's good news,' said Grace. Her job was safe for a while longer then. No one had been more surprised than she had when they had offered her the position of Deputy Manager. She knew that James McAskill talked about fair opportunities for all sexes and ages, but to find out first-hand that he practised what he preached had been very refreshing.

'What was the last boss like then?' asked Christie with a twinkle shining in her eye.

'Brian? Very nice man,' returned Grace.

'He was all right, was Brian,' added Dawn. 'Think he was getting tired though by the end. He left most of the running to Malcolm.' She gave an involuntary shudder when she said his name, which Christie couldn't help but notice.

'Malcolm Spatchcock, that would be?' Christie asked. James had warned her about him. Not that he was one for gossip, he hated it in fact, but he felt it fair to tell her that Malcolm had not been very pleased to be forcibly removed to Cheese, even though it was a promotion. Christie had picked up from that conversation that Malcolm Spatchcock was not one of James's favourite people, although he would never have said as much, not even to her. But Christie Somers liked to make her own mind up about people. Different dynamics between personalities sparked off different sorts of relationships. She might even find that she and Malcolm got on like a house on fire.

'He's gone to be the Business Unit Manager of Cheese,' said Dawn dryly, adding under her breath, 'Appropriate.' She always thought there was a whiff of pongy cheddar about Malcolm – probably her imagination. Or maybe it was something to do with his cheesy flirtations.

Raychel gave a little snort trying to hold a giggle in.

Anna said nothing, just nodded in agreement. In the months they'd been working together, she'd barely spoken. She was a grafter not a talker, the others had each decided.

'It's so lovely to meet you all and share a coffee and break the ice a wee bit,' said Christie, smiling at each and every one of them. 'I like to run a nice cheerful ship. We spend a lot of time on board at work so the last thing I want is for it to be a miserable experience.' She stood up and the others followed suit. She grinned rather mischievously. 'Business Unit Manager – the acronym for that is B.U.M., isn't it? How unfortunate to be known as Cheese B.U.M.'

Chapter 6

Niki was chopping carrots into batons when Christie got home that night.

'Salmon steaks and assorted veg for tea,' said Niki. 'Thought I'd push the boat out a bit seeing as it's your first day.'

'Lovely!' said Christie, kicking off her shoes and wriggling her toes.

'Well?' prompted Niki. 'How was it?'

'Lovely!' said Christie again. 'The women I'm working with are all incredibly nice people and I think I'm going to like it very much.'

'Smashing,' said Niki, pouring out two glasses of crispy and cool Sauvignon Blanc and then adding a big splash of it to his sauce mix. 'How was James?'

'James was James,' nodded Christie. 'Sweet as always although it's very funny to see him through other people's eyes. I get the impression everyone's a little scared of him. They're all in awe of him, that's for sure.'

'Well, he's an impressive man,' said Niki. 'He pays over two thousand people's wages, doesn't he?'

'Oh, much more, Niki. There are now two and a half thousand people working at Head Office alone!' replied Christie, taking a long swallow of wine and giving a contented sigh.

'Bet he's on an honours list before too long as well,' said Niki.

'I think everyone is wondering what my connection is to him,' smirked Christie.

'Let them,' replied Niki. 'Anyway, are any of your girls attractive enough for me?'

'They're all very attractive.' Christie topped up her glass with more wine. Niki hadn't even touched his yet. 'And they're all either married or engaged – no empty ring fingers, alas.'

'Damn!' said Niki with mock frustration.

'Raychel and Dawn are far too young for an old geezer like you anyway. Don't think Anna would be your type either. Now Grace is about five years older than you but stunning. You'd make a very striking couple.' Christie smiled playfully.

'Great,' said Niki. 'I'll wait around until her divorce comes through.' He dropped the salmon steaks onto the grill. 'If you're changing out of that suit, you've got five minutes to do it in. I'm not overcooking salmon for you or anyone.'

Christie laughed and headed quickly for the staircase.

'I'll be down in four!'

Chapter 7

None of them mentioned it, but all four women felt the change in atmosphere the next day when they walked into the department. It was as if someone had filtered out the air and made it lighter and fresher. Christie was sitting at her desk and greeted them all with a hearty 'good morning'. Brian might have smiled a hello, but Malcolm used to dish out 'to do' lists before they'd even got their coats off.

Christie was introduced to a lot of people over the next couple of days. She was all too aware that many of the Unit Managers were curious about her personal connection to James McAskill. But they also knew that he wasn't a fool and would not have brought anyone into the business to head up such a coveted department if they weren't highly qualified. It became obvious to anyone who had a conversation with Christie Somers that she knew her retail onions.

Christie was equally impressed by her team. James had done a good job of picking them. They had lovely telephone manners and were very efficient in their work. Dawn looked after Christie's diary and was obviously a natural organiser. The only thing that concerned her was that there was no interaction *between* them.

She talked to Niki about it after her fourth day.

'Might be the age thing,' he suggested.

'No, it's not that.' Christie shook her head. 'It's as if they're all islands.'

'Islands?' laughed Niki. 'What on earth do you mean by that?'

'I mean, I mean . . .' Christie struggled to explain what she felt. 'There's no bond between them. Considering they've been working together for so long.'

'But that's not unusual,' said Niki. 'Do you remember that dental receptionist I had a few years ago – can't even remember her bloody name now. That's partly my point. She worked for me for three years and none of us knew she'd got married after a year until she told us that her name had changed. Julie spotted she was pregnant before she said anything to anyone. Five months' pregnant and she hadn't said a word about it.'

'Yes, I remember,' said Christie, 'but she was a cold fish. My ladies aren't like that, they're very friendly. Not that I expect them to go off arm in arm to the coffee machine, but you would have thought that they would have . . . bonded a little more. It's unnatural – especially for women.'

'Christie, Christie, Christie,' sighed Niki patiently. 'That might just be the way they all like it. Not everyone thinks of work as a social occasion.'

'True,' said Christie. But still she wondered what was going on in their lives that kept them so tightly bound up in themselves.

Malcolm left it until the end of the week before he swaggered over to Christie's desk, draped his hand over the screen – which Maintenance would be removing within the hour – and introduced himself. He had seen the way McAskill had led her in, and he wasn't an idiot. He knew Christie Somers was obviously someone important. Someone to have on side.

'Charmed to meet you,' he smiled and flicked his eyes quickly over her full-busted figure, thinking she hadn't seen him doing it. He stuck his hand straight out confidently. 'Malcolm Spatchcock, as in the game bird.'

'Christie,' she returned. 'As in the serial killer.'

He gave a high-pitched, nervous laugh, taken aback at her strange humour. It flitted through his mind that she was being sarcastic, but there was a wide, welcoming smile on her face and her handshake was firm and friendly.

'Apologies, it's my attempt at an ice-breaker,' she explained.

'Ah-ha. I see. Very amusing. Well, anything you want to know about Bakery, feel free to ask. I used to run the department.' Malcolm's voice dropped to a whisper. 'Between you and me, the named Head wasn't really interested once he'd got his retirement date. The department suffered, alas. I kept it afloat.'

'Well, thank you. You've done a good job.'

'Worked in Bakery before?' he asked.

'No, never a Bakery department,' Christie replied without elaboration.

Marvellous, thought Malcolm. *Not only do they give the job to a stranger, but to someone who doesn't have any experience in Bakery either! Very strange. Very suspicious.*

The other women were trying to work but the temptation to eavesdrop was just too hard to resist.

'Where did you come from? Morrison's? Handi-Save?'

'Neither of those,' Christie replied. My goodness he was nosey. If his head had been transparent, she had no doubt she would have seen a queue of questions lined up in his brain. She hoped he wasn't the type who would try and undermine her at his earliest convenience. If he was, he was in for a shock. Confrontation excited her. She was good at it. Rather than kicking down the walls of her confidence, it drove up her adrenalin levels.

Malcolm leaned further over the screen. Christie caught a waft of very liberally applied, pongy aftershave.

'We should have lunch. I had some good ideas for the department that I never got the chance to implement. It would be a shame to see them go to waste.'

'Yes, indeed. That would be lovely. Everyone here has been so friendly and supportive,' said Christie, rising to her feet.

'Good, good. We'll get something arranged soon,' said Malcolm with a wink before wending his way back to Cheese, safe in the knowledge that he had had a very successful first meeting with someone who could be a key figure at White Rose Stores.

Christie mused for a few moments. Malcolm was friendly enough, she supposed. A bit forward. Maybe his brashness was over-compensation for nerves. Then her thoughts were hijacked by the sight of the clock. Once again it was 5 p.m. and no one was making a move towards the coat stand.

'Haven't you seen the time, ladies?' said Christie.

They all nodded.

'And?' Christie perched on the edge of Anna's desk.

'Well, we don't usually finish until five-thirty,' said Raychel.

'Why? Are you gluttons for punishment?'

'No, but . . .' began Dawn, before clamming up.

'Go on,' urged Christie.

'Well, Malcolm always made it really clear that we should be putting extra time in.'

'What absolute tosh!' said Christie. 'I know for a fact that James leaves his office as often as he can before six, and he owns the bloody place. Anyway, I'm Head of this department now so we'll have no more nonsense. If people can't do their jobs in a thirty-five-hour week, then we need to look at getting extra staff or conducting time and motion studies.'

'We're perfectly up to date with everything,' volunteered Grace.

'There you are then. Now go – the lot of you. And I'll see you at nine on Monday morning and not before. It's Friday night, for goodness sake. Don't you have men and social lives to go to?'

They all rose nervously and slowly started to get their coats, unable to shake off the feeling that they were sneaking off illegally and some big blokes were going to burst through the doors and force them back into their seats again.

Christie waved them off with a smile. What a lovely bunch of women. She hoped they all did have a smashing weekend. Life was too short to be miserable – as she knew only too well.

Malcolm watched his ex-team file out. He had never left his desk before six and so he didn't see why anyone else should either. In saying that, his extra devotion hadn't exactly been rewarded. And really it was less about devotion and more about not going home to be nagged at by his wife. Whatever sway that Christie woman had with the big boss was huge. He wouldn't rest until he found out what it was.

Chapter 8

One year ago exactly, Vladimir Darcescu, or Vladimir Darq, as he was more famously known in the world of couture, had stunned London by making his English base a house in Barnsley. For years his Business Manager had been buying up chunks of southern building land as investments, plus one very large expensive plot up north in a village called Higher Hoppleton on the outskirts of Barnsley, which the Internet informed him was an ex-pit town in very deepest Yorkshire.

Two years ago, Vladimir decided to go up and see the extent of his Business Manager's madness but instead was pleasantly surprised by the position of the land at the edge of a small but affluent village with its abundance of old stone cottages and shops.

He stayed at the local pub, the Lord Spencer, for three days. Locals greeted him with a friendly 'How do' when he wandered around the shops or took tea in the café in the very beautiful Hoppleton Hall, an old square jewel in the middle of the lovely nearby park. He liked it very much in this village, in fact he felt at home. The people reminded him of those in Tiresti, his Romanian birthplace. He liked to listen to their banter and he basked in their friendliness.

He particularly liked the ambience of the Lord Spencer. The landlady was a very attractive older lady with a droopy chest and sloping shoulders. Vladmir Darq knew that, with the right lingerie, she could look years younger and magnificent. It was there in the pub, in the company of the landlady, on that third night that he had his greatest epiphany.

Within the week, Vladimir Darq had plans drawn up to erect a house on his land and within the year the gothic-type hall – Darq House – was completed. And he was to stun the fashion world again by announcing that he was branching out into the lingerie business with price labels accessible to all women. He wanted to be able to make any female feel fantastic *and* comfortable. He knew he could do that by dressing them in the right underwear.

And so it was that Corona Productions got wind of his intended project and rang him to try and persuade him to star in the flagship TV show *Jane's Dames,* in which a member of the public was transformed without the need for plastic surgery.

Vladimir, however, insisted he choose the woman. But shooting was scheduled to begin in four weeks and he still hadn't found 'the one', though he had trawled supermarkets and shops for her. Then he wondered if he might find his unpolished jewel heading for home at the end of a hard week's work. Which is why he ended up on a Barnsley railway station platform that second Friday in April.

Anna realized that by leaving the office at just after five she could catch the earlier train home. She was probably the only woman in the world who wouldn't have seen that as a treat. It just made the evening stretch even longer in front of her. Whichever idiot said 'the only way is up' didn't have her life. Every day she discovered another record depth to plunge to: another abyss for her spirits to sink down into.

White Rose Stores HQ was a couple of minutes' walk away from the train stop. Five minutes later she was in the main

Barnsley Interchange and from there it was two stops to her home village of Dartley. She preferred to travel that way rather than get snagged up in traffic, especially in a car that badly needed replacing and wasn't the most reliable vehicle. But she didn't want to go home so early and have an even longer miserable night to fill, so instead of turning left onto the platform, she took a right and ended up window-shopping in town for an hour first to kill some time.

She caught sight of her reflection in a glass window. The image it threw back at her was that of the ugliest woman in the world: tired, dull eyes with ghoulish circles, cracked, dry lips and a skin tone that was somewhere between corpse and old dishcloth. It was the face of a woman whom no one in the world valued, not even herself. No wonder her fiancé Tony had run off to the fresh-faced Lynette Bottom with her puppy-plump cheeks and a smile that didn't crease up her face like a contour map of Everest.

She might as well buy a shapeless coat and flat shoes and morph into the Young Granny club that some of the girls from school had joined. As soon as they made it to forty, they dressed like pensioners, left off the make-up, their figures blown and puffed into cheap clothes as they pushed their teenage daughters' children around the market. Not that Anna would even have that pleasure. There would be no grandchildren to wheel about because there would never be any children to wheel about. Still, at least there would be no kids to be embarrassed by a mother with a big, ugly face like this. Her lips stung. No point in moisturising them – no one would ever kiss her lips again, she was sure of it. She was days away from being forty and her life was over. There was nothing to look forward to but more crap.

She waited on the spring-chilly platform, hands stuffed deep into her coat pockets as the breeze coursing down the train track played mischievously with her hair, blowing it annoyingly.

On the opposite platform, other passengers waited for the Sheffield train going south. A man stood apart from them. He was tall, dressed in a long, generously cut, cape-like black coat and a black hat with a wide brim that threw his face into shade. Anna glanced at him to find him staring over at her. She moved her eyes away, flicking them back to see he was still transfixed on her. She folded her arms protectively over her chest. *But then, why would he be staring at me? I'm hardly Gwyneth Paltrow!* she mused. The alarm sounded to warn that the barriers were dropping across the nearby road, for her train was coming. *No, he is definitely staring at me.* He wasn't dressed like a normal commuting passenger from Barnsley. He had no briefcase or laptop bag. It was almost as if he was just hanging out on the platform like a loony. *Come on train*, willed Anna, uncomfortable now. She tried not to look over, but the temptation to see if he was still watching was too much. She found that he was.

The train pulled along the track, blocking his view of her. Anna climbed aboard and slotted into a seat, picking up a discarded *Sun* newspaper to read for her short journey. As the train started up, Anna stole a last glance from her position of safety. The man was *still* looking at her. Her last view was of him doffing his hat at her in a dated, gallant gesture and pulling his lips into an open smile. What's more, she could have sworn she saw the glint of fangs as he did so.

Chapter 9

Grace pushed open the door of the garden centre café. Maltstone was a pretty little village with this lovely café at the side of a country stream. People outside the area – *offcumdens* – wouldn't have believed it was a stone's throw from Barnsley centre. She loved it here because it was the special place where she met her boy. She looked around and caught sight of the strapping young man standing and waving to her and she grinned and walked briskly over to the table he occupied.

'Hello, my darling,' she said, and was enfolded in her son's tight and long embrace.

'Hello, Mum.' She cupped his face in her hand. A strong face, a fine jaw. He had a few premature grey hairs in amongst the dark brown. She hadn't seen those before. He let her go and they sat facing each other at the window table.

'I'm sorry, it's been too long,' he said.

'You're busy, darling, I know,' said Grace with a smile as warm as a lit winter fireplace.

'It's no excuse,' he said. 'You're too nice. I got a bollocking from big sis Laura.'

'Well, we're here now,' she said and touched his arm. 'You're looking well.'

'So are you. But then you always do. I ordered us tea already,' he said, pouring from a waiting teapot. 'How's Dad?'

'Oh, you know, the same,' said Grace. She didn't say he sent his love, they would both know that would have been a lie, but it was a lie she wished she could have got away with. 'Anyway, Happy Birthday.' Grace handed over a sturdy paper carrier bag. 'If you don't like it, I've left the receipt in—'

'Mum, you have great taste and I've never had to change a thing you've given me.' He squeezed her hand and Grace hung onto his fingers for a few sad moments. It shouldn't be like this, skulking around seeing her boy. He should be spending his twenty-eighth birthday embraced in his family home, blowing out silly candles on a cake, even at his age. She had always made a big fuss of them all on their birthdays, the way she wished she had been fussed over by a family.

'So, what do you have to tell me?' she said, sniffing back a threatening cloudburst of sudden tears. She didn't want to spoil this happy occasion with a silly crying fit.

'Well . . .' He reached down, fiddled in a briefcase and brought up a file which he opened. He handed over some photos. 'I've bought it, Mum. That is, myself and my business partner, Charles.'

'You haven't!' said Grace, her mouth wide open with excitement. 'This is the house you were telling me about, presumably?'

'Yep. Which is mostly the reason for the radio silence, Mum. I've been a busy lad.'

Grace looked down at the old manor house set in its own grounds, the one which her talented, caring boy was going to turn into an old people's home.

'It's going to be gorgeous, Mum. Every room ensuite – fourteen, the architect reckons; a fifty-foot conservatory facing east for breakfasts, a library, Internet, webcams, a pool, a cinema . . .'

'Slow down and take a breath,' said Grace, but loving his enthusiasm.

'It will be the most beautiful residential home I can make it.

The place is a mess at the moment, which is why I got it for such a good price – and of course add the recession to the mix. But you should see how many of the original features are still there. And the garden will be lovely with a bit . . . sorry, *a lot* of work. I can't afford to fail at it, that's for sure. Oh Mum, we can't wait to get started. Everything was finalized yesterday so now we can. It's mine, Mum. It's all mine. God, we should both have taken taxis and had champagne instead of tea!'

His face was radiant with excitement. As long as she had known him, she had been convinced Paul would enter a caring profession and on a grand scale too. This was a deal he had been working towards for years. She had no doubt he would be successful at it. He was a fighter, though some of his energies were taken up with fighting things he shouldn't be and that saddened her so very much.

'I'm going to call it Rose Manor, after Granny,' he beamed.

Grace nodded. 'That's a lovely idea. She would have been so proud of you, Paul. And so would your mother.'

'Really? Do you think they would have been bothered by my sexual proclivity as much as Dad is? I often wonder.'

'They would have loved you for being you and been proud as Punch of you,' said Grace definitely. She might not have been able to grow children in her body, but she had grown them in her heart and she felt every bit their mother. But, even though she had never known Gordon's first wife, Rita, Grace had always been careful never to usurp her position as true mother. Rose had once told her that Rita was a feisty little thing who adored her babies, and when she suddenly and tragically died, she left a space that Grace had been proud to fill, but she did so with reverence to the woman who had borne the children she loved as her own. Pictures of Rita still sat in frames in the house and every Mother's Day and on Rita's birthday, Grace had taken the children to her grave in Maltstone churchyard to lay flowers. It was only right she should have the deepest respect for the woman who had given her the greatest gift ever. She had the feeling that Rita would have been her friend had their lives overlapped.

'Your Nana Rose would have laughed her head off to be told she was having a mansion named after her,' said Grace.

'Do you think?'

'I know so,' said Grace. She had fallen in love with Rose Beamish on their very first meeting. She oozed life and love and laughter despite the asthma that crippled her. She never once moaned, taking her illness in her stride. 'Still breathing, aren't I, pet? That's more than them poor buggers in the ground,' she had laughed in her thick Tyneside accent. Grace had been broken-hearted when she died. Gordon had been of the 'it's a blessing' school of sentiment. He wasn't a man for much emotion. But Grace felt the emptiness in the house for a long time after Rose's passing.

They had another pot of tea and then the time came for Grace to make a move to go home. Tall as she was, she was dwarfed by her big, handsome son. When did he become a man? The boy had never given them a minute's trouble in all those years and he was now treated as a pariah by his father because he was gay. The unfairness of it all pained her heart.

'We'll meet again soon,' she said at the door.

'Look, I can't see you next Saturday, but can you sneak off the weekend after – Easter weekend? Meet you here, same time? I'd like to introduce you to Charles. He's been dying to meet you after all I've told him about you.'

'Aw, bless you,' said Grace, adding, 'So is Charles a *partner* as well as a partner?'

Paul grinned. 'He's a partner. He is someone's *partner* but more about that one later.'

'I'll be here, same time,' said Grace. They kissed again. He looked happy. *Her boy*.

'Good. Anyway, I'm relying on you to come and help me

pick out some wallpaper and furniture eventually. I want it to be bright but restful.'

'I'll help you all I can, you know that,' said Grace. She touched his face, his strong, handsome face. His features reminiscent of Gordon, but a Gordon who was pliant, a Gordon who didn't think it was a weakness to *feel*. If only her husband thought about people with as much affection as he thought about caravans.

The weekends were the worst for Anna. A desert where her thoughts tormented her and the bed seemed bigger than ever. Time wasn't a great healer. She was feeling increasingly worse, not better. It had been nearly two months now since she had walked in, needing Tony's arms around her more than ever, but all she found was a strange quiet about the house and saw the note on the table. *Sorry, need some time to think and we need some time apart. There is no one else though – honest.* Obviously, with Tony having an elastic relationship with the truth, there was indeed someone else. Lynette Bottom, aged nineteen with a peachy derrière and bobbly tits. He had taken her on in his barber's shop as a Girl Friday about six months ago. Now she was official bed-warmer. Anna wondered if he'd put her hourly rate up for that.

Anna hadn't heard from him since he had left, which was good in a way, she tried to tell herself, because he hadn't come back for his stuff or asked for a split of assets. And his share of the mortgage and council tax was still going into the bank. But she so wanted to hear his voice and see him. It took every bit of strength she had not to make a detour past his shop on the way to the train every morning. She honestly didn't know what she would do if she saw him. She couldn't quite trust herself not to leap on him, force him to kiss her, beg him to come home. Or worse – fly at Lynette Bottom and grab her by the hair and totally embarrass herself by saying something wild and angry and chavvy. So she let him do what he had to, un-harassed, under absolutely no pressure, and hoped one day that the answer machine would be flashing a message that he'd had his fun and wanted to come home.

It was an effort to get out of her dressing gown at the week-end, let alone put her face on. Whereas a few weeks back she wouldn't have gone out to the wheely bin in less than full war-paint, now she was going shopping in Morrison's without wearing even a blob of foundation. Grey roots were pushing out of her tired-looking chestnut hair. Her hair had always reflected her mood. When she was happy, it was bright and conker-shiny, but it looked dull now, even after she'd just washed it. Her unmade-up eyes were puffy through lack of sleep. She looked knackered and ten years past her age. She was one step away from going to the local shops in slippers and pink terry towelling pyjamas. And *the* dreaded birthday was just around the corner when life apparently would begin, so the saying went. Fat chance. She wondered if slitting your wrists in a warm bath was a painless way to die or if that rumour was as much bollocks as the rest of her life was.

'Wakey, wakey, rise and shine!'

Raychel's eyelashes fluttered open to Ben's gentle awakening. She made a leisurely stretch and he tutted.

'Take your time, why don't you?'

Raychel laughed and shuffled to a sitting position so Ben could put the tray on her lap. Every Sunday morning he made them breakfast in bed. He had done since they had moved in together when they were seventeen, although in those days he hadn't been confident enough to tackle the Full English and it had just been toast and coffee with a daft flower in an eggcup at the side.

He sat down beside her with his own tray and began to tuck in.

'I'll never eat all this!' she said. 'You always give me far too much.'

'Get it down you. You've no fat on your bones. No pudding unless you finish it!' He wagged his finger at her and she speared a sausage and dipped the end in ketchup. She never did finish the huge breakfast he served up; he always had to help her out.

'Just think, there will only be another three Sundays in this house, then we'll be in our own place.'

'Aye, well enjoy it then because once I start paying a mortgage we'll only be able to afford to split a Pop Tart for breakfast,' replied Ben, through a mouthful of bacon.

'I won't mind,' said Raychel, sighing as she thought of the new flat they would be moving into soon.

'As if!' said Ben. 'I like making your breakfast.'

'You spoil me,' smiled Raychel. She leaned over and gave him a kiss on his stubbly face.

'Give me that sausage if you're not going to eat it,' said Ben.

'Get lost,' said Raychel, playfully stuffing the whole sausage into her mouth so Ben couldn't have it.

'I didn't know you could do that!' gasped Ben with a cheeky grin. 'Raychel Love, I think you just might have to stay in bed for a bit longer and show me that trick again.'

Ben abandoned his breakfast immediately and jumped on a shrieking Raychel. Some things were more important than a Sunday morning fry-up.

Chapter 10

'Morning, girls!' said a cheerful Christie to her troupe of four. It was five to nine on Monday morning and they still looked furtive, as if they were sneaking in late. They made her laugh. This job was just what she needed. She was so grateful she had mentioned the fact to James McAskill that she was looking for a full-time job. The ladies intrigued her though, each in their own unique way; they all seemed locked in their own little worlds. Grace, for instance. How many women in their fifties refused healthy offers of early retirement – not once, but twice? What was she running from? And young Dawn was positively schizophrenic. Sometimes she had that glow of a girl in love, only for it to be replaced by the world's biggest worries showing on her face – what was all that about? Little Ray was a sweetheart, but so jumpy. Nails constantly in her mouth, and when there were no more nails, her fingers bled from the skin being ripped around them. Anna intrigued her most of all. Had she ever bloomed? Christie wondered. She had the air of one who never had. That would have been so unfair if she had not. Every woman should have her moment of flowering. Everyone should have days to look back on when they could say, 'I was at my most beautiful then.'

'Morning, everyone,' said Malcolm, swaggering through the office. The ladies returned the greeting politely enough.

'Morning, Christie,' said Malcolm, leaning over her desk. Christie looked up to find a man who was decidedly more orange in the face than she remembered from Friday. Mahogany even. She had the sudden desire to spray some Mr Sheen on him. Poor man, did he realize how silly he looked?

'I thought we might have lunch together. Let me take you through some of the ideas for the department that I never got to implement.'

'Yes, of course,' said Christie. She didn't really like the corporate lunch thing, but the man was making an effort to be friendly and it would have been very rude of her to rebuff him. 'Shall we say twelve in the canteen?'

'Or we could go to the Italian around the corner?' he angled.

'The canteen is fine by me,' said Christie in such a way that brooked no discussion.

'Oh . . . er . . . canteen it is then,' he said and cocked his finger at her. 'Right, best go and sort out the troops. Catch you later.' He clicked his tongue and then strolled back down the office with a satisfied grin.

Christie's eyes dropped back to her work, otherwise she would have seen four grimaces as each of her ladies imagined the prospect of lunch with Orange Malcolm.

At twelve, Christie clocked Malcolm settled at a canteen table with a generous serving of shepherd's pie and salad. She picked up a plate of ravioli, sprinkled it with parmesan, and joined him. Gallantly he stood up while she took a seat.

'Food's not bad here,' he said, unaware of a clot of tomato on his chin.

'Yes, it's very good,' said Christie and speared a cushion of pasta.

'Mr McAskill eats down here a lot. That's a good sign.'

'A very good sign,' she agreed.

'But then I suppose you know that already.'

Christie veered away from the subject that she suspected Malcolm wanted to bend towards. She was quite aware that people were intrigued by her relationship with James, but she had no intention of revealing her private life to strangers. This was a working lunch, not a chat between familiars.

'So, you were saying you had some ideas,' she deflected.

'Oh, yes. Well, James McAskill, *as you will know*, is really into incentivizing. I thought you might like to show him this. I sourced some great promotional gifts before I gave up the department for Cheese,' he said, as if he'd had a choice in the matter. He ferreted in his coat pocket and brought out a clear plastic isosceles triangle. Through the middle was the company logo and across the widest part were the words, 'I spoke and White Rose Stores listened.'

'Very impressive,' said Christie turning it around. She was being kind. It was pretty awful and she couldn't think of anyone who would be inspired to spend their free time trying to improve the business in the hope of getting one of these things in return.

'It's a paperweight,' said Malcolm proudly. He loaded his mouth with potato. 'Yes, I took it on myself to get the example made. It didn't cost the company anything, of course.'

'Very light for a paperweight,' said Christie. 'Wouldn't it have been better in glass?'

'Health and safety issue,' said Malcolm. 'Plus, glass would be way too expensive. These would be made in the Far East at a fraction of the price. Instil a sense of pride though, wouldn't they – glass or plastic? And you could order in bulk to cut costs even further. It would do nicely for when they roll out the idea of taking suggestions for the other departments because it's a general statement – not tied to Bakery in any way.'

Christie made a series of facial gestures that Malcolm took to mean that she was speechless with admiration. 'Well, I'll bear it in mind, certainly.'

'I know Mr McAskill would love this idea and I don't mind if you were to tell him where it came from,' said Malcolm, with a wink. Christie knew James would view it from all angles and say: 'What on earth is it?' before slam-dunking it in his bin.

Malcolm bought two coffees after their meal was finished and more of his mediocre ideas had been imparted, including some very unusual shapes for loaves. Christie watched him holding up the queue at the till as he counted out and handed over a load of change, exact to the last penny.

'How are you getting on with those women?' said Malcolm, imbuing the last two words with all the joy of sniffing off-milk.

'I like them very much.'

'Funny bunch if you ask me,' said Malcolm, coming in so close that Christie was overcome by the fumes from his awful aftershave again. 'That Grace is a snobby piece, thinks she is above everyone. She's fifty-five and I reckon she thought she'd get the Scheme Manager's job. Why else would you turn down retirement? Bit late to start getting ambitious really, so watch your back! Anna's a bit sullen. Never seen her smile yet. And I understand Dawn is getting married, isn't she?'

'Is she indeed?' asked Christie.

'Word of warning, that sort always make too many personal calls. Plus, I don't think she's the sharpest knife in the drawer. Don't know anything about the other one, the young one, Raychel, except I would have thought she was a bit boring to have in such an energy-driven project. Not exactly Miss Personality, if you know what I mean. I'm surprised Mr McAskill picked that lot, to be honest. I'd have had at least one man in there myself.'

Christie wondered if she should write to the *Guinness Book of Records* and suggest an entry for the most number of character assassinations in one minute. Still, she always liked to give people the benefit of the doubt. Maybe he was trying to help her settle in, albeit in a very clumsy way.

'Well, I have to say, I find them all extremely amiable and hard-working,' Christie said brightly.

'New broom sweeps clean,' said Malcolm and his hand closed over Christie's with a squeeze. 'You do realize they've already started taking the mick, coming in at nine and going home as soon as the clock hits five?'

'But that's the working day. Why on earth should anyone do more?'

'Because that's what we do at White Rose Stores, my dear,' he said with a very patronizing smile.

That gave Christie the perfect escape clause.

'I'm totally indebted to you for the insight,' she nodded. 'I had better get back and make sure they're behaving, in that case.' And with that she purposefully picked up her tray.

'Quite,' said Malcolm with a smug grin, pleased that she had taken his comments on board. 'I think I'm just going to have a small portion of apple pie before I get back to the Cheese grindstone. It's been lovely talking to you, Christie.'

'And you, Malcolm. Very useful. Very . . . revealing.'

She really was a very attractive woman, he thought as he watched her wend her way over to where the empty plates were stacked. Her heart-shaped bottom had a natural sashay like Marilyn Monroe. However she had got that job, he would have bet his life savings on it being something to do with that bottom.

'Good lunch?' asked Grace. She was alone in their section. The others were all shopping in town. Separately, not together.

'Pleasant enough,' said Christie, not sure how convincing she sounded. 'I'm going to get another coffee. Can I get you one?'

'Oh, er, yes, thank you,' said Grace. 'Milk, no sugar please.'

'No, I didn't imagine you would take sugar with a figure like yours,' said Christie.

'Oh, erm, thank you,' said Grace with some surprise.

'However, if the truth be told, I have a terrible sweet tooth if I gave way to it. Thank God for yoga. That keeps me on the straight and narrow.'

'I give way to my sweet tooth on a regular basis, as you may have guessed,' Christie returned, smoothing her hands over the curves in her bright, summer-blue suit. She had the most beautiful clothes, none in shy colours. 'My brother is a dentist and he keeps my teeth on the straight and narrow, if not my figure. And I think if I even attempted the Lotus position, my spine would snap.'

'I didn't start classes until I was in my late twenties,' returned Grace. 'Trust me, it's a very gentle wake-up call to the body.'

'I'll take your word for it,' said Christie. 'I get all the relaxation I need from éclairs, an occasional balloon of brandy and the odd packet of Embassy Regals.'

She waited for Grace to wince at the reference to cigarettes. Somehow she thought she would disapprove. Grace didn't. Instead she said, 'Everyone needs to unwind. I think there's nothing more dangerous to one's health than the inability to relax.' And she smiled. Christie suspected that Grace hadn't truly unwound for a long time, not even through the medium of yoga.

'I totally agree,' said Christie. 'Milk, no sugar, you said? Same as me. I manage, at least, to avoid sugar in my drinks.'

'Yes, thank you,' said Grace. A boss had never volunteered to fetch a drink for her in all her working life. But then, like half the building, she suspected Christie Somers was very far from the norm.

Dawn had bought presents in town in her lunch hour. Gold earrings for her bridesmaids – Denise and Demi, Calum's sisters – and a tie-pin for the best man – Rod, otherwise known as Killer, Calum's best friend, although she couldn't imagine he'd ever use it. Maybe it would come in useful for his appearances in court. He was electronically tagged and on a curfew, so he would be leaving the celebrations early. She'd buy Muriel some flowers. Calum's dad, Ronnie, was giving her away. She had said that she would walk down the aisle herself because her dad wasn't there to do the deed and there were no uncles or anyone to ask on her side, but Muriel had said that was stupid and volunteered Ronnie to do it. Ronnie hadn't objected. The Crooke men tended to do what the Crooke women said. She wondered if Calum would take any notice of what she said once she became a Crooke woman.

She was hiring penguin suits for him and Ronnie and Killer. The amount of money she had spent so far was starting to wake her up in the middle of the night, sweating. She hadn't a clue where the rest was going to come from.

Chapter 11

'Ta daaahhh,' said Ben at exactly half past nine on the Tuesday night. 'Finished one room at least, thank goodness.'

'Brilliant,' said Ray, drawing the last brushful of paint across the wall. 'Only two more rooms to go.'

'Ah, man, we'll have it done by the weekend. It's worth it though, isn't it? A free month's rent for a few evenings of this?'

'Well, I don't know. These ceilings are high. There's a lot of wall to paint.'

'The house looks twice bigger in this colour.'

'Remind me not to wear magnolia trousers then,' said Raychel.

'Give over, you've hardly got a bottom,' said Ben.

'"Give over?" You're turning into a Yorkshireman!'

'Aaarrghh!' screamed Ben, as if that was a fate worse than death. But in truth he didn't miss his roots in Newcastle. Sometimes it was as if there was no life before he and Raychel moved to Barnsley and rented this small terraced house in the Old Town district. He felt settled here. He had a good job and Ray seemed to enjoy hers. And if she was happy, he was happy.

'That four hundred quid we've saved will go towards the first mortgage payment.'

They both started to grin at each other.

'Our first mortgage. Can you believe it?'

'I can't believe we're actually excited about paying out a big wodge of money every month. How sad are we?'

'Very.'

'You OK anchoring yourself permanently to a life in Barnsley?' said Raychel, the smile suddenly sliding from her face.

'Where you go, I go,' said Ben, resting his great arms on her shoulders.

'I like it here. Isn't that odd?'

'Why is it odd?' said Ben, giving her a tiny kiss on her head.

'Because of all places to come, we end up here. Where my parents came from.'

'Well, you never knew the place. It's not as if you have bad memories here, is it?'

'I suppose not,' Raychel mused.

'There's loads of work around for me, Raychel. I've never felt as settled as I do here.' Ben squeezed his wife. 'Maybe we're growing up at last.' He nudged her playfully but she wasn't smiling. He knew where her thoughts were. The past was always waiting for their minds to slip back to like a muddy slope with little grip on the sides.

He slapped her bottom lightly to break her out of her reverie. 'You go and have the first bath. I'll get on with making something to eat.'

'No, let's get a curry delivered,' said Raychel, pasting on a smile.

'I won't argue with that,' said Ben. 'Go on, and I'll have the water after you, so no weeing in it.'

'How will you know?' teased Ray on her way out. He pretended to chase her and she squealed.

Ben's smile dropped when she disappeared up the staircase.

'Please God, make us happy in our new flat,' he whispered. He didn't ask to win the lottery or live forever, he just hoped

God would come through for them and give them some peace at last.

'What do you think for the reception, Cal? Roast beef or chicken?'

'I don't know, you pick,' said Calum. He was watching a nature programme. A pride of lions was ripping up a gazelle. Well, the lion was just sitting on the sidelines letting the lionesses get on with it. The gazelle had long, thin legs like Dawn's.

'Are any of your lot vegetarian?' asked Dawn.

'Do us a fucking favour,' said Calum with some amusement.

'Maybe we should have a vegetarian option just in case.'

'Aye, give 'em the option to eat the meat or fuck off.'

'Prawn cocktail or melon, roast beef or chicken, Black Forest or summer pudding?'

'What's summer pudding?' said Calum.

'It's like a bread mould with berries in it.'

'Bread mould? *Bread. Mould?*'

'Not green mould, shape mould, you numpty,' laughed Dawn.

'No, you've put me off that already.'

'Black Forest then?'

'I don't know,' said Calum. 'You decide.'

'We could have black pudding and poached egg starter, turkey and then sticky toffee pudding.'

'That sounds all right.'

'But it's four pounds extra a head.'

'Whatever,' said Calum. 'Ask my mam. She'd know.'

That night Dawn went to bed and dreamed that a giant sticky toffee pudding ate her savings and ripped holes in her wedding dress.

Chapter 12

Mid-week, at eleven o'clock precisely, Christie looked up and saw her ladies all beavering away. She had never worked in a department so banter-free. It unsettled her. Where she had headed other departments in her time that needed pulling into line for their gossip:work ratio, this was unnatural at the other end of the scale and didn't make for the best working environment, in her opinion. They might have all been sitting surrounded by individual barbed-wire fences. She shook her head. Women working in close proximity to cakes and pastries — they should have been in their element! There was an air of disunity about this department she was determined to tackle.

'Staff meeting, in the canteen please, ladies, two minutes, so switch your phones to voicemail,' she called out. She'd begin by plying them with coffee and buns. Always a good start for bonding.

Down in the canteen, a fresh batch of buttered scones had just been put out. Christie piled five onto her tray. Proper elevenses!

'No dieting allowed at the table,' she said, sitting down. 'Help yourselves, girls.'

Anna wasn't all that hungry. She had hardly eaten anything since the weekend, her appetite had absconded with Tony, but everyone else had taken a scone and she would have felt a bit of a party pooper leaving hers untouched. She could nibble at it, she supposed. She really ought to eat something.

'Right, I want to know three interesting facts about all of you – it can be anything – but things that are important to you,' announced Christie, after swallowing a big bite of scone. 'I'll go first. I'm a widow, no children, and I live with my brother who is a dentist and though we used to fight a lot when we were little, as adults we get on surprisingly well. Two: I love clothes, especially vintage ones, and double especially shoes and have far more than I'll ever wear. Three: I love strawberries and I can't damn well eat them because they bring me out in a rash.'

The ladies laughed gently.

'That's cruel, isn't it?' said Grace. 'It's like loving animals but being allergic to their fur.'

'Your turn, Grace.'

Grace racked her brains. Three *interesting* things. She couldn't think of one.

'They don't have to be extreme,' coaxed Christie. 'Just three things about yourself that we don't know. For instance, you were telling me that you picked up a hobby in your late twenties, weren't you?'

'Ah yes,' said Grace, grateful for the prompt. 'Well, number one, I've been doing yoga for nearly thirty years. I start off every morning with quarter of an hour and finish off every evening with the same. I think I'd get twitchy if I didn't; it's become very much my routine.'

'Wish I were that disciplined,' said Dawn. 'I haven't done any exercise for a long time.'

'You've a lovely figure anyway though,' said Grace.

'I'm all legs, which is a pain when I'm buying trousers because they're never long enough!'

'Lucky you. I always need to have mine taken up. Anyway, go on, fact number two, Grace,' urged Christie.

'Right, erm . . . well, I have three children: Laura is

twenty-nine, Paul is twenty-eight and Sarah is twenty-five, and two grandchildren: Joe – who is Laura's little boy, he's five years old and Sarah's little girl, Sable, who is four and there's another brother or sister on the way for her.'

'You married, Grace?' asked Raychel, not hearing any mention of a husband in the family run down.

'Oh yes, I've been married to Gordon for twenty-three years. He was a plastic injection moulding engineer but he took early retirement.'

Interesting, thought Christie. Her husband took early retirement yet she was fighting against it. And from the ages of her children, they were all born out of wedlock. She'd had Grace pigeon-holed as someone traditional too!

'And your third fact?'

Grace thought hard, then she grinned.

'I've had a coffee with Phillip Schofield.'

'You haven't!' gasped Raychel. 'I love Phillip Schofield!'

'Where was that?' asked Dawn.

'Starbucks in Leeds train station about four years ago,' said Grace quite proudly. 'All the tables were taken and he asked if he could sit at mine because I was by myself. I thought he looked like Phillip Schofield, but it never crossed my mind he was the real thing. Then someone asked for his autograph and I could have fainted. He's very dishy.'

'Did you get his autograph as well?' Christie asked, chewing on the other half of her scone.

'He signed my serviette,' replied Grace. 'He was absolutely charming.'

'He gets better with age as well,' said Dawn. 'Was he filming up here?'

'Yes,' said Grace, 'but I can't remember what he said it was. I was a bit star-struck.'

'Starstruck in Starbucks. Say that after you've had a few!' laughed Dawn.

'And on that note, your turn, Dawn?' said Christie.

'OK, well, I'm getting married in two months. Last Saturday in June. To Calum.'

A tinkle of congratulatory noises was the result of that revelation.

'Big white wedding?' asked Christie.

'Small to medium. I don't have any family. I'm having the big frock and the church and the cake, but not hundreds of guests. Can't really afford to.'

'What will your married name be?' said Raychel, wiping her mouth with a napkin.

'Crooke. Not the most romantic name. Not like yours – *Love*!' said Dawn with a smile. Not that she minded. Being Mrs Crooke was good enough in her book and made her insides warm at the thought of it. 'Second: I've played the guitar since I was a kid and my most prized possession is the guitar that my parents gave me on my seventeeth birthday. They were both killed in a car accident a few weeks later.'

'Oh my God, that's terrible,' said Grace with heartfelt sympathy.

'I know,' nodded Dawn. 'I miss them so much, especially with the wedding coming up.'

'You must,' agreed Christie. 'And do you still play the guitar?'

'Not as often these days,' said Dawn.

'You must be good though if you've been playing it all this time. Didn't you ever join a band or anything?' asked Grace.

'No, I'm no way near good enough to join a band,' said Dawn with a smile. A rather sad little smile, thought Christie.

'And thirdly, oh crikey, can't think of anything. Oh yes I can: up until two years ago I was a hairdresser.'

That seemed to surprise them all, judging by the sharp raise in eyebrows.

'What made you change career then?' asked Christie.

'I always wanted to work in an office. I never thought I'd be any good though. I was getting bored with hairdressing and went on a computer course and I really, really enjoyed it. So when I found a vacancy for this place in the newspaper, I applied and got it. Couldn't believe it. Didn't think I had a chance.'

The girl doesn't have a lot of self-confidence, deduced Christie. Funny how it was always the pretty, capable ones who didn't.

All eyes turned to Raychel, who had very pink cheeks as a result. Her co-workers smiled encouragingly.

'Three things quickly, Raychel, then you can escape the spotlight,' said Christie, patting her hand.

'I must be the most boring person on the planet,' said Raychel, taking a deep breath. 'OK, here goes. I'm married to Ben who is a builder.'

'Is he a Barnsley lad?' asked Dawn.

'No, he's a Geordie.'

'Oh, I wondered if you'd moved here to be with him? You're from Newcastle as well, presumably, with that accent, aren't you?' Dawn popped the last bit of scone in her mouth and chewed.

'He moved here for work. We used to live in London and he met a bloke down there that was looking for workers up here,' Raychel explained.

'Funny. Most people are moving down south for work and there's you moving the other way!' Dawn commented. 'Been married long?'

'Ten years.'

'Blimey!' said Anna, her first contribution of the morning.

'How many children do you have then?' asked Dawn, who drew the conclusion that anyone who got married so young had to be pregnant. But Raychel surprised her.

'No children and no plans for them. Right, number two.' She tapped with her fingertips on the table as she thought. 'I like to paint pictures. I've always been into art. I'd have liked to have been an artist.'

'Are you any good?' asked Dawn.

'I don't know,' said Raychel. 'I just enjoy doing it. It relaxes me. Bit like your yoga does for you, Grace. And thirdly, I'm moving into a new flat next month and I can't wait. We've been renting but we've got one of the new apartments in Milk Street, where the old dairy used to be. Right at the top.'

'A penthouse then,' winked Christie.

'It's lovely,' said Raychel with a contented sigh. 'I'm going to measure up for curtains at the weekend and I can't wait, how sad is that?'

'I think it's lovely,' said Dawn, who wished she and Calum could move into a new place. She shuddered when she thought of the state of his windows. A team of Laurence Llewellyn-Bowens couldn't have made those tatty monstrosities pretty.

'Anna?' Christie tilted her head at the quiet woman with the sad eyes.

'Happily engaged to and living with Tony who's a barber, owner of the moodiest cat in the world and aficionado of Hammer Horror films. That's me in a nutshell!' said Anna, nodding her head as if that constituted a full stop.

Christie wasn't going to let her get away with that brief résumé though.

'What sort of cat?'

'Chocolate point Siamese. Male, obviously. You'd think he was Prince Edward the way he looks down his nose at everyone.'

'And free haircuts for you presumably?'

Anna thought of Tony's fingers in her hair and gulped. 'Oh yes,' she said over-brightly.

'I used to love the old Hammer Horrors,' said Grace. 'I had a bit of a thing for Christopher Lee.'

'Once, the nuns at school asked me what I wanted to be

when I grew up,' said Anna, sliding back into a memory. 'They said I should let my imagination run riot, so I told them I wanted to be a vampire. I got a right thrashing for it as well!' She remembered Sister Martin and her smiley face that she would whip off like a detachable mask at the first sign of any insolence. The old bitch had thrashed Anna till she wet herself. Hard-line, frustrated old nuns like her were one of the main reasons why Anna would never send her children to a Catholic school, not that she'd ever have any. Not unless a miracle was somehow bestowed upon her. She'd keep her eye out for a star appearing over her house and a bunch of shepherds knocking on the front door wanting admittance, just in case though.

'You have the look of a gothic maid.' Christie weighed Anna up. Full-bosomed, small-waisted and pouty-lipped, the woman would have been transformed with the right neckline and a bit of red lipstick. She had the look of a woman sadly neglected. By herself more than anyone.

'Werewolf or vampire though. Which would you go for most?' asked Raychel, who had just finished reading *Twilight* and rather fancied the former. The werewolf protagonist reminded her of Ben, all massive and warm.

'No question,' sniffed Anna. 'Vampire every time. Couldn't do with all that werewolf-moulting. It'd block up my Dyson.'

Everyone laughed. Anna had a dry sense of humour, that seemed evident. Christie drained her cup and then noticed that everyone with anything left in their cups followed suit.

'Right, best get back to work then. Thank you for that, ladies. I feel I know you all a little better now.'

Christie led the way out. She was aware that behind her, Grace was twittering to Dawn and Raychel was asking Anna something. She smiled to herself. The thaw had commenced.

Chapter 13

Paul rang Grace on her mobile at work that afternoon.

'Mum, you are aware it's the Grand National on Saturday?' he asked.

'My goodness, it's never been a year since the last one!'

'Time sure does fly when you're having fun,' said her beloved boy. Grace could have wept for him. Life hadn't exactly been a bundle of laughs for him since his father banished him from the family home. She knew he wasn't over the hurt, however much he pretended to be.

'I'll get a newspaper at lunchtime. All the horse names will be in,' volunteered Grace.

'I've looked already. There's one running called The Sun Rose. I'll have to go for it, for my Nana.'

'Oh well, let's do that then. It's as good an omen as any.'

'Same arrangement as usual?'

'Same arrangement. On the nose.'

'You can pick up your winnings when I see you next week. We'll have lots of cake, the full shebang cream tea. I'll pay.'

Grace laughed. He was the most generous soul she knew.

'Oh Paul, I wish you could meet someone who'd love you for the wonderful person you are!' she said.

I wish you could as well, Mum, said Paul to himself.

Gordon hated gambling and so every year, for as long as she could remember, Grace and Paul had had a secret bet. They didn't study form and distance or anything complicated like that, they just picked a horse with a name that meant something to both of them, whatever the odds. They had won for two years running now, firstly with Amazing Grace, then last year on the rank outsider, Laura's Boy. Grace put the winnings in the secret bank account she had opened two years ago and which Gordon knew nothing about. Grace had started squirreling away some of her money to leave to Paul if anything happened to her. Gordon had cut his son out of his will. It annoyed him no end that she hadn't done the same.

'The Sun Rose?' said Christie, looking over Grace's shoulder at the name she had just written down on her pad. 'Are you betting on horses, Mrs Beamish?'

'Just once a year,' said Grace. 'My boy and I always have a bet on the Grand National.'

'Of course! It's the Grand National on Saturday, isn't it?' said Christie. 'Shall we all have a go?'

'What, together or separate?' asked Dawn.

'Together,' said Christie. 'One up, all up.'

'Anyone got a paper?' asked Anna. 'Let's have a look at some names.' Maybe there would be an appropriate *Tosser of a Fiancé*, or a *Big Fat-Titted Scrubber* that drew her eye.

'I have,' said Dawn and got out her *Sun* newspaper. She turned to the back pages and looked at the preview of the race.

'Any good names?' asked Raychel.

'Augustus, Elvis Smith, Chocolate Soldier, Mayfly, Hell for Leather, Royal Jelly, Leapfrog, Silver Lady, Milky Bar, The Sun Rose. Wow, I'm reading the *Sun*!' said Dawn with a little gasp. 'That has to be a sign.'

'Have you been sniffing strong glue?' said Anna.

'Well, it's not much of a sign, I grant you,' said Dawn. 'But it sounds like a winner to me.'

Anna half-tutted, half-smiled. 'No, it's not that. I would have thought with your name being *Dawn* that it would strike more of a chord. Dawn . . . sun rising?'

Dawn gasped, open mouthed. 'Crikey, I never thought of that!'

No, Dawn wasn't the brightest button on the planet common-sense-wise, it crossed one or two minds then. But there was something quite ethereal and unworldly about her – as if she were a simpler, more uncomplicated being, and someone who was meant to have a bit of air between her ears. Her work, however, was immaculate.

'What are the odds on it?' asked Christie.

'Fifty to one,' said Grace. 'That's the horse my son and I have picked.'

'He's a grey. Can't remember the last time a grey won the National. Hmmm . . .' Christie read on. The horse didn't have a lot of form so he was either going to be a total loser or a surprise in the unveiling.

'I love grey horses,' said Dawn. She slid into her own memories then. Her mum and dad always wanted a ranch and horses. They were born in the wrong era and the wrong country, they used to joke to each other. They belonged to the Wild West with all its heroes and cattle and prairies. Her dad had taught her to ride when she was small. They used to borrow a horse from the riding stables up the road for her, a gentle grey called Smoke.

'I'm happy if everyone else is,' said Anna, who knew nothing about horses and wasn't really bothered who won, if the truth be told. Still, she could leave the winnings to charity if she died before Saturday.

'Me too,' said Raychel. 'Fiver each?'

'Count me in,' said Dawn. 'Let's go mad and make it a

tenner.' She was throwing so much money away these days, what harm would another few quid do?

Malcolm watched them from the next section. It was quite obvious they were picking horses out for the National. He spotted McAskill rounding the corner. *This should be interesting,* he thought and waited. McAskill's whole pet department was either reading the horse-racing bit of the newspaper or faffing about with their purses. He wouldn't like that, however much of a flavour-of-the-month Miss Swaggering-Bottom was. As Malcolm watched James McAskill lift up the paper to read from it – *the* Sun *as well* – the smile slid off his face. The big boss and Christie were arguing about something, but laughing too. Open-mouthed, Malcolm saw Mr McAskill open up his wallet and hand some paper money over to Christie. The bloody woman was fire-proof.

Grace got home that night to find that Gordon was in the kitchen looking through a seed catalogue. He had a pad open at his side and showed her the list of fruit trees he was going to order. He was the only man she knew who could get excited over Bramley saplings. Poring over the pages of the brochure had put him in an exceedingly good mood; he even offered to make her a cup of tea. He hummed while he waited for the kettle to boil, but it was a smug sort of hum that implied to Grace he was up to something more than selecting plants. She didn't like it. She didn't like it one bit.

Chapter 14

That Friday night, Anna had a totally believable dream in which Tony came back and had just gone to the bathroom. She awoke the next morning waiting for him to climb back into bed. Then her brain unscrambled the confusion and brutally sorted out fact from fiction. The reality of her true situation hit her harder than ever and the pain in her heart was real and crippling. After making a lunch that she didn't eat, she fell prey to temptation and walked past the barber's shop. There, framed in the window, she saw Tony, *her Tony*, cutting hair with the ease of a man who had no troubles in the world. She didn't know what she had expected to see. Him crying into his scissors perhaps? Looking drawn and pale as if he was a man who had made the biggest mistake in the world? Not only did she see Tony, and it had to be said his hair was looking darker and less grey, and that was a very bright shirt he was wearing, but there was Lynette Bottom in a crop top and jeans that exposed not only a tattoo of something along the top of the crack of her arse but the dainty lace of a black G string.

Anna switched the TV on to watch the Grand National for something to do, but she could barely see the screen for the tears that blurred her eyes and flowed and flowed and flowed.

Dawn had the television on for the big race in the background as she studied the brochure of wedding favour examples which was opened up on her knee. Sugared almonds always looked very pretty but they were horrible things to eat. Her teeth shivered just thinking about the taste. She thought that maybe she should wrap a single chocolate for everyone. It would be a far nicer and much tastier alternative to bog-flavoured nuts covered in sugar, and a damned sight cheaper. She badly needed to cut some costs on this wedding somewhere. She had spent nearly all her savings already and hadn't even thought about flowers or the cake or the honeymoon yet!

The horses were getting into position. She closed the brochure in readiness to watch the race devotedly. Her ears picked up a name of a horse: June Wedding. She wished she'd known that one was running; that would have had to have been her choice. Too late now, obviously. Suddenly they were off. She didn't watch horse races as a rule, scared to see one of them fall and hurt itself and have to be shot. Hell, those fences were exceptionally high. A horse fell at the first. There were thirty fences in all. By the time the horses had got to the Chair at the fifteenth, Dawn was leaning forward and shouting encouragement. The brochure had long since slid from her knee and all thoughts of almonds versus Thorntons had taken second place. Elvis Smith had the lead from the beginning. He was still in first place as they passed the Open Ditch, Bechers – for the second time – then at the Canal Turn he lost the lead to Chocolate Soldier. He slid into third place behind Mayfly but then Chocolate Soldier refused Valentine's. Royal Jelly was belting up on the inside, then the enthusiastic commentary started cranking up her adrenalin levels. She hadn't a clue where June Wedding was. It really was a shame she hadn't bet on that; the jockey had been in peach too, the theme colour for her own wedding. The horses approached the Elbow. Elvis Smith was back in front after a mad spurt. Suddenly The Sun Rose tore up the inside, overtaking everything but the lead horse. The commentator was screaming by the twenty-ninth as there seemed to be nothing between Elvis Smith and The Sun Rose.

'Come on, boy,' Dawn screamed at the screen. 'Come on, you grey sod! I could do with winning some money!'

'Elvis Smith's going to do it,' said the commentator. Just as The Sun Rose burst past in the last nano-second and crossed the line, winning by a short, but definite distance.

'Jesus H!' said Dawn. She couldn't remember the last time she had been as thrilled as that. Her heart was galloping as if she'd just finished running the race herself. She hadn't ridden since she was seventeen though. It had been too painful to even think of climbing on the back of a horse and cantering across the Yorkshire countryside without her parents. Her dad had been so funny, pretending they were all in Oklahoma and yee-haaing like a mad cowboy. Maybe, when the wedding was over, she would visit the riding school in Maltstone and go for a sunny morning hack. Maybe it was time to get back on a horse and revisit a few happy memories.

The tiny Irish jockey on the elegant grey horse was shaking a triumphant fist in the air. He was talking to the camera in a fast, squeaky Irish brogue and no one could understand a word, not that it mattered. He'd led a rank outsider on only his first National to victory. The last grey to win was in 1961, the commentator was saying. No one was interested in the runners-up, although their names flashed up on screen. Dawn hadn't a clue how much money that meant the work's betting syndicate had won but she overrode her initial impulse to tell Calum about it. If he knew she was collecting that sort of money, he'd only put less in the wedding pot. So she kept quiet and sympathized with him when he came in from the pub, having put his money on Mayfly's nose. She picked up her brochure and got back to the argument of sugared almonds versus chocolate truffles in silence.

She learned from the newspaper the next morning that June Wedding was the horse that had fallen at the first fence.

Chapter 15

Grace was staring out of the window after putting all the Sunday lunch pots and pans away. Sarah and Hugo had gone off for an hour or twelve to look for some new conservatory furniture, leaving Sable kicking a ball about in the garden with her granddad and Joe. He was a lovely boy, very much like Paul, kind-hearted and quiet, happiest with his nose in a book or scribbling in a pad.

Gordon had been in a very good mood this weekend. Too good a mood for comfort. He'd been smiling non-stop all weekend. He smiled when he went out to the Legion on Friday night and he had smiled and been Mr Jovial all the way through to Sunday lunch. It wasn't a nice smile though. There was something about the way it sat on his lips that disturbed her.

She was still trying to work out what Gordon could possibly be up to – because as sure as eggs were eggs, he *was* up to something – when Laura handed Grace a cup of tea and interrupted her thoughts.

'Mum? Hello! Tea!'

'Oh sorry, love, in a world of my own there.'

'So much for Sarah being an hour. She's already been over two,' said Laura, joining her mother watching through the window as Sable stormed off in a little strop because Joe hadn't passed the ball to her. 'At least you'll have a break for the next couple of weeks while they are away abroad having their Easter holiday.'

'She's pregnant,' said Grace. 'She needs as much help as I can give her.'

'I'm surprised she didn't ask you to look after Sable while they went abroad by themselves,' said Laura with a tut.

Grace didn't volunteer that Sarah had actually asked her that and she had replied that she couldn't take time off so soon in her new position. Sarah wouldn't have asked her father then, knowing well in advance what his answer would have been. He didn't mind an intensive half an hour playing with his grand-daughter, in a way he had never played with his own children, but he would never have agreed to looking after a child single-handedly during the day while Grace was working.

'She shouldn't have got pregnant again if she couldn't cope,' continued Laura. 'We all know she's having this baby to cement up the cracks in her marriage.'

Grace didn't comment, but she knew Laura was right and it saddened her so much.

'You know she's expecting to go straight back to work after the birth and for you to look after the baby, don't you? She and Hugo are banking on you getting early retirement as soon as possible.'

'Well, they're going to be rather disappointed,' said Grace with a heavy sigh. Yes, she knew that if she ever gave up her job, her workload and domestic drudgery would triple. God help her when she was eventually forced to retire.

'If Sarah and Hugo can afford all those fancy holidays, I can't see why they don't employ a nanny,' said Laura with another tut, then she thought for a second and answered her own question. 'Well, I suppose I can, if I think about it. She's not going to let another woman in the house when she's all pregnancy-fat and risk Hugo's eye wandering again. Where's she off to for Easter? Let me guess – Benidorm?'

Grace laughed. She knew Laura was joking, seeing as Hugo had dropped it into the conversation at least fifty times that they were using a five-star hotel in Lanzarote as their base while they looked around the island with a view to buying a property out there. Hugo was a snob of the highest order, and Sarah wasn't far behind him these days. They were both very concerned with having bigger, better and more expensive things than anyone. Grace hadn't a clue where that trait in Sarah's personality had come from – Paul and Laura weren't materialistic at all.

'They've got a day flight too, so I just hope Sable doesn't get too restless.'

'Sable is a brat,' said Laura. 'She'll kick up, of course, and annoy everyone on the plane and Sarah will see it as her "naturally expressing her feelings" and praise her for it.'

Grace nodded. She felt guilty even thinking it but Sable was quite a difficult child to love. She was spoiled, rather like Sarah. But that had been Grace's own fault.

Sarah hadn't been old enough to remember her real mother when she died and Grace had tried to make up for that by indulging her too much. Add to that all the pretensions that Sarah had acquired since marrying the stuffy, arrogant, workaholic company director, Hugo, and she had become a bit of a monster. Grace loved all her children, but increasingly she felt that Sarah looked down on her and, yes, it hurt.

Laura took a long sip of tea. 'Have you seen Paul recently?'

'Yes,' said Grace. 'And I'm seeing him next Saturday as well.'

'Has he said anything to you?' asked Laura mysteriously.

'Anything about what, dear?'

'Oh, nothing in particular,' said Laura. 'Just anything.'

'He's told me all about Rose Manor,' said Grace.

'Have you seen the pics? Lovely, isn't it?'

'Yes, it is, or at least it will be when he's done all the work.' Grace had no doubt of her son's abilities to turn the wreck of a house into something lovely. He was a perfectionist, a hard worker with vision. She couldn't have wished for a better son, not even if she could have borne her own. She had been only twenty-one when an infection in her womb had resulted in her needing a full hysterectomy. Then, by a cruel irony, she'd had to nurse Laura through the same just after Joe was born. At least her daughter had a little comfort in her memories of one child growing in her body.

They stood and sipped their tea some more, staring out at Gordon in the garden with the children. Both thinking on the same lines.

'It's ridiculous this Paul and Dad thing, don't you think?' said Laura wistfully.

'There's nothing I can do,' said Grace. 'I wish I could. I can't even broach the subject – he just walks out of the room.'

Joe suddenly fell to the ground, clutching his head and crying hard which wasn't like him at all. He was a hardy lad and not at all given to tears. Laura rushed out.

'What's the matter, love?' called Grace a few steps behind her daughter as Joe cuddled into his mum's shoulder.

'He's all right,' said Gordon and grabbed the boy's arm. 'Come and play, Joe.'

'Gordon, what happened?' asked Grace.

Joe struggled against his granddad's grip.

'It's nothing,' said Gordon in that 'don't-make-a-fuss' voice of his.

'He's bleeding, Dad. What happened, sweetheart?'

'Sable threw a rock at me,' said Joe.

'Didn't,' said Sable with her tongue pulled out. She was so like Sarah when she was little. All blonde corkscrew curls and watery blue eyes – a perfect picture of innocence.

'Come and play football and stop being stupid,' said Gordon, pulling Joe away from his mother's embrace.

'Let him go, Dad, he's hurt,' said Laura.

'He's not *that* hurt,' barked Gordon. 'He's going to carry on playing football. Stop crying, Joe. Here, kick that ball.'

Instead though, Joe sprang back to his mother's arms.

Gordon snapped nastily, 'For goodness sake, stop mollycoddling him. He's all right. Joe, come back here and kick this ball.'

'I don't want to play any more,' said Joe.

'KICK THIS BLOODY BALL!' yelled Gordon and stabbed at the ground in front of him with a determined finger. Laura felt her boy wince and she tightened her arms around him.

'Leave him alone, Gordon,' said Grace. 'The boy's hurt. Look at his head. Sable, I am going to tell your mummy what you've done to Joe when she comes back.'

Sable started to cry then. Gordon didn't seem to think that was as inappropriate as Joe crying. Little girls cried, little boys didn't.

'You'll make him soft!' spat Gordon, puce-faced. 'He might as well be a girl. He'll turn out like that other one. That what you want? A poof? Another nancy boy in the family, as if one isn't enough? That make you both proud, will it?'

Gordon pushed, in none too gentlemanly a fashion, past Grace into the house as Joe sobbed against his mum's breast. Laura looked at her father's disappearing back and Grace saw that she was shaking her head with blatant disgust. Grace realized it was the first time she had seen her husband through her daughter's eyes.

Chapter 16

'We did quite well on Saturday, didn't we?' said Dawn, unbuttoning her coat the following Monday morning.

'We certainly did,' said Christie. 'The Sun Rose finished at fifty-five to one in the end. Greys are always rank outsiders, which was lucky for us.'

'Bloody Norah,' said Anna. 'We won a lot of money, didn't we?'

'Don't forget to add on the forty pounds James donated as well. I bet he wished he'd put it on for himself now. All in all, it wasn't bad for an afternoon's work,' added Christie with a little wink.

'You're not joking!' It was the only bit of good news Anna had had in ages. She could buy herself a rocking chair and a lifetime's supply of Horlicks. That's what old farts over thirty-nine spent their money on, presumably.

'Did we win?' asked Raychel, rushing in at just turned nine o'clock.

'You didn't hear the result? Where on earth have you been all weekend?' asked Anna with a good-humoured tut.

'We've been doing house stuff,' said Raychel. 'I think we spent four hours in Ikea alone on Saturday. Sorry I'm late, Christie. I got caught up in a traffic snarl.'

'I hadn't even noticed,' said Christie. God forbid she would ever be the sort of boss who made a fuss over a few minutes!

'Sounds nice,' said Anna, as a memory of moving into her present home with Tony bloomed in her mind. They'd gone mad in Ikea themselves and had to make three trips to take everything home. They had put the bed up first of all and he had insisted on christening it immediately.

'Thank God Ben is such an ox. He should be on *Britain's Strongest Man*. People were looking at him in awe carrying the stuff to the van. He put it all together in no time and all I did was make lots of cups of tea.'

He sounded a good sort, did Ben, thought Anna. How come she never got one like that? How come she ended up with cheating pricks? She had never been lucky in love.

'I'll have the money for you all in the next couple of days,' promised Christie.

'We should save some of it and have a meal out with it or something to celebrate,' suggested Dawn. She knew if she had it in her pocket, Calum would only 'borrow' it from her, with no intention of ever paying it back. And she could never manage to say no to him.

'That's a good idea,' said Christie. 'Are there any nice pubs or restaurants around here?'

'What about that new Thai place next to the Rising Sun pub up the road?' said Dawn. 'It's only five minutes' walk away. Ooh, Rising Suns again. Must be an omen.'

'Fine by me, if everyone is in agreement? We'll arrange something after the Easter break?'

Everyone either nodded or mumbled and Christie was delighted to accept that as a definite yes then.

There was a happy buzz in the office on Wednesday when Christie distributed well-stocked brown packets of horse-race winnings after her brother had accompanied her to pick it up, because she didn't feel comfortable carrying that amount of money around alone. Each of them put thirty pounds into an envelope for their future celebratory meal. Christie mused what the others would do with their balances. She would buy more shoes and had exactly the pair in mind. She would bet that Dawn's would go towards her wedding and Raychel's towards her house, but what of Grace and Anna? They were harder to guess at. She wondered how they spent their treat money when they had any.

Christie would buy a bottle of champagne with it, too, and raise a glass to her late husband, as she always did at this time of year. She revered Easter. She wasn't a particularly religious woman, but she reflected a lot around the anniversary of her widowhood. She wished Peter had died when it was autumn or winter and not when the bluebells that he loved so much were starting to flood the forests, when everything in nature was awakening and coming alive; it seemed so unfair. She made sure she enjoyed this time of year for him, for both of them.

Grace had taken it upon herself to set up a coffee rota, and Christie had insisted on being included on the list; she said she drank the stuff too, and wasn't that much up her own backside that she wouldn't make it when it was her turn. After Malcolm as an acting boss, Christie Somers was like a cold glass of water on a thirsty throat.

Christie liked the smiles that had started passing between the women. It didn't take anything away from their efficiency that they would share a brief natter about 'that shade of blouse really suiting Grace with her colouring' or asking, 'What happened in *Corry* in the last five minutes last night, because the phone rang and I missed it?' Christie was sure that if there had been an office thermometer to check, she would find that it was rising by a degree with every passing day.

That evening, the later Dartley train was in when Anna reached the platform. She had missed her usual one after calling into

Iceland for some bits and pieces. As she ran for it, she noticed the man in black on the opposite platform again. When his eyes landed on her, he looked as if he couldn't believe his luck that he had seen her again. The thing she noticed most was that he didn't just stare over at her, he appeared to be studying her, as Albert Pierrepoint might study a condemned man to determine how much rope he'd need for the drop. Then, to Anna's abject horror, he pointed over at her. He was beckoning. *Yeah, like she was going to go over to him.* Anna's heart rate increased. She jumped on the train, trying to ignore the fact that the man was still trying to attract her attention, waving at her now. She risked a direct look as the train started up. The man had gone. Then she noticed him descending the last step on her side of the platform. How the heck did he get there so fast? He must have flown across the tunnel above the track.

Well, she supposed blackly, if he was a serial killer, what did it matter? Her life was over anyway. All she had to look forward to was an existence of dribbling and smelling of wee in retirement homes. Being forty was the first step on the slippery slope. She hoped, when he did eventually catch up with her, that his method was quick and painless.

Chapter 17

Vladimir Darq watched the train pull out of the station seconds before he had a chance to jump on it. *Damn.* He had found the one he was looking for and he couldn't get to her. The first time he had seen the woman with the long chestnut hair, his inner radar had told him she was a sure contender. He hadn't been able to get her out of his mind that night and knew by the next morning that no other woman would do. Every night he had waited at the train station for her to return and now she had and he had missed her. He thought of all the shopping she was carrying and it came to him then that maybe she usually caught an earlier train? Third time lucky. He wouldn't miss her again.

The building had that happy 'last day before a break' feel on Thursday. Dawn was going to be doing some more weddingy things and was all giddy about that; Raychel was joyfully twittering on about preparing for her house move and, though Anna didn't bubble over like the others, Christie hoped she was looking forward to spending a quiet long weekend with her man and her cat. Only from Grace's corner did she feel a cool draught. Christie noticed her staring into space on a few occasions.

'Everything OK?' she asked.

Grace snapped her mind back to the here and now.

'Absolutely fine,' she said, convincing neither of them, but Christie didn't push and Grace didn't volunteer that she had the most awful sense of foreboding. It was something to do with Gordon, although he wasn't doing anything out of the ordinary she could really put her finger on. Still, it was an annoying feeling that wouldn't go away.

The Easter holiday loomed long in front of Grace. Thank goodness there was a lovely Saturday afternoon with Paul to look forward to and Joe's face to enjoy when he saw how many eggs the Easter Bunny had left for him at his grandparents' house. If Gordon's stupid smile didn't scare away the Bunny from visiting, that was.

Paul had been the last of her children to leave home over three years ago. It was only when he moved out that she realized how buoyant their company had kept her spirits. Once they were all gone, she felt increasingly as if she were struggling for air within the walls.

At five o'clock, Christie bade her ladies a good holiday. The department was to be shut until Tuesday, for Easter. It looked, to Christie, as if Grace especially needed a restful break.

Gordon had volunteered to take Grace to and pick her up from work that day. In fact, he had positively insisted on it. He wanted to take her car in for a service, he said, because he'd heard a rattle. Grace hadn't heard any rattle, but there was no reason not to believe him. They hadn't spoken much since the Joe incident on Sunday. Grace hadn't even brought it up when Laura had gone home. What was the point? If Gordon didn't want to talk about something, he didn't talk about it.

He was already waiting for her in the car park when she came out of work. The car had been washed and polished and valeted inside, she noticed as she climbed into it. They both mumbled a hello at each other as she clicked herself into the seatbelt.

'Did you get the rattle fixed then?' she asked.

'What rattle?' he said absently, then, 'Oh no, there wasn't one. I must have been imagining things.'

Grace knew then that he hadn't taken her car into the garage. He hadn't heard a rattle. He was up to something and her instincts were proved correct when he set off, taking an immediate right turn instead of the left that would have put them on the road for home.

'Where are we going?'

'Just a little diversion,' he said.

Grace was tired this week. Tired of witnessing even more divisions within her family, tired of having to watch her tongue in case she said something to inflame Gordon. She wanted to take the opportunity of a weekend with no babysitting Sable to have long baths, a nice glass of wine or two and a few hours' quality reading time. She felt her batteries badly needed a serious charge-up. 'Gordon, where are we going?' she asked again wearily.

'Never you mind,' said Gordon with that incredibly annoying smile.

'Gordon?'

Gordon didn't say anything and flicked on the right indicator as he approached the roundabout which told Grace they were taking the motorway south.

Anna stood on the railway platform, heart thumping in her chest. The weirdo in black, thankfully, wasn't there. Maybe she should have got any impending attack over and done with. She visualized a touching hospital scene where Tony rushed to her bedside and gently stroked the part of her skull which the stranger had stoved in with an axe. He would pledge undying love and come back to care for her and dab her face with cool flannels and kisses.

The barriers dropped, the train came down the track and

Anna's hold on the new rape alarm in her pocket relaxed. A cool breath puffed onto the back of her neck. She turned to find the man in black behind her, his eyes locking with hers. She saw fangs, clear as day. She was going to feature in the *Chronicle* as the first woman in Barnsley to become undead, she thought, then everything went swirly and, finally, black. His gloved hands came out and caught her as she fainted.

Chapter 18

Anna came to seconds later, though it felt much longer, with a crowd gathering around her, the strange man cradling her in his arms on the ground and some silly cow running up and down saying, 'Help, someone phone the emergency services! There's a woman having a heart attack!'

She remembered being helped to her feet, then the embarrassment set in as her consciousness swam back to the surface. She tried to look *compos mentis* in the same way a totally drunk person attempts sobriety, with about as much success. She kept saying, 'I'm fine, I'm fine,' over and over again. But she heard that daft woman shriek, 'You should have left her lying down. She needs a hospital. I'm St John's Ambulance trained. I know these things.'

But then Anna's brain seemed to fast forward a little and the next thing was that she was being led over to the station café by some nice lady in an apron for a cup of tea with lots of sugar in it. Fast forward again some more seconds and Anna was sitting in a quiet corner, being pushed down on a seat by gentle hands. And Fang-man was sitting opposite her. She did a double-take and shook her head. Did vampires drink Yorkshire Tea, because this one did – and rip open and offer Cadbury's shortcakes? She couldn't remember that from her Bram Stoker edition.

'Are you diabetic?' he asked in a deep voice with a fierce accent reminiscent of black forests and dark castles in East Europe while he proffered the chocolate biscuits.

'No,' said Anna. 'Well, I wasn't this morning anyway.'

'Then you passed out solely because of fear of me,' the man said. 'I am so sorry.' He had pale skin and very black hair, past shoulder length and tied at the back. There wasn't a hint of grey in it but it didn't look dyed at all. His beard was the same colour, a thin, expert line that swept over a strong chin and square jaw.

'I'm sure it's not entirely your fault I fainted,' said Anna, omitting to add that she couldn't remember the last decent meal she had eaten and as a consequence she'd been having moments of light-headedness.

'I have been waiting for you,' the man went on. He had very blue eyes, deep as lagoons, with golden flecks in them, very odd in an attractive way. They were fringed with thick, black lashes that a woman would have killed for. His eyebrows were heavy and black too, arched and masculine, a small space between them above his nose.

'Why? What do you want me for?' said Anna defensively. 'Why are you loitering around interchanges?'

'Not loitering, searching,' he answered. 'And not just stations, but libraries, supermarkets, shops. I look for a woman.'

Anna opened her mouth to reply but she hadn't a clue what to say to that. Apart from '*perv*'.

The man reached into his voluminous coat and pulled out a very stylish business card which he then handed over to her.

Vladimir Darq.

That's all it said, plus a mobile number. How arrogant was that? Or supremely confident anyway. It smacked of someone who should be instantly recognizable. The funny thing was, the name *did* ring a bell although she couldn't for the life of her remember where she had heard it before. *Crimewatch*?

'What do you want with me then, Mr Darq?' She pronounced it 'Dark'. He didn't correct her so she presumed that was right.

Vladimir Darq slid off his gloves to get a better purchase on his mug. He had large but exquisite hands. The nails were black varnished but strangely that only added to his masculinity. He had an enormous gold ring on the middle left finger bearing the word 'DARQ.' It was his only ring, she also noticed.

'You,' he began, staring at Anna with such pale-eyed intensity that she felt herself blushing, '. . . you are the woman for whom I have been searching.'

Nutter alert.

'OK, that's me going home now,' said Anna, attempting to stand but failing.

'Please, hear me out,' he said, his palms open towards her. 'Sit, listen. Five minutes. That's all I ask.'

Anna sat again because she had no choice. Her legs said no to any supporting requests from her brain and the moment she stood, the blood rushed from her head and she felt ever so woozy again. Not that she wanted him to know that, in case he took advantage.

'My name is Vladimir Darq. I am a designer,' he began.

Yes, of course, thought Anna. *That rings a big bell now*. She'd seen him on fashion shows. Gok Wan had dressed some of his women in Darq gowns. If, of course, he was the real Vladimir Darq and not some saddo imposter. After all, Barnsley train station wasn't exactly the place to bump into Laura Ashley, Coco Chanel and the like.

'You may know me as a maker of gowns. Only gowns. But no longer!' He waved away his entire collection of gowns with one sweep of his beautiful hand. 'I have diversified into a new area – lingerie. I don't want to design for A-list divas any more. I want to design for women who want to feel as if they are A-list inside here,' and he thumped his chest where his heart was positioned. 'I have a question: do you watch Gok Wan on the television?'

'Yes,' said Anna cautiously. Oh God, he was going to ask her to walk up and down the railway platform naked!

'And do you watch *Jane's Dames*?'

'I love *Jane's Dames*,' gasped Anna. It was a new programme which competed with Gok's shows, more or less the same formula, and presented by a young, gorgeous, no-nonsense style guru-in-the-making called Jane Cleve-Jones.

'*Jane's Dames* are making a new series. They have approached various designers – I am, of course, one of them – and each of us has a model that we intend to transform. My specialized area will be the lingerie. I need a woman who wants to feel beautiful, earthy – *Darq*, as I call it. I believe that every woman has a Darq side but alas, most women don't even suspect it. Then I see you and I know without a doubt that you are the one. I want you to be my model. I want you to inspire other women to wear my clothes. I want to design for women like you.'

'Old, past-it lumps of lard, you mean?' said Anna, with a mirthless little laugh.

'*Nu*, not at all,' said Vladimir Darq, leaning across the table, stroking one finger down Anna's jawline and making her shiver in the process. 'Women in their late thirties, early forties who think they are no longer sexy or maybe they have never felt that way. I see it in the slump of your shoulders that you do not feel desired. You have not learned that sex comes from within. I would guess that others have not made you feel very good about yourself. I am right, of course. You think that life has forgotten you.' He took a strand of her dull brown hair and let it fall through his fingers.

Anna felt the tears making their way up to her eyeballs and gulped them down. That small gesture in her throat was all Vladimir Darq needed to see to know he was correct in his assumptions. Not that he had had any doubt. He had too much confidence in his intuition for that.

Anna puffed out her cheeks. Was it so obvious she was an unloved reject with about as much spark as a spent match in a canal, even to a total stranger across two railway lines? Boy, she must be a total minger.

'No matter. I can transform you,' whispered Vladmir Darq. His voice was like a velvet caress. 'I can make you feel beautiful. I can change your life in less than eight weeks. And you will inspire other women like you to be beautiful. You will be the first of my beautiful Darq women.'

'Beautiful?' said Anna with a dry snort of laughter. The word had never been applied to her. No one had ever said; 'Anna Brightside, you are beautiful.' Or lovely, or pretty for that matter. In her teenage days, she lost count of the times she had got into conversations with gorgeous guys, only to realize halfway through that they were actually trying to get to her much prettier friend Caroline, with the dimples to die for and eyes like pools of treacle. In her twenties, she drew even less male attention, if that was possible, despite her flawless skin and hair the colour of autumn. Then, in her thirties, she met Tony, with his smooth banter and vociferous sexual appetite. Being the object of his lust had lifted her to some state of desirability. Until he dropped her for Miss Pert-Tits, of course. And now here was a bloke dressed up as a vampire telling her that he had magic underwear that would make her beautiful. At thirty-nine? After being as sexually alluring as magnolia paint all her life! Had he lost his guide dog? Or was he Care in the Community?

'I'm having trouble believing all this,' began Anna, confusion pulling her brows together. 'I mean, this is Barnsley and I'm in a train station. And you say you're Vladimir Darq and want to put me on the telly? I'm beginning to think I'm still on the floor passed out and this is a dream.' Even more so because every time his lips parted, she saw a hint of fangs in his teeth-line.

'What is your name, please?'

'Anna. Anna Brightside.'

'Then please, Anna Brightside, you think it over,' he said. 'Look me up on the worldwide web and see that I am in good faith.' He leaned in extra close and said in a voice that brooked no debate, 'We start filming on Saturday May ninth. You will do this with me.'

'Oh will I?' said Anna. *Cocky git.*

'Yes, you will, and I will expect your call soon to confirm,' said Vladimir Darq. 'It is *soarta* – fate – that we have met. *Soarta!*' And before Anna could say another word, he had stood, lifted up her hand, kissed the back of it, and clicked his heels together like Kaiser Wilhelm. Then he was gone in a swirl of black coat.

'Bloody hell,' said Anna. She couldn't think of anything else to say that better fitted the moment.

Chapter 19

Calum had managed to surpass himself: he delivered a hat-trick. Dawn had come in from work to find that her two-pound coin pot had been raided and the Easter egg from Thornton's she'd had iced with the words 'Foxy Fiancé' was half-eaten on the kitchen work surface. Calum had obviously found them both secreted at the bottom of the wardrobe. She felt more like crying at the desecration of the egg than at the missing money. Thank goodness she'd hidden her Grand National winnings a bit more securely, she thought. Then she found chocolatey fingerprints all over her veil in the carrier bag. She sat on the sofa fuming until he turned up pissed at half past ten. He laughed in that casual way he had, shrugging his shoulders as though totally baffled that she was making such a fuss about a few pounds that he'd borrowed, it wasn't as if he'd stolen it – and a flaming egg that she'd bought for him anyway. She cried that he'd spoiled her surprise for him. Then he shouted back at her that she was a nag and he'd be better off back with his ex, Mandy Clamp, if this was how it was going to be. She screamed back that he was a selfish pig and he slapped her across the face because she was hysterical, he said. Then he went to bed and left her sobbing in the sitting room.

Grace woke up the next morning to the sound of heavy rain

battering against the side of the walls of the tinny caravan in which she had just spent a cramped and uncomfortable night. She turned over to view the clock – ten past six – then she buried her head under the blanket on the narrowest bed she had ever had the misfortune to encounter and tried to get back into the dream she'd been having of swimming in the sea whilst a warm tropical rainstorm gently showered her from above. The bubbling rage inside her made that an impossibility. She struggled on, willing herself unsuccessfully into unconsciousness for another half an hour before getting up to make herself a cup of tea in a very poky kitchen area.

A picture of Gordon's self-satisfied face as he turned off down the motorway the previous evening reared up in her head and flooded her whole being with expletive-flavoured feelings. She'd known instantly then that she was being kidnapped and forced somewhere she didn't want to go. She would have put her life savings on it being Blegthorpe (a place-name which Gordon had been plopping into conversations for months) where she would be systematically tortured with tours of caravan sites. And boy, had she been right! Gordon had been very put out that she hadn't been in the mood for cheery chat over a sandwich and tea as they pulled in for a toilet stop at the service station. He had packed a case for her. It contained a pair of old black trousers that she wore when she was cleaning, a blue skirt and a fawn top, three bras and one pair of knickers. He'd put in her hairbrush and a couple of towels, no make-up but three pairs of shoes. No nightdress, no tights.

She switched on the old portable television and twiddled about with the aerial on top until she found a watchable picture. At least the newsreaders' voices covered the low burr of Gordon's annoyingly contented snoring in the next bedroom. She was half-tempted to take the car keys and drive home. She wanted to spend Easter Saturday with Paul and watch Joe's face light up at the sight of the giant WWE Easter egg she had found for him last week. She hated Gordon for this. What Gordon wanted, Gordon had to have, more so than ever recently since the words 'caravan' and 'early retirement' had started creeping into his sentences. Well, the time had surely come to make some sort of a stand against him. In fact, it was well overdue. She should have done it when he threw Paul out of their home and ignored her son's protestations not to get herself involved.

She texted Paul to say that she couldn't make tomorrow afternoon. Her battery went flat as soon as she had pressed send so she didn't know if the message had gone through. The dead screen on her phone made Grace feel more isolated from the world than she could ever remember being before.

Dawn awoke at ten on the sofa, where she had sobbed herself to sleep the previous night, and drove over to Muriel's house whilst Calum was still wrapped up in his quilt in bed, looking more as if he were hibernating than sleeping.

'Hello, lovey, this is a nice surprise,' said Muriel. Her soft voice made Dawn burst into tears and Muriel gathered her into her plump arms and, patting her back, led her across to the couch. She kicked off the greyhound that was dozing on it and pushed Dawn down onto the dog-furry cushion.

'You and our Cal had a fight, have you?' said Muriel.

Dawn nodded, unable to talk for all the tears clogging up her throat.

'On account of him being given a final warning yesterday for lamping that bloke?'

Dawn looked up.

'Oh, he hasn't told you that bit yet then?'

Dawn's face crumpled. Could this get any worse?

'Not his fault. Our Calum said the bloke had a black eye coming for months.'

So Calum had told his mum about his warning, then went

off to the pub and got drunk before coming home, thought
Dawn. It wasn't hard to see where she sat on his list of priori-
ties.

'It'll be all right, you know,' said Muriel. 'His dad was just
the same when he was younger. Feisty bugger Ron was, especially when he'd had a drink. Took him years to get his act
together, but he did in the end. Look at him now, wouldn't say
boo to a bloody goose. You've just got to hang on in there, girl.'

'He hit me across the face, Muriel,' said Dawn.

'You should have hit him back,' said Muriel, amazed at her
apparent stupidity. 'He wouldn't do it again so quick then, I can
tell you.' She laughed, then she took a close look at Dawn's
tear-stained face and her voice hardened.

'He couldn't have hit you that hard, there isn't a mark on
you. What did he hit you for anyway? You must have given
him a reason.'

'He said he'd be better off with Mandy Clamp.'

'Well, he would say that if he was trying to get your back up
in a row. You should have told him to bugger off and go to her
then; I would have.'

Dawn wouldn't though. Mandy Clamp was a big, nasty
thorn in Dawn's side. She and Calum had had an on/off relationship for years. Then, when Mandy dumped him for the last
time, he'd taken up with Dawn in that fateful window of
opportunity. Then Mandy decided she wanted him back and
had chased him blatantly on several occasions. Dawn always
took an obvious delight when Muriel said that none of them
liked her very much. The Crookes were all deliciously bitchy
about her wonky eye.

But, wonky eye or not, Calum might have visited Mandy,
just to teach Dawn a hard lesson. And Mandy Clamp would
have been happy to get one over on Dawn and open her door
to Calum. And her legs.

'He shouldn't have hit me,' wept Dawn.

'You want to grow up, Dawn,' said Muriel, a sudden sharp tone to her voice. 'He's told us that you nag him to death. Sooner or later a man will blow if you nag him like you do, we've all said as much.'

Dawn drew in a shock of breath. It had never crossed her mind that Calum had run to his family and moaned about her and then that the family had discussed her behind her back. What else had they said about her? It was obvious they would believe his side of things, but still, surely they didn't think he was entirely blameless? She wanted to say that she didn't nag and that asking him to put some money towards the wedding instead of spending it all across the bar wasn't nagging, was it? And it wasn't nagging to tell him off for raiding her savings bank. But, for the first time, she felt that Muriel wouldn't listen to her counter-claims. A Crooke's word to a fellow Crooke was gospel, it seemed. Even if one had gone so far as to slap one's girlfriend in the process.

Dawn's parents had been so easygoing, kind to each other, loving, respectful. Unlike some kids who went to sleep with a lullaby of their parents arguing, she had never heard them raise their voices to each other. She was sure they must have had their moments of disagreement, but she hadn't witnessed them. She had had a sweet, gentle upbringing with a family who loved and laughed together and the pain that she felt at being left alone took her years to recover from, if she ever had. Then the Crookes had stormed into her life and like a dry sponge she had sucked them up like a pool of clear water. But their world was so very different from the one she had been used to. Screaming to get her point across had never been her way and sometimes mid-argument she didn't feel like herself at all. She wondered if she would ever be able to adjust enough. She often hated that she had adjusted so much already.

Unlike Muriel though, she did accept that there were two sides to a story. Maybe she *was* coming across as a nag, even though she didn't mean to. Maybe she did need to cut Calum some slack. The more she nagged, the more she would drive him away, maybe to his waiting munter of an ex. She didn't want to fall out with Muriel on the point, so she conceded it for the sake of their continued harmony and said, 'You're probably right, Mu, I do nag a bit.'

'Get yourself back home,' said Muriel. 'Go and make it up with him. You're getting married in a few weeks. He's a good lad, Calum. He just needs a bit of love and support, not someone on his back all the time and moaning about him going out. If you want a caged animal, love, buy a hamster.'

Calum was Muriel's little blue-eyed boy. He could do no wrong. Dawn would do well to remember that.

Chapter 20

A few determined holiday-makers in cagoules were walking on the beach the next day, their umbrellas blowing inside-out; a full aerobic session's worth of wrestling with them followed, turning them into the wind to reform them into umbrella shapes. Grace decided to throttle back her rising temper and play Gordon's game. One, because she was too tired to resist him and two, because then she could at least say she had tried to like blustery, boring Blegthorpe but, surprisingly enough, had failed dismally.

So, while she should have been sharing tea and scones in the lovely Maltstone Garden Centre café with her son and the person he was keen for her to meet, she was taking refuge from a force eighteen gale in a basic, no frills dump, eating a sandwich made from tasteless cheese, cheap white bread, spread with even cheaper margarine and drinking tea from a mug that had a big chip knocked out of the rim. Gordon was tucking into a greasy fish the size of a small whale.

'Can't beat good old seaside fare,' he said, hooking a fishbone out from in between his teeth. The café sign outside was blown into the window with a bang. 'By, that's a hell of a sea-breeze,' he chortled.

'What time do you have to be at that caravan park?' asked Grace. She took a sip of tea and hoped Paul had got her message and that he didn't think anything was wrong because she hadn't turned up to meet him.

'Half an hour,' said Gordon, checking his watch. 'I've just time for a pudding. Want anything?'

I want to scream, thought Grace, but she answered tartly: 'No thanks. I'll pass.'

After he had eaten a monster-sized portion of treacle sponge and custard, they braved outside to find the wind had dropped and the sun was playing peek-a-boo behind very grumpy-looking clouds.

'This will be bonny in the summer,' said Gordon, zapping the car open. He whistled an annoying loop of 'Oh I do like to be beside the seaside' all the way to *Bayview* Caravan Site, three miles down the coast road.

They called in at the caravan reception office and a lady with a too-small suit straining over a very generous apple-shaped figure welcomed them warmly and led them over to caravan number one after a chirpy bit of sales banter. It had flower pots outside containing plastic plants and a staged barbecue next to the steps. Inside, Grace had to admit it was impressive. Twice as big as the one she had spent two uncomfortable nights in. Four rooms, three with double beds and built-in wardrobes, and a bathroom that a cat could have looked forward to a fair swinging in. It was very nice, just not her sort of thing at all. She was sick of camping and caravanning holidays, the only sort of 'breaks' Gordon acknowledged. She wanted a change, she wanted holidays where someone else was making her meals for her and there was guaranteed sunshine. She wanted to spend a week or two in a place where she could truly unwind instead of merely transferring domestic chores from one destination to another. Gordon might have had the chance to relax on the holidays, because he never lifted a finger while Grace cooked, cleaned, washed up and made the beds. *Women's work*.

'This is our new model, the "Monte Carlo",' said Small-Suit.

'Twenty thousand pounds, but if you buy it this weekend we have a special offer of eighteen.'

I'll get my cheque book immediately, thought Grace sarcastically. How many weeks in Sorrento wandering along the paradise of streets would eighteen thousand pounds buy? She watched Gordon's shoulders flinch at the price. He knew how much the caravans were because he'd done his homework. Said aloud though, it sounded scary to a man who had never flashed his cash about freely.

'I don't think we'd need as much space as this,' said Gordon. 'Can you show us something else?'

'Certainly,' said Small-Suit. She had gauged now that this couple weren't going to be the biggest spenders and showed them the 'Cannes'. It had had one lady owner for the last five years. *A colour-blind one at that*, thought Grace, judging by the ghastly mix of orange soft furnishings. It was like being inside a giant rotting mango.

'Twelve thousand, three hundred pounds for a quick sale, this one,' said Small-Suit. 'It's a six berth, one of those being a double. But it does boast a separate dining area.'

The shower room was generously proportioned and Gordon obviously hoped Grace would be impressed by the galley kitchen – her future domain. She could see his brain working behind his glittering eyes, imagining them there in tropical sun-shine British summers, Grace happily baking apple pies while entertaining the children and feeding the new baby and load-ing the washing machine and sweeping the floor with a broom stuck up her bottom, while he read yet more seed catalogues and waved amicably over to the neighbours.

'I think we'll be saying yes to this one,' said Gordon. 'It's got a lovely feel to it.'

'Gordon!' said Grace crossly. 'Excuse me, could I just have a word?'

She pulled Gordon's sleeve, leading him into the corner, and

Small-Suit melted into the background to allow them to discuss.

'It's a lot of money, Gordon,' said Grace.

'You'll be getting a lump sum soon, I'm sure of it,' said Gordon.

'You can't rely on that,' said Grace.

'Well, OK then, we can still afford it from the savings. No pockets in shrouds, Grace. It's a good price and we're having it.'

What a time for him to suddenly become extravagant, thought Grace. She wanted to scream at him that there was no way she would spend whole summers in Blegthorpe. No way would she be dragged from a set of pots and pans that needed cleaning in Barnsley out to the coast to do more of the same, but she knew the fight was lost before it started. Gordon didn't lose arguments, instead he wore his opponent down with persistence and she was too tired to fight back after a second night of rubbish sleep. She felt trapped, imprisoned by Gordon's will more than ever since Paul had fallen out with his father.

When Gordon barred Paul from the house, there had been a change in how she saw her life, as if, for the first time, a big light had been shone onto it. She had realized then that there was no parity in her marriage. Gordon mowed the lawn, mended things and took care of the money; she cooked and cleaned and saw to the children but, where he expected total respect for his male role, hers was taken for granted as 'what women did'. Her opinion did not matter. *She* did not matter. Gordon was a dictator, not a democrat.

Grace watched helplessly as he opened his cheque book and wrote out the 10 per cent deposit. He was smiling while his pen moved. 'Chirpy' wasn't a word Grace would ever have associated with her husband. It was weird to see him so elated, as if someone else was inhabiting his body but the fit wasn't quite right.

They spent that night in the 'Robin Hood Club', listening to a mediocre singing duet, 'Paradise', accompanied by resident organist, 'Trevor Starr', who was wearing a suit so glittery that it could have come from one of Liberace's car boot sales. Then Blegthorpe's own Celine Dion, 'Lynn Laverne', took the stage and warbled out some power ballads. Then there was a break for bingo. Then Lynn Laverne came back on with a costume change and Gordon ordered scampi with chips and side salad for two while LL shattered some more glasses. Gordon picked up a couple of die-hard caravanners at the bar who came over to join them. They enthused over sea-air and camping life and invited Gordon and Grace over for morning coffee and to look over their brand new de-luxe Rolls Royce of Caravans, the 'Monaco'. Grace tried to smile but inside she was screaming. Gordon Beamish, however, had come home.

Chapter 21

Ben had left a huge chocolate egg for Ray in the fireplace late Saturday night so she would find it on Easter Sunday morning. He'd had it iced at Thornton's with her name on it and three kisses. He had made pink potato prints of bunny's feet across the tiles the previous night whilst Ray was sleeping.

'Hey Ben, look, the Easter Bunny left me an egg!' said Ray, waking him up by jumping on him.

'Well, I hope you're going to share it with your husband,' he smiled.

'You might have your own,' said Ray. 'He might have left yours in the kitchen, for instance.'

'Oh, might he?' said Ben. He leaped out of bed and ran like a child to the kitchen where he found a big nest made out of brown cardboard. It was full of mini eggs and cream eggs and a big chocolate mama chicken sitting on them all.

'You daft lass,' he said affectionately, giving Ray a big kiss on her head. He loved her for these sweet, considerate things she did and was careful to make sure he afforded her the same courtesies. After all, they were in control now. Big and grown-up. They could make all the lovely things happen that never happened when they were kids.

Dawn and Calum had made up, after she had apologized for

nagging and watched him go out with his mates on both Friday and Saturday night without questioning him, and she buttoned her lip when she heard him come in at after two on Easter Sunday morning. He rewarded her with an early morning perfunctory bonk and an eventual 'sorry that he had eaten the surprise egg'.

Then they went over to Muriel and Ronnie's for lunch. All the family were there, squeezed around a big table like the Waltons. Like the sort of family she had always dreamed of belonging to, and now she was about to – legally. She was squashed in between his younger sister, Demi, and his older sister, Denise. Denise, Demi and Dawn – even the alliteration of their names made her feel like one of theirs.

'Got some good news for you two,' announced Muriel. 'Bette across the road is going to make the bridesmaids' frocks. That'll save you an arm and a leg.'

'Oh!' said Dawn, trying to muster up a diplomatic refusal. 'Well, actually I've seen some lovely ones in Laura Ashley—'

'Laura Ashley!' scoffed Demi. 'They'll be poncey.'

'No, not at all, they're lovely and—'

'Bette will make anything at a fraction of shop prices. You just tell her what you want and she'll sort it. She's a brilliant sewer.'

'Oh well, thank you,' gulped Dawn. Mu had already decided that Bette was doing the dresses and she felt ungrateful turning her down. And if Bette was so brilliant, she could make the same ones that she had seen in Laura Ashley.

'Oh, and another bit of good news. Your Auntie Charlotte in the home is giving you a cheque for a thousand quid. You'll have to go and see her to get it though.'

There was a round of wolf-whistles from everyone except Calum who said, 'Fucking hell.'

Muriel gave him a crack with the spatula that she was using to apportion her meat and potato pie.

'Who's Auntie Charlotte?' asked Dawn.

'Well, it's my auntie really,' said Muriel. 'Our Calum's middle

name is William; I named him that after her husband. He was
very high up in the pit, Uncle William.' She rubbed her finger
and thumb together to indicate that Uncle William and Auntie
Charlotte certainly weren't without a bob or two. 'Anyway,
he's dead and she's got no kids. I tell you, it was a very good
move calling him Calum William. I thought it might come in
handy one day and seems I was right. Ever such a nice man he
was, my Uncle William.'

'You're just like him then, aren't you, Cal? Ever such a nice
man?' said Demi across the table to her brother. 'I heard you
thumped Dawn.'

'Chuffing hell, you lot know more about my life than I do!'

'You didn't thump her, did you? What for, you rotten git?'
said Denise, screwing up her face with disgust.

'Bloody nagging me, that's what for,' said Calum, taking a
big slurp from his can of lager. 'Anyway, it weren't a thump.
She were hysterical. I hit her for medical reasons!' He smirked
at his own wit.

'For God's sake, Dawn, don't start going all bunny-boiler,'
said Denise, sympathetic to her brother now.

'Anyone would think I'd turned into Peter Sutcliffe!' said
Calum. 'It's her fault. She nags and nags and nags.'

'Aye, lad,' said Ronnie, making a rare contribution to the
conversation. 'And now you've given her something else to nag
you about.'

They all laughed. Dawn felt herself dragged into their jollity
and seeing herself through their eyes. So what if they were a bit
rough? So what if they had a brown sauce bottle permanently
on the table and drank whatever lager was on special offer by
the crate load? They were an old-fashioned family who loved
and laughed together and stood side-by-side with each other.
Like the ones in Catherine Cookson's books. Her heroines
were always feisty and fighting and making up, weren't they?
She really did need to lighten up.

Chapter 22

Maltstone churchyard was a serene place for the dead to sleep, was Raychel's first thought as they threaded through the bumpy grass and stone crosses and angels to a pretty corner, a mass of bright and faded colours, flowers, teddy bears and cards: the children's graveyard.

'What do you think?' said Raychel.

'I think it's perfect,' said Ben. 'It's a lovely spot. Aye, here, pet.'

There was a tree at the edge of the grass border where a wood started. Raychel opened her handbag and took out a small cross and a tiny, fluffy toy rabbit. She parted the grass at the side of the tree. Bluebells were in flower and the air was full of their musty scent.

'Here?'

'Yes,' said Ben.

Raychel kissed the cross and lifted it to Ben's face so he could do the same.

'Happy Easter, my darling Angel,' she said, kneeling to anchor it between the sweet blue flowers in the soil. 'Dear God, please look after her for us. Amen.'

'Amen,' said Ben, helping Ray to her feet. He wrapped his arm around her as tears bubbled in his eyes and he sniffed them down hard.

'I'm OK, really,' she smiled. 'I know she isn't there. I know she's up in heaven but I need somewhere to come that's nearby and pretty like this.'

'You don't have to explain to me, darlin',' said Ben. 'Come on, let's go home. We'll come again. She knows we will.'

As they turned to go, Ben blew a kiss heavenward and hoped it would be delivered to her. The baby had died before she had been given a name, so they had picked 'Angel' for her. Ben and Raychel, her big brother and sister, were the only ones who would ever remember and grieve for little Angel.

Chapter 23

According to the Internet, Anna read, Vladimir Darq was forty-two years old and originated from Romania. He had enjoyed huge success as a designer of exclusive gothic gowns and wedding dresses for A-list clients before he disappeared from the face of the earth for a year, emerging recently in Milan with a breathtaking taster-display of sumptuous lingerie. According to an *Observer* article that she also found, he no longer wanted to design exclusively for the very wealthy, already-beautiful people. His new market was to be '*the forgotten woman*', the one who thought herself ordinary and who had carved her niche in the background of life. The price points would match her purse too! Vladimir Darq maintained that it was possible to make any woman feel sexually powerful with the right underwear beneath her clothes – *his* underwear. He had designed a bodyshaper that no woman could afford to be without, he proclaimed confidently.

There were quite a few sites featuring him, even an online fan club and forums trying to find out things about him, although no one seemed to have much information other than what was reported in the newspapers. He was, it seemed, a real international man of mystery. Or was he indeed a man? There was a weighty amount of speculation on a few gothic sites that he was, in fact, not marketing himself as a vampire, but was the real thing. It accompanied obviously Photoshopped pictures of him with pale golden eyes, bleached white skin and exaggerated fangs. Apparently, he preferred to do all his business in the evening because he hated the sun, which added fuel to the fire. All tabloid newspaper nonsense really.

Unmarried, childless, he was pictured alongside a few beautiful models and with his arm around his 'friend', the photographer Leonid Szabo. Anna might have known Vladimir Darq would be gay. Let's face it, any man who was interested in her couldn't possibly be heterosexual.

Anna spent the rest of Easter Sunday watching a Jesus film and getting tipsy on too much wine. She cried a lot as Jesus went up on the cross and, once the floodgates were open, she cried about Tony and the big, painful hole he had left inside her heart. She cried about her cat abandoning her for another woman, seduced away by Edna the widow who served him smoked salmon. She cried hard and unashamedly that no one in the world loved her at all and at the thought that when her own death day came, no one would turn up at her funeral. There would be no headstone, and the grass and big, ugly weeds would grow rampant over her plot and dogs would crap on it. She would be even more forgotten in death than she ever was in life.

She caught sight of her face in the mirror as she staggered to the sink after throwing up in the toilet. A moment of clarity in her alcohol-clouded brain told her that this was no way to carry on. She looked like she had died, been buried, dug back up and hit with the gravedigger's shovel. There had to be something more than this for her. She truly was the forgotten woman that Vladimir Darq was talking about. She fell asleep with his business card clasped in her hand.

Chapter 24

'Hello, everyone,' said Christie, breezing in. 'Had a nice long Easter weekend?'

'Lovely, thank you,' came a ripple of consensus.

Anna hoped she wouldn't have to elaborate. What could she have said? *Cried a lot, got totally pissed with Jesus – oh, and fainted in the train station and was asked to dress up in underwear by a gay vampire.* Easter just didn't get better than that. And to top it off, she'd seen that scrubber Lynette Bottom and Tony pass her in the car that morning. And she had a belting headache from crying herself to sleep. Well 'sleep' was pushing it a bit. She couldn't remember when she'd last managed to have a full night's kip. Last night, she'd had an hour, if that, before sinking into a dream about Tony and a very heavily pregnant Lynette getting married in front of Sailor Sid's sweet stall on Barnsley market. She woke up with a start. Ache roared inside her body and she sobbed hard into her pillow, hoping sleep would come and be kind to her, but it didn't. In the end she conceded defeat and got up to make herself some hot milk, but that only served to make her feel sick. She slumped on the sofa and clawed the time into morning, watching rubbish cable comedies that didn't raise a single smile. Two large coffees and ibuprofen for breakfast had done bugger all to shift the pain in her temple that was making it difficult for her eyes to keep functioning. It felt as if someone was stabbing her brain with a screwdriver.

Malcolm's nose was once again sniffing in the direction of the department. As Anna went to the loo, she noticed him watching to see what the boxes were that Maintenance had just brought up to Christie. If he paid as much attention to his own department as to theirs, he might have ended up actually giving Cheese a chance to survive independently. It was looking more and more likely that it would be merged with Deli within the year.

Anna went into the deserted toilet and sat on the closed seat, resting her head against the coolness of the partition wall. The pain went much further than her temple. It reached down into her guts, squeezed tightly and kept the pressure on until she felt she could bear it no more. Not content with haunting her dreams, she had opened a second-hand *Barnsley Chronicle* on the train to see that Tony had won an award for his barbering. He was there on the front page 'pictured with his partner, Lynette Bottom'. Tony's arm was around her back, a peep of his fingers at her waist.

Partner! She wanted to ring up the *Chron* and say, 'It's not his partner, it's his slaggy tart! *I'm* his partner!' *Partner.* That one word, applied to Lynette Bottom, hurt – so much. And just to pile on the insult to the injury, they were smiling like love's young dream. Her own life was in bits and she had apparently been whitewashed out of Tony's. Everywhere she looked, he was there – in her vista, her nightmares, even her bloody newspaper.

A fresh wave of pain engulfed her as she imagined Tony and *her* in bed, and she groaned aloud. Tony liked a lot of sex. He would do all the things with Lynette that he and Anna used to do together. Probably more, driven by her energetic teenage hormones. Anna burst into tears; the drops fell fat and warm down her cheeks and she didn't care that they were cutting through her foundation, dragging her mascara with them. She couldn't live with this tearing agony in her heart any longer; it was killing her. In fact, she wished it *would* kill her and there would be an end to it, because she knew she couldn't recover from it. There was nothing to live for: she couldn't sleep, couldn't eat, couldn't concentrate, she couldn't find any joy or hope in anything. And, if that wasn't enough, in three days she would be forty – Mayday in every sense of the word. Fat, frumpy, forgotten-and-forty day. *Life ends, not begins Day.*

The boxes contained lots of new and innovative gifts to reward those colleagues who sent in good suggestions to improve the business. Dawn volunteered to pack them all away in the store cupboard and Christie encouraged her to get on with it. The girl was in her element when she was organizing. It was only when the task was finished and Christie called a coffee break that they noticed Anna had been missing for a considerable time.

'Where did she go?' asked Christie.

'I thought she'd gone to the toilet,' said Raychel.

'Not for all that time, surely?'

'I'll go and have a look, shall I?' volunteered Dawn.

She entered the loo which was deathly quiet, but the end cubicle door was locked.

'Anna, is that you in there?' She knocked quietly on it. There was no response.

There was barely more than a slit between the door and the floor to look under and so Dawn went into the adjacent cubicle and climbed on top of the toilet seat to look over into the next. There she saw Anna, sitting on the loo lid, head against the partition wall, tears cascading down her face. The silent way in which they were doing so was the most disturbing thing about the scene.

Dawn almost fell off the seat when the main toilet door opened, but thankfully it was only Christie.

'We thought there was a Bermuda triangle in here and you'd disappeared as well. What's going on?'

Dawn opened her mouth to answer, then the thought hit her that, however nice Christie was, she was still their boss and Anna looked as pissed as a fart. Or, worse, drugged.

'Is she all right?' said Christie. 'What's up?'

'She's not really,' Dawn hedged. If Anna was inebriated, she didn't want to drop her in it.

Christie rapped on the door.

'Anna, love, open the door. Are you ill?'

Anna leaned forward, her head dropping into her hands.

'We need to get inside,' said Christie. She whispered through the door, 'Anna? Anna, can you open the door?'

'No, please just leave me,' said Anna.

'I'm coming in,' said Dawn, tucking her skirt up in her knickers, springing from the loo seat and hooking her long leg over the top of the cubicle. 'Oops – bang go my tights!'

Christie heard Dawn land and a second later the door was open. She came in and bent over Anna, who looked like a zombie.

'Anna, Anna love, whatever is it? Have you taken anything?'

'No, no. I am so sorry, Christie,' Anna sobbed.

'Why, love, what's happened?' Christie stroked Anna's hair back from her face and that kind, gentle action smashed the last few bricks holding back the mother lode of Anna's grief. She fell forward into Christie's arms and a confession poured out of her.

'I lied to you all. I'm not happily living with Tony. He left me in February. There was a note saying there was no one else and there was. I'd just come home from hospital after a miscarriage. I needed him so much and he wasn't there.'

'Oh, love,' said Christie, squeezing Anna into her.

'It was my fourth. I can't seem to carry babies longer than six weeks.'

'God,' said Dawn, at a total loss for anything constructive to say but feeling the need to say something at least in a sympathetic tone.

'I'm going to be sick, I'm sorry,' said Anna, quickly pushing Christie away to a safe distance and throwing open the toilet lid. Yellow liquid poured violently out of her mouth. She looked like something out of *The Exorcist*.

'Sweetheart,' said Christie with a pitiful sigh.

'I'm a wreck,' said Anna, spent now and reaching weakly for the loo roll and finding none. Dawn pulled loads of toilet paper from the next cubicle and handed it to her.

'Men can be such thoughtless bastards,' Dawn said kindly. Her skirt was still tucked up in her drawers.

'Oh God, look at your tights,' said Anna. 'I am so sorry.'

'Anna, it's only a pair of tights. Get a grip!' she replied, mock-harshly. 'I'll go and get you a cup of water. Sit down before you fall.'

She left Anna in the capable hands of Christie. Anna looked down to avoid eye contact and wished she hadn't.

'Oh no, Christie, you've got sick on your skirt.'

'Don't you worry about that. It's only a splash anyway. I'm driving you home, young lady. You're not well. When was the last time you ate something? There was nothing but bile in your stomach to throw up. You've been running on empty, haven't you?'

'I'll be fine.' Anna dropped down onto the toilet seat again. Her legs were as shaky as a new-born foal's. She realized that she must look a total sight.

Dawn came back in with a cup of water and a packet of wet wipes which she handed over to Christie.

'Grace sent these in,' she said. 'Here, get this down you. I got it from the water cooler, so it's nice and cold.'

Anna gulped at the water while Christie pulled out a couple of the wet tissues and gently began to wipe Anna's face as if she were a little girl.

'I'm so sorry,' Anna said again.

'Shush,' whispered Christie. 'Are you OK to stand? We're going to get your coat and your bag and I'm taking you home now.'

Anna opened her mouth to protest that she'd get a taxi and not put anyone to any more trouble, but she was too weak. 'Thank you,' she relented.

'Good girl,' said Christie, helping Anna to her feet.

Anna felt as frail as a kitten as she walked back into the office where Grace was waiting, holding Anna's coat open and ready for her to slip her arms into. At her side, Dawn was holding her bag. Anna looked at them both, so much kindness shining in their eyes that she wanted to sink to the floor and sob with shame and gratitude in equal measure.

'I'll see you later, ladies,' said Christie, leading Anna down the office. 'Come on, pet, let's get you home and tucked up.'

It was a nice, quiet road end where Anna lived, very close to Dartley train stop. Courtyard Lane was well-named as it was a square of narrow, terraced houses around a neat courtyard garden at its centre.

The house gave out so many mixed signals. It was a lovely mix of heavy old furniture and matching reproductions. Quite dark and gothic in its taste: a strong red on the walls, a brave blue showing through from the hallway. But the surfaces were dusty and the carpet could have done with a good vacuum. It looked *tired*. A place someone was once proud of, had put together with great style, and now lost the ability to care for. It looked a perfect reflection of Anna at that moment in time.

The small kitchen was clean, if a little untidy. Cat bowls hand-painted with the wording 'Butterfly's Food' and 'Butterfly's Water' lay full on the floor. Christie hunted in the cupboards for some cups after announcing that she was putting the kettle on. There was a shelf full of bone china mugs with pictures of Siamese cats on them. She made two coffees and returned to the lounge where Anna was sitting on the sofa looking drowsy now.

'I used the de-caff,' said Christie. 'Looks like you need a good sleep.' She opened her handbag and brought out some tablets. 'Here, these'll take the headache away with any luck.'

'I feel a bit better after being sick,' said Anna, but she took the tablets anyway. She felt as if she had been turned inside-out.

Christie noticed the many photographs displayed around the room: Anna snuggling up to a good-looking guy, Tony presumably, and lots of pictures of a sharp-faced Siamese cat in various stages of growth.

'That your cat?' Christie asked. 'He's very beautiful.'

'He moved in with the widow across the Courtyard. Edna. I can't even keep the bloody cat from straying. Thank you, Christie, for bringing me home. I'm so sorry to put you to all this trouble.'

'If you say that once more I'll thump you,' said Christie. 'You're not well and shouldn't have been at work. Didn't you take any time off when you had your miscarriages?'

'I didn't need to,' replied Anna. 'I lost them so early. Except for the last one. But even then I was in hospital Friday night and out Saturday morning. I didn't want a fuss.'

'And *he* left you that Friday night?' Christie affirmed calmly which belied the disgust she felt.

'It's been hard for him too, to cope with losing so many,' said Anna. She knew she was making excuses for him but she wanted to believe that he was hurting and weak rather than a total bastard with a pipe cleaner for a backbone.

'Yes, of course, poor him,' said Christie tightly.

'I'm so sorry,' said Anna, bursting into a hard, primal sob. Her dignity was long gone. She was just a mess of tangled up feelings. 'I'm forty on Friday. That isn't helping!'

'Good grief,' said Christie. 'You should be flinging open the door to that fortieth year and dragging it over the threshold.'

'I'll be old,' said Anna.

'Will you hell as like,' snapped Christie. 'Women at forty should be formidable creatures. What on earth makes women think forty is old? Half of them get reborn at that age because they've not lived until forty comes and kicks them up the backside.'

Anna found herself smiling at Christie's force of argument.

'And another thing, I don't want you coming into work until you're well,' warned Christie.

'I can't rattle around this house any longer than I have to, Christie. It depresses me so much. I need to get you a cloth for your skirt.' Anna made to stand but she was gently pushed back down onto the sofa again.

'Look, I can brush it off. Do you want something to eat?'

'No, I couldn't face it.' Anna shuddered at the thought. 'I just want to sleep.'

'Then you sleep, love,' said Christie. She pulled a couple of throws from the other side of the sofa and tucked them around Anna. Anna's eyes started to shutter down. She heard the front door close and the key being pushed through the letter box. Then she slept.

Chapter 25

Anna walked into work the next day. She felt a wee bit shaky, even though she'd been sensible and eaten some toast. But as she told Christie, she didn't want to spend any longer in a house full of memories than she had to. Plus she wanted to give Dawn some new tights.

'You silly beggar,' said Dawn when Anna handed them over.

Christie gave Anna a wide, kind, welcoming smile.

'You've got a bit of colour in your cheeks this morning. I hope you had a good sleep.'

'I can't remember getting up and putting myself to bed, but I must have because that's where I woke up,' Anna replied. 'I feel much better today. Thank you for taking me home, Christie. And for listening.'

'Don't mention it at all.' Christie waved it away. 'I'm just glad I could help.'

'Look, it's not much. It's just a gesture to say thank you, everyone, for being so kind yesterday . . .' Anna took out of her handbag four boxes of chocolates that she'd bought at the train station newspaper shop.

'You're getting paid too much,' Dawn grinned, her hands full of Anna's presents.

'You really didn't have to do that at all,' said Grace. 'I only picked up your coat.'

'I only picked up your bag!' said Raychel.

'You did more than that,' said Anna. She couldn't put it into words without sounding over the top. She remembered the warmth in their eyes – not pity, but support. There was a difference.

Dawn had already eaten three chocolates. 'You'll have to get ill in the office more often,' she said through a coffee cream. Then she corrected herself. 'I don't mean really ill, just ill enough to feel bad enough to bring choc—'

'Yes, we know what you mean, Dawn,' put in Christie. There wasn't an ounce of malice in the girl but she had a very clumsy line of expression. 'Anna, I shall take your chocolates and enjoy them with my coffee, seeing as you've been kind enough to buy them,' she went on. 'And we've been talking. Seeing as it's your birthday on Friday, how about we use our horse race winning kitty and celebrate with you?'

'That Thai place up the road. It'd be smashing!' said Dawn.

'Oh!' was all Anna managed, because that invitation came from left field. But the accompanying smile gave Christie the answer she wanted.

'Marvellous,' she said.

Chapter 26

'I can't believe Dad did that to you!' said Paul angrily down the phone as he talked to Grace from his office. 'What right does he think he has to force you to go somewhere you don't want to go like that? I tell you, Mum, he's getting worse as he gets older. He's a control freak. '

'I'm just glad you got my message,' said Grace, mobile to her ear as she sat on the park bench having her sandwich lunch. 'My phone died on me when I was texting you. I was so looking forward to seeing you and Charles too.'

Grace was terrible at lying and she knew Paul wouldn't really have been convinced by her text message that she and Gordon had taken an impulsive trip to the seaside, especially to a place they had often joked about as being a coastal hell-hole. Despite her best efforts, Paul had winkled the truth out of her within a minute of talking to her and he was furious.

'You'll see Charles soon, I promise you that,' Paul growled. 'Mum, I hate to say this but Dad's losing it.'

'Don't be silly, love—'

'I mean it. Laura told me what happened with young Joe and the football.'

'Don't, Paul, he isn't that bad,' said Grace, feeling more disloyal by the minute because she wasn't feeling what she was saying.

'The trouble with Dad is that he was always nice Dr Jekyll when things were going his way, but as soon as they weren't, out comes Mr Hyde with a vengeance. And Mr Hyde has been coming out more and more these days, Mum, because we've all grown up and he can't tell us what to do any more. Why was there always so much anger in him? It's as if he was perpetually just waiting for any excuse to kick out. I've never understood it.'

Grace sighed. She knew why, of course. The anger was born out of frustration. Years and years of sexual frustration, of being impotent and being too stupidly proud to seek help. Not something she could tell her son, of course.

'Paul, love—'

'I'm telling you, Mum. I don't know how you've stood him all these years. You can't have been happy.'

'Of course I have,' said Grace. 'You have made me the happiest woman alive.'

'Just tell me something, then: if he hadn't had three young kids when you met him, would you have ever married him?'

Grace opened her mouth to answer that of course she would, but she knew it wasn't the truth and so would Paul. Her marriage was as dry as dust, held together only by her children's love. His children's love.

'I'm fine, we rub along in our own way,' said Grace, changing the subject swiftly and attempting cheeriness. 'Now, when am I seeing you? I still have your Easter egg to give you.'

'Mum, I'm a grown man!' he said in the same way he had last year while laughingly accepting the big chocolate egg she knew he would enjoy.

'You're never too old for an Easter egg,' she said. Although Gordon had always been too old for silly things like that.

'I've only got one empty box left after this,' said Raychel, packing up the canvases she had painted. Ben had often told her she should sell them, but Raychel didn't want to do anything to draw attention to herself. She was happy enough painting them purely for the enjoyment of it. She had always been so clever at arts and crafts. She had sewn all their bedding and made the fancy curtains that they were leaving behind for the next tenant because everything in their flat was going to be fresh and new and clean.

'There's loads at work,' said Ben. 'I'll ask the boss if I can take some; he'll let me, I know he will.' Ben liked his boss. He was a huge bear of a man who didn't cut corners in his work and paid good wages and on time. They were lucky in having plenty of work on when a lot of building firms were going down the pan. But John Silkstone had a good reputation locally as a craftsman who charged fair prices and didn't muck anyone about breaking promises.

'Smashing,' replied Raychel, and bent to empty the sideboard next. She opened the top drawer and took out the treasure box which she kept there. She slid off the lid and at the top of the pile of letters and cards from Ben sat the little yellow cardigan with the duck buttons in a crinkly plastic bag. It had never been worn. She had knitted it herself in preparation for their baby sister's arrival when Raychel was just a girl herself. She could hardly bear to look at it, but neither could she ever throw it away.

Ben watched her trembling fingers reach out to tenderly stroke it through the plastic and he stepped in quickly.

'Come on, let's stop packing for today, pet. Enough for today.'

When Anna got to the train station after work, there was no man in black facing her. Nor was he behind her, about to breathe on her neck. She felt an unreasonable stab of annoyance that he wasn't haunting her that night. How bizarre was that?

There was a bing bong, preceding a train announcement that

hers was delayed by fifteen minutes. She sat on a bench on the platform and pulled out her mobile phone to check on the time. The black-edged card bearing Vladimir Darq's name was next to it in her handbag. *Go on, ring it*, an imaginary voice whispered seductively in her head. She thought of his promises to locate her 'Darq' side. She thought of Tony and winning him back with her revitalized inner goddess. It was worth a try; anything was worth a try. She pressed down the first two numbers on her phone and then cancelled it. Then she thought of standing in front of Tony in a velvet basque, feeling his hands on her once again . . .

She steeled herself and dialled once more, the whole number this time. She lifted the phone to her ear and heard it burr three times, then a man's voice – *his* – answered with a clipped, 'Hello.'

'Erm, it's me, from the train station.'

'Ah.'

'Anna Bri—'

'Yes, I know who you are.'

'I'm ringing to say—'

'My address is Darq House in Higher Hoppleton,' he cut her off. 'What is your address?'

'Erm, two, Courtyard Lane – that's Dartley.'

'Be ready Saturday night at seven p.m., please,' he interrupted with a no-negotiating East European accent. 'A car will be sent for you. You will come here and I will prepare you for filming. Wear your most comfortable, not your best underwear. I repeat, your *most comfortable*.'

And with that, the line went dead.

Chapter 27

Dawn ironed Calum's best shirt. He'd compromised and said he would wear it, but only with jeans. He'd looked at her as if she was daft when she'd held out a tie.

'She's fucking barking anyway; it won't make any difference to her giving me any money if I turned up in a tie or a full clown suit,' he moaned.

'When was the last time you saw her?' asked Dawn.

'Not fucking long enough ago.'

'Do you have to swear so much?'

'Yes, I fucking do,' said Calum. 'You're nagging again.'

Dawn shut up. Now he'd discovered the 'N' word, he was using it as an excuse for everything. It was the verbal equivalent of a 'one size fits all' T-shirt. He'd accused her of nagging earlier when she'd told him to turn the volume down on the TV. He didn't accuse the neighbours of nagging though when they started thumping on the wall five minutes later.

Dawn twisted her hair up into a crocodile clip and pulled out some stray locks at the sides to soften the effect. 'I just want us to look nice to see her. It's the least we can do if she's giving us that sort of money towards the wedding.'

Calum grunted and put on the tie, tying it in a low, sloppy knot, rebelliously pulling it to one side. He was so handsome in a shirt and tie. He was going to look gorgeous in his penguin gear at their wedding. He had a boyish face with big, grey-blue eyes and that sexy smile that had roped her in from the first.

Dawn drove to the old people's home: Greenfields in Penistone. It was an old Victorian double-fronted house with a very wide girth and a big, glassy conservatory extension to the left. Neat, frilly curtains hung at the windows and a closely clipped garden at the front impressed to visitors that this was a well-cared-for residence. Calum was bored and moaning before they'd even got to the reception desk. Dawn felt like his mother, pulling him in and doing all the talking to the receptionist. It wasn't the first time she'd felt like that. Her fiancé wasn't exactly Mr Get-up-and-Go.

The receptionist led them to a lovely sunny lounge at the back of the house which looked out onto a long, flowery-bordered lawn. A couple of old men in sun hats were playing croquet in the middle of it. It was all very old-fashioned and English and gave Dawn the impression that someone had turned the clock back to the 1930s.

Aunt Charlotte wasn't the tiny little withered thing Dawn had visualized. She was very nicely dressed, healthily slender and sitting straight-backed in her armchair, and when she said her hellos, it was obvious she'd had a fair few elocution lessons in her time. She spoke like a lady as well as looking like one. Her hair was frost-white, pinned up into an immaculately neat pleat and her eyes were bright and sparkly and grey-blue. She smiled at them and proffered her cheek to Calum and then to Dawn. The old lady smelled of a sweet and delicate perfume that Dawn had never come across before.

'I thought we'd have scones,' said Charlotte, leaning forward as if divulging a big secret. 'Do you both like scones? The food is very good in here.'

'I love scones,' said Dawn.

'Likewise,' said Calum like a bored teenager. Dawn wanted to kick him.

Right on cue, a lady wheeled in a rattling trolley with a big pot of tea and cups and polished silver cutlery and a china plate of tiny, round buttered scones and pot ramekins full of jam and cream. The old people's home experience wasn't at all like Dawn imagined, dull and scruffy and smelling of wee. But then, this was a very upmarket one. Muriel had made some comment about it eating away at Charlotte's savings like a swarm of locusts devouring a picnic.

'Would you pour, dear,' said Aunt Charlotte. 'Those teapots are far too heavy for me.'

'Yes, of course,' said Dawn. Calum had already started on the scones without offering them to anyone else first.

'It's Dawn, isn't it?' asked Charlotte. 'Such a lovely name. A sunny name.'

'Yes, Dawn Sole.'

'S-O-L-E?' Charlotte delicately plucked a small scone from the plate. She had long, straight fingers with beautiful nails.

'Yes, that's right.'

'Italian for sun too,' nodded Charlotte. 'Not pronounced the same, but the spelling is identical.'

'Oh, really?' said Dawn, deciding then and there that Calum was totally wrong about Aunt Charlotte being loopy. There was a bright shrewdness in her eyes that said she was very switched on.

'You're going to be a June bride. Like I was,' said Charlotte.

'We'll bring you some wedding cake,' smiled Dawn.

'Thank you.' Charlotte leaned in close and whispered, 'But I don't like it. The icing is too sweet, I've never liked marzipan and I'm not a lover of that dark fruit cake.'

'I don't like it myself to be honest,' Dawn sighed.

'You should have a chocolate cake instead then. Or some of the young ones these days have towers of cupcakes. Such a lovely, pretty idea.'

Calum reached for another scone. Seeing as Dawn wasn't cutting to the chase, he did it.

'Auntie Charlotte, Mum said something about a cheque.'

'I haven't forgotten,' Charlotte said coolly, taking a sip of her tea as Dawn cringed with embarrassment. 'It's all ready for you, don't you worry.'

'I'm just nipping off for a pee,' said Calum, stuffing the rest of the scone in his mouth. *A fag more like*, thought Dawn.

'It's by the front door,' Charlotte called after him. 'You can't smoke in the grounds, you have to do it in the lounge.' She winked at Dawn. 'He has smoker's twitch. My husband William had exactly the same. Dreadful habit.'

Dawn reflected the smile back. What a lovely old lady. She bet her mum would have grown into an old lady like that, given the chance.

'How are your plans going? I hope Muriel isn't taking over too much. She's a very strong personality,' said Aunt Charlotte with natural diplomacy.

'She's been a great help,' nodded Dawn.

'Well, you be careful. She was always the same, even as a girl. It was her way or no way and this is your wedding day, you are the star. Here, have another scone. They're home-made with clotted cream.'

'I shouldn't but I will. You're a bad influence. That tea's good, by the way. Shall I top you up?'

'Yes, thank you. My hands aren't as strong as they were.'

'You have beautiful hands.'

'I played a lot of piano. It kept them very supple. And my mother always made me wear hand cream from a very early age. I had to sleep in cotton gloves. Mother had the most beautiful hands too.'

Funny to think this very old lady had a mother, thought Dawn. Did she ever think that one day her daughter would be ninety? Better to see your children grow old though than die before you. Her own grandmother had been devastated to lose her only son. She had never recovered from the shock of it.

As if Charlotte were reading her thoughts, she asked; 'Do you think you and Calum will ever have children?'

'I don't know,' said Dawn. 'We haven't talked about it. Certainly not for a while.'

'I think he may need to grow up a little more himself first. Don't rush it, that would be my advice.' Charlotte looked towards the door to check he wasn't coming back. 'I hope you're very happy, but you're not what I imagined.'

'Oh?' Dawn gulped, not sure how to take that. Old people could be brutally blunt, she knew that from her hairdressing days.

'You seem a very gentle, nice person. You must stand up for yourself, you know. Especially in that family. They're a *pack.*'

'Oh, I do, don't you worry.' Dawn laughed with some relief that a compliment not an insult had come her way.

Calum swaggered back into the room. It was obvious from the smoky scent around him where he'd just come from.

'I'll get your cheque.' Charlotte bent to pick up her handbag from the floor. It was a lovely vintage purse with a big central clip. She brought out her cheque book and hunted around for a pen.

'It's very kind of you,' Dawn said.

'It's a ridiculously expensive business getting married these days, I know. And I understand you're quite alone in the world. I thought that was very sad when Muriel told me about the wedding. I just need to write the payee name on.'

She clicked on the pen and filled in the missing details with a flourish.

'Denise and Demi will get a cheque when it's their turn, but not this much.' Charlotte ripped the cheque out of the book. 'So keep the details to yourself. I told Muriel I'd give you all one thousand. I'm giving you two.'

Calum became animated then. 'That's really nice of you, thank you, Auntie Charlotte.'

'There you go. I've made it out to Dawn Sole. The bride will know how to spend the money for the best.'

Calum had a moment of annoyance, but it passed quickly. He'd get it out of Dawn when it cleared in a few days.

Dawn was delighted. This way she could make sure the money went on the wedding and not straight into the tills of the Dog and Duck. Along with her horse-race winnings, she was back on course for getting the best that money could buy for her big day.

'Have you picked your dress yet, Dawn?' said Charlotte, stifling a little yawn. She was getting tired, Dawn could see that.

'Yes, and it's gorgeous. Would you like me to bring you a picture of it?' said Dawn.

'That would be lovely,' said Charlotte. 'Obviously I won't get to the wedding, I'm afraid. But I would like to see your dress very much.'

Calum didn't relish the idea of coming up again, obviously, so for his benefit Dawn said, 'I won't bring Calum when I show you the photos. I'll come early one afternoon, then I won't tire you out.'

'I do get tired very early,' said Charlotte. 'Trouble is, I wake up so damned early too. It's not much fun getting old. Enjoy your youth whilst you have all that energy.'

'We won't tire you out any more. Come on, Dawn. Auntie Charlotte's sleepy,' said Calum, grabbing at Dawn's sleeve and making himself sound thoughtful in the process.

'I'll come again soon.' Dawn kissed Charlotte's cheek. Her skin felt so fragile and thin and soft under her lips. That lovely perfume wafted towards Dawn and made her think of an autumn walk in a wood after the rain.

'Drop us off at the pub, I'm calling in to celebrate,' said Calum as they pulled out of Penistone.

Dawn bit down on what she was going to say. He would only accuse her of nagging for the millionth time. She put up and shut up, as she realized she might have to do quite a lot in the future.

May

Chapter 28

Without exception, all five women were really looking forward to their night out together, albeit for different reasons. Dawn knew that every Friday she expected to stay in with Calum and every Friday, without fail, he would promise that he'd come back in after a couple of pints only to turn in long after she had gone to bed. So it would make a refreshing change to go out and enjoy herself. Anna was so dreading being alone on her birthday that even an evening with four relative strangers seemed like a gift. Grace wanted to have a night off from Gordon's incessant talk about their future life in Blegthorpe. And young Raychel knew she was far too reliant on Ben for company. Sometimes, though he never said so, she felt as if she was choking him with her neediness.

They all found themselves in the ladies' toilet at work competing for the mirrors as they reapplied their lippy and fluffed up their hair a bit. There was more than a little pleasant thrill running through each of them.

The Rising Sun pub was only up the road from White Rose Stores HQ at the edge of the industrial estate. They called in for a drink to whet their appetites for the meal later in the new Thai restaurant next door, aptly called the Setting Sun.

The Rising Sun had recently had a refurb to make it look like a cowboy saloon, albeit with more comfortable seating than rickety old wooden chairs. Lots of saddles and cowboy paraphernalia were nailed on the walls, and posters at either side of a small stage announced that 'The Rhinestones' were playing the following week. Dawn was quite sorry they wouldn't be performing that night; she loved any sort of country and western music. She only had to hear the first few bars of a Jim Reeves song to be back to her childhood with her singing-mad dad and his gee-tar. She used to sing a lot around the house herself until Calum told her to shut up because he couldn't hear the telly.

They found a conveniently empty table to sit at by the side of an unlit fireplace. No sooner had they sat down than a waitress with a silver bucket full of ice and a bottle of champagne turned up and another waitress followed behind with a tray bearing five long glass flutes.

'A little present from James McAskill,' explained Christie to her party of open-mouthed administrators. What was this woman to James McAskill that she had such sway? they thought. But they took advantage of his kindness and raised their glasses in Anna's direction and said in unison. 'Happy fortieth birthday, Anna!'

'So how come you haven't any mates or family to go out with tonight then?' said Dawn. Anna coloured.

'My dear girl, you have such a way with words,' said Christie, shaking her head from side to side.

Anna knew that Christie had spoken to the others about the split with Tony because she had acted above board and told her that she had. She wasn't the type to gossip but she wanted them to know something of Anna's story so that no one put their foot in it. Even though Dawn still seemed likely to do exactly that.

'Well, you know about my errant partner of course,' Anna began to explain. 'Mum and Dad are divorced. Mum got remarried and lives in Ireland with her new fella, Dad got remarried and lives in Cornwall but we've never really been close. I've got a much younger sister, Sally, but she dyed her hair green, changed her name to Rainbow Storm, started doing strange things with crystals and went to live on a French commune. Anyway, she never did believe in monogamy so she wouldn't have been the best support. I've had a few cards from couples that Tony and I used to go around with, but they're more his mates than mine, so they're being loyal and staying away, I expect. And I appear to have lost all the friends I did have when they all went on to have families. I think they started to feel awkward that I was having such a bad time con-ceiving and they were churning kids out on conveyor belts. Having children and not having children is a bit of a divider,' said Anna. 'So I drifted apart from everyone except Tony and now he's gone and that's why I'm a Billy-No-Mates saddo today.'

Grace nodded supportively. She knew how easy it was to find yourself isolated. She had devoted her life to her family and lived a friendless existence after her best friend Ellen died six weeks before her wedding to Gordon. 'Please don't marry him, Gracie,' had been the last lucid words she had heard from her friend's lips.

And Ben had been Raychel's only companion. Friendship outside their close circle of two was an alien concept. How could she have friends when she could never trust anyone but Ben? Ever. They were united by things that set them apart from everyone in the world.

'Friendships are so important,' said Christie. 'I feel for you being alone. Which is why you are going to have a wonderful meal with us tonight and toast the fact that this day is the first day of the rest of your life.' Christie had been thinking a lot about her ladies and was so glad they were here around this table – together. Man was not meant to be an island. Once upon a time she had been wrong in cutting herself off from everyone and floating out into a sea of loneliness. She had been lucky, at least, in being pulled back to shore by wonderful people who cared for her.

'This is a nice place,' said Christie, expressing the view of them all. Stained-glass windows with suns on them threw shafts of gold light into the room.

'Malcolm noticed us all going out,' said Raychel. 'He won't be off for at least another hour. He hates it that we leave on time. You can tell he thinks we're skiving.'

'Well, we aren't, so sod him,' said Christie. 'He doesn't run the department, I do. It's Friday night! What on earth is so bad for him at home that he won't leave until six and get snarled up in the weekend traffic?'

'Must have a right old bat for a wife.'

'Bet she's relieved he stays out of the house as long as he does.'

'I did hear,' began Grace, aware that the champagne had gone straight to her head and she was about to gossip but enjoying the mischief all the same, 'that his wife is a high achiever and he doesn't quite come up to her standards. I think there's a lot of resentment on both sides that she's surpassed him.'

'Interesting,' commented Christie. It sounded very believable. 'Who did you hear that from?'

'Someone I worked with who retired last year. He lived near the family.'

'Has he any kids?' Anna asked.

'One, a mini-me Malcolm,' said Grace again. 'Apparently they have trouble with him at school. Bit of a bully, I heard.'

'If he's like his father, he'll be feeling up girls' bums in assembly,' said Dawn, shuddering at the thought of Malcolm's hand brushing against her own bottom. 'How old do you reckon he is?'

'Ah, now that one I know,' said Christie. 'He's the same age as I am, forty-seven. Perfect age for a mid-life crisis. I'm picking my leather trousers up tomorrow, when I've had the triple spray tan.'

They all laughed. His Oompah Loompah-coloured skin was the talk of the building.

'Don't you think "Spatchcock" sounds like a sexually transmitted disease?' said Anna, adopting the tone of an eminent doctor. '"I'm sorry, sir, you have obviously slept with some dirty women because you've developed a serious case of Spatchcock".'

'He's quite proud of his name though,' said Dawn. 'He must think it makes him sound like a macho superhero.' She extended her arm in Superman-flight style. 'I am Spatchcock, saviour of the universe, and I hail from Planet Penis.'

Christie nearly spat out her champagne with laughter. 'I shall have to tell James that one!'

'He wouldn't find that funny, surely!' gasped Dawn. She could never imagine Mr McAskill finding a penis joke funny; he was far too dignified for that.

'Trust me, he would,' laughed Christie, putting on her glasses so she could read the label on the champagne bottle. In true Christie flamboyant style they were vintage Bakelite-shiny with diamanté stones down the arms.

'Anyway – happy birthday, Anna. This is a little something from us all.'

Grace lifted a bag from under the table and put it down in front of Anna, who was genuinely taken aback. She hadn't expected a present at all.

'I don't know what to say!' she said breathlessly.

'Oh, just get it opened, girl,' said Christie.

Anna reached tentatively into the bag, prompting Dawn to joke that it wouldn't bite her. There were cards inside, a book, bubble bath, chocolates, a bottle of champagne and all sorts of ribbons and sweeties and a pen with a wobbly '40' on top.

'We thought there might be something in there at least you liked,' said Raychel. 'We had a stab at what your tastes are.'

'Seeing as we hardly know each other,' added Dawn. 'By the way, the book's all about a woman who gets revenge on a cheating louse; we thought you'd like that! I picked it myself this afternoon.'

'Thank you all so much,' said Anna. She was genuinely touched. A lot more thought had gone into the girls' presents than the cheques her parents had sent her.

'You've done us a favour,' said Dawn. 'You gave us the kick up the bum to organize this meal.'

'Oh well, my rotten love-life is good for something then,' said Anna with a good-humoured tut.

'I bet I could give you a run for your money with some of my exes,' Dawn huffed.

'Bet I'd win,' said Anna. 'I've had every rotten trick in the book played on me. And even some that weren't in the book because they were too bizarre.'

'Ooh, like what?' asked Dawn, leaning forward eagerly.

'Well,' began Anna, wondering which disaster to start with, 'before I met Tony, this guy called Wade asked me out and I thought, *This is it. For once – a decent bloke.* He had a great job, loads of money, dressed gorgeous, had lovely manners, paid for me in restaurants, held doors open for me.' Anna took a glug of champagne before continuing. 'Then, just when I thought I'd landed Mr Right, he starts sending me really dirty texts. But the sort that a young kid would send who'd just found some naughty words in a dictionary. One just said *SPUNK*.'

'Yuk,' said Raychel, screwing up her nose.

'I thought he had Tourettes. He was forty-five, for goodness sake; I presumed it had to be medical. Turns out it floated his boat to write filth on his mobile. The texts got worse, he got more excited and I felt increasingly sick.'

'I hope you told him to piss off in the end,' said Dawn.

'I daren't,' said Anna. 'I might have turned him on.'

They laughed, all of them, together. It was a nice sound. More than one of them was trying to remember the last time they'd laughed in the company of a group of women.

The champagne finished, they gathered up their coats and bags and moved next door to the Setting Sun. A beautiful Thai waitress in a blue kimono met them at the door with her palms pressed together in greeting.

'Dinner for five in the name of Somers,' said Christie and they were smoothly led over to a beautifully set table in the corner and given the biggest menus Anna had ever seen. It would have been quicker to read *War and Peace*.

'Pad Prik Sod?' Anna said dryly. 'I'm not having any more pricks, thanks, I've had enough.'

'Have a Poppia Poo then!' Raychel snorted.

'Pla Kraproa!' Dawn contested, barely able to breathe for giggling.

'Wank Cum Cock,' said Anna.

'You're joking! Where's that?' said Dawn, laughing so much that the tears were running down her face.

'I made it up, you dipstick,' said Anna. 'In honour of Wade.'

'Oh stop it, I'm going to die,' said Dawn. Her sides were sore from laughter.

'Children, children!' said Christie, in fake headmistress mode. Even Grace was giggling away. She was having a lovely evening. It made her think how much she had missed out on over the years, though.

'OK, OK, we'll be sensible,' said Dawn, drying her eyes on a serviette. 'Let's be serious, now what are we ordering? Grace, you start us off.'

'Pad Pong Galee,' said Grace, as the youngest two started giggling again.

'Will you behave!' said Christie. 'Honestly – it's like taking a bunch of nursery kids out.'

'I thought she said "Bad Pong Galee",' said Dawn. Anna's face muscles ached. It felt so liberating to act her shoe size for once. Or rather, Tony's willy size.

Miraculously they managed to order their meals and drinks without collapsing again and relaxed into the merry warmth around the table. Dawn thought how nice it was to have a night off wedding preparations. She hadn't realized until she let go of them for a little while just how much they were taking over her life. She took a long sip of sparkling water and felt the coolness spread inside her.

Likewise, Grace savoured her glass of cold fizzy water too and let it swirl around and work on relaxing those parts of her that hadn't rid themselves of tension since that horrible trip to the coast. A letter had arrived that morning offering a further 5 per cent off the Monte Carlo caravan model if they wanted to change and upgrade their choice.

'Here's hoping our horse-race win changes your fortune then,' said Christie kindly to Anna.

'Here, here,' said Anna. 'In fact . . . no, it doesn't matter.'

'Oh go on, you can't start something and then stop it,' said Dawn. 'I'm far too nosey for you to do things like that to me.'

'Well . . .' began Anna again. She really ought to tell some-one about her visit to Vladimir Darq tomorrow, as a security measure if nothing else. 'Something strange happened to me recently. This bloke followed me in the train station . . .' And she proceeded to tell them the full tale.

'Goodness me!' said Grace. 'He does live in Higher Hoppleton, though. I've read about him in the newspapers.'

'Isn't he the one that looks like Count Dracula?' said Dawn.

'Wow! A Transylvanian vampire in Higher Hoppleton,' mused Christie.

'You make it sound like the sequel to *American Werewolf in London*!' said Dawn, with a snort.

'Should I go, do you think?' Anna asked.

'Of course you must go,' said Grace adamantly. 'It's just what you need: an adventure. Perfect timing on his part.'

'But being on TV in my underwear? I'm not sure I could. And they always feel you up on those shows, don't they?'

'No one seems to complain when Gok Wan grabs their hooters,' said Christie. 'And I warn you, if the man gives you anything like a proper fitting service, you're looking at something akin to invasive surgery.'

'Oh God, no. Really?' Anna paled.

'Oh yes, you'll have to strip off and let him look at you.'

'Get away! You're having me on.'

'I am not, my love,' said Christie, highly amused by the look of horror on Anna's face.

'Oh, just go for it. I mean, what would your alternative plans for the evening be?' said Dawn. She wondered if gay men had good foreplay techniques. Calum was straight in there like Flynn usually, if the beer let him keep it up. Sex wasn't that big a part of their relationship.

'Fair point,' conceded Anna for comic effect but still thinking inwardly, *Bloody hell fire! Stripping right off! In front of millions of people*. It was all a bit surreal. Her life was starting to make the world of Spongebob Squarepants seem normal.

'Just be careful though,' said Dawn, shaking her finger. 'Those celebrities are all druggies. Don't let them stick anything up your nose except a Vick's Sinex nasal spray.'

'I've never taken drugs and I'm not starting now,' replied Anna vehemently.

The Thai food was good and plentiful. They followed it with creamy ice creams and coffees.

'What a lovely way this has been to round the week off,' said Christie, popping the last half of her mint chocolate into her mouth. 'We should do this again.'

'I'd like that,' said Anna. 'I've had a great evening. Thank you all so much.' She meant it too. Their company had given her spirits such a lift. She dreaded to think what her birthday would have been like had she been alone in the house.

'Me too, I've had a smashing time,' said Dawn. It was a nice change from the Crookes' company. Their wit was so caustic and always seemed to involve slagging someone off, which could be uncomfortable to listen to sometimes, however funny their delivery.

Yes, thought Christie. This evening had done them all good.

'Well, happy birthday, Anniepoos,' said Dawn and raised the last of her coffee in the air. Four other cups nudged against it. 'May this day be the start of better times ahead for you.'

Anna just wished she believed it could be.

Chapter 29

Calum was hungover the next morning and wouldn't be shaken out of bed to go for his penguin suit fitting. Instead, Dawn drove to Meadowhall to look at some decorations for the tables at her reception. She played country and western music all the way there and back and sang out her heart to Tammy Wynette and her '57 Chevrolet.

Paul had a beautiful apartment on the posher outskirts of Sheffield which he had, luckily, paid a pittance for in an area that would see a triple return on his outlay. It was all money which would go towards Rose Manor when the time came for him to sell up. Grace rang the intercom and Paul buzzed her in cheerfully. He greeted her at his door, taking all the big bags of belated Easter eggs from her with good-hearted humour and his usual loving hug. She was pleasantly surprised to see Joe there with his uncle.

'Hello, sweetheart,' said Grace, giving her grandson a kiss on his head. He looked quite sorry for himself.

'He's got a bit of toothache,' Paul whispered. 'Laura's just nipped out for some oil of cloves for him and milk for me. His big Uncle Paul is taking his mind off it by playing a game of cards. Aren't we, Joey?' He gave the boy an affectionate squeeze on his shoulder.

'Paul, where are . . . oh hello!' A tall, smart, incredibly handsome black man came into the lounge from the dining room.

'Mum, this is Charles, meet Mum, Mum meet Charles, my business partner.'

'Oh, hello,' said Grace with a broad smile. 'How lovely to meet you at long last.'

'Mrs Beamish, delighted,' said Charles in a beautifully plummy English accent. 'I've heard a lot about you.'

'All good, I hope,' said Grace, with a hint of a blush.

'Every single word,' said Charles.

'Charles is an absolute sweetie,' said Paul. 'And a damned fine architect too.'

Then a buzzer went and Paul's intercom camera showed Laura holding up a four-pint carton of milk.

'She volunteered to go fetch it,' said Paul. 'We were gentlemen and offered but she wanted to cool off. She's been ringing around for a dentist for Joe and getting nowhere.'

When Laura came in, she gave Grace a big hug.

'Calmer now, sweetheart?' said Charles, pulling her to him and giving her a squeeze.

'Oh, I see!' said Grace.

'We've just started courting, Mum. I was dying to tell you but I didn't know if he'd want to see me again after the first date,' said Laura.

'I didn't know if you'd want to see *me* after the first date,' said Charles. 'I was so nervous I spilled my wine all over her skirt.'

Charles and Laura looked at each other sweetly and Grace couldn't help but mirror their smile. *What a lovely man*, she thought. She just hoped it would last. Laura was a bit like poor Anna in the love department. She'd always had a rotten deal when it came to boyfriends, Joe's father being the cherry on the cake. He had left Laura when she was five months' pregnant, saying he had changed his mind about being ready to be a father (at forty-four) and had written himself out of the boy's life before he was even born. Laura was well overdue some love and attention.

Laura's mobile rang and she grimaced on recognizing the number. She clicked the connection button.

'Hi, Sarah . . . No, I can't at the moment, I'm a bit busy trying to find a dentist for Joe . . . No, don't know where she is . . . Oh, she hung up. I presumed you didn't want me telling her you were here, Mum. Just for once, I insist that you don't shoot off to rescue her; you're having a late Easter lunch with us.'

'Don't tell me, she wanted someone to take Brat-Girl off her hands,' said Paul.

'Paul, that's your niece!' said Grace.

'I know but . . .' He didn't have to say any more. Sable was a nightmare. Even Joe didn't enjoy being in her company and young Joe was as placid as they came.

'If Sarah can't cope with one child why on earth did she get pregnant again?' said Paul. 'Rhetorical question, I know, but what a stupid thing to do. It's not going to stop Hugo's eye wandering, is it? In fact, quite the opposite, I would have thought, with two screaming, spoiled brats in the house.'

'Three, you mean. *Miaow,*' said Laura, uncharacteristically bitchy.

'It can't be easy for her,' said Grace, feeling the need to redress some balance. She hated the fact there were more and more factions in this family which she had nurtured so carefully over the years. And she had always been so soft on Sarah who had been too young to have any memories of her real mother, unlike the other two who had at least something to savour of her.

'I hope you aren't thinking about leaving your job in order to be dedicated granny-babysitter,' said Paul to Grace. 'You'd better stay firm, Mum. You've done more than your fair share for all of us.'

'Don't be silly, you're my family and I help where I can,' said Grace. She loved Sarah, but the thought of being cooped up at home with two babies and Gordon made her feel as if she was drowning and they were weeds around her feet, pulling her further down and holding her in the water until her lungs burst. The more she struggled against them, the more they seemed to gain purchase.

Laura put the kettle on. Paul had bought cakes and made sandwiches and picnic fare because he had decided they were going to have a high tea on his roof terrace. It was a summer haven up there, an organized chaos of plants and trellis and water-features.

'So we're all good for caravanning holidays in Blegthorpe then,' said Paul, delicately popping a small pastry into his mouth and giving Grace a wink.

'Oh, don't even joke,' said Grace wearily.

'You and Dad, alone together 24/7 in a giant can. Lovely.'

'Don't ever retire, Mrs Beamish,' said Charles. 'That's the key.' Laura had obviously been filling him in with some details.

'On that note, how's the new boss?' enquired Paul.

'She's a very nice woman,' said Grace. She'd enjoyed the previous night more than she could ever have guessed at. It had been like throwing a dusty cover off her life and allowing a little fresh air to blow through it. 'We all went out for a meal last night. I've never eaten Thai food before. It was beautiful.'

'Good for you, Mum,' said Paul. 'I presume Dad didn't have any objections?'

'Goodness, Paul. He wouldn't stop me going out anywhere.'

'Apart from here. He wouldn't like it if he knew you visited me,' said Paul.

'He must know that I do see you.'

'Maybe he doesn't. Maybe he thinks you wouldn't dare,' said Paul, which awoke Grace to the idea that her son just might be right, even though she couldn't admit it.

'That's ridiculous.'

'Well, you won't be able to go out with your new friends if you're stuck in Blegthorpe!' Paul wagged his finger at his mum.

'You have to start saying no,' said Laura. 'No one's ever said no to Dad, that's the problem.'

'I did,' said Paul with a proud smirk. 'Hence the reason why I am banished from the family home. He thinks I'll be "cured" when I meet the right woman.'

Grace was surprised Paul could laugh so objectively about that day. She knew how hurt he had been when he told his father he was gay, not hoping for endorsement, just acceptance, and Gordon had refused to listen, then stormed out of the house and said that Paul was to have left by the time he came back. In all the years they had been married, Grace had never heard Gordon swear before, but he more than made up for it that day. A stream of the vilest language came effortlessly from Gordon's lips as if he had been possessed of an evil entity. Paul hadn't let her step in to intervene. And if the truth be told, she was glad, because Gordon had scared her with his ferocity.

She often wished she had been brave enough to walk out with Paul then.

After that lovely interlude of lunch with one half of the family, Grace landed back on terra firma with a resounding bump. She came home to find Gordon wearing a path in the hall carpet. He was carrying a crying Sable whom he pushed into Grace's arms as soon as she had walked in through the door.

'Where've you been?' he demanded.

'I told you, I went for a walk around the shops,' she lied. She didn't want to risk his reaction by telling him the truth.

'Sarah's been phoning you. Said it kept going onto voicemail.'

'Oh, did it?' Grace searched her bag to find her phone was switched off. She grimaced to discover there had been twenty-four missed calls: ten from her daughter and fourteen from Gordon. 'I thought I'd left it on.'

'Well, you obviously didn't, did you? What's the point in having a mobile phone if you switch it off when you're out? She's been having pains. She was thinking about going up to hospital!'

'Oh goodness me.' Grace felt panicked. 'I didn't . . . should we go up there? Have you rung?'

'I had to go over and pick Sable up. Sarah was going for a lie-down and she said she'd ring if things got worse.'

Grace immediately rang Laura on her mobile. Laura was remarkably unsympathetic and explained why.

'Mum, I've just passed her in the car. She looked fine to me as she was pulling into the multi-storey in town. She's having as many birth pains as I am!'

'Are you sure it was her?'

'Like there is any mistaking her flash numberplate!'

Grace really was going to have to learn how to start saying no, before those weeds pulled her down any further and robbed her of her last breath.

Chapter 30

It was amazing the things that crossed your mind when you were standing in a pseudo Transylvanian castle having two men scrutinize your knockers at point-blank range, thought Anna. She wondered what Tony would think if he knew what she was up to. Would he have her bang to rights on grounds of adultery, even if the men in question were gay?

Leonid Szabo was small, slight, very camp in his gestures, and with his frilly shirt and long waistcoat he looked like Adam Ant in his highwayman days. In stark contrast, Vladimir Darq was looking very alpha male in slim-cut black trousers and the whitest shirt Anna had ever seen. She hadn't realized what a big man he was. Not ridiculously tall, not in the least fat either, but wide-shouldered, large-chested and solid. He wouldn't even have wobbled in a hurricane, that's for sure. He wasn't exactly classically handsome close up, with his pale skin, square jaw and thin, precise line of beard on it, but there was something very 'man' about him. Ironically so, given his sexual proclivity.

His eyes were his second most striking feature: ice-blue with tiger flecks of gold in the iris. Probably contact lenses though, she decided, because they were far too strange to be natural. First prize had to go to the hint of fangs which she caught tantalizing glimpses of as his lips spread. Just small ones, not like those on sale in joke shops, but his canine teeth were definitely elongated all the same. And though she wouldn't have put ponytails on her list of most desirable must-haves on a man, seeing as they were usually rats' tails grown to lead the eye away from a fast receding hairline at the brow, his luxuriant, wavy black hair tied back behind him was straight out of Prince Charming land. All part of the dramatic charade of pretending to be a romantic vampire for the benefit of the press, no doubt.

She'd arrived at the house in a black Mercedes which had drawn up outside her home exactly as her grandmother clock in the lounge was chiming 7 p.m. The Romanian driver was sullen and uncommunicative, but later it emerged that he'd had the excuse of not being able to speak much English. Black electronic gates gained them entry to a long drive on the outskirts of the cottagey village of Higher Hoppleton. They had pulled up in front of the biggest door Anna had ever seen, and it even opened with an Addams' family-style creak. She half-expected to find Lurch behind it but there was only a much smaller man with a bald head and eyeliner whom she recognized immediately from the Internet as Leonid Szabo: the 'friend' of Vladimir Darq. The door opened out into a huge galleried room. Darq House was a new build made to look like it was a relic from the Middle Ages. With a mixture of clever architecture and *trompe l'oeil* painted walls, it looked eerily like a fifteenth-century vaulted castle.

'You must be Anna, come on in,' Leonid said in a strong accent. He helped Anna off with her coat, all the while appraising her like she appraised lumps of cut beef on Baxter's meat stall in Barnsley market. Then the man himself made an entrance, shook her hand politely and cut straight to the chase.

'Please, Anna, we need to look at you. Stand up straight and stay still.'

Both men circled her, looking at her unextraordinary body from all angles. Anna felt surprisingly detached. It was all very medical and such intense scrutiny could not have made her feel more hideous than she did already. All she could think was that two homosexual men staring primarily at her chest was bizarrely healthier for her than a night in, alone, watching *Casualty* and sobbing into a box of tissues.

The two men spoke to each other rapidly in their native language. Anna could only guess at what they said to each other. It didn't exactly sound as if they were comparing her to Cindy Crawford.

'Ah, before we commence,' said Leonid, bringing a small, elaborately painted tin out of his pocket which he opened and proffered to Anna. It was full of small white pills.

'I don't take drugs, thank you,' said Anna stiffly.

'It's mint,' said Leonid, waving and wafting the air between them. 'To overcome the much garlic.'

'Oh,' coughed Anna. 'Sorry.'

OK, it might have been a bit daft but she had rather overdone the garlic in the small chilli she had made for herself that teatime. She'd actually put enough in there to make her old maths teacher keel over unconscious, and he hadn't had a sense of smell. She couldn't decide if it had been wise or silly to take a few precautions. Silly, she decided now.

Vladimir had quickly turned away, but she was sure she'd seen him grin and then immediately stamp on it. Anna felt herself blushing. It must be obvious to them both why she'd eaten so much. She took a couple of mints and said a meek thank you.

Leonid put the tin away in his pocket.

'She's perfect,' Vladimir commented, as if Anna wasn't there. 'Her underwear is of course awful, that is obvious, and doing absolutely nothing for her at all.'

'Can we see, please?' asked Leonid.

'What? You want me to strip off?' said Anna.

'Just to your underwear,' Vladimir said.

Anna took a deep breath and started unbuttoning. She didn't

feel as embarrassed as she thought she would. Then again, next week she was going to be standing here with these two and a film crew, including the very gorgeous, slim, cellulite-free Jane Cleve-Jones looking at her. That was a much scarier thought.

'This bra isn't a cheap one, I can see that. But it's rubbish. Why do women buy comfortable rubbish?' Vladimir despaired.

'I won't have to strip off totally, will I?' asked Anna. 'I don't think I could.'

'Not for the cameras,' replied Leonid, although Anna wasn't quite sure what *that* was supposed to mean.

'What bra-zire size are you?' Vladimir asked, stepping back from Anna and studying her chest.

'Thirty-six C.'

'*Nu!*' he said with a humph. 'You aren't.'

'I am!' said Anna. 'I'll prove it. Have you a tape measure?'

'I don't trust tape measures,' said Vladimir, wearing the expression of a man who had just smelled something foul. 'And stand up straight, please.' He rushed behind her and gripped her shoulders, pulling them back. Her boobs seemed to rise twelve feet when he did that.

'Ah, eez better. Posture is everything,' said Leonid.

'Posture and confidence go hand in hand,' said Vladimir, 'and she obviously has no confidence, so she has no good posture.'

Vladimir stroked the skin down her neck to her shoulders as if she was made out of clay and he was smoothing it. The gentle reverence with which he was treating her body told her without a doubt that he was 100 per cent homosexual. She couldn't remember the last time Tony had been as gently attentive. He could roger for England, but stroking and softness didn't turn up on the menu. She coughed away the thought of Tony for now and amused herself by looking around the room while she was being discussed in fluent Romanian.

It really was a cleverly built house. The walls looked as if they were fashioned from ancient stone. Huge iron torches were bolted to them. A cavernous unlit fire awaited colder months and a huge black dog that was part Great Dane, part Zoltan Hound of Dracula reposed in a basket at the side of it. He'd given Anna a perfunctory glance when she first came in, but didn't deem her important enough to rise up and investigate her. No change there then. She wasn't exactly the darling of the animal kingdom, as Butterfly and his unfaithful nature would surely testify.

A great wide staircase ran up the middle of this cavernous room and split into two on its journey upwards, to Vladimir Darq's four-poster coffin, no doubt. Everything was so large: the table, the sofas, the candlesticks. And apparently her tits as well, because Vladimir seemed to be arguing with Leonid that she was at least a 40D as the dispute dipped in and out of English.

As the conversation between them got even more inflamed, Vladimir Darq flounced off, only to appear minutes later with an armful of corsets and bodyshapers still with long uncut threads. He clicked his fingers impatiently at Anna to hold her arms out and step into the bodyshaper that he was stretching for her. Then, when he had pulled it up over her drawers, much to her surprise he whipped off her bra with the ease of an expert magician snatching a tablecloth from under a stack of crockery. She gasped but he didn't acknowledge her shock because he was too busy hooking her up at the back. Once that was done, he plunged his hands into the front and positioned Anna's breasts precisely into the cups as if he was an artist arranging fruit in a bowl and Anna stood and let him because she was too stunned to move. How he managed to avoid giving her impromptu acupuncture treatment while he was pulling the material in and pinning darts in it like a madman was anyone's guess.

'See?' he said to Leonid. 'I could tell from looking at her she was all wrong. This is much better. Look! Of course you can see the difference already that good-fitting underwear can give her,' said Vladimir in an animated voice.

'Can I see?' asked Anna tentatively.

'*Nu*,' replied Leonid, obviously speaking for Vladimir as well by the looks of it.

'Anna, the filming will take place over the next five Saturdays and chart your progress. Now I have your shape in my head I can make more for the show. It will be very good. You are the perfect choice to demonstrate to other ladies that you don't need to be aged twenty and a size zero to be a siren. I will show you how. Any lingerie I make for you, you can keep. The production companies do not pay a wage, only expenses if you incur any. Are those terms acceptable to you?'

Anna nodded. Being able to keep just one piece made for her by Vladimir Darq would be payment enough. He began to unpin the bodyshaper so Anna could slip out of it. Her bra made her feel extra saggy and blobby when she put it on again.

'Try to stay much the same weight as you are now, Anna, please,' asked Vladimir. 'Dress exactly the same next week as you have tonight and bring a bag of your other underwear with you – they may want to see it.'

'When will the programme be on the TV?'

'I don't know, but they are hoping to turn it around very quickly. I will send a car for you at quarter to seven next Saturday evening.'

'So late?'

'I don't work in the daylight,' he said, as if that were obvious.

'Oh no, I suppose not,' said Anna. *Blimey*, she thought. He couldn't really be a vampire, could he? They didn't exist. Then again, she half-believed in the Loch Ness Monster and ghosts. And an after-life, because Derek Acorah was too convincing on that front not to.

'Would you like some refreshment before you go?' said

Leonid, pouring something very red from a decanter into a long pewter goblet.

'Er, no, thanks,' said Anna. 'I'll pass.'

Leonid helped her on with her frumpy jacket. Once again she was back to being a middle-aged, ordinary Barnsley bird who wouldn't stand out from a crowd if she'd painted her hair green, her face orange and wore six-foot stilts.

The Mercedes dropped her off at home and zoomed off into the night, leaving her feeling slightly tingly all over. Strangely, for once, a Saturday evening did not stretch quite as torturously empty in front of her.

Chapter 31

Anna caught sight of herself in the wardrobe mirror as she roused herself from bed the next morning. She looked like that spooky girl from *The Ring*. She was overdue a hair dye and some new nightclothes. Her nightie, comfy as it was, had bleach splashes on it and was stretched enough by washing to accommodate another three people and Vladimir Darq's dog.

And Vladmir Darq was going to give her back her lost pride and turn her into Sophia Loren? All in a few weeks? Yeah, right — 'course he was. Still, at least she could do something about the hair and her night attire.

Dawn went upstairs to rouse Calum at 11 a.m. He'd been drunk again the previous night, even though it was supposed to be her night for drinking and his for driving. He seemed incapable of having one or two, he had to get totally blasted and excuse himself that 'it was the weekend and he was allowed to let off steam.' He'd told her to leave the car and they'd get a taxi. It wasn't just the twenty pounds plus that would cost, it was the principle. She always ended up driving. Then they'd bumped into his mates and sisters and Calum wanted to go on to a club with them. Dawn was too tired by that time and annoyed with him, so she'd driven home and he'd ended up getting a taxi back in the wee small hours anyway.

'Has that cheque cleared yet?' were his first words to her.

'Give me a chance, I haven't even banked it yet,' she replied.

'How about a sub off it?'

'I can't, Calum, I haven't got enough funds. This wedding is costing me a fortune!'

'Oh, here we go,' Calum said, burying his head under his pillow. 'She's starting to nag already.'

'No, I'm not nagging,' said Dawn, a little tearfully. 'I just wish you'd contribute something.'

'I will,' he said. 'Now go and get me two paracetamol and a cup of tea, there's a good girl.'

Dawn's eye caught her guitar in the corner of the bedroom: the only thing of value she had. Her mum and dad had bought it for her seventeenth birthday. *Dee Dee, we have a surprise for you. Close your eyes and open your hands.* She asked herself would they mind if she sold it, to pay for the most important day in her life? After all, she never played it these days. The question wasn't given more than a split-second of head-space though. However broke she was, however desperate for her day as a princess-bride, she could never do that. It held all their dreams within the strings. She'd sell a kidney before she sold her guitar.

They were at Muriel's half an hour later with a bottle of the sweet white wine she preferred and some perfume for Denise because it was her birthday. She was there with her long-standing boyfriend, Dave, who was like a younger version of Ronnie: quiet and virtually transparent when placed next to the formidable Crooke women. Demi met them at the door, sporting a sulk because she had fallen out with her fella in the club the previous evening. Demi was always sulking about something or other though. Nothing ever seemed to please her. Even when she was happy her mouth never lost its downward swoop of misery. Muriel was busy in the kitchen, juggling a dozen pans and a steamer tower in between pressing at her head. She had a hangover as well, and the lunch, when it was served, was evidence of that.

The veg was limp and boiled to death, the beef was hard on the outside and too pink on the inside for Dawn's taste by far, plus the Crookes liked fatty meat and this joint hadn't been cooked slowly enough to tenderize it. The potatoes were lumpy, the gravy was lumpier; only the Yorkshire puddings stood superb, puffing proudly out of the tin moulds.

'This is a bit shit, Mam,' said Demi, whose sour little face said she was prepped for taking out some of her hurt on a third party.

'Now, now! Just 'cos you were dumped, no need to make everyone feel as bad as you do,' said Calum, rapping her arm with a serving spoon.

'And you can shut up,' said Demi, cutting off as Calum hit her harder with the spoon and flashed a warning at her.

'For fuck's sake, just eat it or leave it!' said Muriel. 'Look at them Yorkshires. Bloody gorgeous they are. Cheers, everyone!' She raised her glass of plonk. 'You should have had me doing the catering at your wedding, Dawn.'

'Well, I'm not coming if you are,' said Demi. 'Did you actually put any gravy granules in this hot water, Mam?'

'That reminds me,' said Dawn, turning to Calum. 'We have to go to the Dog and Duck and finalize the menus.'

'Oh, I did that for you on Friday. More or less, anyway. I just need to know if you want sloppy peas or carrots with the beef. Didn't you tell her, Cal?' announced Muriel.

'I forgot,' said Calum.

'He's chuffing useless,' said Denise. 'Are you sure you want him, Dawn? Wouldn't you prefer something with a spine and a brain?'

'Sandra – the landlady – wanted to know quick, so me and our Calum picked whilst we were up there,' said Muriel, flashing her thumb at her son and shaking her head in despair at the same time.

Dawn gulped down her annoyance. 'What . . . what menu did you pick then?' she asked Calum, but Muriel answered.

'Vegetable soup to start, beef dinner, then treacle sponge or fudge cake. Sandra's given you a right good price an' all. And she's putting a karaoke on and a buffet at night.' She cracked Calum again with the spatula that she'd used to lever the Yorkshires out of their tins as she saw Dawn's face drop. 'Don't tell me dopey lad hasn't told you that bit either? He said you'd be OK with it.'

Dawn gulped again. At this rate her gulping muscle was going to beat a previous world record. 'A karaoke?'

'Ooh, I love karaoke,' said Denise, who was a bit of a local star behind a mike. In her own eyes at least.

'The buffet sounded OK,' said Calum, forking up another Yorkshire pudding. 'It'll be cheap an' all.'

'Why didn't you ring me first so I could have had a say in it?' Dawn said between her teeth.

'Me mam said it was the best menu,' shrugged Calum, as if that answered the question sufficiently.

'We'll put a bit towards it because we're inviting some of our friends as well,' said Muriel, looking proudly over at Ronnie.

'Aw, thanks, Mam, Dad,' said Calum, reaching for more meat.

Dawn fell quiet. She didn't want a load of strangers there or a karaoke. Her worst nightmare was a karaoke after her wedding. She wanted a live band and dancing. And she wanted to pick her own menu.

'I don't think I want a karaoke,' she braved quietly.

It was as if the atom bomb had landed in the middle of the gravy. Everyone stopped chewing and rotated their heads in her direction.

'Why not?' said Denise. She was usually smiley but when that smile dropped it altered her whole face to a replica of Demi's.

'What's wrong with a karaoke? Is it not good enough for you?' said Demi with an unpleasant sneer.

'No, it's not that . . .' Gawd, Dawn found herself wishing she hadn't opened her mouth. The men had resumed stuffing their faces but she had just witnessed the Crooke women swapping raised eyebrows. Even Denise, who was miles softer than her sister, was looking at her with something akin to bitchy amusement.

Dawn immediately felt herself backing down rather than be ostracized from good family feeling. 'It's just that, well, would everyone like a karaoke? I was thinking more of a live band but if more people are happy with a karaoke—'

'Live band?' scoffed Calum. 'Who'd you have in mind? Take That?'

There was a ripple of laughter around the table and it contained unkind tones that chilled Dawn to the core.

'OK then, a karaoke it is. That'll be fun,' said Dawn, forcing a smile. She felt like she'd just escaped a savaging by a pack. It did the trick though. Muriel beamed and the temperature of the room leaped up by several degrees.

'Oh, and you'll have to go and see Bette this week about those dresses. She wants to crack on.'

'We should have a karaoke after this dinner, cheer your miserable face up a bit,' said Denise to her sister.

'I don't need cheering up, he were a knobhead anyway. I'm well shot.'

'He were king of the knobheads,' said Calum. 'It's not like it's the first time he's cheated on you and you've only been going out two minutes.'

'Hark at Mr Faithful!' said Demi. 'Ow, you shit. What did you kick me for?'

'Will you two watch your bleeding language when we're eating!' snapped Ronnie.

'What's this?' said Dawn, suddenly picking up on a nasty vibe. There was something zapping between Calum and his sister that she didn't like the look of.

'It's nowt, she's a stirring little cow,' said Calum, giving his sister a look that could have quite easily killed her had his eyeballs been loaded with bullets.

'It's nothing, really,' said Denise, adding to the impression Dawn had that everyone around the table knew something she didn't, and that nothing was, in fact, a very big something. And that something had happened after she drove home last night and Calum went off clubbing.

'It's not my fault I'm so damned attractive,' admitted Calum with an open grin.

'What isn't?'

'Ignore them all,' said Denise kindly. 'It's that cow Mandy Clamp. You know what's she like around our Calum. A fly around shite.'

That didn't make Dawn feel any better at all.

'Wh . . . what do you mean?'

'She's after my body,' said Calum, treating it like a big joke. Like he treated everything.

'I didn't exactly see you pushing her off,' sniped Demi.

'She only moved in because you weren't around, Dawn,' said Denise.

'Jesus, he's like a dog on heat,' said Muriel.

Tears rose in Dawn's eyes and she was outed before she could push them down again.

'No point in getting upset,' said Demi. 'He won't change. They don't. If they've got away with it once, they'll get away with it again. Everything with balls is a twat.'

With tears in her own eyes, she flounced off, sending her plate zooming across the table to clash into her brother's.

'Is she on the blob?' said Calum, still grinning. 'Nothing happened, Dawn. I swear. Did it, Den?'

'Not that I saw,' said Denise, keeping her eyes down on her dinner. *That was a very careful diplomatic answer*, thought Dawn.

'Oh ho, I know that look: nag-alert!' said Calum, pointing

at Dawn who tried to protest that she wasn't going to do anything of the sort.

'You need to get a grip, lady.' Muriel's voice came quiet but hard across the dinner table. It hurt, especially because Dawn had deliberately made a conscious effort *not* to say anything. Calum had used her to deflect attention away from himself.

'Oh, chuffing hell, happy bleeding birthday, Den!' said Den's man, Dave, lifting up his can of lager and raising it in his girlfriend's direction.

'Oh, I'm glad someone remembered!' said Denise with an annoyed sigh.

'Happy birthday, sis!'

'Aye, happy birthday, love.'

'Happy birthday.' Dawn joined in the family chorus but felt nothing like a part of them at all.

Chapter 32

Grace was just finishing her Sunday dinner. She hated the fact that her table wasn't a complete representation of her family. Joe was there with Laura, Sarah and her husband, Hugo, and Sable, Gordon at the head of the table taking the meat carving very seriously as usual. Paul should have been there; lately she had found herself wanting to scream that at Gordon. But Grace had not been built to rail against social order. And she definitely hadn't been built to rail against Gordon.

'How's the job going, Mother?' said Sarah. 'New boss not too much of a bitch, I hope?'

'It's very enjoyable and the new boss is lovely, thank you, dear,' said Grace. She suspected Sarah had an ulterior motive for enquiring about her job satisfaction.

'You scared Mum silly yesterday, Sarah, saying you had pains,' said Laura, with blue-eyed innocence.

'I did have them,' said Sarah. 'I was very worried, which is why I rang for Dad to pick Sable up. Thank goodness they subsided just before I was going to drive up to hospital.'

'Yes, that was lucky,' said Laura with more than a touch of sarcasm, adding to herself, 'And in plenty of time before the shops shut.'

'Anyway, you were saying about your job,' said Sarah, ignoring her sister.

'Are the people there nice, Nana?' said Joe.

'They're all very nice, thank you, Joe,' said Grace.

'Are they all your age?' asked Sarah, reaching for the gravy boat.

'No, Raychel is in her twenties, Dawn in her thirties, Anna was forty just last week and my boss is late forties.'

'So no competition if an early redundancy comes up then?' said Sarah.

'Can't be long,' said Gordon. 'I've a good mind to ask them myself what's going on.'

Grace looked at him, horrified. 'You can't do that!'

'What's the worst they can say?'

'You could affect any payout I get,' said Grace, thinking on her feet. 'If they think I'm desperate to go they won't pay as much.' *Whew!* Whatever muse had put that in her head, Grace owed them a stiff drink.

'A very good point,' said Hugo, shovelling in a huge roast potato and chomping on it sloppily.

Thank goodness, Gordon seemed satisfied by Hugo's endorsement. That thankfully closed off that avenue of conversation. At least for the afternoon.

'No pud for me, Mum,' said Laura. 'Joe and I are off for a walk. It would only mean more calories to burn off.'

'We're taking a dog with us!' said Joe excitedly.

'You haven't eaten all your dinner, so you wouldn't have got any pudding anyway,' said Gordon. Even with Joe he was getting snappier, Grace thought, yet she didn't comment.

'He's having a bit of on-and-off toothache. I doubt he'd have wanted a pudding,' replied Laura stiffly after seeing her boy's face drop.

'Well, take him to the dentist then,' said Gordon with a humph.

'Mine's on holiday and I can't get anyone to look at him before next Friday. I should have lied and said it was an emergency.'

'I'll ask around,' said Grace. 'I'm sure my boss said her brother was a dentist. He might be able to help.'

'What's this about a dog? You haven't gone and bought one, have you?' asked Hugo.

'No, he belongs to my friend Charles,' said Laura.

'Oh, starting courting, have you?' said Sarah. 'Do we know him?'

'You won't know him,' said Laura.

'And what does he do?' pushed Sarah.

'He's an architect,' said Joe, butting in proudly.

'Oh really,' said Sarah, impressed by that.

'As a matter of fact he'll be here any minute to pick us up. Joe, get your shoes on, love.'

'Bring him in,' said Grace.

'No chance!' laughed Laura. 'That'd be too scary for him. Maybe a few weeks down the line.'

Joe had barely got his first shoe on when there was a car horn beeping outside.

'I think he's here, love,' said Grace, giving her daughter a goodbye kiss before she bent to help Joe tie his second shoe.

'Let's have a look at him.' Sarah rushed to the window. 'Damn, you can't see much of him! He's parked the wrong way round.'

'Oh dear,' pouted Laura. 'You'll have to wait then.'

'Have a nice time, you two,' said Grace. She kissed Joe on his cheek. She knew they were in for a lovely afternoon because Laura was loved-up and smiley and Joe was dog mad.

With a flurry of byes and waves they went out down the path towards the waiting car. Gordon moved to the window as Sarah sat down and said, 'Well, she's a dark horse, isn't she?'

Grace wondered what Gordon had seen out of the window to make his back stiffen and his eyes lock like a Rottweiler before an attack.

Chapter 33

'Christie, do you mind me asking?' said Grace as soon as she laid eyes on her boss. 'Did you once say that your brother was a dentist? And if so, is he a local one?'

'Yes, he is and yes, he is. He's a private dentist and very local,' said Christie. 'What's the problem?'

Grace told her all about Joe. Laura had rung to remind her to ask because Joe had had a fitful night's sleep.

Christie made a quick phone call and a couple of minutes later she said to Grace, 'He can see your grandson at twelve, is that OK for you?'

'Oh, thank you so much,' said Grace. 'I'll try and get in touch with Laura. I didn't expect you'd get him in so fast. Where's his surgery?'

'Prince Street. Opposite where the old St George's Church used to be.'

'I know it.'

'You could take him if she can't,' said Christie. 'Have a long lunch break.'

'Thank you,' said Grace. 'I'll make up the time.'

'Don't be ridiculous, Grace,' replied Christie, both amused and affronted by Grace's offer.

What a kind woman you are, Christie Somers, thought Grace, after ringing Laura to ask if it was OK to take Joe out of school.

She wondered what the story behind her boss was. She was a shining example of what management should be like. Someone considerate and flexible got so much more out of their workforce than little Stalins like Malcolm did.

The plaque on the door read 'Nikita Koslov and Robin Green' alongside a string of qualifications that looked incredibly impressive. Grace and Joe rang the bell and then went into a spacious and tidy reception room with a central table full of magazines and comics. Joe picked out a *Dr Who* mag while Grace spoke to the receptionist and filled in a form. Then she went to sit next to Joe opposite a middle-aged man who was tapping his foot almost maniacally.

'You scared then?' the man asked, getting eye contact when Joe looked up to see why the floor was vibrating.

'A bit,' said Joe shyly.

'Ah, you'll be all right with Mr Koslov. Won't he?' he said to the receptionist, who nodded. He didn't say any more because the phone buzzed and the receptionist sent him up. His footfalls were heavy going up the stairs; all went quiet, then there was an almighty scream.

Joe looked at his nana in horror.

'It's all right,' said the receptionist. 'Mr Koslov gets all the nervous ones. He's so good with them.' She lowered her voice a little. 'The bloke that's gone up has only come for a check-up and he has to be numbed down to his knees.'

'It's awful to be scared of the dentist,' said Grace, remembering the rough old ogre she'd had as a child. She thought of that awful gas mask descending over her face and the fat old dentist telling her she'd dream of fairies when she was asleep. She didn't. The gas brought images of wild, swirling people that made her feel sick when she awoke. She had never since managed to feel entirely comfortable at the mercy of a dentist. That's why she had taken great care to choose a sympathetic one for the children because of her own experiences.

Soon it was their turn to go up the grand old oak staircase, which led to a waiting area on one side and two dentists' rooms on the other. It smelled of polish and flowery air freshener rather than the scary gas Grace remembered from old.

'Well, hello there,' said a booming voice, as rich and deep as an expensive Christmas cake. The owner of it strode forward with a hand outstretched. 'You must be Joe. Come and take a seat, Joe, while your big sister sits on that chair and waits for you.'

'Oh Gawd,' said the pretty young dental assistant, raising her eyes heavenward.

'And you're Grace,' said Niki, seizing Grace's hand firmly. 'I mean, of course, "you must be Grace", not "your Grace", because of course you look nothing like an Archbishop.'

Grace smiled both at him and the dental assistant doing a fresh roll of her eyes behind him. This man was instantly recognizable as Christie's brother by his twinkly blue eyes. His hair was established silver-white, as if it had lost its pigment a long time ago, short and spiked up, with no thinness on the crown. He was a completely different body shape to his smaller, rounder sister though, being long-limbed, slim and straight.

'Now then, young man, relax and go for a nice ride on this chair, totally free of charge. Can you open your mouth for me? Fan-tas-tic! Ah ha – I see the little devil! That's going to need to come out, I'm afraid. But don't worry, Joe, because I am the best dentist in the world and you aren't going to feel a thing.'

He injected Joe's mouth so gently that the boy never made a murmur. And whilst the numbing was building, Nikita Koslov encouraged Joe to concentrate on the spot-the-difference pictures that were stuck up on his ceiling. The tooth was out in a jiffy and a couple of minutes later, Joe was rinsing out his mouth and picking out a lolly from a container which the dental assistant was holding out for him and a sticker with a lion on it saying, 'I've been super-brave'.

'Thank you *so* much,' said Grace. 'I can't tell you how grateful we are.'

'No problemo at all,' said Niki. 'Joe has been absolutely brilliant. A star patient. And any friend of Christianya's is a friend of mine, of course.'

'I didn't know that's what Christie was short for,' said Grace, thinking, *What a beautiful name.*

'Russian ancestory,' said Niki. 'Noblemen who escaped the homeland in the Revolution. Who knows, if we'd stayed, I might have been Czar by now. That's the King of Russia to you, Joe.'

'Really?' said Joe, wide-eyed with fascination.

'Absolutely,' said Niki, winking at him. He had a lovely smile, just like Christie's. Genuine and friendly, spreading right up to his eyes.

He held out his hand to Joe and shook it manfully.

'Well, Joe, I hope the next time I see you will be in less painful and happier circumstances.'

Joe returned the handshake with a medically lopsided grin.

'Right, Joe, let's go and pay our bill,' said Grace, taking the little boy's hand.

'Absolutely not, wouldn't hear of it!' said Niki.

'No, please. I couldn't let you do this for nothing.'

'I insist and it's my surgery so I'm the boss and I win this argument,' said Niki, holding up a shushing finger. 'A favour for a friend of my sister.'

'That's incredibly kind of you,' said Grace, thinking that his heart was as generous as his sister's, it seemed. But she was already planning to ask Christie what his favourite tipple was. It wasn't in her nature not to pay her way.

'Pleasure. Goodbye, Your Grace,' smiled Niki. His fingers closed around Grace's hand. They were strong and warm. It was the oddest feeling but it was as if something passed between them like a soft, benign electrical current.

Grace was aware of an involuntary increase in her heart-rate as Christie's brother courteously showed them out.

Chapter 34

From the way Ben answered the door, it was obvious that it was to someone he knew. Raychel could hear a pleasant interchange taking place and then Ben was ushering a man into the sitting room. The visitor was invisible under a stack of thick, empty boxes.

'Here, put them down here,' said Ben.

'Right,' said the man, who was obviously a big, strong bloke to have carried that pile in.

'Ray, this is John, my boss.'

'Hello, Mrs Ben,' said John, straightening up, but when his eyes touched on Raychel's face, his mouth dropped open like a dead fish's.

Raychel started to go hot in that familiar way whenever anyone had prolonged eye contact with her.

'Forgive me for staring,' said John. 'You just look so much like . . . Do you mind? Can I ask? Are you from round here? Originally?'

'Newcastle,' said Raychel, frozen in his headlight gaze.

'No family at all down here then?' said John.

'No, we're all from up there,' said Raychel.

'Wow, that's so . . .' John shook his head. He seemed genuinely winded by the sight of Raychel.

'Do you want a cuppa, John?' said Ben.

'No, lad, don't worry. I'll let you get on. Nice to meet you . . . Raychel,' said John, taking a last lingering look at the young woman and really making an effort not to make her feel any more uncomfortable than she obviously was, but *My God*, it was hard to keep his eyes off her.

Outside, John Silkstone instinctively pressed the home number on his mobile, then clicked off before it connected. The lass had said she had no connections with Barnsley, so was it worth getting the missus upset or excited? But the likeness was uncanny – there simply *had* to be a connection. He needed to think very carefully before venturing anywhere near this giant can of worms with a tin opener.

Chapter 35

'So, are we going out again tomorrow?' asked Anna. 'Only I've got such a busy schedule I need to pencil it in the diary.'

Dawn laughed. Once upon a time, she'd thought Anna hadn't any sense of humour, but quite evidently she did. It was subtle though, the dry and deadpan sort. Very unlike her own 'in your face' kind.

'Well, that would be nice,' said Christie. 'We can celebrate you being forty and one week old.'

'No thanks,' said Anna. 'That means there's only fifty-one weeks until I'm forty-one.'

'Or five hundred and nineteen until you're fifty,' added Raychel.

'Stop, I'm feeling ill!' said Anna, feigning a headache.

'It will have to be a quick one for me,' said Raychel. 'We're moving into our new flat this weekend and I'm busy, busy, busy. But it would be nice to have a drink in that pub again.'

'You can count me in,' said Dawn. 'You can tell us all the details about your night with the Darq one as well.' It had been a very busy week. They hadn't had any chance to chat.

'Wasn't much to tell,' said Anna. 'I—'

'No, save it!' said Dawn. 'We don't want a drive-by account. We want detail.'

*

So the following night saw them chattering and walking around the corner together to the Rising Sun. The small stage in front of the bar wasn't empty this time. It was full of equipment and men in cowboy shirts and hats faffing around with mikes and instruments. Presumably these were 'The Rhinestones'.

'Are we all driving?' said Christie.

'I'm not,' said Anna. 'But one alcoholic drink will be enough for me. I can't hold my booze very well.'

'Well, let's get a bottle of wine and five glasses,' said Christie. 'That won't send us over any limits.'

'Shall we have a kitty?' suggested Dawn, opening up her purse and holding up a fiver. 'I haven't any change, but it could go towards next week if this is to be a regular occurrence. What do you all think?'

The others seemed to agree and tipped up a fiver each, then they went to find a table away from the tuning-up band, a little to Dawn's disappointment, while Christie ordered the wine at the bar.

'So come on then,' said Raychel, once they had all taken off their coats and the wine was poured. 'What happened with the designer?'

'Oh, where to begin?' said Anna. 'A Merc picked me up and took me to his house which is absolutely gorgeous, like a castle off a Hammer Horror set. And then he had a good look at my bra and told me it was appalling.' Anna left out the embarrassing garlic episode.

'Not one for much elaboration, are you?' said Christie, with a mischievous grin.

'The filming is starting tomorrow though. That's when I'll have "stories" to tell.'

'Are you scared?' asked Raychel.

'I wasn't that bad at the beginning of the week but I'm terrified now.'

'It must be so exciting,' said Dawn, grinning. 'I looked Vladimir Darq up on the Net. He's rather dishy, isn't he?'

'Gay blokes always are,' sniffed Anna. 'Look at Gok, he's gorgeous. You just want him as your best friend, don't you?'

'You must fancy Vladimir Darq though, surely?' said Christie.

'What's the point?' replied Anna.

'Can't wait for the next instalment,' smiled Raychel. 'What time are you going?'

'He's sending a car at quarter to seven. He said he doesn't work during the day.' Anna shifted forward in her seat and whispered as if he could overhear her, 'And he's got fangs.'

'Fangs?'

'Like a vampire. Not great two-foot-long ones at the front, but there are definite fangs there. On his teeth.'

'As opposed to on his ears?' twinkled Christie.

'No, really, he has,' Anna insisted.

'He plays on the image of being Romanian then, obviously,' said Christie. 'As one would.'

'What do you mean?' said Dawn as the others groaned.

'Romania – vampires – Dracula,' explained Grace.

'Never been one for all that gothic stuff. That's more my sort of thing,' said Dawn, pointing to the band who had started playing and were really very good from the off. Especially that tall rhythm guitarist at the back. She'd had the brilliant idea of asking them to play at her wedding as soon as she heard his fingers on the strings. At least that would make the evening karaoke more bearable.

'Grandson's tooth doing OK?' Christie asked Grace.

'Thanks to your brother, yes,' replied Grace.

'I remember you saying once that your brother was a dentist,' Dawn recalled.

'Yes, and a very good one,' Grace said.

'He's a lovely man is my big brother,' smiled Christie. 'Why he never found the right woman is totally beyond me. He's kind, generous, patient, faithful.' She shook her head. She had never understood why he wasn't settled with a brood of children. She would have loved to have seen him in a sweet, caring relationship.

'Well, there's your answer then,' sighed Anna. 'If he'd been a total bastard, he'd have pulled a nice bird, wrecked her life and been instantly attractive to loads of other women.' Wasn't it unfair how relationships worked? Some lovely people had no one and all the gits had the pick of the crop.

'And are you ready for the big move tomorrow then?' Christie asked Raychel.

'More or less. I've just got a bit of cleaning left to do for the next person in the house.'

'Yeurch. I shan't be asking to swap you weekends,' said Anna.

'Me neither. I'd rather get felt up by a gay vampire than scrub out ovens,' said Dawn.

They downed their glasses and put their coats on and said their goodbyes and 'have a nice weekends'. Dawn volunteered to take the glasses back to the bar because she wanted to listen to the band for another five minutes. And as she came near to the stage, she fell instantly in love. She noticed that the tall rhythm guitarist was playing a vintage Fender Stratocaster: the same guitar her dad had. She closed her eyes and listened to the sound and imagined her dad on the stage, his fingers on the strings.

There was applause as the song ended but Dawn was locked in a bitter-sweet daydream and swayed, and when she toppled, it was the rhythm guitarist whose hands steadied her.

'You OK there, ma'am?' he drawled in a voice straight off a John Wayne western. It seemed the band had stopped for a break.

'Oh yes, sorry,' said Dawn, feeling a bit of a twerp then. She hoped he didn't think she was tottering because she was drunk and so launched into an explanation. 'I was listening to your guitar. My dad used to have a vintage Stratocaster too. It's got such a great sound. It's so nice to see one again.'

'*Used to?* He had one of those and he let it go?' questioned the guitarist.

'Not really. He was buried with it. Which is a bit of a conversation stopper, sorry,' sighed Dawn.

'Oh, jeez, I'm sorry to hear that. It must have been real special to him.'

'Oh, yes it was.'

'And do you play like your daddy, ma'am?'

His voice was gorgeous. It was like sunshine warming up her ear. It was nearly as gorgeous as the sound of his guitar playing.

'Oh, I'll never be as good as he was,' said Dawn bashfully.

'Which guitar do you have?'

'A Gibson Les Paul. Nineteen fifty-seven.'

He whistled respectfully. 'Wow. You in a band yourself then, ma'am?'

'No, my father was though,' said Dawn.

'The Beatles?' he teased.

Dawn laughed. 'Of course. He was George.'

'Then may I buy you a drink, Miss Harrison?'

Dawn opened up her mouth to say, *No, thank you, I'm just going*. But what came out was, 'Yes, please. Just a Diet Coke though because I'm driving.'

One soft drink wouldn't do her any harm. It wasn't as if she was missing a passionate night in with Calum. He'd crawl in beside her in the wee small hours and attempt sex if he didn't fall asleep first. She was aware that she gave a shudder at the thought of it.

'So, what's your everyday name then, Miss Harrison?' said the tall, dark guitarist as the barmaid put two Diet Cokes in front of them.

'Dawny. Dawny Sole.' She added the 'Y' on to make her feel like a different person to the Dawn Sole who had a fiancé and was in the midst of imminent-wedding preparations.

'I'm Al Holly. Miss Dawny Sole, it sure is nice to meet you.'

The cowboy held out a large, slim-fingered hand and shook her own. Although she could have just held it out and it would have shook by itself. His voice was having the same effect on her that the lead guitar on Chris Isaak's *Wicked Game* had. It was bouncing around inside her, twanging her own strings and stirring up all sorts of things inside her that it shouldn't have.

'I wondered . . . how long you were going to be around for?' stuttered Dawn. She bit off the part about asking if he'd be available to play for her wedding.

'Well, Kirk – the bass guitarist right there – has come to spend a few weeks with his parents who moved back over here a couple of years ago, so we're playing a few gigs in the area and we're hoping to head home at the end of June. Why? You thinking of coming and joining us?'

'I wish!' said Dawn. The idea of running away from all those wedding bills with just her guitar and a few pairs of knickers in a bag flashed through her head and felt very attractive.

'You could bring your guitar along and show us all how it's done,' said Al Holly. 'Maybe I don't believe you can play at all and here you are just trying to chat me up.'

His soft hazel eyes were shining like a naughty little boy's on April Fool's morning.

'No, no I'm not, really,' said Dawn, thrown into a sudden small panic. Was she flirting too much?

'Then you'll have to bring your Gibson along and prove it before we leave,' said Al Holly.

'I might just do that,' said Dawn, grinning back.

She stayed for that one drink, talking guitars. She hadn't done that with anyone since her dad. What a square she would seem to outsiders, but it was so interesting to her. Al Holly went back on stage after fifteen minutes and she went back to the car park wondering what the heck had happened in such a short time to make her grin to that degree.

Chapter 36

Raychel twirled around in her lovely new flat that afforded views over the whole town. Not exactly a New York skyscraper but it was so light and airy up here, and quiet. Everything was so clean; the walls were all snow-white with fresh paint and no one had ever cooked in the kitchen oven or put their dirty clothes in the washing machine.

Their new bedroom was so cosy. The second bedroom was going to be a kind of all-sorts room with their computer and Raychel's painting paraphernalia. There was no point in using it for a bedroom; it was unlikely that there would ever be guests. And it would never be a nursery.

Dawn called at Muriel's bright and early as arranged to sort out the bridesmaids' dresses with Bette across the road. Then she had to have two cups of coffee because Demi wasn't yet awake and when she did venture downstairs, it wasn't a pretty sight.

'What position did you sleep in?' laughed Denise. 'You've got hair like a Maori's hut!'

'Go arse,' said Demi, pinching some of her dad's toast.

'Dawn's been waiting forty minutes for you, you lazy cow.'

'I'm up now, aren't I?' barked Demi at her sister. Dawn heard her muttering, 'Anyone would think it was the bloody Royal

Wedding!' under her breath as she went upstairs to put on a bit of make-up.

Five minutes later, they were marching across the road. Muriel obviously knew Bette well enough to open the door, go on in and then announce: 'Only us, Bette.'

The largest woman Dawn had ever seen waddled towards them in a poky front room filled with smoke fug. She had a choice of chins to put out on display and was dripping in so many gold necklaces that she looked like a cross between a Lady Mayoress and Mr T. Strangely though, she had delicate, tiny, plump hands and beautiful nails painted red; the two little ones were pierced with jingly charms hanging from them.

Bette greeted Dawn warmly, after killing her cigarette in the ashtray on a coffee table heaped high with tripey women's weekly magazines. Muriel sat on the sofa arm while the others squeezed themselves down on Bette's sofa and the big lady herself occupied the armchair which creaked in pain when she dropped into it.

'I've collected some patterns for you to look at,' said Bette, her voice sounding as if it was coming out of her voice box via a cheese-grater. She emptied a carrier bag full of pattern packets out on the coffee table. Most of them looked as if they were out of some 1970s' nightmare. The fact that neither Demi nor Denise was cooing either told Dawn they were of the same mind.

'This is all right,' said Muriel, tapping her nail-bitten finger at a long, swishy number.

'I'm not wearing that!' said Demi. 'I'll look a right chuffing frump.'

'Take that bottom frill off and drop the neck a bit and it's lovely, that,' said Bette, lighting up again. 'I've done that dress before and it looked beautiful. I did it in shell-pink for a woman up Ketherwood last year.'

'Trust Bette, she knows what she's doing.' Muriel nudged Dawn from behind.

'I suppose if you drop the neck it would look all right. I don't want to look like a doll,' said Demi, who was rubbing her head and would agree to wearing a black bin-liner in five minutes' time just to get out of there and back to bed.

'Well, I'm OK with it,' said Denise. 'If you take that frill off for me an' all.'

'Well, that was easy,' said Bette, reaching into another carrier at her side. 'Here's your material samples. You wanted peach, did you say? Here you go then, cocker.'

Dawn passed around the squares of peachy materials. She was pleasantly surprised to find the lovely shade that matched the tiny roses on her own dress. She intended to make sure it was replicated on the wedding stationery and chocolate favours. Then, fresh fag-a-dangle, Bette measured Denise and Demi's vital statistics. She was wheezing as though she had completed a full body work-out by the end.

'Leave it with me, kid,' said Bette, giving Dawn a big wink on the way out. 'What Bette can do with a needle isn't worth talking about.' Which was all mixed up. At least, Dawn hoped it was all mixed up.

Chapter 37

The Mercedes arrived for Anna exactly on time. Leonid once again answered the door and pulled her excitedly into the vaulted room which was now populated with a small film crew who came over to introduce themselves: Mark, the director, who was dressed very grungily and would have made a great Jesus in a play with his long, thin face and beard, a young, leggy runner called Flip (short for Philippa, she explained in a very confident but smiley voice), a punky cameraman with a white Mohican hairdo, who introduced himself as Bruce, and a plump and pretty make-up lady called Chas. Vladimir was standing at the back of the room with a tiny, white-haired, pinch-faced woman of about sixty and the tall, gamine Jane Cleve-Jones who was even more gorgeous in real life than she was on screen. Seeing that she had arrived, the trio came over and Vladimir nodded a welcome. Jane introduced herself with two alternate air kisses at Anna's cheeks. Everyone seemed very friendly. Even the dog rose out of the basket and came over with a slow walk, tail wagging, and pushed his head into Anna's hand, sniffing her.

'What's his name?' asked Anna.

'Luno.'

'I've got a cat. He can probably smell that,' said Anna.

'Maybe he isn't frightened by the presence of garlic this week,' Vladimir said with a little sniff. Anna puffed out her cheeks with embarrassment but he ignored her and introduced the stern-looking woman with the white hair. 'Anna, this is your make-up lady: may I present Maria Shaposhnikova.'

The tiny woman held her hand straight out and shook Anna's with the strength of a WWE wrestler. Close up, Maria looked like an ancient-faced snow pixie with anger management issues.

'Maria is a master. I work with no one else,' said Vladimir, going on to translate what he had just said for Maria. She nodded, without smiling, at the compliment.

'Can I get you some refreshment?' Leonid asked, looking at Anna's shaking hands. 'A glass of wine maybe?'

He held up a long crystal decanter full of dark red liquid.

'Maybe just a little one,' said Anna, receiving the pewter goblet that he handed to her. It was strange drinking out of something which had a taste of its own. But it was a lovely, fiery wine.

'That's nice,' said Anna. 'What sort is it?'

'It's a wine local to the part of Romania where I come from. *Sânge de virgina*,' said Vladimir.

'What's that mean?' said Anna.

'The nearest translation would be "Maiden's Blood",' said Vladimir with a twinkle in his eye, as Anna had a sudden choking fit and then tried to explain that her wine had gone down the wrong way.

'We've been doing a few shots around the house,' said Jane, flicking her long caramel-highlighted hair over her shoulder. 'It's absolutely fantastic. I am *so* in love with it. It's going to make a great programme. Vladimir tells me he discovered you at a railway station.'

She said 'discovered' like Anna was a top model, like Twiggy was 'discovered' in a hairdressing salon. Anna had to clamp down on the sudden urge to giggle.

It was late and the film crew had a lot to get through, so Anna was shoved in a chair and stripped of make-up by Maria and a lot of swoops of cotton wool.

'Aarrgh, I've got no make-up on – get the crucifixes out, everyone!' laughed Anna, then she clamped her hands over her mouth. Not the most appropriate joke to make in this house.

The camera was quite a frightening piece of equipment, Anna decided, as its big lens-eye trained on her for the first shot. Everything went quiet and Anna did as she was directed, which wasn't difficult because all she had to do was stand there while Jane and Vladimir talked about her.

'Why did you pick Anna to be the face of your "Every Woman has a Darq Side" project then, Vladimir?'

'I could see instantly that Anna feels she is much older than she is and as a result her confidence has gone. I am going to show women that whatever their size or age, there is always a goddess in them waiting to show herself.'

'Cut!' said Mark.

There were a lot of short 'action' sequences, Anna noticed. It was quite fascinating to be part of a TV show. Not as glamorous as she had imagined by any stretch though.

Anna was feeling quite relaxed until the moment when the director asked if she could strip off now. She had a sudden and awful vision of Malcolm seeing her norks on the box.

'Just to your undies, Anna. We need to ask Vlad why he thinks they are so bad.'

Anna took a deep breath and slipped off her shirt and skirt. She imagined that everyone would burst out laughing, or throw up. What she didn't bargain for was, and unfairly so she soon realized, that they were professionals doing a job and they'd probably seen more boobs and bras and backsides in their time than the porn king Ron Jeremy.

Leonid took some shots of Anna with a very big and heavy-looking camera. They needed some stills, he explained. She hoped those pics wouldn't turn up on any *Readers' Wives* pages.

Filming commenced again.

'So, Vladimir,' began Jane. 'What is wrong with Anna's underwear?'

'What is right with it?' He laughed without humour. 'The bra is too small, she is wearing the wrong size completely, and there is no support at all for a bust.'

'It's pretty though,' put in Jane.

'Pretty bad, you mean. Look how the straps are making a groove in her shoulders,' he carried on, lifting up the said strap and showing the camera the indentation it was making on her skin. 'As for the pants . . .' He made a sound of despair.

'Cut,' called Mark. 'Excellent. Anna, there's a screen in the corner; can you change into some more underwear and we'll do the same.'

It appeared Vladimir couldn't find words bad enough in English for the second and third lots of undies. There seemed to be a lot in Romanian though. Then Jane held several coloured scarves against Anna's face and she went through which shades would work with her skin tones. That was interesting. Apparently black worked very well, which was lucky because that was more or less all that Anna had in her wardrobe. Vladimir waved away the 'colours' theories. He said that if a woman had inner confidence she could carry off the most inappropriate hues and still look fantastic. Anna tried to imagine herself pulling off clothes in bright colours the way Christie did. She concluded that she wouldn't stand a chance.

Then Anna had to stand in front of the mirror and tell Jane what she saw in her reflection. Where to start?

'My bust is too big, my waist isn't thin enough, my hips are too wide . . .' The list went on and on. By the time she had got to her knees looking like crêpe paper the tears were shining in her eyes. She tried to stuff them back but couldn't. They plopped down her cheeks as she 'fessed up that she felt totally worthless and hideous and old. She was so deeply embedded in her self-massacre that she forgot the camera was there.

'Cut!' called Mark. 'I think that's enough for today, boys and girls. Let's get this equipment packed up and out.'

'Sorry,' said Anna as Jane pulled a tissue out of her pocket and handed it over.

'You were fab and so natural,' said Jane supportively, rubbing Anna's shoulder. 'Women everywhere will identify with you.'

'Anna, before you go, please try something on for me,' said Vladimir. He held up a stiff, dark red corset. Even keeping her eyes forward, Anna could tell that her chest was three feet higher with the garment on than it was without it. Vladimir leaned over her from the back and she could smell his cologne. Something she had never come across before: exotic and spicy but at the same time as fresh as wild Christmas trees.

He expertly laced up the back then stepped away to look at her. Then he marched forward again and straightened her shoulders.

'*La naiba!* As soon as I look at you, you try to curl into a ball! You are wearing a Vladimir Darq exclusive, how can you wilt like a dead flower?' he said crossly. He backed off again, only to come striding forward, growling, 'Stop doing that, you are driving me crazy!'

Thus reprimanded, Anna pulled her stomach in and pushed out her chest. He nodded by way of approval. At least she assumed it was approval. It appeared that if he wasn't disapproving, then he was approving.

'You are married?' he asked.

'No,' said Anna. 'Engaged.'

'I couldn't work out if you were unhappy because you are with a man or unhappy because you are without a man.'

'Both,' said Anna as she placed her hands on her waist, which felt very much smaller. Where had all the flab gone? No doubt it was all crushed up inside the material, but she couldn't feel it if it was.

'What does that mean?'

'My partner left me in February.'

'For another woman?'

'Yes. Don't pull any punches, will you?'

He ignored the barb.

'That explains the sloping shoulders.' He pulled the ribbon tighter at the back of her and made her yelp.

'Ow! His aren't sloping.'

'No, he is parading like peacock, huh?'

Yep, that just about summed Tony up. A peacock. One with two dicks as well.

'Men can be such monsters,' Vladimir then said in a surprisingly soft way. Which, she thought, was a bit rich coming from a bloke who probably got his nutrients from draining people of their blood. 'OK, that's enough for today for me too.' And he started to unlace her. She hadn't noticed the camera was still rolling and Bruce was smiling behind it. He'd get major brownie points for this when Mark saw the footage.

The next day, Grace was washing up the Sunday dinner plates when there was a knock at the back door and she opened it to a smiling Charles in a smart, pale blue shirt and jeans. He really was a good-looking man.

'Come in, Charles, Laura won't be long. Would you like a cup of tea?'

'Thank you, but no, I won't,' he said. 'Oh hello, Mr Beamish . . .' Gordon had walked into the kitchen. He stared at Charles's hand that was outstretched in greeting, then his eyes lifted to Charles's face.

'Who are you?' said Gordon coldly.

'I'm Charles, Charles Onajole. I'm a friend of Laura's, and young Joe's, of course,' came the courteous reply. His hand was still outstretched but more awkwardly now as Gordon had not come forward to return the greeting. There was an uncomfortable silence in which Charles was eventually forced to let his hand drop back down. Gordon's jaw tightened and he said in a quiet voice, which was nevertheless full of menace, 'I think you'd better get out of my house, lad.'

Charles's eyes flickered as his brain tried to fathom what on earth he had done to earn such a reaction to his cheerful greeting. But it was painfully obvious, because there was really no mistaking that look on Gordon's face. Silently, Charles turned and went out of the door. Grace, watching this interchange, was dumbstruck by Gordon's rudeness to a guest.

'Gordon, what on earth—'

Then Laura came down with Joe's bag and Joe trotting behind and Grace bit down on what she was about to say.

'Was that Charles?' she asked, then picked up on the vibe in the room. 'What's up?'

'There was a nigger in my house, that's what's up!' snarled Gordon, not seeming to care that Joe was present.

'For God's sake, Gordon!' Grace was horrified at the words coming out of his mouth, the swear words that followed.

'Joe, go and join Charles in the car,' said Laura quickly, pushing her son out of the door. She was shaking when she turned back and Gordon rounded on her immediately.

'I don't want you in here either, if you're sleeping with *that*!' He was stabbing his finger in the direction of where he supposed Charles to be now.

Laura looked from Grace to her father, unable to really comprehend why he was being like this and where this hate had suddenly come from. They were all right as rain less than two minutes ago.

'Dad, what's the matter with you?'

Gordon laughed as if everyone in the house was being obtuse. 'Well,' he turned to his daughter. 'All I can say is – thank God you can't have any more kiddies!'

'Gordon!' Grace cried out in disgust.

Laura burst into tears. It was beyond cruel, and Grace leaped to her daughter's side.

'God forgive you for that, Gord—'

But Gordon was in no mood for listening. He made a none-too-gentle grab at his daughter's arm.

'You. Out!' he raged. Grace stepped forward to put herself between father and daughter and ended up being pushed into the table where a cup fell off and covered her skirt in cold tea.

'Mum, are you OK?' said Laura, coming forward to help her mother.

'Laura, love, go,' said Grace, pushing Laura safely out of the house. 'I'm fine.' Although she wasn't fine at all, she was shaking with the worst mix of emotions, but her priority was to get her daughter out and away from this awful atmosphere and any more vicious, wounding words.

Grace closed the door and turned to face her husband who was standing frighteningly still and breathing tightly. He looked like a bomb due to explode at any minute, a dangerous, harmful one full of nails and burning sugar, intent on causing the most damage it could.

'Did you know? Did you know he was a blackie?'

'Stop it, Gordon. Stop talking like that!'

Gordon shook his head in disbelief and stared at Grace as if she was insane. 'The world's gone bloody mad.'

He marched out, towards the soothing calm of his allotment no doubt, leaving Grace still in shock, her heart thumping and her limbs quivering. She didn't know this man, swearing and hating like something out of the Deep South in the 1920s. Yes, she had witnessed his temper spill on a few occasions over the years, but not to the extent that she was seeing it these days. And now it seemed that two of her children weren't welcome in the house. 'Whatever next?' she said, still shaking as she swept up the remains of the cup, a present from Sarah that read: 'World's Best Dad.'

Chapter 38

'Oh, come here, you're useless,' said Elizabeth Silkstone, reaching up to straighten the knot on her husband's tie as they were about to go into church. John Silkstone was a big man and he carried a suit well. He made her knees knock in a suit, still. She was aware that he was staring intently at her while she unloosened his clumsy effort and started again.

'What are you staring at?' she snapped.

'I'm not,' he lied. Had she not opened her mouth then, he would have told her his burning suspicion that Raychel Love, the wife of his newest worker, young Ben, was closely related to her – was possibly the child of her sister who went missing nearly thirty years ago. It was bursting out of him to say something. But it wouldn't be fair, not today. They would be witnessing their friend Helen's wedding in less than half an hour. Helen was marrying a gentleman solicitor, Teddy Sanderson, although not so much of a gentleman, they'd laughed, seeing as Helen would be saying her vows with a five-month-old son growing inside her.

What John had to say would have to wait until later. There was a time and a place – and this was neither.

Chapter 39

'Crikey, did you see that programme last night?' said Dawn as she breezed into the office after the weekend. The next part she directed at Anna. 'If you thought your love life was bad, wait till you start wanting to hump buildings!'

'Thanks for that, Dawn,' said Anna, smiling. Dawn was the most verbally clumsy person she thought she had ever, or would ever, meet. But there was something simple and totally non-malicious about her that was refreshing and funny. She didn't know much about the woman, but she was pretty sure that Dawn would be gutted if she ever thought she had upset anyone with her gauche way of speaking her mind.

'What do you mean "hump buildings"?' asked Grace.

'There's this condition where people are sexually attracted to buildings.'

'Get away,' said Anna.

'Honest! This woman was married to the Eiffel Tower. People were having relationships with fences and banisters and everything.'

'That's so made up,' said Anna, shaking her head. 'It must have been a spoof programme.'

'No, Dawn is right,' put in Christie. 'It's called "objectum sexuality" or "animism". It's the belief that inanimate objects have feelings.'

'Oh aye, and how come you know so much about it?' grinned Dawn. 'You've not been knocking off the coffee machine, have you?'

'My father was a lecturing psychologist,' said Christie. 'You'd be surprised how many strange and wonderful people conditions there are out there.'

'I wish he was here now,' said Anna. 'I have this recurring dream that David Attenborough is a zombie but I really fancy him. I've always wondered what it means.'

'It means you should stop eating strong cheddar after nine p.m., that's what my nan used to say,' laughed Grace.

'I don't get how anyone could fancy a building,' said Raychel, downing tools and joining in with the conversation.

'I didn't get it and I watched it!' said Dawn. 'I thought it was a wind-up at first. There were even some women who were in love with the Berlin Wall and when he, I mean it, got ripped down they went nuts.'

'So the Berlin Wall had more than one lover?' said Anna with a naughty glint in her eye. 'He was unfaithful? Gawd, there's no hope for any of us if a pile of bricks can't even keep it in its trousers.'

'Well, Anna,' said Dawn with a cheeky look on her face, 'I just thought that if you don't pull soon, you could always go and try to chat up the Town Hall.'

'I wouldn't want anything that big,' said Anna with a sniff. 'The bus shelter on the end of my street has nice slim windows. He's more my type.'

'You two should be on the stage as a double act,' said Grace with a chuckle.

'OK, here's a question for you: which would you rather snog – a garden fence or Malcolm?' asked Dawn mischievously.

'The fence!' they all said in unison and laughed just as they spotted the rejected choice make his way down the office on an obvious bee-line course for Christie.

They all had to sit hard on their giggles as his first words were, 'I love the new furniture in here. My, Mr McAskill has really splashed out, hasn't he?'

Christie didn't give him the satisfaction of an answer. She gave him a fixed, courteous smile. She suspected (rightly) that he had finally started to realize that his attempts to charm a friendship with her had fallen on stony ground and, as a result, something dark and bitchy was forming in his psyche.

'I just came to tell you that there's a meeting for Heads of Department at two, were you aware?'

'I have the email, yes,' said Christie.

'Lovely desk,' said Malcolm, smoothing his hand over the surface before turning to grease back up the office to his own department.

'Bet the desk would say "I'm not that desperate",' giggled Dawn, sending them all into fits.

The laughter caught up with Malcolm and he didn't know what had been said but he suspected he was the subject of their hilarity. His growing resentment towards McAskill's teacher's pet shot up a few notches. The connection between her and the big boss was blindingly obvious and he would show up that blonde tart as McAskill's fancy-piece the first chance he got.

Chapter 40

John Silkstone was trying to find the right words as he worked with Ben, skimming adjacent walls with plaster. He couldn't get Raychel out of his mind but he needed a bit more to go on before he told his wife about her.

'Finding it different from London then, lad?' he began as an opening gambit.

'Aye. A lot quieter.'

'And how's the new flat?'

'Smashing. Although it'll take a bit of time to put a stamp on it. It's all too *clean* at the moment.'

'Well, enjoy it being clean before any bairns come along.' He laughed. For a little boy, his own son couldn't half make some mess.

He saw Ben flinch slightly, not much, as if John's words had passed very close to a raw nerve.

He carried on plastering for a couple more minutes before starting up again.

'So your wife's from Newcastle as well then?'

'Aye,' said Ben after a telling pause.

'Your family still up there?'

'We've got no family. There's just Ray and me.'

'How old is your wife?'

Ben whisked around to John; he was gripping his trowel so hard that his knuckles were white.

'Why all the questions about my wife, John?'

'I'm just making conversation,' said John, holding his hands up in a gesture of peace. Placated, Ben started plastering again.

'OK, I lied,' confessed John. 'It's Raychel. She's the spitting image of my wife and she's been looking for her sister, Bev Collier, who ran away from home in the seventies when she was pregnant. That bairn would be about twenty-eight now. Can you see where this is going?'

Ben kept his back towards John and carried on working. His voice, when he answered, was calm. Too calm, too measured.

'Aye, I can see what you're saying. But it's not Raychel.'

John had no choice but to let it drop for now. He didn't want to push too hard, too soon. But he felt Ben's tension from across the room and knew without any doubt now that the lad knew more than he was letting on.

Chapter 41

Things were far from normal at Grace's house. She was still suffering from the seismic shift that Gordon's outburst the previous week had caused. Then, in the middle of her ironing on Thursday night, Paul had rung to talk about Laura and made her think even more.

'He's cracking up, Mum, and I think you might need to get him to a doctor,' said Paul. 'I know he's always had a temper but this is getting ridiculous. Laura said you got hurt in the crossfire.'

'It was an accident,' Grace replied quickly.

'Do you know, I was only little but I still remember him and Mum having blistering rows. She stood up to him and he just blasted her down. I remember her crying – a lot.'

Grace gasped. 'You never told me that before.'

'Well, it's funny, but with all that's happened recently, it's like parts of my brain have been woken up and things have been coming back to the surface. I know you'll say that time's distorted what I remember and it probably has, but not that much. You're so different to her – she fought him. You always backed down and let him have his own way. He never had any reason to shout and bawl at you.'

'I've been married to your father for nearly twenty-four years, love; I think I know him quite well myself,' Grace said, desperate to underplay this and not fuel any more bad feeling between father and children.

Paul sighed at the other end of the phone. 'You married him for us, Mum. Laura and I know that. We're not thick.'

Grace opened her mouth to answer but nothing came out. Her son was a wise and insightful man and he had known the truth of her situation, if not the whole story. Even when she had first come into their lives, she had realized there was a rift between Paul and his father and she had hoped to heal it. She never had and now they were totally estranged with little hope of ever reconciling.

'We know he has never liked people breaking ranks, but this is something else. You must see that, surely?'

'Paul, love—'

'All I'm saying, Mum, is please, just humour me and take care, will you?'

The way he said it sent a shiver down her spine.

The next morning, as Grace was reaching for her coat, she was aware of Gordon's scrutiny.

'Haven't seen that dress before, is it new?'

'Yes, I got it yesterday in my lunch hour.'

'Where from? There aren't any clothes shops on your industrial estate, are there?'

'No, but there's one in Maltstone. It's only a ten-minute drive up the road.'

'Bit posh for work, isn't it?'

'It was only fifteen pounds in the sale. It's hardly a Stella McCartney, Gordon.'

'Who?' said Gordon.

'She's a fashion designer.'

'I'll bring in fish and chips for tea,' said Gordon, rattling the creases out of his newspaper and not acknowledging her answer.

'Well, I'd be better picking them up on my way home,' said Grace. 'I'm going for a drink after work with the girls.'

'Again?' said Gordon. 'How come you're going out all of a sudden?'

'It's only a quick drink, Gordon. All five of us go after work. It's nice.'

'Getting some fancy ideas from them women you work with, aren't you?' he said with more than a hint of sarcasm. 'Talking about designers and getting dolled up. Aren't you a bit old for all that?'

Grace bit down hard on her lip. *Old, old, old.* Gordon hadn't grown old, he was born old. She was fifty-five, *only* fifty-five. She liked clothes and yoga – and laughing.

She picked up her bag and said that she would see him later. Something about that last conversation she'd had with Paul stopped her dignifying his barb with anything else. Gordon was not a man to antagonize at the moment.

'Hi, is that Anna?' trilled the voice down the mobile into Anna's ear.

'Yes,' said Anna. She didn't recognize the incoming number and hoped this wasn't a 'we're doing a customer survey' because they really got on her nerves.

'It's Jane Cleve-Jones. Listen, Anna, slight change of plan. Vlad's taken a lightning trip to Milan so we're going to be shooting at your place tomorrow. We'll have a good look at your wardrobe. We'll be there first thing in the morning – that OK? Say eight?'

'Really?' Anna was flown into sudden panic. The house was a tip. And she couldn't show them her real wardrobe because it was full of total crap!

'Really. See you tomorrow,' said Jane. '*Ciao.*'

'Oy, are you part of this conversation or what?' said Anna,

nudging Dawn whose eyes were drawn to the cowboy guitarist and his sexy black quiff. He looked like he'd just stepped out of a 1950s film. He had waved at her when they first walked in and she was lost in watching him play.

'Sorry,' said Dawn. 'I just love those guitars.'

'Not in a "wanting to have sex with one" way, surely?' said Christie.

'Oh, don't start all that again,' laughed Dawn. 'I'm still traumatized from watching that woman fondling a piece of fence. Not sure I'm ready for this week's episode – it's about women who have five hundred orgasms a day.'

'Lucky cows,' said Anna. 'I'd settle for five hundred in a lifetime.'

'There's no cure either,' said Dawn.

'Who the hell would want to look for a cure?' replied Christie with a snorty laugh.

'Hope she doesn't have a celebratory fag after every one,' Dawn giggled.

'Hey, Dawn, how are your wedding plans going?' asked Raychel.

'Oh, so so,' said Dawn, the laughter dying quickly to a sigh. 'Calum's auntie gave us two thousand pounds towards things, so that was nice.'

'It won't go very far with the price of wedding paraphernalia these days,' said Grace. Sarah's wedding to Hugo had cost over thirty thousand. But then she had to have 'designer this' and 'designer that'. She had every indulgence known to man that day. But a big wedding didn't necessarily make for a solid foundation. Her son-in-law had an affair before he'd reached their second anniversary.

'You don't look very thrilled about it,' said Raychel. 'I was so excited when I got married, although we only had a register office do and none of the trimmings.'

Dawn hummed a little bit. 'It's not that I'm not excited . . .' *How to put this sensitively?* 'I just feel . . . like . . . as if . . .'

'Spit it out, lass,' said Christie.

Dawn huffed and came straight out with it, feeling immediately disloyal to her in-laws-to-be as soon as the words had left her.

'I just feel that it's not my wedding any more. I feel that it's been taken over and my choices have been pushed into second place.'

'Who's doing that to you?'

'Well . . .' Dawn felt almost as if Muriel was looking disapprovingly over her shoulder. But who else could she talk to? And she badly needed to open up to someone and get a fresh perspective on things. 'My new mother-in-law is quite a force to be reckoned with. She's paying for some of the stuff and she thinks that gives her the right to choose. They've booked a karaoke and a beef dinner in a dingy pub and I wanted a band and chicken in white wine in a bistro . . .' Dawn snapped her mouth shut before any more came tumbling out. She was already feeling painful prickles behind her eyes.

'And what's your fiancé had to say about it?' asked Christie gently.

'Oh, he's a bit under the thumb. His mother's, not mine. He just agrees with whatever she says. God, I'm sorry.' A big fat tear broke through and rolled down Dawn's cheek and she felt Grace's hand upon her own.

'Weddings are very stressful,' she said in that lovely calm voice she had. 'You try and make sure you get what you want though. Your mother-in-law has had her big day. This is your turn.'

'I half-wish we'd just carried on living together and not bothered with all this palaver,' said Dawn, blowing her nose on a tissue that she pulled out of her jacket pocket. *But you leaped on that drunken proposal Calum made, didn't you, and you ran with it before he could sober up and change his mind?* She shook the thought away. Brains could be very cruel sometimes.

'It's your day, so stand your ground,' said Grace. She would never have dreamed of interfering with Sarah's plans. Not that she would have been able to. Sarah even dictated the colour Grace had to dress in.

'What's your Calum like then?' asked Anna.

'Quiet,' said Dawn, thinking how to describe him. Quiet sounded more acceptable than comatose. 'Laid-back, too laid-back really. He's a fork-lift truck driver. Five years younger than me, medium height, slim build, blond hair, likes a pint.' *Pub every night, pub every Sunday lunchtime. Nap on Sunday afternoon and goes to his mother's house for his tea every Monday for the Sunday dinner leftovers . . .*

'He sounds very . . . stable,' said Christie, nodding kindly. Dawn knew what was going through all their minds though. Try as she might, she couldn't sex him up in her description. Nor did she want to at that moment. She thought of how young Raychel spoke about Ben and his gentlemanly ways, and how Christie's brother came across as being lovely when she spoke about him, and then how long Grace had been married, so she *must* be really happy. Even Anna's estranged bloke sounded sexy and interesting, but there was no getting away from it – Calum was pure shades of grey. It was his family who were colourful and lively. Calum had no *passion,* that was the problem. He drank beer, he ate food, he watched TV and he slept and that was enough for him. But it wasn't enough for her. She was quite aware she was killing the fizzy Friday feeling but she couldn't stop herself.

'What made you fall in love with him?' asked Raychel.

'I used to do his mum's hair when I was a hairdresser. She's lovely, really,' Dawn recalled. 'She asked me along to a night out with a busload of women. Her daughters went along as well and we all had such a laugh. Then she asked me to tea at theirs and there was Calum, all killer smile, floppy hair and work overalls. He'd just broken up from his girlfriend and his mum suggested we went out. So we did and suddenly I was part of their family.' They were all listening intently, Grace especially.

'How did he propose then? Was it the down-on-one-knee job?' asked Anna.

'Nope. We were all out one night and he . . .' *got absolutely hammered*, 'got a bit tipsy and just came out with it and suddenly we were all celebrating.' Dawn smiled. 'It was fantastic. I was so happy. Me and his sisters were dancing on tables and Cal's mates were all there being loud and funny and Denise – that's my future sister-in-law – rang her parents and they came down and joined in . . .' It was just a shame that her new fiancé was catatonic under a table five minutes after asking her to marry him. She thought it best to leave that bit out as she painted a romantic and merry scene for her work-mates. But all of them, without exception, picked up on the fact that the 'other half' in this relationship seemed to be the family, not the man himself.

'The big question is – do you love him?' asked Anna.

' 'Course I do,' replied Dawn quickly.

'Then that's all that matters,' said Christie. 'You'd be surprised how many people marry someone they don't love because they have other reasons for doing so. And I'm afraid they'll almost always be disappointed if that's the case.'

Grace felt her lip tremble. She volunteered to go and fetch the second round from the bar before those tears pricking at the back of her eyes made a show.

Dawn stayed behind when the others had gone, watching Al on his guitar. He had the same rapturous look on his face that her dad had whenever he got lost in his music. As the song ended, a soft rock ballad with a Western twist, he came back to the present world and smiled at her and held up a finger. *One more song, then we break*. She knew that's what he meant.

She could have listened to their music all night, even though to most people in the bar they were just a pleasant background hum. The lead singer was obviously a relative of the bass guitarist, both sharing lean, blond and blue-eyed looks. Then there was the good-looking older guy with the beard who was playing another guitar. Then there was Al with his black hair and lips so full and red they should have been illegal on a man. She made up her mind to ask him that evening to play at her wedding. That would put an end to any flirtation.

'Hello again, Miss Dawny Sole,' came that smooth caramel voice over her shoulder as she ordered two Diet Cokes at the bar.

'Oh hello, Mr Holly. And how are you today?'

'I'm just fine, ma'am, just fine. You bought that for me? Thank you, that's very kind.'

'I didn't want you thinking I don't stand my round,' said Dawn. 'I might find myself bad-mouthed all over America.'

'Shame on you!' said Al. 'I'm a Canadian. British Columbia born and raised.'

'You all sound the same to me,' Dawn smiled playfully, quite aware that whatever her gracious intentions had been, she had opened international flirting barriers, no passports required.

Al laughed and took a long drink of Coke. Dawn watched his Adam's apple rise and fall in his throat. There was dark chest hair poking out of the top of his shirt and she had the impulse to reach out and touch it.

'So what brings you here again? You got a recording contract you want me to sign?'

'I only wish I had,' said Dawn. 'We come here every Friday after work, just for an hour or so, to end the week on a jolly note.'

'What do you do?'

'I work in an office,' said Dawn, keeping it short. 'Are you a full-time musician?'

'I am now. I was a carpenter but my parents died and so I

decided to live out my dream for a few years. I'll retire at thirty-five and buy a small farm and strum my guitar in the evenings on the porch and frighten all the animals.'

Dawn laughed. He had wit like Anna, all the funnier for the dry delivery.

'You're like me then, an orphan,' she said. Something else they had in common.

'I guess so.' He leaned down and whispered conspiratorially in her ear, 'But I'm living my dream and I suspect you're not.'

'Oh, and what do you think my dream would be then?' Dawn asked. He'd hit a nerve and it showed in the shake in her voice.

'I think you'd like to be strumming alongside me on that stage.'

'Yeah, right,' said Dawn. 'I'm not good enough by half.'

'I'll be the judge of that. Bring your guitar and come along on Sunday morning to our practice session.'

And that's how, despite all her best intentions, Dawn found herself agreeing to meet Al Holly on Sunday at the Rising Sun with her guitar in tow.

Chapter 42

Anna had no time to feel lonely that Friday night. She had a house to scrub. OK, it wasn't that bad, it just needed a bit of TLC, especially from a caressing duster.

The crew had arrived by seven thirty, although there was no Maria because apparently she was with Vladımir in Milan. It looked like Jane didn't do mornings because she was puffy-eyed and not in a very smiley mood at all. It took the make-up lady, Chas, quite a while, and a lot of *Touche Éclat*, to sort her out.

Anna's wardrobe was totally garbaged, as she expected. Jane had brought some clothes with her that she thought would suit Anna, including V-necks which Anna never wore.

'Why not? They accentuate your bust perfectly and lengthen your neck!' enthused Jane. 'There are women out there who would kill for the breasts you were given!'

She dressed Anna in red and dark blue and purple outfits and matching killer heels. But Anna wouldn't admit that the reflection in her wardrobe mirror was pleasing to the eye. Her confidence levels were too damaged to accept any praise.

Mark was setting up a laptop in the corner when they had a break for coffee.

'Do you mind me asking, are you OK?' Anna said to a very glum Jane, mentally away on another planet while she sipped at a coffee.

Jane turned to Anna, said that yes, she was absolutely fine and promptly burst into tears. Anna was straight over with a comforting hug and a tissue. She had lots of tissues in the house. She'd bought them in bulk on the first supermarket shopping expedition after Tony left.

'Sorry,' said Jane, blowing her nose. 'It's nothing. Oh God, I'm messing up my make-up!'

'Sod the make-up, what's the matter?' Anna drew a few more tissues out of the box; it looked as if Jane was going to need them.

'This is my last series. They're thinking about replacing me with Elaine Massey.'

Anna's brow furrowed. 'What, Elaine Massey, the bird from the ex-girl band that were so crap I can't even remember their name? That can't be right; she's only twelve.'

Jane let loose a very teary snort of laughter at that. 'No, she's twenty-two, I'm twenty-eight. Six is a big number in television years,' she sniffed sadly. 'She's so gorgeous and young . . .'

Anna couldn't believe her ears. 'Whoa there,' she cut in. 'You're twenty-eight? What's that if it's not young? And you're far more gorgeous than she is!'

Jane smiled. 'You're very kind, but "fresh" is the order of the day and I'm nearly thirty. There's a meeting on Tuesday to decide who's going to be fronting the next series.' More tears rolled down her cheeks.

Anna leaned in close.

'Then you're going to have to convince them not to fix something that isn't broken, aren't you?'

'I only wish I could,' Jane croaked. There was no point in damage limitation to her make-up now; it would have to be totally redone.

Anna took a big breath. 'Do you know, one of the reasons that I never blossomed was that I didn't appreciate my youth. I took all that freshness and energy for granted. When I was twenty, I looked back at my teens and wished I was still at school. When I was thirty, I wished I had my totally fresh twenty-year-old skin and the stomach that snapped back to flat when I'd lost some weight. And now I'm forty, I'm looking back at my thirties and wishing I'd just *appreciated* what I had then. I was always looking back and regretting things. I was quite pretty when I was a teenager, but I didn't realize it at the time and I only wish I had.' She put her hands on Jane's arms and pulled her squarely in front of her.

'You are in your twenties and I am telling you now you need to appreciate how gorgeous and clever and fabulous and popular with the public you are. And you need to do it whilst you're living it, not ten years later. Go fight!'

Anna saw her words sink into Jane's brain. She saw fluttery activity behind her lovely blue eyes. Jane nodded slowly.

'My God, you're right,' she said with a pleasing bit of strength in her voice. 'I should, shouldn't I? I've never thought that I'm *only* twenty-eight.'

'Precisely – you are *only* twenty-eight.'

Jane's face broke into a huge smile. 'Anna, I'm going to fight my corner like you said.'

'Good for you,' said Anna with a wink.

'Girls, we're ready for part two,' Mark interrupted. 'Anna, park yourself in front of this laptop. We've got something fab to show you.'

It wasn't fab at all. In fact, it was hideous and Bruce captured every horrified arrangement that Anna's features made as she watched the huge image of her in crap underwear being projected onto the side of a big building in Leeds. Jane then proceeded to stop passers-by and ask them what they thought of Anna's semi-naked figure.

Anna watched through gaps in her fingers and waited for Joe Public to pass comment.

What a wobbly-arsed woman!

Glad I don't look like that ugly cow!

Chuffing hell — who is it? Has Hattie Jacques come back to life?

Imagination was a powerful suicidal weapon. In fact, the people of Leeds said nothing of the sort.

Nice full bust, I'd kill for that.

The underwear doesn't do her justice.

Good womanly figure, the way a bird should look.

A good-looking woman. I'd say about forty-five years old.

'OK,' started Anna. 'Tell me all the nasty comments about my blobby stomach that you've cut out.'

'No one mentioned your stomach, which isn't surprising considering you don't have that much of one,' replied Jane. 'The most negative thing anyone said was that you were older than your real age and that your underwear wasn't good, and I didn't think that was critical.'

'Oh!' Anna was shocked. Were there a lot of blind people in Leeds then?

'Right then, let's wrap that for today,' said Mark. 'Back at Vlad's next week, Anna, for a seven o'clock in the evening start.' He shook his head at the thought of filming at night. 'Bloody vampires!'

'Thanks for the pep talk,' smiled Jane. 'I feel so much better and I am going to give it my all in that Tuesday meeting.' She gave Anna a big hug as she climbed into the crew van.

Anna waved them off and wished someone had let her into the big secret about valuing her youth years ago. She wondered what track her life would have taken if she had.

Anna caved in to temptation and drove past the barber's on Saturday afternoon en route to the chemist to buy a hair dye. Tony and Lynette were both cutting hair and looking very jolly. Why was it that he was the bastard and everything was all right in his world? Even the cat, when she saw him in the communal garden shared by the small courtyard of eight houses, was looking at her like she was something that he had just imparted to his litter tray. Damn seductive women – bobbly-bosomed ones like Lynette and salmon-buying ones like Edna the widow. Women should be looking out for each other, not coveting males that belonged to someone else.

Hurt and angry as she was, when she stormed back into the house, she realized that for the first time she had survived seeing her estranged other half without crying. It was a tiny step forward, but at least she was going in the right direction. She rallied herself and mixed up the hair dye. She had knocked five years off her appearance by the time she had rinsed it off.

Grace was babysitting Sable while Sarah went to Meadowhall to buy things for the new baby. Once Sable had landed, Gordon disappeared to his allotment, of course, and Grace got on with her washing while Sable was playing with an old Fuzzy Felt of Paul's.

When Grace emptied the laundry basket, she saw at once that her new dress was ripped at the front. That upset her because she had really liked it. She couldn't remember tearing it on anything and how was it that she hadn't noticed it when she took it off last night and put it in the wash basket? She shook her head, realizing that the way it was ripped meant that it couldn't possibly be mended. She would have to throw it away. What a shame, she thought. She really couldn't work out how it could have happened.

Dawn had driven Calum over to Muriel's house because 'some more DVDs had arrived that he needed to sort out.'

'More? Are you opening up a shop?' Dawn had asked.

'Keep that out, Missy,' had been his reply, gently flicking the end of her nose.

She sat on the sofa with the lazy greyhound while her fiancé faffed about upstairs.

'Bette's shown me the frocks. They're coming on lovely,' said Muriel. 'Not be long now before you're a Mrs Crooke like me.'

'No,' smiled Dawn, but it was a smile she had to lift up at the corners with some effort. What the heck was the matter with her? Once upon a time, the thought of sharing their name would have set her off sighing wistfully. She hadn't even practised her new signature once this past week. Her head was full of music instead of marriage.

The doorbell rang.

'Get that, will you, love,' said Muriel, hunting around for her cigarettes only to find that the greyhound was sitting on them, which set her off swearing.

'I want to speak to Calum Crooke about some DVDs,' said the official-looking man on the doorstep. 'Is Mr Crooke in?'

Oh God, he's police! Dawn froze. She'd had an idea from day one that the DVDs Calum was getting from Killer weren't strictly kosher, despite the 'house clearance' story. There were a frightening number of boxes full of them up in his old bedroom in Muriel's house, all looking suspiciously brand new.

Dawn blanched. What the heck should she do? She opened her mouth to say something ridiculous like, 'Who?' Then she almost burst into tears of relief when Calum appeared at her shoulder.

'Calum Crooke?'

'Yep, that's me.'

'I understand you've had a delivery of DVDs.'

'So?' said Calum, cool as you like. Dawn had visions of his being carted off to the police station at any minute. Her heart was battering against her chest wall with fearful anxiety.

'I see,' said the man sternly. 'Calum Crooke . . . have you got a spare *Kung Fu Panda*? The kids are desperate to see it.'

They were still laughing at Dawn half an hour later because she hadn't stopped shaking.

'He's all right, is Gav. He's always getting stuff off me,' said Calum. 'You need to chill. He did that stern routine to wind you up.'

'I thought he was the police!'

'Police? Gav? He's a bloody fag smuggler.'

'I didn't know you sold pirate DVDs!'

'And CDs, don't forget the CDs!' said Calum with a gloating smile.

'I didn't know you sold those either!' Dawn drew her breath in tightly. Could it get any worse?

'Well, it would only have given you something else to nag me for,' said Calum. 'Like you haven't got enough already. You're best staying out of my business.'

'You'll have to jump off that pedestal of yours if you want to be part of this family,' said Muriel, laughing still but with a hardness in her voice that Dawn was hearing more and more these days.

Dawn resented that pedestal comment, even though she didn't say it. She wasn't on one at all. She had just always hated rip-off merchants. Her mother and father had been hard-working, decent, solid people. They'd never so much as taken a week's dole in their life and always paid their way. And they wouldn't have dreamed of buying a pirate CD and ripping off a fellow musician. She just wasn't crook material and never would be. Maybe that meant she wasn't Crooke material either?

Chapter 43

Calum was still asleep in bed when Dawn drove off to the Rising Sun at nine o'clock without her Gibson. She couldn't find it anywhere. Calum had obviously moved it, because she knew she hadn't. She didn't have enough time to look for it now and waking him would only bring her more 'nagging' accusations, plus she didn't want him asking her where she was going. So she picked up her old acoustic guitar instead.

'What am I doing?' she asked herself when she pulled up outside the pub. It suddenly didn't feel as innocent as just going and strumming along with some other like-minded musicians. She really did need to stop the flow of chemistry between herself and that cowboy. It wasn't honest. She would tell Al, definitely that day, that she was getting married, she decided. Then again, she couldn't remember the last time she had felt as excited about anything as she did about playing guitar with him that morning. It felt right and wrong in equal quantities.

The boys had already started practising when she got there. The acoustics of the room were so much better than the bar, and the twangy guitar sound made her feel a strange longing for something way out of the world she was presently living in.

Al waved over and the music stopped.

'Boys, I'd like you all to meet Miss Dawny Sole. Dawny – this is Kirk, Samuel and Mac.'

They all said a really friendly hello and Dawn noticed that they'd already got a stool ready for her. She took her guitar out of its battered old case.

'I've had to bring this one,' she said. 'I seem to have temporarily mislaid my Gibson.' She was aware she had missed the opportunity to say that her 'boyfriend must have moved it'. Deliberately missed the opportunity.

It was still a very nice instrument and she sat fine-tuning the strings on it while the band members asked her questions about her dad and his band and Samuel fetched her a coffee. It was obvious that Al had filled them all in on quite a few details. They strummed idly and then Samuel led the music into a tune she recognized because her dad used to play it and her mum used to sing it. *I Took My Chance With You*. And just as all the horses had started to run together in the Grand National, the band and Dawn were suddenly all playing it and Samuel started singing and Dawn opened her mouth and her voice joined his and her heart lifted from her shoes back to where it should be residing. It was the most exhilarated she could remember feeling in years. She felt as if she was standing in sunshine and it threw the rest of her life into dark shade.

'You have a lovely voice, Dawny Sole,' said Samuel. 'What else do you know?'

'Crikey, loads of things. Anything from Tammy Wynette to Chris Isaak.'

'We once opened for Chris,' said Al.

'NO!' said Dawn, who had rather a thing about Chris Isaak. And for the same reason she had a bit of a thing for Al Holly: because they were from similar moulds, physically as well as musically. 'I wish I could afford him to play at my wedding.' It was out before she could stop it and she could have smashed her own mouth in for it. She always did have the clumsiest gob in the world. Al's head made the smallest jerk, but she still saw it. There was nothing else for it but to say what she'd been putting off.

'I'm getting married at the end of June, you see, and I wondered if you'd be around to play at my wedding. Obviously I'd pay you. I'd rather have you than Chris Isaak anyway. It's Saturday the twenty-seventh.'

'Ahhhh – that's the day we leave for London. That's a real shame. I'm sorry, honey, no can do,' said Samuel.

'Oh, never mind, it was just a thought,' said Dawn. She tried not to sound as disappointed as she felt. There would be no relief from the karaoke now. Then again, did she really want Al Holly to play the background music while she twirled around a dance floor with Calum?

'How about this one?' suggested Al. The strings of his guitar gave birth to an echoey, haunting Chris Isaak intro and Dawn joined in softly in the background, feeling that wavelength she had shared with Al slip out of sync. Sometimes she felt that life was playing its own *wicked game* on her.

Sunday lunch at Grace's house was a strained affair to say the least. That week there were just the two of them. Grace hadn't done any of the fancy vegetable dishes she usually did when the table was surrounded by family. She had no desire to make an effort to do her lovely cauliflower cheese and mustard or her leeks in cream sauce. Gordon would just have to put up with plain mash, plain carrots, plain cauli and broccoli. She couldn't even be bothered to chop up any onions to put in the gravy.

They ate in silence. As usual, he had his Yorkshire puddings first as a starter. As usual, he carved the roast and Grace dished up everything else. Sarah and Hugo were out having lunch with friends. Paul was having lunch with Laura and Charles and young Joe. Grace looked down at the dinner she had just spooned onto the plate for Gordon and she had the greatest desire to spit on it. What he had done to the family was unforgivable. But Gordon would never apologize, even if he thought he was in the wrong for what he had done. Not that he did. He had crossed an emotional Rubicon with every one of them now except Sarah. Her family were on different banks and the bridge, it appeared, was irreparable.

Dawn's smile couldn't have been wider as she waved goodbye to the band when their practice session came to an end. She couldn't remember the last time she had spent a morning as sweet, lovely, enjoyable, wonderful. Maybe she never had. Certainly not as an adult anyway. It was one of those mornings she knew she would be reliving all day. Although it would have been even nicer had she not opened her trap about her wedding, she thought.

She walked to the door with Al, who was gallantly carrying her guitar for her. They made it as far as the porch because a flash flood was in full pelt and Al pulled her back when she attempted to walk out in it.

'You'll get drenched,' he said.

'I live in England,' laughed Dawn. 'This is what we're used to.'

But still, the opportunity to stand next to Al Holly and talk to him was there for the taking. And despite the fact that she knew she really should start to distance herself from him, she would no more have made a second attempt to run to her car than she would have asked Muriel for a loan of her flip-flops to walk down the aisle in.

'Do . . . do you have rain like this in Canada?' asked Dawn, attempting to say something in the thick silence that surrounded them. Then immediately afterwards she said, 'I'm sorry, that was the world's most rubbish question, wasn't it?'

'I don't know,' said Al in that slow, calm, dry way of his. 'I think comparing the rainfall of different continents is very interesting.'

'You don't really, do you?' said Dawn, unsure if he was being sincere or sarcastic. He gave her the slightest raise of his eyebrows that told her he didn't think comparing rainfall of different continents was in the least interesting and she let loose a bark of laughter.

'So, you're getting married, Dawny Sole,' said Al, which pulled the brake on that laugh.

'Yes,' said Dawn. Of course it was right that she had told him but still, she felt so disappointed that any flirtation would stop now.

Al nodded slowly as if all sorts of things were running through his mind. She wished she knew what they were.

'And is your fiancé in a band?' said Al at last, and in such a way that the answer would be of heightened importance.

'No, he's not,' answered Dawn. She wanted to laugh though. The image of Calum on stage in cowboy gear playing an instrument tickled her. The words fish and bicycle came to mind.

The rain stopped so suddenly it was as if a tap in heaven had just been switched off. They fell into step across the car park.

As they reached Dawn's car and she fiddled in her bag for her keys, Al asked, 'Is he into your music?

'God, no, he's not into music at all.'

Al handed Dawn her guitar and said, 'Then he isn't for you. Any fool would see that. Have a good week, Dawny Sole. Hope to see you again Friday.' And with that, Al Holly turned and strode back inside, leaving Dawn numb, speechless and feeling that she had just received a precisely aimed waking-up slap across the face.

Chapter 44

There was a hand-delivered letter in Raychel's mailbox when she went down to collect the Sunday newspapers. It just had her name on the front in a lovely scrolling font. She waited until she was back in the flat again with Ben before she slit it neatly open with a knife. It was a short letter written on pretty, pale pink paper.

'Dear Raychel,' it began.

'Please read this letter. I am Elizabeth, the wife of John Silkstone who Ben works for. I believe I may also be your aunt. My husband, who isn't a man to say these things lightly, is convinced you are the daughter of my missing sister, Beverley. He tells me that the likeness that you have to me is too much to be a coincidence. I will know as soon as I see you if he is right or wrong. I wish you no harm or distress but I have been searching for my sister for many years with no success at all. Please, meet with me just once and then I will bother you no more. *Please*.

Kindest

Elizabeth Silkstone.'

*

Ben read over her shoulder. He noticed how she gripped the letter as she read it over again.

'I think we made a mistake moving to Barnsley,' Raychel said, with a cross edge in her voice.

'Oh, don't say that, pet,' said Ben. He liked this lovely new flat, and the friendly, buzzing little town and working for John Silkstone.

'Will you tell your boss that I can't help his wife,' she said. 'My mother didn't have a sister.'

'But you know she did.'

'She said she did and then she said she didn't. Who knows which bits were lies and which bits were the truth. It's not as if I can tell your boss's wife anything of comfort, is it?'

Ben pulled her round to face him, his big hands warm on her shoulders. He bent so he could look into her large grey eyes. His voice was soft when he began to speak.

'Ray, you know that I would never let anything or anyone hurt you again. John Silkstone is a really good man. If his wife has been looking for her sister for all these years, let her see you once, then, like she says, she can put it to bed.'

'And what if it's true?' said Raychel. 'What if I am the person she's looking for? The answer is no, Ben. *No.*'

The strength in her words belied the tremor in her voice.

When she reached home, Dawn was determined to find her missing guitar. Calum was in the pub by that time. He hated it when she rang him there but on this occasion she didn't care. He didn't answer. She stabbed in a text, telling him to ring home because it was important.

Her mobile phone rang within the minute.

'What's up?' Calum's impatient voice jumped down the receiver.

'Have you moved my electric guitar by any chance?' asked Dawn.

'I thought you said it was important, for fuck's sake!'

'It is to me!'

'Why would I move it?'

'Well, I don't know, but I thought I'd check, seeing as it's gone missing.'

'No, I haven't seen it. I'll be back in a bit. I'm having my usual one pint only, then I'll be in for my dinner.' And before Dawn could ask anything else, the line went dead.

'Yeah, OK,' she said into the air. The 'one pint only' joke was so thin it was positively threadbare. In fact, more and more she was feeling that it was better when he *was* in the pub. He seemed to have only two states when he was in the house: half-drunk or comatose. She wondered how long he used to sleep as a teenager if he was this bad as a man. He slept more than a dead sloth.

Sure enough, a good hour and a half passed before Calum showed his face. In that time, Dawn had turned out every cupboard in the house, even searching places where the guitar couldn't possibly fit, but still she didn't find it.

'Put an insurance claim in,' was Calum's only suggestion, watching her standing there, scratching her head.

'What, and say that my guitar got stolen by aliens because it can't have just vanished?'

'Well, it has, hasn't it? What do you want it for anyway? You never play it.'

'I'm going to start playing it a lot more.'

'Well, wait till I'm out before you do, for Christ's sake!' he said, muttering about her playing being akin to a 'right row'.

He went to bed immediately after his Sunday lunch which he ate alone because Dawn was, once again, checking around just in case she had missed an obvious hiding place. He got out of her way very quickly, suspecting this was something else she wouldn't let drop.

Dawn didn't want a new guitar. She wanted her Gibson. She

would never have let it go in a million years. How could she? She could still recall her dad's face when he brought it from behind his back and presented it to her on her seventeenth birthday. Her parents hadn't wrapped it because they knew she wouldn't have wanted to waste time ripping paper off when she could be playing it. *Dee Dee, take good care of it and it will last you a lifetime.*

A crazy idea came to her. Maybe if she went through the motions of replacing it, it would suddenly turn up. That had happened to her before with a bracelet she had once lost. She bought another and then found the original down the sofa. Giving up all hope of finding things maybe invited the cosmos to make them appear again. It was worth a try because her guitar couldn't have just vaporized. It must be in a stupidly silly place she hadn't yet thought of.

She went into the kitchen and pulled the laptop out from the drawer to get a street value. She typed in the make and model and the first entry took her to eBay. She wondered what other people were selling on there. She couldn't believe how many guitars were listed. A gorgeous Kirk Palomino Archtop, and even ones signed by AC/DC, Paul McCartney and Jeff Beck. There was a Gibson, like her own, at a ridiculous bargain starting price of £304.00 – although twelve bids had driven it up to £1,400. There were five days to go before the auction ended. Wow, she thought, there was going to be an exciting war over that one in the final half an hour. The postage was £60. Blimey, where was it being shipped from, Pluto? She looked at the item location: Barnsley. *Barnsley?* Her eye flashed over the screen, trying to find the seller. *Cal412.* Calum's birthday was 4 December. Dawn's head started to spin and prickle with anxiety. He wouldn't have done that, would he? Not knowing what the guitar meant to her. Her confusion segued into anger at the realization that, yes, he apparently would because this was no coincidence and that wasn't an exact replica of her own guitar, it *was* her guitar. He wouldn't get out of this one by accusing her of nagging.

Dawn tried to compose herself and keep calm, but her whole body had become a racing heartbeat and there was no way she could stop herself running up the stairs and shaking Calum awake. It took a couple of attempts.

'What the fu—'

'My guitar is on eBay and you put it there, didn't you?'

He yawned and stretched. The fact that she was starting to cry with rage didn't phase him in the slightest.

'I knew you'd say that, that's why I didn't tell you.'

'Wha . . . at?'

Dawn was so gobsmacked by his easy admission that she laughed, but it was a very hollow laugh. Then she rubbed at her forehead as if that would make some sense of the scene she was in. It didn't.

'You're selling my guitar! My last ever birthday present from my parents! What did you expect that I'd say?'

'Calm down, you silly tart!'

'I will not calm down, Calum, how could you—'

'Shut up, you hysterical cow, and listen. No, I'm not selling it actually, so button it for a minute, will you. I just wondered what it was worth. I was going to pull it off sale at the last minute, saying it got damaged. But I thought that if it were worth a lot, you might – *might* consider selling it so we could go on a nice honeymoon or something. It's not as if you play it any more so I didn't think there was any harm in just testing the water. It's safe, at Empty Head's house – he took the photo and put it on for me. BUT I WASN'T SELLING IT – OK!'

Dawn's breathing slowed. Was he telling the truth? She could never tell when Calum was lying because he was so good at it. She wanted to believe him so much. She didn't want to think that the man she was marrying would do something as rotten as sell her precious guitar. He even sounded quite selfless and honourable until she remembered how often he was at the pub. He could have taken her away to the Bahamas for three months if all his money didn't go over the counter of the Dog and Duck.

'I want that guitar back,' Dawn said, her voice shaking with anger. 'I will never sell it, ever.'

'Fair enough,' said Calum, shrugging his shoulders and settling his head back down on the pillow. 'Can't see why you're making such a fuss; it was only an idea! God, Dawn, get a grip.'

He had drifted off again before she had reached the bottom of the stairs. He looked as innocent as a child in sleep.

They had make-up sex that night after Calum had made some attempt at an apology cushioned in excuses that he was 'only thinking of ways to raise some money'. Dawn didn't turn down his advances but she found herself merely going through the motions. Not that he noticed. She wanted to believe him, but she was having difficulty on this occasion. There were too many questions that kept interfering in the logic of his story. Why didn't he admit that was what he was doing instead of lying and saying that he knew nothing about the whereabouts of her guitar? And what if she had put an insurance claim in? She could have been arrested for fraud! He would have found that funny. She could imagine him laughing as the police came to cart her off. The Crookes would have enjoyed her falling so dramatically 'from her pedestal' too. She blushed with hurt and shame as she thought of that happening.

Dawn lay in bed with doubts circling in her head like vultures on speed. She also wondered about her gold belcher chain that had gone missing since she had moved in with Calum Crooke.

Chapter 45

At home the next night, Raychel was modelling for Ben the snazzy red shirt she had bought when Anna invited her to wander around the shops with her at lunchtime. It wasn't something she would normally have picked. She tended to be drawn to dark colours that kept her in the background. But Anna had convinced her that it would suit her and it did. And lovely Ben, of course, agreed. It was great to see his wife in something that wasn't dull. Those women she worked with seemed to be coaxing her out of her shell and he loved that. Then the buzzer rang and Ben picked up the intercom phone. Raychel heard him press the entry button.

'It's only John, he's dropping off my tool kit. I left it on site by mistake.'

'Did you tell him that I wouldn't see his wife?'

'I did.'

'What did he say?'

'Nothing,' said Ben. 'Nothing at all.' He was telling the truth for John had silently nodded in a way that said he understood.

Raychel walked warily into the kitchen in order to stay there while Ben's boss was around. She didn't want him staring at her like last time.

There was a knock at the door and Ben opened it to find John standing there with a tool kit, but he wasn't alone. In front of him was a small woman, one with dark curly hair and grey, grey eyes. Ben immediately saw the likeness of this woman to his wife. He could see why John had been transfixed now.

'Can I see her, please?' asked the woman. Raychel stole a glance around the doorframe and when she saw the surprise visitor, the plate she was drying dropped from her hand and smashed on the floor.

'Jesus Christ, it is you, isn't it? I'm sorry. I know you didn't want to see me, but wild horses wouldn't have stopped me. You're Bev's daughter, you have to be!' said the woman, coming into the room past Ben and patting her breathless chest. 'I'm Elizabeth, I'm Bev's sister.'

'You're mistaken,' Raychel said, but she was evidently flustered.

'Your mother must have been called Beverley. The likeness is too much to ignore.'

'No . . . no . . . she wasn't. I'm sorry.'

Raychel looked to Ben for back-up, but he was shaking his head with resignation.

'Tell them, Raychel. Tell them they're right.'

Elizabeth burst into tears and then struggled to rein them back. 'Oh my God. You're so beautiful, Raychel. I've always wondered if you were born and where you were. I've tried so hard to find you and your mother. Where is Bev? Is she all right?'

Raychel covered her ears. 'Please, please, Ben. I can't . . .'

Ben strode to Raychel's side and put a strong, protective arm around her.

'I think you had better leave,' he said. 'I'm sorry to have to ask that, John. This is upsetting Raychel too much. There's a lot to think about.'

'I'm so sorry,' said Elizabeth, the tears plop-plopping from her eyes. 'I had to come.'

John tugged gently on Elizabeth's arm, even though he

could see she was drinking in the sight of Raychel with the thirst of so many missing years. 'Come on, love, enough for now.'

'I don't want to bother you, I just wanted to see you. Please come to me,' said Elizabeth. 'Ben knows where we live. When you're ready.'

Ben didn't say anything, just squeezed Raychel hard into his side. He was surprised when he felt her nod that she would.

'Soon,' said Elizabeth. 'I don't mean you any harm at all. I wouldn't hurt you for the world.' Then she let her husband lead her out of the door and shut it gently behind them.

Ben and Raychel stood entwined, still, silent. Then she looked up at his kind face and said in a calm and conceding voice, 'I will go and see her, Ben. I'll tell her what she wants to know. Maybe the only way we can get peace is to fight for it.'

Chapter 46

'You're very quiet today, Raychel,' said Christie the following morning. 'Everything OK?'

Raychel snapped out of her reverie. 'Sorry, yes, I'm fine.'

'No need to apologize, I'm just enquiring.'

'She'll have got her first mortgage bill,' Anna shouted over. 'That's enough to drive anyone to despair.'

'It's just my time of the month.' Raychel went for an obvious excuse. 'I'll go and get some sugar in my blood. Anyone want anything from the chocolate machine?'

'Just bring the whole chocolate machine back with you,' smiled Christie. 'We'll share it out between us.'

'Back in a tick then.' Raychel made her way out of the office. She didn't really want anything from the machine but she'd go through the pretence of enjoying something. What she did need was for this day to be over. She was going to Elizabeth Silkstone's house that evening and she was absolutely dreading it.

John Silkstone had taken his son on a ride to a building site after tea so that Elizabeth and Raychel could be alone to talk. Elizabeth had been on tenterhooks all day but that last half-hour of waiting made her anxiety levels flare up. When the bell rang, she opened the door to a whey-faced Raychel with her grey, nervous eyes. The same eyes that she had seen so many times in the mirror before John Silkstone put peace behind them.

'Come in, love, come in.'

Raychel moved slowly over the threshold. It was a beautiful house, the sort of house that she and Ben used to dream of having when they were little. Lots of rooms and light and polish-smelling wood and a big kitchen like the one Elizabeth was now leading her into and telling her to sit down at a massive, thick-topped pine table while she put the kettle on.

There were pencil sketches on the table of a small boy being copied from a photo.

'Is this your baby?' said Raychel.

'Yes, that's my little two year old, Ellis,' said Elizabeth. 'He's out with his dad,' she added. 'Can I get you a coffee? Tea?'

'Coffee, please. Black.'

'And . . . and have you any plans for children?'

Raychel's eyes flashed towards her.

'If you're truly my aunt, then you'll know that I can't,' she said and with a dry little laugh added, 'Well, I can but I can't.'

'Did you say you take sugar?' said Elizabeth, with a shake in her voice.

'My mother told me who my father was,' said Raychel. 'Is it true?'

'I don't know what she told—'

'She told me that my father is my grandfather. She and you and I all have the same dad.'

'She told you that?' said Elizabeth in shock, but still she didn't deny it.

'That's why I can't have children,' said Raychel, her voice hard like a protective shell. 'Because I'm dirty. I have *dirty blood*, was how she used to put it.'

Elizabeth's face dropped into her hands as she stood waiting for the kettle to boil. She had only been a little girl when her sister, Beverley, ran away, pregnant at fifteen. Elizabeth had been too young to realize that her father had been abusing her sister. Only when his attentions turned to Elizabeth did her juvenile brain tell her that she needed to run to the safety of her Auntie Elsie, who brought her up, loved her and kept her safe. It wasn't this beautiful girl's fault that her parentage was so warped.

'You aren't dirty,' said Elizabeth. 'None of this could ever have been your fault.' She felt guilty for a reason that wasn't clear. She had tried to trace Bev but her National Insurance number had never been used. After drawing a blank for so long, she could only presume she was dead. She could find no avenues left to explore.

'I searched for your mother for years and years.'

'You wouldn't have found her,' said Raychel, wrestling with a shake in her voice. 'She didn't want to be found. She changed her name to Marilyn Hunt, then Marilyn Lunn. Then she went to prison when we were thirteen. She's been out for a few years, of course.'

'Prison? What for?' said Elizabeth, wiping at the fat tears plopping down her cheeks. 'What happened to her?'

'God, where to begin!' Raychel shook her head. Earlier on that day, she had seen Grace with her eldest daughter in Reception and seeing them embrace had sparked something within her. She had no one to hug her like that. No woman-family to walk along with, arms linked, chatting, laughing, warmth boomeranging from one to the other. She had Ben, of course, but working with the women in her office had awakened something in her. Their budding friendship had given her another source of acceptance, other than his. It began to feel good, to feel *right,* to let people be close to her and know they weren't judging her or winning her over so they could hurt her.

Elizabeth slumped into a chair, the kettle forgotten, and Raychel took a deep breath and began.

'My mother said on many occasions that she should have aborted me and she was right. She should never have been allowed to have children. When she wasn't smacking me because she was drunk and didn't know what she was doing, or leaving me by myself all night, she was abusing herself – drugs, alcohol, men. My name was Lorraine then and we were always moving, one scruffy place to another. I can't remember much before we ended up in Newcastle except being alone and watching a lot of telly. Isn't that strange? It's as if my early childhood never existed.'

Elizabeth nodded, understanding that sort of loveless childhood. Before her auntie had taken her in.

Raychel went on in an even, emotionless voice.

'Then she moved in with the perfect soul-mate for her – a match made in hell – a man called Nathan Lunn and he had a little boy my age – David. I remember thinking that I didn't like him much either, he was nervy and quiet, but then he would be because Nathan Lunn used to thrash him stupid. He was a bastard.' Raychel's voice failed her. Elizabeth got her a glass of water.

'Did he hit you too?' She had to ask, but she didn't want to hear the answer.

'Oh yes. I got it as much as David did when he was in one of his rages. Though David used to try and take the beatings for me. He'd get in the way and divert Lunn's attention to him – all for me.'

'Didn't Bev . . . stop him?'

'Once. She was usually too out of it or she left him to it because she was scared she'd get the same. But once, I remember when he was whipping me across the legs with a garden cane, my mother said, "You'll leave marks!" and he stopped. We were too scared to tell anyone and as long as there weren't any visible signs that we were living with a sadist, no one was any the wiser.

'I don't seem to have any time perspective about it all, but David and I became inseparable. We shared a bedroom and we'd talk at night about all the things we were going to do when we were big enough to run away. Then one day the school rang up because they were concerned about some bruises on David's legs and Nathan Lunn, being the sensible type, went mad and nearly killed him for that. He broke one of David's ribs and it punctured a lung in the beating he gave him. I ran to the shop up the road to get the police and Lunn came chasing after me and I felt as if I was in a nightmare.'

Elizabeth clutched her throat. She felt as if she were being choked by memories of her own, of being back in the place of a terrified, helpless child, running from a man intent on doing her harm.

'I didn't get to the shop; Lunn dragged me back home screaming, but the shopkeeper saw him and, thank God, she rang the police, otherwise he'd have killed us both,' Raychel carried on. 'The police took me to hospital, an ambulance came for David; he was in intensive care for weeks. Nathan Lunn ran off, but they caught him soon enough. Mum missed all the action, she was comatose upstairs. Heavily pregnant and totally wrecked on heroin. I don't know how that little girl survived so long inside her. She was still-born at seven months while Mum was on remand. She tried to use her sad circumstances to get herself a lighter sentence, when really she didn't give a toss about anybody but herself. And it didn't wash with the judge anyway.'

Elizabeth was crying, but now her tears were of rage. She thought of her own son and what she would be galvanized to do if she found out that anyone was hurting him.

'David and I got put into care. Some idiot decided that it would be best for us if we were parted. But we'd always had this pact that if we were ever split, we would meet each other under Big Ben on my sixteenth birthday at midday, just as the clock struck. And when I turned up, he was there waiting for me. He was huge. He'd started beefing himself up so that he could always protect us both. He's obsessed, even now, with staying big and powerful.

'David took the name of that big, dependable clock and I became Raychel, because that was the name of the shopkeeper who rang the police. We changed our surname to Love, just because we liked it. We moved around but we never felt really settled anywhere, until Ben got the job here.'

Elizabeth couldn't think of a single thing to say. Her world had been turned upside-down by these revelations, old loyalties and loves smashed in an instant. She hadn't imagined any of this, not even in her worst nightmares. And Elizabeth Silkstone still had terrible nightmares.

'So you see,' said Raychel, smiling strangely and dry-eyed, 'I don't know if you're my aunt or my sister because you're both, aren't you? And Ben is my husband and yet we share a sister.' She laughed and that laugh slid without warning into hard, gulping tears.

'My mother traced me last year and wrote to me,' Raychel began again, wiping her tears away with the heel of her hand. 'She wanted to meet up, she said she had things to tell me. I didn't reply. I didn't want to have anything to do with her or anyone connected with her ever again. I would never have children, even if I could. I'd be too terrified of hurting them.'

So many feelings coursed through Elizabeth, she had no hope of separating them and defining them. But she knew what was most troubling this beautiful young woman standing in front of her because she had lived through the same. She had been terrified that the pattern would be repeated in her, that her rotten genes would out. For a long time she had thought that women coming from 'stock' like her had no business procreating. Then she had got pregnant and inside her a tigress roared that would protect her child at any cost.

'My darling girl,' she said, 'I would kill anyone who tried to hurt my son like you were hurt. Never think that you would make the same choices as your mother. Good God.' She felt her head spin and a sick feeling descend on her stomach. The monster that was Raychel's mother was the same sister she had worried about and cried for all those years. She steadied herself with the back of the chair.

'Where was Bev living when you got that letter?'

'She returned to Newcastle when she was released and was calling herself Bev Hunt again. I threw the letter away and I didn't keep the address.'

'Thank goodness you have Ben, and he has you,' said Elizabeth, wanting to cry for Ben too. She thought of him in the gym, ensuring he was always at the fittest and strongest state his body could achieve. A little boy's fears still present in the big, grown man.

'We're happy now,' said Raychel softly. 'We do lots of nice, daft things together. Things we missed out on. But he still has nightmares and it breaks my heart. I've always felt that we are separate from the rest of the world, as if we don't fit in and shouldn't try.'

All these years she had been duty-bound to keep people away from her. She felt so unclean that she had been one step away from carrying a leper's bell.

'Letting people close to you can be hard,' said Elizabeth gently. Once she too had felt not worthy enough to be treated kindly. 'But never think that you don't deserve friendship and love because of other people's mistakes. I understand what you're going through.' Elizabeth took the young woman's face in her hands. 'Oh Raychel, I can't tell you how glad I am that you came to see me. But I never imagined any of this.'

'Can I come and see you again?' said Raychel in a quiet, hopeful voice. She surprised herself by asking. She hadn't planned to.

Elizabeth pulled the younger woman into a firm embrace. She didn't say anything, neither did she need to.

They held each other for a long time. They had both found something in each other they didn't expect. There was no word for it, just a feeling of peace.

Chapter 47

On the Thursday evening, Gordon glanced over the top of his newspaper at Grace and said, 'You look tired,' with an alien, gentle note to his voice. 'Has this week been a bit rough?'

'I'm fine,' snapped Grace by way of a response. She wasn't though. She hadn't been sleeping particularly well, with the events of the past few weeks racing around her head and denying her brain any rest. Paul and Laura no longer rang the house in case Gordon answered and her mobile was set on silent so that Gordon wouldn't know when they sent a text. Sarah was the only one who rang, but only when she needed a baby-sitter, yet an answerphone always greeted Grace whenever she rang her youngest daughter to see if she was feeling fine in her pregnancy. Sarah hadn't asked about or mentioned her brother or her sister to Grace, not that Laura and Paul would have expected Sarah to ring them and offer her support. Grace could never work out how she had turned out so much more cold-hearted than her siblings. If anything, she had been more indulged, more cosseted.

'You should get an early night,' said Gordon. 'Go on, off to bed with you.'

Grace sat on the retort that was rising in her throat. It was half past eight, for goodness sake. Why on earth would she want to go to bed at half past eight?

'I might look tired, but I'm fine,' said Grace again with a tight smile.

'What about going part-time?' he asked, rattling the broadsheet sports page into a readable shape. 'You should ask.'

'Maybe later,' said Grace. 'I'm enjoying this job and I don't want to start making demands so early on.' Work life was the only thing keeping her smile muscle alive and giving her brain some respite from the family situation. Since Laura and Paul and Joe were banished from the house, there were no moments of light relief from Gordon's suffocating presence. She was beginning to have nightmares about being in a tiny airless caravan with him. There were no doors or windows in it and she couldn't move without touching him.

'I'll make us some hot chocolate,' said Gordon.

Grace didn't resist. It was easier to let him do what he wanted. Then again, it always had been. Plus it stopped him rattling on about how tired she looked and got him out of her sight for five minutes.

'There now, that's just the thing to relax you,' he said, delivering a mug to Grace's hands. She had barely got halfway through it when she started yawning and felt distinctly drowsy. Maybe Gordon was right for once, she conceded, after saying goodnight to him. Maybe she was more tired than she thought.

Chapter 48

When Christie came in early the next morning, Grace was already there, sitting at her desk, resting her head in her hands. She had a killer headache, worse than any hangover.

'Goodness, Grace, are you all right? You looked drip-white!' said Christie immediately.

Not you as well, was Grace's immediate thought. First Gordon telling her she looked tired, now also her work colleagues. She had been asleep by quarter past nine the previous night and barely remembered her head touching the pillow. It had been a solid, dreamless sleep and she woke up at five-thirty with her head booming. She felt as if she had only had half the amount of rest she should have had. Extra strength paracetamol had taken the edge off the pain but they'd worn off now and her headache was worse than ever. She had just swallowed two more and hoped their power would kick in quickly.

'Here, have my coffee,' said Christie, parking it in front of her. 'I haven't touched it and you take the same as me, don't you – milk, no sugar?'

'No, I'm fine,' said Grace, but Christie wasn't one to take no for an answer. 'OK, thank you, Christie. I just had a very heavy sleep. I feel more drained than if I hadn't had any at all.'

'Why on earth did you come in if you're not well?' said

Christie, wagging her finger. 'Go home and let your husband cosset you!'

'God forbid!' said Grace quickly. She would rather try and work through the headache than be at home with him.

'Home not a good place to be at the moment?' asked Christie tentatively.

Grace pressed at her head which stopped the throbbing pain temporarily.

'You could say that,' said Grace. 'I think my husband is having a late mid-life crisis.'

'Is he going out clubbing in leather trousers?' Christie asked gently.

'No, quite the opposite. He wants me to retire and live happily ever after in a caravan, knitting socks and sucking on Werther's Originals.'

'Oh dear,' said Christie. 'Bit early for all that, isn't it?' Grace was the sort of vibrant woman she could imagine being still beautiful and wearing high heels in her nineties. She couldn't visualize her ever wearing Devon Violets perfume or dowdy hats. Funny, she hadn't pictured Grace with an 'old-headed' husband either.

'It's a nuisance,' said Grace. 'He's got so much worse of late. I don't know what's the matter with him at all.'

'How long did you say you'd been married?' asked Christie.

'Twenty-three years. You'd think in that length of time you'd know someone pretty well, but . . . lately . . . it's as if he's a different person. There's something . . . strange going on in his . . .'

She tapped her temple, then realized that she was saying too much. She was so preoccupied with her headache that her tongue was running away with her.

Malcolm's chirpy appearance chopped that conversation off.

'Morning, ladies.' He did a double-take at the sight of Grace's face. She looked as though she'd been whacked on the nose; her eyes were puffy with dark shadows underneath them. *Ooh, is the graceful Grace a bit of a boozer on the side, then?* 'Day off today for half the department, is it?'

'No,' replied Christie, with no attempt at a returning smile. 'But then it is only early.'

There were ten minutes to go before the official working hours began. It wasn't their fault Malcolm turned up at a ridiculous hour. Just because he was *at* work eighty-seven hours a day, didn't mean he *did* any work, except when Mr McAskill was hovering. Then he could have got an Oscar for over-acting the part of a busy Cheese B.U.M.

Malcolm opened his mouth to give a smart retort but was headed off at the pass by Christie upping and breezing past him.

'You'll have to excuse me, Malcolm, but I have a meeting with James. See you in a little while, Grace. And remember what I said. You are to go home if that headache gets any worse.'

'If you have a minute later . . .' Malcolm called behind Christie, but she appeared not to hear him. He suspected she had chosen not to.

Grace's head was down now and she too seemed to be ignoring him.

Malcolm bristled. He hated that Christie Somers's department held him in such obvious disdain. Bitches.

'How's things with you then?' Grace asked Anna later when she was distributing the coffees. Thank goodness the tablets had driven away her headache and she was feeling much brighter.

'Not bad, not bad at all,' replied Anna, nodding, surprised actually that it was the truth and not just something she felt she ought to say. Things weren't that bad. At the moment anyway.

'Any word from Tony?'

'Nothing,' said Anna. 'Not a dicky bird.'

'You seem to be coping a lot better with it.'

'Well, the trouble is, Grace, I never know when a big

thought of him is going to hit me. Sometimes I can be at home and thinking about some daft thing that Dawn's said and then – whoosh – this big tidal wave of Tony hits me and knocks me for six. He's still paying his half of our bills into the bank, so all isn't lost, I suppose.'

'And how are things going with the vampiric designer?' asked Grace, sipping gratefully on the coffee. Her throat had been horribly parched all day.

'It's all quite fun actually, though I'm not sure how I'll feel when I turn on the TV and see all my widescreen cellulite on display. Can't wait for that night.' Anna shivered at the thought of it.

'You talk about yourself as if you're an enormous horror, and nothing could be further from the truth,' Grace chided her gently. 'And by the way, that colour on your hair is lovely.'

'Thanks, I did it yesterday. It was well overdue.'

'You're a lovely-looking woman. Vladimir Darq must think you have something special, otherwise he wouldn't have picked you out.'

'No, he picked me because he thinks I'm a "blank canvas". You can't get much blanker than this,' and Anna gestured towards her body. 'Still, I'm intrigued to see if he can put me in touch with this sex goddess that's apparently inside me. Needle and haystack are words that come to mind.'

'You know, you should wear a bright red lipstick, like Christie does.' Grace visualized the effect. 'You could easily carry it off with your colouring.'

'Hmm . . . I just might go and buy one at the weekend then,' mused Anna. Jane Cleve-Jones wore a very brave fire-engine red lippy and it looked gorgeous.

'My daughter wears one by Mac. Makes her lips look lovely and soft. But you'd have to go to Meadowhall for that.'

'Like I've anything else to do?' said Anna with a grin. 'The weekend will be long enough as it is with Bank Holiday Monday added to it. I think a little shopping trip to Meadowhall will do me good. Grace, are you OK yourself? You're very pale today.'

'I'm fine, thank you,' said Grace. 'I had a bit of a headache this morning, but it's just about gone now.'

'Here,' said Anna and delved in her bag, pulling out a little bottle. 'Lavender oil. Put some on your temples. I don't want it back, there's a few drops left in. I've got more at home.'

'Thank you,' said Grace, warmed by Anna's kindness. She so enjoyed working here, with these women, and hoped she wouldn't have to give it up for a long time. Since coming to this department, she was increasingly aware that her life was running the opposite to how other people's did – work is what she rushed to, home was what she rushed from. No, she wouldn't be asking for part time, as Gordon suggested. Not in a million years.

That afternoon, en route to a meeting, Malcolm just happened to be passing Reception when he saw one of the ladies at the desk having an increasingly heated conversation with a man in a brown coat and a trilby. He looked like an extra from the black-and-white version of *Brief Encounter*, very British and upright. Kathleen, the receptionist, was shaking her head and whatever she was shaking her head at, the bloke in the hat wasn't having any of it. Malcolm quite fancied Kathleen. She was a tidy, trim piece and he seized on the opportunity to earn some brownie points.

'Can I help?' Malcolm enquired.

'This "gentleman" wants to speak to the head of HR but, as I've explained, she's on holiday,' said Kathleen in a polite but spiky voice.

'Well, I'm not leaving here until I've spoken to someone with authority in that department,' said the man. Kathleen looked both vexed and exasperated and her eyes were pleading with Malcolm to help her.

'May I ask what it's regarding?' said Malcolm smoothly, with a calming, plastic smile.

'And you are?' demanded the man rudely.

'My name is Malcolm Spatchcock. I'm a Business Unit Manager.'

'You're not in Personnel though or whatever they call it these days.'

'We're all interlinked,' bluffed Malcolm.

The man mused for a few moments, then obviously decided to trust in the smiling manager in front of him, 'I'm here about my wife. She works in Bakery. Her name is Grace Beamish.'

This was all getting more confusing by the moment. As Gordon turned his back to the Reception desk, Kathleen was mouthing at Malcolm, 'Did he want her to call security?'

But Malcolm was too intent on being the hero of the hour.

'Ah yes, I know Grace. Until recently I was her manager in Bakery. Why don't you come and sit down over here and tell me what it's about, and then we can see if I can help you, and your wife.'

'I don't want to sit down, I want something sorting,' said Gordon, stabbing his finger in Malcolm's direction. 'I want someone to tell me why my wife has been passed over for early retirement again and again. If you *were* her boss, you can explain that to me, can't you? Eh?'

Malcolm drew Gordon back away from the Reception desk where Gordon's raised voice was beginning to attract attention.

'I'm slightly confused,' said Malcolm smoothly, rather relishing the fact that he might be about to drop someone in the smelly stuff. 'We are talking about the same Grace Beamish? The lady who is now the Deputy Manager of Bakery?'

'We are indeed,' said Gordon stiffly.

'But . . .' Malcolm knew he shouldn't be saying this. It was confidential. Then again, he could always worm his way out of it by saying he was tricked into releasing the information, if it came to it. '. . . Mrs Beamish was offered the chance of early retirement on two occasions that I'm aware of and turned it down.'

Malcolm watched Gordon's jaw tighten. He wouldn't have put the graceful Grace with an old, unsmiling man like this. He thought she would have more taste in husbands. He had always imagined her with an ex-army officer type with money, not Mr Mothball 1930. He looked more like her dad than her husband.

'She turned it down?' said Gordon, as breathless as if he had been winded. 'She turned it down?'

'Hmmm . . . yes. Maybe she's regretting it though. She was looking very tired this morning when I passed her. I do hope she's all right.'

'She turned it down,' Gordon said again. He seemed to be having trouble absorbing the words.

'Well . . . I really can't say any more. I shouldn't divulge a colleague's business. Even to their spouse.'

But there was nothing more to say. Gordon had been told everything he needed to know. He silently turned his back on Malcolm without saying another word and marched out of the building.

Malcolm winked over at Kathleen who blew him a grateful kiss. Now should he say anything to Grace or should he wait for the drama to unfold over the next few days? Malcolm decided on the latter form of action. That would teach one of the snotty cows a well overdue lesson.

Malcolm made his apologies for arriving late. He took a seat opposite to Christie across the table and she noted that there was a smile playing on his lips for the full length of the meeting, however much he tried to stifle it. She would have loved to have known what was going on in his brain. He had the look of a child who had kicked a wasps' nest and was waiting for the reaction.

Chapter 49

The Rhinestones playing in the background of the pub added to the mellowed-out feeling that visited the women after work that night. This was only the fourth time they had been out together yet already it felt an essential part of the week's end. There was that rare sensation that everyone around the table was comfortable with each other, accepting of each other, and liked each other.

It was the first time that Dawn had relaxed since Sunday. It had been hard work feigning being cheerful at work, trying extra hard to push down a whole nasty cocktail of emotions that felt as if it were poisoning her.

Calum hadn't rushed to bring her guitar home. When it was returned to her on the Tuesday night, she could have wrapped her arms around it and kissed it. In fact, she did. The sense of relief brought tears flooding to her eyes. The euphoria was so extreme she almost forgave Calum everything. What a weird psychological state that was. There had to be one of those documentaries about it: where someone took everything from you but managed to make you feel they were bloody marvellous when they deigned to give you back a crumb. When did she become so easily pleased?

And now Dawn was here again, staring at Al Holly strumming away and thinking about his parting shot to her last weekend about Calum not being the man for her. She was surprised her head hadn't exploded all over the office walls this week it was in such a mess.

'Dawn's been getting friendly with the band,' said Grace mischievously. Dawn had let it slip that she had stayed behind for a drink with Al Holly last Friday, although she omitted to add that she had met him on Sunday as well.

'Oh yes?' said Anna. 'That one at the back that looks like a cross between Elvis and Chris Isaak is a bit of all right.'

She meant Al of course. He looked all mean and moody playing a complicated riff. Dawn's body betrayed her engaged status by increasing its heartbeat as she watched him, willing his eyes to find hers. He hadn't looked at her once so far, though. He was lost in his music and it was a beautiful sight.

'Do tell us more,' said Christie.

'Oh, there's nothing to tell. I just got chatting to one of them about music and we had a drink,' shrugged Dawn.

'And are you staying for another tonight?' asked Grace.

'With the Chris Isaaky one?' asked Anna.

'Yes and yes,' said Dawn, as nonchalantly as she could manage.

'Have you had a go on his amp?' dirty-laughed Anna.

'Do you mind, I'm an engaged woman,' said Dawn.

'Anyone doing anything exciting this weekend, ladies?' asked Christie, raising her glass and issuing a smiley 'Cheers' to them all. She needed the comfort of a hit of red wine after sitting opposite Malcolm's smirk for so long.

'No doubt I'll be preparing to make more of a fool of myself in front of the whole nation,' sighed Anna.

'And I'm looking at brochures for honeymoon ideas,' said Dawn.

'Aren't you leaving it a bit late?' said Christie.

'We'll just go for a cheapy, last-minute thing, I think,' returned Dawn.

'Where do you fancy going?' asked Raychel.

'Dunno. Where did you go?'

'We couldn't afford the big honeymoon thing,' said Raychel. 'We were only teenagers. We came home from the registry office and had fish and chips by candlelight. We were just a couple of skint kids.'

'Aw, how lovely,' sighed Dawn. 'What about you, Grace?'

'I didn't have a honeymoon at all,' said Grace. 'We had the children to look after and Gordon's mother was poorly at the time.'

'Didn't squeeze in a belated one then?' asked Raychel.

Grace shook her head. A honeymoon would have been too romantic for Gordon. Their marriage had been more of a business alliance than anything. Gordon gained a housekeeper and companion and she got to borrow some children. Anything as romantic as a honeymoon had no place in a relationship as cold as theirs.

'Where would you have gone, if you'd had the chance, Grace?' asked Dawn. So far she hadn't had any clues as to an ideal honeymoon destination.

'I've always wanted to cruise,' said Grace without any hesitation. 'Then I could visit a few places. Hot and sunny places – Spain, Italy, Sardinian beaches, that sort of thing.'

It sounded divine, if a dream. Dawn turned to Christie for an alternative destination. Cruising was way out of her budget. Unless it was cruising down the Manchester Ship Canal in a blow-up dinghy. 'Give me an idea, boss.'

'We eloped to Gretna Green, then went to Loch Ness.' Christie smiled. 'It was wonderful. We didn't get out of bed for a week.'

That was more like it, thought Dawn. Calum wouldn't have any problem with staying in bed that long. It was just that he wouldn't notice she was in there with him. Ho hum.

'Anyway, what are you doing this weekend, Raychel?' asked Christie.

'Shopping for a tumble drier. How's that for romance?'

'Yeah, but I bet you and Ben stop off for a nice tea somewhere and turn it into a less boring task,' said Dawn. They had all gleaned that Ben and Raychel did such sweet things together, like going for a drive, or to the cinema or visiting the ice-cream parlour out near Penistone, comfortable, coupley things. And when Ben dropped her off and picked her up from work sometimes, they always looked so in love. He tweaked her nose or held her hand and never failed to give her a kiss. Dawn wondered if they were passionate behind closed doors or had been married so young that all that side of the relationship had fizzled out. Must have been nice to have had something in the first place to fizzle out, she added dryly to herself.

'Grace?'

Grace had barely thought about the extended Bank Holiday weekend to come. She just wanted to get it over and done with. There would be no family get-together to lighten her spirits. Just an extra day of Gordon's scintillating company and the post bringing catalogues of Stannah stairlifts and hearing aids, no doubt. She wasn't sure she could stand her life with him any longer. She finally felt near the end of the line and needed to do a lot of thinking.

'A belated spring-clean beckons,' she replied. Doing the beds and bottoming the upstairs rooms would both fill a lot of time and allow her brain to roam. She sighed and Christie caught a strong whiff of boredom.

'Not doing anything exciting with your hubby then?' said Raychel, who wanted Grace to be married to an older version of Ben because she deserved someone like that.

That amused Grace. 'No, not this weekend,' was all she said, although much more could have come tripping out so effortlessly in this comfortable corner with these women ready to listen.

'Well, I shall be doing nothing at all,' said Christie breezily.

'The forecast is bright and sunny and so I intend to sit in the garden, read magazines, drink Pimms and let my big brother cook a huge Sunday lunch for me.'

'That the dentist?' asked Anna. 'Good cook, is he?'

'Superb,' said Christie.

'He sounds lovely,' said Anna wistfully. 'He must be gay.'

'Nope,' laughed Christie. 'Straight and wonderful and frustratingly single.'

'Shame he's not my type then,' said Anna. 'I only go for wankers.'

'Tell you what you need,' said Christie. 'A bored, married lover on the lookout for a mistress to spoil.'

At that Anna spun.

'What, and do to some poor cow what Tony is doing to me! Why would I want a man that did that to his wife? I wouldn't touch a tosser like that with someone else's ten foot bargepole!'

'Whoa,' said Grace, holding up her hands in a peace-like gesture. 'I don't think Christie was being serious, Anna.'

'It was a joke,' put in Dawn, suddenly desperate to preserve the precious harmony. She didn't want it spoiled. She had come to love these Friday evenings with all their shared banter.

'Of course it was a joke,' said Christie quickly too. 'I'm sorry, Anna, it was a clumsy thing to say. I didn't mean—'

'No, no, it's me that should be sorry,' said Anna. 'Christie, I apologize. I'm too sensitive for my own good at the moment. It's our anniversary today, you see – well, the anniversary of our first date. We used to celebrate it like a proper wedding anniversary, you know, with cards and pressies, even though we aren't married – obviously. ' *God, I'm a mess*, she thought.

'Oh, Anna . . .' said Christie and gave her hand a comforting squeeze.

'You weren't to know,' said Anna. 'It's not your fault. I need to take a bit of control of myself.'

'Maybe if this married bloke was living with a right old dog who didn't give him any sex,' added Dawn, trying to help to make things right again between everyone. '. . . And she never washed her bottom and had brown teeth,' she went on.

Anna laughed gratefully. She knew what Dawn was doing and felt ashamed that she had overreacted. Bloody Tony, he had a lot to answer for. He was sending her loopy. 'Well, yes, it might be nice to rescue the poor man from that.'

Dawn hung behind when the others had gone. She was more than relieved when Al raised his eyes at last, saw her and smiled. She smiled back at him and sat at the bar waiting for him to take his break. She wondered, after his parting shot last week-end, if he would come over. She needn't have worried.

'Hello there,' he said in his deep drawling, voice. 'You find your guitar?'

'Yes, thank goodness,' said Dawn and went on to tell a lie. 'Silly me, I put it in a safe place and forgot about it.'

'And how was your week?'

'Good,' said Dawn. She felt suddenly guilty. There she was sympathizing with Anna about her adulterous fiancé and she was full of floaty feelings for this tall guitar-man in front of her. 'And you?'

'Good too. Played a lot of places and travelled around,' he replied. 'We won't be practising on Sunday though, otherwise I would have said come along again. We all really enjoyed your company.'

'Oh, shame,' said Dawn. She shouldn't have been, but she'd been hoping they would invite her to join them once more.

'The guys are going sightseeing instead. They want to see something of Yorkshire.'

'And you're not going?' asked Dawn.

'Not with them,' he replied. 'I wondered if you'd like to show me your favourite places, Dawny. How are you fixed for escorting a cowboy round your county? As friends, of course.'

Her insides were a sudden battleground. *No, you can't. That's too intimate. Yes, yes, go, you bloody idiot. How can you turn that invitation down? Danger, Danger! It's just as friends – his words.* The Nos were so greatly outnumbered, they were virtually in the Valley of Death.

'Yes, that would be lovely,' she found herself saying, even though inside her there were still thin protests that she should-n't be encouraging his attentions. She should be picking out honeymoons, she should be sending off invitations. But instead she made arrangements to pick up Al Holly at nine o'clock outside the Rising Sun on Sunday morning in order to spend the whole day with him.

Chapter 50

When Grace got in from the pub, she picked up a vibe that something wasn't quite as it should be. Her senses went on red alert because she felt exactly as she had last time, when Gordon forced her down to Blegthorpe. She made tea, Gordon read the *Chronicle* while she washed up and it all seemed, on the surface, a very typical Friday evening, but still she felt an odd undercurrent.

The music for *Coronation Street* ended, which was Gordon's usual cue to go up and get changed for the Legion, but he didn't. He was such a creature of habit that this prompted Grace to ask, 'Aren't you going out tonight?'

'No, not tonight,' he said quietly.

'Are you feeling all right?'

'Just because I'm not going out, it doesn't mean I'm ill.' He stabbed the remote and switched the television over to *Sky News*. Grace never failed to bristle when he swapped channels without doing her the courtesy of asking. She realized she had been bristling about it for over twenty years, yet not once had she ever countered him about it. That small action of switching channels set off a massive chain reaction in her brain.

She looked at Gordon, weirdly absorbed in the news stories, and she knew she had to leave him that weekend. Funny, she had been waiting for a massive event to give her the energy to walk out and, in the end, it was a mere button on the TV remote. It didn't matter that she had nowhere to go or little time to plan, she could bear his presence no longer, sucking all the oxygen out of her life, pushing her where she didn't want to go, making choices for her, smashing up her family with his prejudices and anger. She had been here before, near the end of the line and praying for the strength to go, but somehow this was different. She knew she would not change her mind this time; the line had been crossed – it was over. The sudden thought of the freedom to come gave her an injection of euphoria. How should she tell him? She wasn't the type to sneak out like Anna's Tony, leaving a note on the table. She would have to face him head-on. A prospect she wasn't looking forward to at all.

Tuesday, she decided. She would go on Tuesday in the most decent, honest way she could. She would spend the weekend cleaning the house and filling up the food cupboards for him. She would pack a suitcase in readiness and tell him first thing Tuesday morning that their marriage was over. Then she would walk out and go to work and think about the next step from there; she couldn't think any further than that without panicking. She watched *Sky News* but her mind was miles away, making a mental list of things to do.

When Anna got home, she found a rectangular brown paper parcel waiting for her, propped up against her step. It had obviously been hand-delivered because there were no stamps on it. She opened the door and got the scissors out of the drawer before she'd even got her jacket off. It had enough brown tape around it to withstand a nuclear blast. Even the Stanley knife she turned to for extra assistance was having trouble getting through the wrapping. Then there were about twelve layers of bubble wrap to contend with and finally a square polystyrene case. Puzzled, Anna prised it open to find the white back of a plate with a hanging ring on it. She turned it over to see that the front had a photograph of herself and Tony on it, arms around each other, he sporting that cocky God's-Gift grin. It was the photo he used to have as the wallpaper on his mobile. And under the photograph on the plate there was a single word printed. *Together.* What the hell did that mean? Was this an anniversary present? She felt a sweet surge of excitement at the thought he might have remembered the date. But if he hadn't, why was Tony sending her photographs on plates when they weren't together? They were about as apart as Lynette Bottom's legs. Or was he coming home? Dear God – was this his way of telling her that he was on his way home?

Gordon did not go out to his allotment on Saturday. He growled at Grace when she asked him why that was.

'Anyone would think you were trying to get rid of me!' And so she didn't rouse his suspicions by asking again. She changed the sheets on her bed and tried to look like a woman interested in her house, not like one preparing to leave it.

She very quietly pulled down her small suitcase from the top of the wardrobe, threw some underwear, a couple of shirts and skirts and shoes into it and slid it quickly under her bed. Then she carried on busying herself with vacuuming the landing for a while before deciding she needed some air.

'Think I'll get a bit of shopping done,' Grace said, popping her head around the lounge door. 'Shan't be long.'

'I'll come with you,' Gordon said.

Chapter 51

Anna had danced around the house for twenty-four hours now. She had thought about that plate and the only possible conclusion she could come to was that Tony's heart was on its way back to her. The anticipation that he could open the door at any moment made every single moment delicious. She lost count of how many times she reapplied her lipstick during the day and then imagined Tony kissing it all off.

She wished she didn't have to go to Vladimir's; Sod's Law dictated that Tony was sure to come when she was out filming. But she couldn't exactly let the crew down. She'd leave a note on the door to tell Tony, if he called, that she would be back at 10 p.m. and hope a burglar didn't see it first.

Jane was waiting for her at Vladimir's front door. Her lovely face was almost bisected by the length of the smile she wore. Anna was barely out of the car when Jane grabbed her in the tightest hug someone less than eight stone could perform.

'Dear Anna, I found out yesterday – guess what, a new series of *Jane's Dames* has been commissioned and I'm still going to be fronting it. And they're talking about doing some variations on the theme after that.'

Jane looked taller. Anna checked down to see if she was floating on air.

'You should have seen me, Anna, I was magnificent. I was

young and fired up and irresistible. Elaine Massey had no chance
against me.'

'I'm thrilled to bits for you,' replied Anna, who was wearing
a big smile of her own too, half-thanks to Jane's good news,
half-thanks to her anniversary plate present.

But Vladimir Darq seemed rather annoyed by that smile.
Not as annoyed as Maria who was saying '*la dracu'* a lot – obviously swearing – as she tried to apply Anna's face make-up.

'Maria says you are smiling too much,' Vladimir said with a
huff.

'Right, I'll look miserable then.' Anna assumed an exaggerated pout.

'No, not miserable. Like a statue. Neutral. It is good that you
don't seem nervous today, Anna, but what is going on in your
head? I presume' – and here he gave a haughty sniff – 'that it is
something to do with your adulterous man, *Tony.*' He imbued
the name with all the qualities of a bowel movement. 'Ach, and
I thought you retouched the colour on your hair because you
want to look good for yourself!'

'Well, actually I did dye my hair for myself,' said Anna,
giving a haughty little sniff of her own back. 'I did it before
Tony sent me a present that tells me he is getting fed up of his
fancy woman.'

'What present?'

'A plate.'

'A plate! *O farfurie*?' He made a round gesture, plate-sized, to
double-check that's what she meant. He didn't look as
impressed as Anna by the prospect of a plate as a symbol of
romance.

'Not any plate. A special plate. With our photograph on it.'

Vladimir's right eyebrow lifted so high Roger Moore would
have been envious. It wasn't a gesture lost on Anna.

'You wouldn't understand.' Maybe gay blokes weren't as
romantic as straight ones after all, she reasoned.

'Why? Why would I not understand? Maybe because I am not as human as you?'

His strange-coloured eyes twinkled at her as if offering proof of that.

'I meant no such thing,' she said. She knew it amused him that she, and half the fashion world, wondered if the stories about him being a vampire had more than a foothold in the truth. But on this occasion she was being honest. That wasn't what she meant at all. 'Look, I don't know what passes for romance in the gay world—'

'And I do?' he cut her off, his voice losing the amused quality.

'Well . . . yeah,' said Anna. 'I would have thought so.'

'And why would that be?'

'Well, because you're . . . I thought you were . . . aren't you? Well, you're, erm . . . you're gay, surely, aren't you?' said Anna, less confidently now.

'You think I am gay? Because I am a designer – you think I am gay?' She couldn't tell if that spark in his eyes was anger or amusement.

'I thought . . .'

It was amusement. He threw back his head and laughed.

'*Nebunatico!* You silly girl – oh no, no, no, Anna. I am not gay.'

Anna looked up at this newly re-classified, non-gay, big Romanian bloke and pulled her robe a little tighter around her. God, he'd felt her boobs. How embarrassing!

Vladimir Darq's mouth curved up at one side as he watched her.

'Believe me, Anna, if I had wanted you, you wouldn't be safe. I am a very dangerous *straight* man. Now, please, stop smiling and let Maria put your make-up on.' And he issued a '*la dracu*' of his own as he walked away to impart their conversation to Leonid, who was setting up big, umbrella-shaped reflectors.

Anna heard them laughing together and she fumed silently as Maria got to work on her face. Jane came over with a coffee for her, not that Maria would let her drink it.

'I apologize but I was eavesdropping,' Jane admitted. 'Who's Tony?'

'My fiancé,' replied Anna with a loaded sigh. 'Well, at least I think he's still my fiancé. He ran off the day after Valentine's Day with the teenage Girl Friday who works in his barber's shop.'

'Great timing, men, haven't they? I got dumped last Christmas Eve.'

'Dumped – you?' said Anna incredulously. She couldn't imagine how anyone could dump someone as gorgeous as the woman in front of her.

'It's OK though,' said Jane with a big, sloppy smile. 'Bruce gave me a shoulder to cry on and, well, we've been together ever since.'

'Really?' Anna gasped with delight. 'You're very professional then at work because I would never have guessed.'

'That's the idea,' winked Jane. 'But don't be fooled. At home, he's an absolute tiger. Incidentally, Dumping-Boy turned up at my front door, like the proverbial bad penny, on New Year's Eve and I had the great satisfaction of kicking him to the kerb.'

'Brilliant,' laughed Anna. She wondered if her own 'dumping-boy' had turned up at her front door while she was here.

'Were you very hurt?' Jane then asked softly.

'Crucified,' Anna replied. 'I couldn't see any way round the pain for a long time. It hurt like hell.'

'How are you feeling now though? Is time a great healer like they say?'

'Not for the first few weeks it wasn't,' Anna answered, thinking back to that awful lake of pain and not being able to even see the bank, never mind swim to it. 'But I feel a bit of ground beneath my feet now, although I still have my moments. This programme has made the weekends seem not so long and lonely, and the women I work with at the day job are fantastic and really supportive. It's very strange, because we're all different ages, but we get on. The age thing doesn't get in the way at all.'

'Oh, that's interesting.' Jane's ears seemed to prick up. 'Where do you work?'

'In the White Rose Stores' headquarters on the Eastings business park. I'm in the Bakery department there.'

Maria started on Anna's hair, piling it into a huge, gravity-defying tower.

'Do you think you'd take him back?' asked Jane, half-transfixed by Maria's skill.

'Yes, I think I would,' replied Anna. The brain which should be throwing up all the rotten things he'd done – like bugger off while she was having her miscarriage – was annoyingly remembering his positive points instead: his physically gentle nature, his lust for her body, his career ambition, his generosity with money. He had a lot of good points as well as shitty ones. She hoped they could get back on track if he returned.

Twenty minutes later, Jane was deep in conversation with Anna, for the camera this time.

'So, here you are wearing a 99p value T-shirt, Anna, on top of a Vladimir Darq bodyshaper – how sexy are you feeling?'

Anna looked into the mirror. Maria had built her hair into a beehive that would have given Amy Winehouse a run for her money. She had also given her smoky eyes and glossy pink lips, but it wasn't the make-up that was filling her body with electricity. Vladimir Darq's bodyshaper had given her the knockers of a nineteen year old and a waist that swooped in and out to a grand pair of hips. For once, instead of curving her back to minimize her chest, she was sticking it up and out. Even wearing the cheapest T-shirt in the world, Anna was looking hotter than she thought possible.

'I can't believe it, Jane,' said Anna. 'I didn't think I could have my boobs back up here again. I thought they were destined to loll around my waist.'

Bruce suppressed a snorty giggle.

Jane's attention switched to the designer. 'Vladimir, talk us through what you've done for Anna.'

'It's very simple. I have made a bodyshaper, which I call "The Darqone", which is both comfortable and sexy,' he said confidently. 'It's not impossible to be both.'

'How can you do that for every woman and keep the price point low?'

Vladimir gave a small laugh as if the answer was obvious. 'The trouble with these firms who say "Yes, we have G sizes and H sizes" is that they have 32G and 34H but they don't have 44G and 46H,' he went on to explain. 'I will have ALL sizes available. "The Darqone" which Anna is wearing now will become a wardrobe basic, just you wait and see. I will sell so many that I can keep the price down, of course.'

'You seem very sure, Vladimir,' parried Anna, playfully. 'What if you don't sell as many as you project you will?'

'I will,' said Vladimir Darq. His answer scored 300/10 on the confidence chart.

'Cut,' called Mark. 'We need to see the body thing now, Anna. We'll just get a few shots of it before we call it a day.'

'That's all you lot ever seem to say to me: "get your kit off,"' smiled Anna.

'Yes, and you love it,' said Mark, blowing her a kiss.

Grinning, Anna slid the T-shirt over her head.

'Your tits really are fantastic in that top, Anna,' called Bruce from behind the camera.

'Hands on waist, Anna,' instructed Mark. 'And I agree.'

Anna laughed. If someone had said that to her a month ago

she would have thought he was a deranged pervert with cataracts. Now she nearly allowed herself to accept it as a genuine compliment, albeit with a blush.

Vladimir Darq said nothing. He stood by Maria, arms folded, a saturnine glower on his face. But he noted that Anna's shoulders were back and how long her neck looked when she wasn't trying to hide herself away.

'So, how was Milan? Was it a fashion week?' said Anna, slipping into her robe after the shooting had finished.

'I didn't go for the fashion,' said Vlad. 'I went for the Italians.'

'Italians?' Anna gulped.

'Yes, I was hungry and Italians taste so good.'

'You're joking, right?' said Anna.

'*Vampiri* – they don't joke about their food,' said Vladimir Darq with such an intense stare that Anna felt mentally ravaged. Then he turned to liaise with Mark, leaving Anna to fan some cool air onto her heated cheeks.

Vladimir sent Anna home with her smoky eyes, big hairdo and 'The Darqone' on. He told her to keep wearing it and walk around her house feeling like the woman she had seen in the mirror. He gave her a parcel of more in various gorgeous colours and told her to wear nothing but those all week under her clothes.

The note she had left for Tony was still there on her door when she got back home. He had not called. 'Ah well,' she sighed, in a hurry to have a look at herself in her make-up. She made a bee-line for the long mirror in her bedroom and posed seductively at her reflection, trying to imagine what Tony would think if he saw her now, all pouty-mouthed and attitude. Lynette Bottom would be launched into the nearest wheely bin and he'd have leaped on her. She smoothed her hands over her curves. She felt magnificent. Tony wouldn't have had a chance at resisting her, looking like this.

Chapter 52

Calum had been out at his mate's thirtieth birthday do all Saturday night and was just going up the stairs to bed on Sunday morning as Dawn was coming down them.

'Where you off to?' he slurred.

'Meadowhall. Wedding stuff,' she lied. It wasn't even eight o'clock but Calum's eyes couldn't have focused on a clock.

'Have a nice day,' he waved behind him. 'See you at Mum's for chicken.'

Drat! She had forgotten they were supposed to be going to Muriel's. Not that, ashamedly, it would alter her decision on how her day would be spent. She was giddy as a kipper and any feelings of guilt she should have had were being squashed with all her might. She would ring, supposedly from Meadowhall, and tell Calum to send her apologies but she was too busy shopping and had lost track of time. More guilt to add to the mix. *But then, why should you feel guilty?* asked her brain. After all, she was only showing a cowboy around some Yorkshire countryside. A friend. *Yeah, but a 'friend' who makes your heart gallop,* came a counter-argument. A 'friend' who would be gone from her life in a couple of weeks and whom she was never likely to see again, fired back her brain. It was one argument too far.

Al was waiting for her, sitting on the wall in the sunshine. He was wearing faded denim jeans and a black T-shirt that made his chest look wide and his waist look small. She found herself smiling as soon as her eyes touched on him.

'Good morning, Dawny Sole,' he said. His presence seemed to make the sun shine brighter. He had a lazy grin that made her feel as if she had swallowed some of that sunshine and it was making her stomach glow.

'Hi, y'all,' she drawled back and he laughed.

'So, where are you taking me?'

'Wait and see,' she said casually, belying the fact she had pored over the Internet for ages the previous night. There were so many places she could have taken him, but she had made sweet, gentle choices rather than wildly exciting ones. Places she liked, places she would go to when he had gone back to Canada and remember him.

'How about we start with a walk in a nice park?'

'Sounds good to me, honey,' said Al, swinging his body into her passenger car seat. Dawn's foot was very shaky on the clutch.

The ducks and geese at Higher Hoppleton were so well-fed they looked at the breadcrumbs scattered by little children with total disdain. Dawn had often been the recipient of their disgusted glances, so this time she had lovingly prepared two bags full of Madeira cake.

The ducks waddled forward, quacking a 'that's more like it'.

'Do you feed ducks in Canada?' said Dawn.

'Only to diners,' said Al, grinning again.

'Oh, that's awful,' said Dawn, laughing.

'Sure is a lovely house,' said Al, looking over his shoulder at Hoppleton Hall. 'Can we go in and take a look?'

'Yes, it is on my to-do list,' said Dawn.

'Is an English cream tea on your list too?'

'Of course,' said Dawn. 'I'm going to blow your mind with my choice for that later,' she said.

'You're my kind of guide, Dawny Sole,' he said, saluting her.

They fed the greedy ducks and then walked around the lovely old Hoppleton Hall, looking at all the military memorabilia, and Dawn's imagination played with the idea that they were a couple on one of many days out. Like Ben and Raychel. Calum never wanted to go anywhere but the pub or, occasionally when his mates dragged him, the football ground. Even when they'd gone to the seaside last year, he'd spent the afternoon in a beer garden, saying it was too hot to walk around. And sand bored him. He'd looked at her as if she were daft when she'd suggested that they take off their shoes and go paddling.

It was just over an hour to the coast. Cleethorpes wasn't the busiest seaside town, but it had sun and sea and sand, some of the things that Dawn wanted to share with Al. She had always wanted to live by the sea or some water. Al, apparently, lived by a lake so big it was like an ocean, he said, making Dawn sigh. Again. She sighed a lot in his company. They chatted, played daft games like 'comparing favourite things' and 'being the first to spot a . . .' for the whole journey, driving along roads which were surprisingly clear for such a beautiful day – and a Bank Holiday weekend to boot. Cleethorpes itself was busy but they dropped on a good parking space just as a family with a screaming toddler were leaving it.

Dawn headed straight for the nearest novelty shop and bought two Kiss Me Quick hats.

'It's illegal not to wear one of these at the seaside,' she said, and then dragged Al off for his first taste of British fish and chips, doused with salt and vinegar, and they ate them from the paper as they sat on a bench and looked out at the sea and kids with buckets and spades and donkeys with tinkly bells and teenagers showing off to each other with skimpy bikinis and sloppy shorts and volleyballs.

'I love water,' said Al, finishing off the half of fish that Dawn couldn't manage. 'The lake I live alongside is full of fish. Ever been fishing, Dawny?'

'Dad used to take me fishing,' said Dawn, sliding into a memory that was as cosy as a pair of old slippers.

'Your mom ever remarry?' asked Al, licking his fingers.

'Mum and Dad died together. Car crash. Some idiot boy racer.' She shook her head as she thought of the community service 'sentence' which the dangerous little teenage twit got for destroying three lives. He had arrived in court with his face all sorry and a theatrical neck collar. He had ripped it straight off when he left court with his celebrating mates.

'I'm so sorry,' said Al. 'I didn't realize.'

'They're buried next to each other. Dad and his guitar, Mum and her piano.' Dawn's smile was fond and sad. 'I'm joking, of course. Mind you, it was the only thing that wasn't in her coffin. It was like a car boot sale with all the flowers and bits of music and poems and stuff that all their musician friends put in.'

'How old were you?'

'Seventeen.'

'That's young.'

'Too young at any age to lose people like them.' Dawn felt her eyes getting a bit watery and gave her head a little shake as if to settle the tears back to the waiting place.

'Come on, let's hit the beach,' said Al, scrunching up the empty fish and chip papers and launching them perfectly into the nearby bin. He grabbed Dawn's hand and pulled her down the steps to the sand. He held her hand for the length of six steps only but the effect on her was catastrophic. It stirred up everything she was doing both now and would be doing at the end of June. It was sending feelings that she shouldn't be having to every part of her, feelings that she couldn't muster for the man she was marrying. It brought everything she was into question.

Al tugged his boots and socks off and Dawn slipped off her

sandals. They walked along the wet sand, the flow of the sea washing over their toes and thrilling them with the chill.

'You get to the seaside often, Dawny?'

'Not that much,' she said. 'It's a bit far away from Barnsley.'

'Far away? Naw! Everything is so close together in England,' he said. 'You want to try living in Canada.'

'We were going to live in the States,' said Dawn. 'Mum and Dad were getting ready to emigrate. They wanted to live the simple life and play music in bars. They just wanted me to get through school first.'

'And would you have enjoyed that?'

'Yes,' she said, without needing to think. 'My parents would have been happy and so I would too. I wish they hadn't waited. I would have adjusted. We should have just gone. I would have loved it.'

'Then why aren't you doing it now?'

'Because my dreams died with them.'

'Why?'

'Because . . .'

The words dried up; she couldn't expand on her answer. Strangely enough, she had never asked herself that. When her mum and dad died, she hadn't even considered that she could move there without them. And live the dream for them, if she couldn't live it with them.

'I know, it's easy for me to say,' Al conceded. They were at a stretch of beach where the crowds had thinned. He suddenly stopped and turned to her. A sea breeze blew a strand of her hair across her face. He reached out and took it in his fingers and tucked it behind her ear. She wanted to push her face against that hand and feel his long fingers on her cheek. It was so wrong to let such thoughts trip down that road, she knew. But Canute couldn't hold the sea back, and she couldn't hold those feelings back. She looked up and found that his eyes were locked onto hers. He reached out again and tapped the side of her head gently.

'. . . But all your dreams are sleeping in here still, Dawny. Just sleeping.'

Dawn's heart was booming. She daren't move. Was she imagining things or were they leaning closer to each other with every second that passed?

'Sorry!' said a young boy, diving between them for a big inflatable beach ball and spraying them with sand. It stopped whatever was going to happen next. It was the equivalent of having a bucket of cold water thrown at them. They sprang back from each other and started wandering back to the car park in virtual silence.

Dawn slid the sun roof fully open once they were in the car.

'I am now going to drive you around some of our finest countryside,' she said, trying to get back into Dawn-The-Tourist-Guide mode.

'Sounds good to me, girl,' said Al. He slid in a CD and they both sang along to Nicolette Larson and her smoky, soft-rock voice while Al played air guitar. She knew that had he he had a real guitar in his hands, his fingers would be note perfect.

'You have a beautiful voice, Dawny.'

'No, I don't,' she said. She thought she used to have a pass-able voice, but she had lost all confidence in her ability. 'She's always fucking howling. She sounds like she's being strangled,' Calum had said many a time at Muriel's table, making everyone laugh. Dawn had stopped singing aloud when anyone was around.

'Do you do everything to music?' she asked.

He raised his eyebrows mischievously and she tutted.

'I mean, are you like me? Do you like music in the back-ground when you're eating, do you cook to music, do you sing in the bath?'

'Yep, all of those. And sometimes I sit doing nothing and listen to it too.'

It sounded lovely, just lying back, eyes closed and doing

nothing but listening. She could imagine what the answer would have been if she'd suggested to Calum they try that one day. Then she forced Calum out of her thoughts; it wasn't that difficult to do today.

They crossed moors and hopped down country lanes, taking a long and winding road back to Barnsley.

'Now the *pièce de résistance* of your stay in England,' she said, as they pulled into a car park by a row of old buildings. 'The Yorkshire cream tea.'

'This place is Italian though!' said Al, laughing at the huge, stripey flags hanging outside.

'Nope, it's pure Barnsley,' returned Dawn. 'You won't get portions like this anywhere in Italy.'

She pushed open the door and the first sight that met their eyes, as was intended, was the largest sweet cabinet in the world. The cakes inside it looked as if they had been prepared to a much larger dimension than the world they served.

'Oh, wow!' said Al. 'There are so many. How will I choose?'

'Try the eeny meeny miny mo method, if all else fails,' said Dawn, laughing with the waitress who showed them to a niche and handed them long green, red and white menus.

Ten minutes later, they still hadn't decided what to have.

'Why don't you go for the "Mamma and Papa"?' suggested the waitress. 'It's for two people and has tasters of eight cakes of your choice.'

'We have to narrow it down to eight?' said Al, shaking his head. 'I'm not sure I can do that!'

He loves his food, just like me, Dawn thought. She came from a family where people enjoyed a heaving dinner table and socialized around it; that had been a big attraction of the Crooke family. When the cake plate arrived, Dawn said, without thinking, 'Blimey, there's enough here for my reception!'

She wished she could have snapped the words back. All day

she hadn't mentioned her other life and now she had to drag it right into the limelight.

Al silently poured out two coffees from the giant cafetière.

'When's the big day then?'

'June the twenty-seventh,' she replied uncomfortably.

He sat silently for a moment or two. Then he dropped another question into the still lake of quiet between them.

'What's he called?'

'Calum.' She didn't want to talk about him. This was a different world, a different universe and one in which Calum Crooke didn't exist.

'What kind of a man is he?'

He sleeps a hell of a lot, he's lazy, he drinks too much, he deals in dodgy gear, he thinks I nag and he hates me singing. But, according to my future mother-in-law, all I have to do is wait a few years and he'll turn out OK.

'He's, er, nice-looking, he's got a great family; they've been really kind to me. He's quiet. He's a family man. He's close to his parents and his sisters. They're all very funny.' She took a long glug of coffee.

Al ladled a spoonful of chocolate cake towards his mouth.

'Sounds like you're more in love with the family than you are with him.'

'No, I'm not,' said Dawn, with a defensive edge to her voice that shocked even her. 'It's just that they come as a package. That's the sort of family they are: very close. I like that.' That was twice now he had said things that were too near to the bone for comfort.

'I see,' said Al, but she could see that he was pondering over her words as he dived in for half the coffee meringue.

'Would your mom and dad have liked him?'

Would they? She had avoided asking herself that question. She didn't want to consider it now either. She probably knew what the answer would have been.

'Mum and Dad would have wanted me to be happy. And I am. Really.' She stuck her chin out as if that added extra weight to her statement.

She couldn't read what was going through Al Holly's head as he tucked into the cakes, but she felt that something most definitely was, though he didn't say any more on the subject.

He picked up the bill. She protested because he'd paid for the fish and chips too but he said that he didn't feel right that a lady would pay for him, especially when she'd used her petrol to give him his day out. Calum never saw any problem in her paying, she thought. Then she wondered how many times during that day she had compared Calum to long, lean Al Holly? And how many more points Al Holly was in front? Maybe it was just as well that it was time to go home now. It was time for this to end.

They pulled out of town and headed towards the Rising Sun. She took the long way along country lanes, aware that she was squeezing out every last bit of his company. Down one of the lanes, Al suddenly asked Dawn to stop the car.

'Here?' she said. 'What for? There's nothing here.' But she pulled in all the same, by a gate leading to a wood. They walked where the last blur of spring bluebells carpeted the ground. Late bloomers that would be gone within days.

'Look at that, it's just so pretty,' said Al.

'It is,' said Dawn. 'Don't you have them in Canada?'

'Not British ones. We have hybrids but they aren't the same as these.'

He closed his eyes and breathed in the delicate scent as a soft breeze blew towards them.

'This has been a beautiful day,' he said at last, not looking at her. 'I know we can only be friends, but I'm wishing there was a parallel universe somewhere out there and in it . . . you're free . . .' He thumped his thigh hard with his fist as if to snap himself out of the place where his imagination had taken him. 'I'm sorry. I shouldn't have said that. Dawny . . .'

Dawn gulped at the way he said her name as he slowly turned towards her. She couldn't have cut the sexual tension arcing between them with Darth Vader's light sabre as Al Holly picked up her hand, laid a small kiss on the back of it and said, 'You may think this is a corny chat-up line, but it isn't. Today has been one of my favourite days ever and I'll always remember it. Thank you.'

Dawn couldn't reply. Her breath was all tangled in her throat. She was glad then that he made 'let's go' noises and headed back to the car because she was able to wipe a rogue tear away unseen. She wondered what she would feel like next year when she saw bluebells. She wondered if they would make her smile or cry.

When she dropped him off at the pub, he gave her a big lop-sided grin and told her that he had a surprise in store for her on Friday so she had better come to the Rising Sun and meet him as usual.

That night, Dawn dreamed of dancing at her own wedding. But she wasn't in Calum's arms. She was being spun around the dance floor in a breathtaking waltz by Al Holly in his cowboy gear. The scent of bluebells was heavy in the air. She woke up at the moment when Al Holly's lips were about to descend onto hers.

Chapter 53

Grace rolled her neck around on her shoulders and tried to focus on the clock. She'd give anything to stretch her arms back, but that was impossible seeing as both her hands were tied with a belt to the table leg. She tried to think what was happening to her and her last point of recall. She had been ironing. There had been a Bond film on, so it must have been Bank Holiday Monday afternoon. Gordon had made her a hot chocolate and she had sipped at it while she was doing his shirts, even though he'd put too much powder in and made it overpoweringly sweet – too much to finish it. She wanted to leave him with a clean house and all his washing done. She remembered feeling sorry for him while she was putting the shirts on the hangers. Would he manage without her? She hoped they could split up civilly. She could remember nothing after that.

He'd drugged her, she knew he had. Then she realized he must have drugged her the other night too, disguising whatever he had used in the hot chocolate. That's why she had slept so hard and been so tired at work. Was he testing out the quantity that would render her unconscious? It was laughably unbelievable, not the sort of stuff that happened to fifty-something suburban couples in real life. But she wasn't laughing and it was happening, because she was tied to a table leg on the floor and Gordon was sleeping on a chair with his head on the table above her. She noticed the phone had been unplugged in the corner and the connection was snipped off, lying next to the cord. She tried to push the table leg up so she could unloop the belt strap, but it was too heavy, plus she noticed, mid-struggle, that he had nailed the belt to the wood. *How long have I been like this? What time is it? What day is it?*

Grace tried to think but any detail eluded her. The only thing she knew was that she had to stay calm. Gordon was no longer acting like a spoiled child who wasn't having things his way; this behaviour was in another league. He had totally flipped. She didn't know what he was capable of in his state of mind. She had only drunk half the chocolate – what if she had drunk it all? He could have killed her.

She didn't know if it was the right tactic but she needed to take some control. She had to get out of that front door and safely.

'Gordon,' she called softly, though her throat was even drier than it had been at work the other day. 'Gordon, love.' The 'love' stuck in her craw. She felt anything but affection towards the man sleeping nearby. She had never studied him in sleep before. His face looked old and quite different from the animated man. He looked peaceful and untroubled, even though he had no right to.

'Gordon,' she called again and again, until he snorted and his eyes sprang open and he sat up as if he didn't know where he was or what he'd done. Then his wits caught up with him and Grace saw in his face that he knew exactly what the situation was.

'Gordon, I need the toilet,' said Grace.

'You'll have to do it there,' he said, stretching the creaks out of his back.

'Gordon, I can't do that. Please, let me get up.'

Gordon rubbed at his temples as he sighed wearily. 'I don't know what to do with you, Grace, I really don't.'

'What do you mean . . .' her voice began to rise and she had to force herself to throttle back on the volume '. . . you don't know what to do with me?'

He looked at her then as if she should have known what he was talking about. Then he was up on his feet, railing at her.

'You lied to me, Grace. You lied to *me*.'

'Gordon, I don't know what you mean!' Grace cowered as his fists curled up and rose, but they didn't make contact with her on their descent, only the top of the table, and the reverberations travelled all the way down her arms.

'Well, you've no excuse now. You'll pack in your job, retirement or no retirement, that's final.'

'I can't miss out on a retirement package, love,' said Grace, trembles taking over her voice. 'It won't be long – there's some coming up, I heard.'

'You've turned down two, you lying bitch!' This time the back of Gordon's hand came crashing into the side of Grace's face. And she wet herself on the impact.

'Oh God,' she managed. Grace was afraid now. He knew. How had he found out? She was to discover the answer to that in his next breath.

'I went to your work and had an interesting talk with someone about you,' he said in a horribly knowing way.

'Who?'

'Never you mind who,' said Gordon. 'But he told me you'd had your chance to retire, not once but *twice*, and you wouldn't. You turned it down *twice* and took another job.'

Grace knew that he wasn't bluffing. He couldn't have guessed she had turned down retirement twice. But HR wouldn't give out details like that. *He told me*, Gordon had said. *He*. Surely he didn't mean Malcolm?

Grace groaned. She was frightened and sore and her dignity was in shreds around her.

'Gordon, I'm in pain. Please!'

'And why are you suddenly going to the pub on Friday nights? Don't tell me it's with those women you work with. You must think I'm stupid.'

'It *is* with the women I work with!'

'You don't buy new frocks to go to the pub with women!'

Again Gordon's hand came soaring down towards her cheek. Grace cowered, waiting for the sting, but his hand hovered an inch from her, shaking with anger.

'Look what you're making me do!' he screamed at her, then burst into tears. They ran through the fingers that covered his eyes. Then, just as suddenly they stopped and he spat at her, 'You're ruining everything! You can't leave me, Grace. I won't let you.'

Despite her predicament, Grace looked at him with a sudden implosion of bitter hatred. Years of pent-up anger and frustration were suddenly unleashed in her. He had got it all twisted. He thought *she* was having an affair – with someone at work? *He* was the cheat. He had cheated her out of a marriage. He had never tried to make her happy, even though he told her he would in their short courtship. Once that ring had been put on her finger, he had reneged on every promise to try and work at being a proper family. Her own desire for children had locked her into a loveless, sexless relationship.

Grace battled against responding to him. She wasn't in a position to inflame the situation any further, but if she had been untied, she knew she would have flown at him with every bit of strength she possessed. Instead, she forced herself to remain as still as she could. She let him think she might have slipped back into unconsciousness.

He wiped his eyes roughly with the back of his hands and gave himself a mental shake.

'Yes, of course I'll get you a cloth and a towel,' he said, as if she had just asked for them. 'Shan't be a minute, love.'

Chapter 54

'You lost weight?' Raychel asked Anna as soon as she had taken off her coat.

'Nope,' said Anna, smiling because she hadn't but looked decidedly trimmer thanks to Vladimir's 'Darqone' creations. They really did work. They gave her a lovely shape, even under her crappy clothes. That had a knock-on effect of making her feel, dare she admit it, *sexier*. They brought the swagger back to her step as she walked.

Over the next hour, Christie and Dawn would ask her the same question about her weight. Grace didn't, because she hadn't come in, which was strange.

'Has Grace rung in yet?' Christie asked as she came out of her meeting with the Buyers at 10 a.m. It wasn't like Grace to be late for work.

'No, she hasn't,' answered Raychel.

'It's a bit funny, isn't it?' said Dawn. 'I haven't known Grace that long but I wouldn't have thought she'd be the type not to turn up without saying anything. She's far too much of a pro'.'

'I totally agree,' said Christie. Grace was *not* that type at all. And no, they hadn't known each other all that long, but a warm current flowed between these women and pulled them together a little closer with each day that passed.

Christie retrieved Grace's home number from HR which

she hoped would give them a result, even though they didn't have any record of her mobile number. She was aware that ringing Grace would be viewed by HR, if they'd known what she was doing, as a form of harassment and strictly not to be done, but Christie would make her apologies to all concerned after she found that her colleague was all right. She rang and, as bad luck would have it, all she got was a dead line. Then she had a brainwave. She rang Niki at the surgery. He must have her grandson's details on file. She could get hold of Grace's daughter that way – it was a start at least.

'What do you want her number for?' he asked.

'Grace hasn't come in. I'm a bit worried about her. I'm thinking of going round to her house if I can't get hold of her.'

'Christie, for goodness sake—'

'Niki, you of all people know what I'm like.'

'Yes, unfortunately I do,' said Niki with an exasperated sigh. 'Where does she live?'

'Thirty-two Powderham Crescent in Penistone.'

'You shouldn't really go up, you know. It's not what a manager is supposed to do.'

'I wouldn't be going up as her manager, Niki. I'd be going up as her friend.'

'Look,' Niki sighed, recognizing that unnegotiable, stubborn note in his sister's voice. 'If you're serious about going up, I'll meet you there. I don't want you getting into trouble or coming to any harm.'

'I *am* going, but there's no need for you to be there,' Christie protested, but she knew he was as obstinate as she was. One of their ancestors was definitely a mule.

Christie rang Laura's mobile. It burred so many times she felt sure it would click into voicemail at any moment, but at the last second a female voice answered.

'Hello,' said Christie. 'Look, you don't know me, but I work with your mother and we're a little worried that she hasn't arrived yet. Do you have a contact number for her, so I can check we have the right one on file? And her mobile number, please?'

'Yes, yes, of course,' said Laura hurriedly. 'We're just driving back from—' Annoyingly, the phone cut off. Then, seconds later, it rang again in Christie's hand. Laura dictated the home number, which was unfortunately the same as the one on Grace's HR file, then Laura supplied Grace's mobile number and just as she finished, the line cut off again and however much Christie rang back, she couldn't get past the voicemail.

She rang Grace's mobile and that too went straight onto voicemail. Her lovely voice invited the caller to leave a message, which Christie did. 'Grace, it's Christie. I'm at work. Can you let us know that you're all right? Can you ring me on my direct line?' Then she left the number. She rang the home number again. It was still that flatline burring sound. Her intuition was strongly telling her that something was very wrong. Especially when coupled with that recent conversation she and Grace had in the office that all wasn't well at home. She would risk being told that she was overreacting later.

'I can't get through. Anyone know where –' she read again the address HR had just supplied '– Powderham Crescent is? No bloody postcode! Stupid sodding idiots in HR!' Christie growled at the ineptitude of the department immediately below her feet.

'It's on that huge estate near Penistone,' said Raychel. 'Just before you get into the town after the big roundabout and it's on the left. She told me that's where she lived.'

'I think I might just take a drive there,' said Christie.

'Isn't that a bit . . . over the top?' said Anna tentatively.

'I don't know,' said Christie. 'But something isn't right and I know it isn't. Yes, actually, it probably *is* over the top but I won't get any work done for worrying so I might as well go.'

'So long as you don't go barging in like the SAS to find her watching *Morning Coffee*,' said Raychel. But she sensed as much as the others that Grace would never have taken a day off without letting anyone in the department know.

'Here's her daughter Laura's number, just in case,' said Christie, scribbling on a pad and ripping off the page. 'I'll be back as soon as I can.'

'Are you really that worried?' asked Raychel, shivering with the sort of chill tripping down her spine that was said to denote when someone was walking over her grave.

'Yes, I am.' Unfortunately there was no doubt in Christie's voice. 'If James asks where I am, tell him. If anyone else asks, tell them it's none of their bloody business.' Then she grabbed her coat and walked down the office towards the stairs.

The estate was easy enough to find, but it was positively labyrinthine, and street signs seemed to be non-existent. Frustrated, Christie threw the brake on and hurried over to the nearest house.

'I am so sorry to disturb you,' she said to the householder, a woman in slippers mid-vacuum, 'but where is Powderham Crescent? I'm looking for number thirty-two.'

'You're on it, love,' said the woman. 'It curls round in a big arc. For thirty-two, you'll have to keep going to the other end. You'll see a row of shops and it'll probably be somewhere around there.'

'Thank you so much,' said Christie, getting back in the car and doing a perfect three-point turn to follow the directions she had just been given. The house numbers reduced to 74 then broke for the shops. She counted down and pinpointed a quiet little house on a corner, innocently standing there surrounded on three sides by a perfectly snipped lawn and five-feet conifers. Christie parked in front of it and walked tentatively down the path.

She stretched her hand towards the door knocker, then pulled it back at the last second. She stole across to the front window and peered through. There was no sign of any disturbance. She would have liked to get around to the back but the tall side gate was locked. She returned to the front door and pressed the flap of the letterbox open. There was a faint noise of a radio and voices so soft that Christie wasn't sure if she was imagining them or not.

She heard a car draw up and turned to see that it was Niki, still in his white dentist's tunic.

'You're too protective for your own good,' she levelled at him.

'I know what scrapes you've got yourself into since you were old enough to walk,' said Niki. 'You never did err on the side of caution.' He took a long look at the house. 'Nothing seems untoward. Are you sure she hasn't just broken down in the car and can't get a signal on her mobile to let you know?'

'I hope that's the case,' said Christie. 'But you know me and my intuition.'

Niki nodded in the manner of a man who did indeed know about his sister's intuitive feelings.

Christie rapped on the door knocker and rang the bell at the side too for good measure. Through the door glass, she saw a flash of light as if a door at the end of a passage had opened slightly and closed again.

'Someone's in, I'm sure of it,' she said and bent to the letterbox, pushed it backwards and shouted through it: 'Grace, are you in there? Grace, are you all right?'

Just then, a brand-new Volvo pulled up at the side of the road and stopped behind Niki's bumper. A young man with a concerned look on his face hurriedly got out.

'Hi. Are you Christie? I'm Paul, Grace's son. My sister's just rung asking me to call over and check on Mum, then her phone cut off and I can't get her back again. What's happening?'

'Hello, Paul, I don't know what's wrong, if anything. Yes,

I'm Christie, I work with your mother but she didn't come in today and that worried me. There's someone in the house, I'm sure of it.'

Paul looked through the windows and tried the side-gate also. Then, with no other option available, he rapped on the door too.

'Mum, Dad, let me in. It's Paul.'

A man's blurry silhouette appeared behind a slim rectangle of patterned glass in the door and an impatient voice said, 'Go away. What do *you* want?'

Despite everything, Paul was relieved. It had been crossing his mind that his parents were tied up at the back, victims of armed robbers.

'Dad, is Mum there? Let me in.'

'Go away, you.'

The relief was starting to slip. 'Dad, what's going on? Are you all right?'

'Of course we're all right,' said Gordon. 'Why shouldn't we be?'

'Mum should have been in work today,' said Paul.

'She doesn't go to work any more.'

Christie and Paul looked at each other.

'Dad, what's happening? Where's Mum?'

'I said, go away and leave us alone,' said Gordon, and his silhouette disappeared.

Paul raked his fingers through his hair. 'This is surreal,' he said. Had he been watching this on the telly he would have been shouting at the characters, *Why don't you ring the police? Why don't you smash a window? Why don't you . . . do SOMETHING?*

'What now?' said Niki, no longer thinking that his sister had overreacted.

'I'll ring the police,' said Paul, even though it felt rather dramatic to do that, to ring the police about your parents. He shook his head at the scenario he was in the middle of as his finger landed on the first 9. He gave it another second for it all to make sense – it didn't – then he dialled the remaining 99 and lifted the mobile to his ear.

'God, this is weird,' he said, as he waited for the call to connect.

'I think you're doing the right thing,' encouraged Niki.

Curtains were twitching across the road. Paul wished the police would hurry up. His mother would be mortified if she came out to find this spectacle at her front door. But she wasn't coming out and he was scared stiff at what he would find when he got inside the house. These were his parents after all and, even though he knew what his dad thought about him, he would have fought tooth and nail to save him from getting hurt by anyone. He had visions of a man with a gun at his mum's head telling his dad to get rid of the people at the door. Was the 'Mum doesn't work any more' line a clue to tell him that they weren't all right really? All sorts of awful, insane explanations were flashing through his mind. He tried talking through the letterbox again.

'Dad, let me in. Is Mum OK?'

There was no answer.

Paul tried to climb over the solid wooden gate, but it was too high even when he dragged over the compost bin to stand on as Niki held it firmly in place for him, and it was too heavily locked from the inside to crash open with his shoulder. He could just see over into the back garden but there were no clues there as to what was going on inside the house; nothing disturbed, no broken glass. The three of them stood around listening, not sure of what to do in the ten minutes until a police car rounded the corner.

A corpulent police sergeant and a younger male constable emerged from their car. Paul filled them in on the few details he had to hand. The sergeant checked for himself that the front door was locked and the gate could not be accessed. He called through the letterbox and rang the bell but there was no response. He made the decision on what to do then quickly.

'Best get the number one key ready,' he said, in the manner of a man who had been here many times before. The constable immediately went to the car boot where the large door ram was kept. He put on the protective helmet, goggles and gloves stored alongside it as the sergeant rapped hard on the door and called through the letterbox again.

'Mr Beamish. It's the police. Can you please open this door now, sir?'

There was no response. The sergeant pulled out a steel ASP baton and flicked it down so it extended in readiness. Then he nodded to the constable and stepped aside. The constable crashed the ram next to the keyhole and the whole building seemed to vibrate with the intense noise it made. The door swung instantly open into a house so quiet it could have been deserted. The sergeant quickly checked the lounge for activity, then stepped cautiously forward to the kitchen door at the end of the hallway. He pushed it open, called out both Gordon and Grace's names again and then, holding the ASP firmly in a position that was ready both for defence or attack, he moved forward, the young constable at his heels, Paul and Niki close behind, despite being urged to stay back.

But the sight that greeted them was the most surreal part of it all. Gordon was sitting at the table drinking a mug of tea and reading a magazine, and underneath that same table was a barely conscious Grace, her arms tied in front of her to one of the thick wooden legs. Niki doubled-back down the passage and out of the house. He knew there was a surgery up the road. Grace needed a doctor, if not an ambulance, and quickly, that much was obvious.

Gordon looked up at the people who had suddenly poured into his kitchen. His eyes scanned them and stopped at the young constable. He pulled himself up onto his slippered feet.

'What do you want?'

'Come on, sir,' said the sergeant as he saw Gordon's fist begin to shape. Whatever he'd expected to find, it wasn't this, thought the policeman. He quickly assessed the situation and grabbed the arm of the man he had thought he had come in to rescue and twisted him around whilst reciting his rights. Only when the cuffs slid on his wrists did Gordon start struggling, as if he had come back to the real world and realized what was happening to him, but he was no match for the big sergeant who pulled him easily out of the room as he muttered, 'What's going on? What do you think you're doing? Get off me! Grace! Grace!'

Paul and Christie sank to their knees around Grace and while they untied her, the constable spoke down his radio asking for another unit to come and take Gordon down to the station. Grace cried out at the sweet pain of being able to move her arms. Then Niki barged in with a doctor from the nearby surgery, who introduced himself to the constable as Dr Mackay and said that he knew Mrs Beamish because she was one of his patients. Paul and Christie moved away to give him space to tend to Grace. She was in a terrible state. Limp, bruised, her clothes in damp and suspicious disarray and her muscles crippled from being in one position for so long. Niki left the room, instinctively aware that Grace wouldn't want to be seen like that by anyone she barely knew, least of all a male.

'You need an ambulance,' said Dr Mackay, pulling out his mobile phone.

'I don't need an ambulance,' croaked Grace. 'I just want some water.'

Paul and Christie helped Grace gently to her feet and she immediately fell backwards onto a chair.

'You're going to hospital now,' said the doctor in a soft but no-nonsense Irish brogue, putting his phone back into his pocket. He rubbed at her cold, stiff, aching hands. Grace doubted the blood would ever flow back properly into them.

'Dear God, woman, how long have you been like this?'

'What day is it?' Grace asked. Her whole body throbbed. She could barely think.

'It's Tuesday morning, love,' said Christie, lifting a glass of water to her lips.

'Since yesterday then,' said Grace breathlessly, gulping greedily at the drink. She had lost a whole night. 'Yesterday afternoon.' As soon as the water hit her stomach, she retched and Christie grabbed a towel and held it to her mouth.

'Mum, I'll get you some things for hospital,' said Paul softly. He was wiping his eyes. The panic that anything could have happened to his father had turned in on itself and become something he couldn't even define. *His own father*. He couldn't absorb any of it. He just wanted to concentrate on his mum for now. He didn't want to think about his father.

'No, Paul, I don't want to—'

'You're going, Mum. That's an end to it.'

'I'll come and help you,' said Christie.

Grace pulled her clothes tighter around her, aware they were torn in places.

Paul shook his head. It was as if he had been lifted out of this world and put in another where nothing made sense.

'The ambulance is here,' called Niki from the hallway. He couldn't equate the smiling, elegant lady holding the hand of her jolly little grandson with the poor, pitiable, half-dressed creature he had just seen. He wanted to smash his fist into the perfectly plastered white wall behind him. How could a man do that to such a lovely woman? His own wife?

The ambulanceman and the doctor started to lead Grace gently outside but her legs were so stiff that she had to surrender to the wheelchair they had brought out for her.

Paul was answering the young constable's questions but wanted to break off to go with his mother.

'Stay, Paul, help the police,' said Grace.

'You can't go by yourself, Mum.'

'Christie, will you come?' It was pure instinct. She wanted a woman with her. A friend. She wanted Christie Somers.

'Do you want me to come, love?' Christie came rushing forward.

'Please,' said Grace.

'I'll follow on in my car,' said Christie. 'Niki, will you let the girls at the office know I shan't be back today?'

'Of course I will,' said Niki.

'I'll be there as soon as I can, tell Mum that,' Paul called to Christie. The police would be at the house for a while and he would need to sort out the front door which was shattered. At least he could do these practical things for her, so she had one task less to worry about. He had to keep his mind busy before it exploded.

The second unit had arrived to take Gordon to the police station. A van with a caged facility in the back which horrified him when he was put in it. 'I'm not an animal,' he said with disgust.

But first, the ambulance drove slowly away, followed by Christie in her car. Even Niki was shivering as he made the call to the girls in the office.

In the hospital, Grace allowed her bruised face to be photographed, despite repeating that she didn't want to press charges. But apparently that might not be her decision, said the policeman who came to take a statement. He very kindly and expertly explained that the incident had not been a simple domestic. Dictated and read back to her, her statement sounded like some poor soul's story out of a downmarket magazine, not her own. She was ashamed that friends and neighbours and strangers had seen her in that state. Despite everything, Grace hadn't volunteered the information that she had been drugged as well. She didn't want to sully Gordon's name with his children any more than he had done himself, but then a nurse took blood tests and Grace realized that the full extent of her husband's control would probably come to light anyway.

When Laura arrived, she burst into tears at the sight of her mother's injuries. Like Paul, her emotions were ricocheting between anger and relief, confusion and hatred.

'You can't go back to that house. You must come and stay with Joe and me.'

'I shan't go back, no, don't worry,' said Grace. 'But I'm not coming to move in with you. I'm going to stay with Christie for a while.'

Her son and daughter protested gently but, much as Grace loved them, she wanted the generous, uncomplicated company of Christie Somers. She didn't know why she would turn to a woman she barely knew really, but she was in no state to question her own logic. She just went with the flow of what her mind was saying she needed at this time. She didn't want to be a constant reminder to her children of what their father had done. They were hurting enough as it was. Paul was feeling terribly guilty that he hadn't done more to keep his mother safe from his father's meltdown. Grace could see that he was torturing himself about it.

'How could you have predicted this, son?' She had cuddled him tightly into her neck as if he were still a little boy, and she knew that every time her children looked at her as she healed, they would suffer a fresh wave of pain. So, when Christie asked her in the hospital if she would like to stay with her and Niki, she had accepted with gratitude.

'Don't tell Sarah yet,' said Grace to her children.

'She'll have to know!' said Paul.

'No, don't, Paul. She's got enough on her plate with her pregnancy. Protect her as much as you can.'

'You just think about yourself, Mum,' said Laura. She loved

this woman so much it half-killed her to see her lying on a hospital trolley with wounds her own father had caused. She had cried a lot after he had thrown her out of his house, but had still been prepared to forgive him, because he *was* her father after all. Now, after this, she never wanted to see him again.

Chapter 55

'Are you all right?' said Christie, turning to Grace in the car as she pulled up at the top of her drive, then she immediately reprimanded herself. 'No, of course you're not all right. What a bloody stupid question.'

'You're very kind,' said Grace, managing a smile. 'I didn't want to sleep in hospital, Christie.' Her face ached when she talked, her shoulders ached, all of her body ached. She wanted to sink into a bath up to her nose and wash away the memory of Gordon clumsily trying to dry her. She felt totally violated. She doubted there was enough soap in the world to rid herself of the feel of Gordon's hands on her.

Christie helped Grace out of the car, linked her arm and led her carefully into the beautiful old house. It had been advertised as a 'gentleman's residence' when Christie's father bought it many years ago, and there would never be a more apt description of it. Standing in its own generous grounds and affording the most fabulous views over the surrounding countryside, West House had a soothing, relaxed air about it. As soon as Grace stepped into it, she could feel the protection of its big safe walls.

Christie pushed Grace down gently into a large, soft chair by a set of French windows.

'Now you just sit there and I'll get us a cuppa.'

Grace let the quiet rush over her. Three days ago, her world was a very different place. Now here she was in a strange house and her husband was in a prison cell. The thought of Gordon's breakdown brought with it no feelings of sympathy. He wasn't an ill man not in control of himself. It was his selfishness that had smashed her family apart. He had seen them all as extensions of himself with no right to their own will. She should have left him long ago, when the children had moved out, then they would have been spared this hurt and confusion. She should have left when they thought he was merely a nasty old goat, then they would never have had to see this . . . this monster he had become.

Christie arrived with an old-fashioned tray of tea with a nice teapot and china cups and a plate of chocolate biscuits. A tea that was made to comfort.

'We have a choice of four spare rooms, but I think the Rose Room would be the prettiest. It's en-suite so you'll be private and at the back of the house so it'll be lovely and quiet. I expect you want a big bubble bath. There's a heap of my softest towels waiting on the bed for you.'

It was then that an animal-like noise of distress came from Grace's throat and as Christie moved forward to comfort her, Grace clutched at her and cried and cried and cried.

Chapter 56

Understandably, Grace was not at work the next morning. Dawn, Anna and Raychel rushed forward as one when Christie came through the door to ask about her. Intuition, again, had told her that she should disclose to these women what had happened to Grace. Her secret would be safe with them. They were her friends now and, being in the know, would be armed to fend off any gossip or questions being circulated.

'She's fragile,' said Christie. 'I don't think she slept very well last night, but at least she was sleeping peacefully when I left this morning.'

'I can't believe it,' said Dawn. 'It's like something in a film. What a psycho!'

'Her kids must be in bits,' said Anna. 'I mean, what do you feel when your father does something like that to your mother? Then again, why does it surprise me after all you hear on the news?'

'I have to agree, sadly,' said Christie. 'Who knows what goes on behind closed doors?'

'The bastard,' said Raychel, which made the others stare at her. They'd never heard her swear before, nor envisaged there could be such a hard edge to her soft voice.

'Well, obviously, let's keep it quiet,' said Christie. 'I know I don't need to say that. Grace isn't someone who would want anyone knowing her business. God knows what she'll feel if it hits the newspapers. Officially, Grace is off with a cold.'

The figure of Malcolm and his perma-tan crept into her peripheral vision. Christie turned her full stare onto him.

'What's up?' asked Anna. 'Why are you staring at the walking Caramac like that? If looks could kill!'

'I'm sure he had something to do with what happened,' snarled Christie. 'Someone – a man – apparently told Grace's husband that she had twice turned down early retirement. I very much believe that triggered him off.'

'And you think that man was Malcolm?' said Raychel.

'Oh yes, I'd put money on it, Raychel,' said Christie.

'If it is him, then that's so evil,' said Dawn, staring at him also with eyes narrowed to slits.

'What is his problem with us?' said Anna. She felt so fiercely protective over Grace at that moment. She thought that if she caught anyone gossiping about her, she was capable of bashing their face in.

'You don't think Grace will go back to her husband, do you?' asked Raychel.

'How could she?' said Anna, her face creased up in disgust. 'How could you go back to someone who treated you like that?' However, her voice toned out at the end as she remembered her own situation. How ironic: this show of strength from a woman who was waiting pathetically in the wings for an adulterous fiancé to return to her.

At lunchtime, Christie rang home to see how Grace was. Paul and Laura were with her. Christie had told them that they were welcome any time. Grace was remarkably calm considering her ordeal. Christie suspected she was still in shock though.

Niki came home to find Grace asleep in the chair. She woke up with a start when he tried to sneak past her into the kitchen and the door stirred up a whisper of cool air.

'Oh, Grace, I'm so sorry. I didn't mean to wake you.'

'Sorry,' she said, adjusting her aching bones.

'Sorry? What are *you* sorry for?' said Niki. 'You're a guest in our house and must treat it like home. If you wanted to drop off in the chair, the garden or the fridge, you'd be very welcome.' He smiled at her. He had such a calming way about him, which was strange because his voice was low and deep and made for booming. He was a natural at putting nervous patients at their ease.

'How do you take your coffee? Let me guess – you're a milk, no sugar girl.'

'I'll do it,' said Grace, not used to having anyone run around after her.

'No you won't,' said Niki. 'Now give me the formula and don't make me force you back in that chair.'

'Then yes, milk, no sugar,' said Grace, surrendering her will. She felt so tired and numb. Much more so now than she had done this morning when her mobile had rung and awoken her. It had been Paul and Laura, desperate to know how she was and to see her. They had been round within the hour and sat with her all day. She could barely remember what they had discussed over many pots of tea. There hadn't been much talking about what had really happened, that much she did remember. How could she tell her children those details? Grace didn't want to think about it, nor did she want to plan where she went from now. She was happy to sit with her children and talk about Charles and Rose Manor and little Joe.

Niki delivered a frothy coffee to her in a china mug.

'Grace, I'm cooking pasta. You aren't a vegetarian, are you? Please tell me you're a die-hard carnivore like my sister and me.'

Grace opened her mouth to say, 'Oh, don't worry about me,' but she knew that she would be an awkward guest for protesting against their every kindness.

'I'm a die-hard carnivore,' she confirmed.

'Marvellous,' he said. 'Don't mind me then. I unwind by cooking. Please forgive the singing.'

Grace sipped her coffee and listened to Niki clattering about in the kitchen, singing opera. She rather thought it was his usual routine, not one staged for her benefit.

Dawn was also cooking pasta. She had set the table with candles and made a prawn cocktail starter and had a cake defrosting from the freezer. She opened a bottle of wine and was just pouring out two glasses when Calum came in from work.

'What's all this then?' he said.

'I just thought I'd treat you,' she said.

'Smells lovely,' he said. 'But don't bother with that wine for me, I'll have a beer.'

She pushed herself into his arms and kissed him though he laughingly told her to 'Give over, you soppy cow.' This was the man she was marrying. She couldn't get Al Holly and the kiss that never was out of her head and she had to. She needed to concentrate hard on being the future Mrs Crooke.

'The girls all send their love,' said Christie across the dinner table. 'And don't worry, no one outside our department seems to know anything. There's been no gossip that I've heard of. I told HR you'd rung in and were off with a cold.'

'There will be gossip,' said Grace, shaking her head at the thought of it. 'The local newspaper will get wind of it.' She thought of all those curtains twitching at the arrival of the police and the ambulance, and the quiet end of the crescent suddenly heavy with cars and lots of people.

'Well, if they do, sod them,' said Christie. 'Today's newspaper is tomorrow's cat litter tray-liner. James McAskill said to take off as much time as you like.'

'Does he know?' gasped Grace.

'Not the full story. He trusts my judgement on things.'

'I shall be in work tomorrow,' said Grace.

'You will not!' said Niki. Not in the same dictating way as Gordon. Her interests, not his, were paramount.

'The sooner I get back to normal the better. Foundation will cover this bruising if I put it on thickly enough.'

'Whatever you think best,' said Christie, shushing her brother as he opened his mouth again. 'I'll drive you in if you decide to go. And, I'll say this now, if you feel it's too much – you come straight back here.'

Grace nodded but stayed silent. The warmth around the table brought a surge of tears to her eyes. She felt protected and safe in West House and was clinging to that feeling of security for her life. She also knew that if she didn't step out of its big front door soon, she might never do so again.

Chapter 57

When Grace walked into work, she was immediately surrounded by her work-mates asking, 'What the hell are you doing in?' But it was a rhetorical question. They didn't need an answer. Instead, they sat her down with a coffee and a big plate of biscuits and the office box of tissues, because their caring concern brought the tears racing up to Grace's eyes.

'How are you feeling, or is that a totally daft thing to say?' said Dawn, when she came around with the elevenses. 'Not that I say many daft things, of course,' she added with a self-deprecatory chuckle.

'I feel OK,' said Grace calmly. And strangely enough, she did. She felt remarkably detached from the events of the past few days. She wasn't even panicked by the inclusion of a paragraph in the *Evening Star* about a local woman in Penistone who had been falsely imprisoned by her husband and was then rescued by police. 'An unnamed man has been held in connection with the incident,' it was reported. It did not say that the unnamed man had been sectioned under the Mental Health Act, as the police had informed the family.

Grace knew that it was just all too big to sink in and her brain was protecting her, keeping the horror at arm's length until she was strong enough to deal with it. This composure was a temporary benefit. But the night was a different matter entirely. She needed the sleeping pills the hospital had sent her home with to knock her into the sort of deep sleep which dreams didn't enter.

'Coming to the pub with us tomorrow?' asked Anna, giving Grace a matey nudge. Close up, the bruising was visible through Grace's make-up, though Anna didn't mention it. 'Totally understand if you don't want to, but it wouldn't be the same without you.'

'I'd like to,' replied Grace.

'Great,' said Dawn. To her inner shame, Friday nights could not come fast enough for her.

To Dawn's horror, the stage was empty when the five of them walked into the Rising Sun the next evening.

'Aren't the band playing tonight?' she asked a passing waitress as she stood at the bar.

'I think they've finished,' she said, whizzing past with a basket of condiments for some diners.

Dawn felt hot and faint. She ordered the wine for them all, feeling adrift. Was that why Al Holly wanted to spend the day with her last weekend? Was that his way of saying goodbye without mentioning the actual word? Was that 'the surprise' he said he had for her tonight?

'My mistake,' said the waitress, appearing at her shoulder. 'They've been held up on the motorway apparently. They'll be here in a bit.'

Dawn's mood lifted instantly. Actually it didn't just lift, it shot up to orbit with G-force. God knows what she'd be like when she saw him. Since Sunday, the days had crawled towards this weekend like a tortoise with arthritic knees.

'What's happened to your husband since?' Anna tentatively asked Grace. 'Don't talk about it, if you don't want.'

'He's in hospital,' said Grace, with no emotion in her voice.

'He's under psychiatric observation.' She could imagine Gordon being furious about that. He wouldn't want to be judged mentally ill and not in control of his faculties.

'You're not going . . . I mean, will you go back to him?' said Raychel softly.

'No,' said Grace with not a hint of a waver. She would never forgive him for his obsessive and dangerous selfishness. Being away from him for even these few days had given her a lot of perspective. She saw the big picture now, how things she had lived with for so many years and accepted as the norm were, in fact, far from it. Every lungful of breath she had taken since leaving Powderham Crescent was sweeter than the last.

Dawn arrived with a tray of glasses and a bottle of Merlot and slipped into the stream of conversation.

'Has he been violent towards you before?' she asked.

'No,' Grace said with a long outward breath. 'He always had a ready temper but I never thought he'd be capable of anything like that.'

'That's scary, isn't it?' Dawn shivered. 'Remember that bloke who flipped and shot all those kids up in Scotland? What leads someone to meltdown like that?'

'I suspect in a lot of cases it's a very long, slow-burning fuse to the dynamite,' Christie sighed. She wondered what sort of marriage Grace had that her husband came into work to enquire about her retirement prospects. Even from that snippet alone, he sounded a very controlling man. That type usually broke rather than bent under pressure.

Grace took a sip of wine; it felt warm at the back of her throat. Nearly as warm as the thought that she would be going home to West House that evening and not to her marital home. Although she would have to go there soon enough.

'Knowing Gordon, he is now probably saying to himself, "What a load of fuss over a simple domestic argument". I wouldn't be surprised if he expected me to have his tea on the table when he gets home and say no more about it.'

'You're joking!' Raychel said, but straight afterwards she remembered how quickly Nathan Lunn recovered from his rages and carried on from the point just before he lost it. It was as if the beatings existed in a loop of time that wasn't ever to be acknowledged after they had happened.

Grace knew she wouldn't be far off the mark. She wasn't a seasoned psychologist like Christie, but she did know her husband, who would be her *ex*-husband as soon as was humanly possible. Gordon would fight her all the way, she knew that. He would think she was overreacting and being 'a silly woman' and that 'she should stop all that nonsense'. His brain had no chamber for accepting blame, it never had. He would not see he had done anything to apologize for, he was 'merely keeping order' in accordance with his role as head of a respectable household. She thought of Gordon walking away from Paul, railing at little Joe, throwing Laura out of the house and then of all he had done to her. She had been lucky to get out. Yet she also knew that, in Gordon's head, his behaviour would be completely rationalized. Grace took a deep breath and prepared to share a secret she had told no one yet.

'I was going to leave him.'

'Did he know?' Anna said.

'No, but I think he suspected and hadn't a clue what to do about it. He more or less accused me of having an affair at work.'

'What? Who with?' snorted Dawn.

'No one in particular. He made the evidence fit to excuse his behaviour.'

Christie nodded. 'Rejection can be a huge trigger for violence.' She watched Grace's brain whirring and she nudged her. 'You're safe now,' she whispered. 'And amongst friends.'

'Yes,' said Grace. 'And I want to say that I do regard you *all* as my friends. I can't . . . can't put into words how much you've all come to mean to me in such a short time.' She took a deep breath to steady her rising emotion.

'Sounds like he did you a favour,' grinned Dawn, then seeing the jaws drop around her, she gasped. 'Oh hell, that came out all wrong. I meant that . . . that . . .'

Grace rescued her with a tinkly laugh.

'Dawn, you're a tonic.'

'How far ahead have you thought?' enquired Anna softly. 'Must be terrible, I wouldn't know where to start planning.'

'One day at a time,' interrupted Christie. 'I don't think you plan longer than one day at a time when you're in the middle of something like this.'

'I'm going to have to start planning soon,' said Grace. 'I can't stay with you for ever.'

'For goodness sake, Grace, the house is enormous. I am sure there are people living with us that I have never seen,' smiled Christie. 'Besides, I think Niki rather likes having someone to show off his cooking skills to. I've got rather blasé, alas. Chicken, mushroom and asparagus spears risotto is on the menu for tonight. It's one of his thirty signature dishes.'

Anna thought back to Tony's culinary skills with a fresh stab of pain. He was very flamboyant in the kitchen: Laurence Llewellyn-Bowen meets Jean-Christophe Novelli. She liked a man who enjoyed cooking and his was so good it was like fore-play. Which was just as well, because it was the only place she got any. What a waste, because she doubted Lynette Bottom's palate could have appreciated anything fancier than chicken nuggets. She probably thought Asparagus Spears was Britney's younger sister.

'Must be nice!' said Dawn with a little laugh. 'Calum made me a chip butty once. Micro chips. That's about as

adventurous as he gets.' Then she remembered that she was
dissing the man she was going to marry in a month and tried
to turn it round. 'Mind you, he made quite a good job of it.
He buttered the bread right up to the edges.' Somewhere in
her head she heard a pair of hands giving her a slow clap.
Wow!

'Calum's talents must lie elsewhere,' smiled Christie kindly.
She wasn't the only one left wondering why Dawn was marrying someone whom she would have to spend her whole life
kicking up the bum.

'Oh *yes*,' said Dawn, laughing a little too raucously and not
pulling off the intimation that Calum was a wild animal in
bed. She just hoped they didn't press her for details because
she wouldn't be able to supply any. Then she was distracted
as, from the corner of her eye, she saw Samuel arrive on the
stage and rush to set up, followed by the others and finally
Al.

'What's up with you?' said Anna. 'You look like someone's
just switched on a light inside you.'

'Me?' said Dawn, trying to will her heartbeat to slow down.

'It's one of those guitarists, isn't it?' said Raychel with a teasing smile. 'You fancy him.'

'I don't!' she protested.

'What are you blushing for then?'

'I'm not,' said Dawn, all flustered. 'I just think they're nice
blokes, that's all. I like their music.'

'Sorry we're late, folks,' Samuel's voice blasted down the
microphone. 'We got held up in your wonderful British traffic,
but we're here now and we're starting with this one.' And they
slid effortlessly into their first number.

'Have you booked them for your wedding then?' asked
Anna.

'No, they're leaving on that day.'

'Oh, that's a shame.'

'Yeah,' said Dawn. She didn't want to think about that. 'I'll go up and get some crisps, shall I? I'm a bit peckish.' She thought she would get out of the way of the others because she felt three questions away from her voice cracking.

The bar was more packed than usual. Dawn had only just managed to order a couple of bags of cheese and onion by the time the first song was completed.

'This one is a special number,' drawled Samuel. 'It's called *I Took My Chance With You* and we have a guest singer to perform it. I'd like you to give a warm Rising Sun welcome to Miss – Dawny – Sole.'

Absently, Dawn began to clap along with everyone else. It took three seconds for her brain to engage, then her head whisked around to the stage to see the band members beckoning to her.

No, no, no, no, no! she thought. This couldn't be happening. *What the hell . . .?* Her head was planning an escape route but she was surrounded by people moving aside to let her through. Her legs, totally disconnected to her panicking brain, were betraying her and moving forwards. She was mouthing at the band, 'I can't, I can't,' and they were totally ignoring her and pulling her onto the stage. It was like being in a nightmare. The only thing worse would have been if she was naked as well.

Al slipped his guitar around her neck and picked up another from behind him.

'Go, girl,' he whispered into her ear. His breath puffed on her neck and fanned flames in her heart.

The intro began. Dawn looked around at the sea of faces staring at the local woman, and her only option was to open her mouth and sing and get through it, and then leave the stage and die in a corner. In the background, she could see Christie, Raychel, Anna and Grace standing to watch her.

Dawn opened her mouth and heard the first shaky bars

leave her. Then it hit her that she was singing in a band, *a real band,* and if she didn't get a grip and belt out the sound she knew she was capable of, she was going to look a total clot in front of an awful lot of people. She thought of watching her mum and dad perform this, then she thought of her mum and dad watching her, now, at this moment, and a strength gathered in her voice. She saw people in the audience smiling, their heads absently nodding. Her voice floated out past them to the walls and she saw Anna sticking up a congratulatory thumb at her. And she was aware that her fingers were moving across the guitar strings in perfect harmony with the rest of the band and it all felt so *right*. And as Al played the final riff and the applause and cheers rose in the air, Dawn found herself grinning as she turned to Al and fought the surge of euphoria that made her want to fling her arms around him by saying that she was going to kill him. And he winked at her and said, 'You're wasting yourself, honey. Wait for me.' And for a moment she didn't know if he meant 'wait for me' when her friends had gone, or for ever.

'Workin' that voice or what? You *are* a dark horse,' said Anna with true admiration, as Dawn came back to the table. 'They sent another bottle over for us. On the house, so double well done. And you told us you weren't that good!'

'That was wonderful,' said Grace. 'You looked so at home on that stage. How can you hide that talent away so secretly?'

'Oh, give over,' said Dawn, blushing and beaming at the same time.

'You have a true gift.' Christie patted her on the arm. 'You're a total natural. It was fabulous, Dawn. Your voice is perfect for that kind of music.'

'Honestly, you looked as if you were born to it,' added Raychel. 'You really enjoyed doing that, we could tell.'

'You're joking! I was shitting myself,' said Dawn.

'Oh, please no, don't spoil your newly cultured image!' laughed Anna.

Dawn decided she would stay for one drink only with Al Holly. She was in serious danger of getting involved with him and if he tried to take up where he had left off last Sunday, she didn't know if she could resist. There wouldn't be any little boy with a beach ball to get in the way of the kiss that nearly happened in here.

But Al surprised her. He talked about banal things like motorway hold-ups and transport cafés. He didn't invite her to practise with them on Sunday and Dawn didn't ask to. They parted that night as friends who would soon go their separate ways and had just shared two Cokes together. It was how it should be, said Dawn to herself, it was right that it should be that way. But, as Al returned to the stage and she went out to her car, disappointment weighed her footsteps down and her heart wasn't feeling it was the right thing at all.

Anna found she was smiling all the way home. What a lovely evening that was; better still because Grace came too. And there was Anna thinking *her* relationship was crap! At least Tony didn't have a violent bone in his body. Actually, thinking about it, he didn't have any bones in his body, he was a walking jelly. She thought of a jelly-shaped Tony wobbling down the road and giggled. She slipped into a fond memory of him accidentally head-butting her during a love-making session and how gutted he was that he might have hurt her. She gloried temporarily in his inability to intentionally mash anyone – at least not physically. Then a sharp ache squeezed at her heart and a big sigh came from that place also.

She crossed the road from the railway station. Her lonely little house was in sight. But there was a film on that night she would enjoy and, bugger it, she'd ring and get a Tandoori

Butter Chicken delivered and enjoy it with a glass or two of that Riesling presently chilling in her fridge. She got her key out of her handbag and almost stepped on another surprise-Tony-present – a single red rose lay on the doorstep.

Chapter 58

Sarah rang Grace on the Saturday afternoon to ask how she was, but her opening tone was luke-warm. She always addressed Grace as Mother. It lent a distance between them that Grace had tried, but failed, over the years to close and it felt a particularly chilly word to use at the moment. Out of all her children, Sarah had been given the most – attention, toys, leeway. But she was the coldest of them all, with her father's gift of being able to shove a stopper in his bottle of emotions.

Paul and Laura had told their sister most of what they knew. They hadn't been that surprised at her cool response that 'Dad was obviously ill and Mum must have antagonized him.' Gordon's genes held strong in her.

'I've phoned the hospital but they don't know when Dad will be coming home,' Sarah said. 'Have you been to see him?'

'No, Sarah, I haven't,' said Grace. 'Nor will I be going to see him. I don't even know if I'm allowed to see him.'

'Haven't you rung?'

'No.'

Sarah gave an incredulous laugh. 'You can't leave him in there!' she said. 'He's sick – he needs help.'

Sick, yes, that was an apt description, thought Grace, but she didn't want to get into an argument with her daughter.

'I can't get involved, Sarah. It's a police matter,' said Grace in an even voice that masked the hurt that Sarah's attitude was causing her.

'What on earth happened? What did you say to make him flip like that?' Sarah suddenly railed.

'I don't really understand why he did what he did,' said Grace. She had tried not to think about it on a detailed, analytical level. She didn't want to put herself back in that awful place.

'Laura said he wouldn't let you out of the house!' said Sarah with a note of scoffing in her voice, as if all Gordon had done was say she couldn't go out to the shops and had to suffer the indignity of a police raid because of it.

'There was a little more to it than that,' said Grace, bristling now. She knew that Laura wouldn't have made light of it. If anything, Laura would have made sure Sarah knew exactly what her father had done. What part of the story Sarah chose to believe was another matter entirely.

'Who's going to look after him when he comes out?' said Sarah. There was a touch of panic in her voice that intimated that she, as the only child still accepted by her father, would be in line for that particular duty.

'He's hardly in his dotage, love.'

'Yes, but he doesn't know how to do washing or ironing or anything like that, does he?' Sarah snapped, unaware of how pathetic she was making her father out to be.

'I don't know,' said Grace, suddenly tired. 'I don't know if the police will hold him or release him. I don't know if he'll go to trial or—'

'Trial?' screamed Sarah. 'You can't let him go to *trial*! He's my *father*!'

'It's not for me to decide, Sarah, I have no control over what happens.'

The thought of a trial made Grace's head ache. She could not be disloyal to *their father* whatever she thought about *her husband*. She, herself, could stand the heat of the spotlight if Gordon had to go to court and was vilified in the newspapers, but she didn't want her children and grandchildren hurt any more than they had been. Lawyers, she knew, would rip the details of her marriage apart merely to prove technical points without any care of what that would do to her loved ones. And truth could be viewed from so many ugly angles.

'You'll have to both pull yourselves together,' said Sarah with a long, impatient exhalation of breath. 'You can't split up at your age. I'll see if I can source a good counsellor.'

'We already have split up!' A shot of anger added strength to Grace's voice. 'There isn't a counsellor alive who could fix this one. And, Sarah, even if there were, I wouldn't want to engage him.'

'Don't be silly,' said Sarah. 'You've been together for over twenty-three years. Twenty-three years! You can't just leave him to rot!'

Grace took a fortifying breath.

'Sarah, I *have* left him,' she said definitively. 'I won't be going back to him. I have made an appointment to see a solicitor and I am divorcing him. It's something I'm afraid you'll have to accept, love. Your mum and dad have split up.'

'Except you're not my mum, are you?' said Sarah spitefully before she slammed the phone down, leaving Grace so wounded that she wondered if she had been the eventual destruction of the Beamish family and not, as she had wanted to be all those years ago, its salvation.

Chapter 59

'Well, look-ee here!' whistled Bruce as Anna walked into Vladimir Darq's house at the tardy time of ten past seven.

'What? What's up?' replied Anna quickly.

'You, that's what's up!' said Bruce. 'You look different.'

'You're wearing a V-neck that isn't black too, well done!' said Jane, giving her the customary two-cheek kiss. 'I think that shade of blue is definitely your colour. What do you think, Vladimir?'

Anna felt her cheeks flare up at the amount of attention she was receiving from the whole room. Especially when Vladimir strode over and started studying her intensely.

'Yes, it's good on you, Anna.' Then he groaned. 'The shoulders, Anna, they are dropping again. *La dracu!* You drive me crazy!' And he flounced off as if in a very bad mood.

Bruce pulled a face and mouthed, 'What's up with him?' at Jane, who shrugged her shoulders.

'He's been pacing about for ten minutes,' she whispered to Anna.

'It wasn't our fault we were late. We had to take a detour because a lorry had broken down and blocked the road,' Anna explained.

'Maybe it's his time of the month. Full Moon,' giggled Bruce until Jane slapped him playfully.

'You do look different though,' Jane smiled. 'Really straight–backed and sassy. And thinner. Have you lost weight?'

'Can't, can I?' said Anna. 'He won't let me. I weighed myself this morning and I'm exactly the same as every other week.'

'Fantastic stuff then,' grinned Jane. 'I think you've been hit by "Darq" magic.'

'We want some footage of you in that bodyshaper and then some higher price point corsets tonight, Anna darling,' said Mark. 'Leonid's knocking around somewhere, so we can get some stills.'

Anna stripped off and put on her robe. It felt so natural now. The crew had seen all she had and still remained mentally intact. It was only like stripping down to a bikini on the beach really, when she thought about it. Give or take a vampire re–arranging her knockers at regular intervals.

Maria worked her magic on Anna's face in her surly, silent but wonderfully efficient manner. Then Vladimir came in to view 'the finished product'.

'You have the smile under control this week,' he observed. 'I take it you haven't heard from *Tony* since the *plate.*'

He was so wonderfully sniffy Anna wanted to giggle but she reined it in.

'Actually he left me a rose. A red one. On my doorstep.'

Vladimir stood stiffly in front of her, legs astride, arms folded, hair magnificent behind him. His voice was very sour when he spoke. 'I must remember that one. The next time I drag a woman's heart through the mud, I will send her a plate and a rose and she will forgive me everything.'

'I didn't say I'd forgiv—'

'Presumably he still lives with the other girl. Still he goes home with her every night and then deceives *her* once a week by leaving presents for you at your door.'

Ouch! He punctured Anna's puffed–up spirit with one expert dart. Smack in the bull's-eye of her ego. Anna felt her body slump as if someone had whipped out her spine.

Vladimir pulled Anna fiercely in front of him and when she raised her eyes, they locked into place with his.

'Why do people do this?' hissed Vladimir, passion throttling up the volume. 'Why do they sell themselves so cheaply and wonder why they feel undervalued? I don't understand!' Softer now. 'Anna, this *Tony* shines a light on you and you flower, he turns it off and you wither – you are an emotional marionette! I want you to feel your worth *here.*' He placed the flat of his hand on her breast, above her heart, and yet it was in no way a sexual gesture.

Of course he was right. If Tony came back, she would feel victorious, for a time, whilst he was in between her legs. And in the morning? Would she feel all-powerful if, with his thirst slaked, he got dressed and returned to Lynette Bottom and her gravity-defying tits?

Vladimir took Anna's chin in his hand and lifted it. He saw that his words had sunk in and was satisfied – temporarily at least. Anna made a conscious effort to keep her back straight in front of him and her trembling lip as controlled as possible.

Vladimir called to Mark, 'We are ready.'

Leonid took some shots of Anna posing, then she changed into some absolutely gorgeous corsets in sumptuous velvets and heavy satins. Vladmir wasn't very gentle lacing her into them that night, but she didn't give him the satisfaction of complaining. Artistic temperament, she supposed, was his excuse.

'So, how have you felt this week dumping the old drawers and wearing only "The Darqone"?' Jane asked, for the camera.

'People have definitely noticed and asked me if I've lost weight,' replied Anna with utter sincerity. 'It's been very comfortable and I have felt more confident that everything seems to be in the place it was when I was much younger.'

'And going to the loo? How easy has that been, Anna?'

'Surprisingly easy,' came the answer. 'The poppers on the gusset are very good. I've had bodies before where they were uncomfortable and not very easy to fasten. And I've thrown them in the washing machine, tumble-dried them and they've come up good as new.'

Jane looked very impressed at the bonus information. Anna answered her raised eyebrow look. 'Well, I got picked for this programme because I'm just an ordinary woman and how these things wash is important to us. 'Course I wouldn't risk the higher end ones in the tumble-drier but, well priced as "The Darqone" is, it wouldn't be a good buy if it all fell apart after a couple of washes.'

Mark gave her a big thumbs-up and then called for a cut.

'Thank you, Anna,' said Vladimir in a less thorny voice now. 'That was a point worth mentioning.'

'Happy to help,' said Anna, trying not to look as if she was thinking about Tony and wondering if he had turned up at her house this week whilst she was filming.

'That's it then, thank you, everyone,' Mark clapped. 'Same time next week for the big finale.'

The last one. Next week was the last time she would be in Vladimir Darq's house. It blindsided her how saddened she was by that thought. Weekends really wouldn't be the same. She wasn't sure what the next chapter in her story would be. Maybe in two Saturdays she would be sharing a takeaway with Tony on their sofa? She really didn't know how slumped her shoulders would be, or wouldn't be, by then.

Chapter 60

Early Sunday morning, Grace unlocked the new front door to 32 Powderham Crescent. Paul had organized the replacement as the policeman's ram had left the old door irreparable. The key slid into the lock like butter, she didn't have to pull it slightly out on the turn to gain entry, which in itself felt odd. Something else that heralded a change, an end to a past life with all its suffocating routine. Inside the house, there was the evidence of Paul and Laura's recent clean-up to make everything as untraumatic for their mother's temporary return as they could. A strong smell of bleach pervaded the air. Bless them, they'd tried to leave no trace of that weekend, but even they could do nothing about the big nail hole in the table leg.

'Mum, pick up what you have to and get out of here,' said Paul, putting a comforting arm around her shoulder.

Grace found that the case she had started to pack in readiness for leaving and then hidden under the bed was smashed in, as if it had been stamped on. Gordon had found it, it seemed, which explained a lot. It didn't matter, she had other cases and Paul and Laura had brought spares.

Grace went to the drawer and pulled out her passport and building society book. From upstairs, she packed a suitcase of clothes and a make-up bag. She collected her treasure box of photographs and homemade cards from the children that she had saved over the years. Her diary and address book, spare glasses and hairdryer, mobile charger: she didn't want much else. It was amazing how minimalist one could be when one was happy to leave one life for another. Laura was busy checking all drawers and cupboards for things her mother might have missed.

Grace opened the kitchen cupboards to see the plates she would never eat from again, cutlery she would never use again, pans she would never cook in again. It would cost her a fortune to start afresh, but she didn't want to take anything but the bare essentials. When she moved into a new home, everything would be unused. Things that Gordon had not touched. Things that Gordon had not chosen.

Looking at the house objectively now, she saw how his choices dictated everything, from what sofa they sat on to what table they ate from, from what wallpaper they looked at to what colour carpets they walked on.

Gordon. She wondered how he would cope on his own after a lifetime of living only the alpha male role. There was a big basket full of his underwear. The instinctive thought flashed across her mind that she should put it all away tidily in his drawers, only to be quickly overridden by more sensible ones. Ghosts of twenty-three years' worth of duty were much harder to cut off than her feelings, it seemed.

Gordon was being held for a month in hospital for assessment. She didn't know if the Crown Prosecution Service would force him to court. As she understood it, they would take into account the hospital's findings. She knew in her heart of hearts though that Gordon wasn't mad. He was a bully of the worst sort. She had been too easygoing – never rebelling against him to keep the peace. She suggested a red sofa, he had wanted the brown one and so they had bought the brown one. It was the same in all things. He hadn't bargained for the fact that his children would one day grow up and do things out of the nest that he could no longer control. How could she not have seen all this before? It was hardly as if she was blinded by love for him. In the early days she had hoped they would grow close and have a proper marriage. But he had killed that idea early on, not wanting even to discuss his problems in the bedroom. And she had been forced to accept that too. He could have sought help instead of letting it twist his life out of shape. He could have been a very different man. Maybe she should have revolted so much earlier. Maybe if she had, things might have been very different.

Paul's caring voice reached her ear.

'I know what you're thinking, Mum, but you couldn't have done anything to change him. None of this is your fault.'

'Oh Paul,' said Grace, her head falling against her son's strong shoulder. 'I just want to go.'

Grace hoped that one day she would be able to filter out the bad memories of this house and once again see the children drawing at the kitchen table, running in from the garden; see their little clothes hanging up on the washing line. All she could think of now was the smell of bleach and that nail hole in the table leg. It had been her home for nearly twenty-four years and she had been a prisoner in it for twenty-four hours – yet the memories of that Bank Holiday Monday far out-weighed the pleasanter, sunny days of raising her beloved children.

June

Chapter 61

Dawn wasn't her usual chirpy self by half and hadn't been all week. She hadn't once breezed in as usual to talk about a bizarre programme she had seen on the TV. Not even on the Thursday morning when she came in with four wedding invitations did she seem like an excited bride-to-be.

'I'd love it if you could come,' she said. 'It's not as if my side of the church will be heaving. I've only got a couple of great-aunties and uncles and I haven't seen them for years. That's if they turn up. They might even be dead.'

''Course we will,' said Christie, thinking, *poor love*. She so wanted to whisk Dawn to one side and ask if she needed to talk. She suspected the girl was suffering from more than pre-nuptial nerves. But would she be taking her interfering skills a tad too far? 'Grace and I have been discussing your wedding present. Is there anything you'd like? It's always difficult buying things for couples who have already set up house.'

'Oh, I'm not bothered about a present,' said Dawn. 'I wasn't inviting you for that.'

'Do you have a wedding list?'

'Er, no,' replied Dawn. She had asked Muriel to let her borrow her Argos catalogue at the beginning of the week so she could start writing out a list. Muriel had raised her eyes and clicked her tongue at that.

'People will buy you what they want to buy you,' Muriel had laughed, rather humourlessly. 'It's a bit bloody cheeky telling people how much money to spend!'

Dawn had tried to backtrack then and say that it was just in case people wanted ideas. It was the done thing.

'Done thing?' Muriel had scoffed, raising one side of her lip like an insulted Elvis and making a lah-di-dah-type 'oooo' sound. 'Not with our lot it isn't the *done thing*! I tell you this, Dawn Sole, I'm seeing a bit of a different side to you with all this wedding stuff. I hope you're going to get off your high horse when you're one of us.'

Dawn knew without a doubt that Muriel would later relay to her daughters just how 'up herself' her future daughter-in-law was getting. She had felt herself getting so ripped up over their dinner table lately that she contemplated changing her name to 'Tear-and-share'.

'It never crossed my mind that you were inviting us to get a present,' tutted Christie kindly. 'But you must have one. I tell you what, leave it with us.' Her suggestion to Grace would be to give the newly-weds an envelope of money rather than risk buying something they wouldn't like and have to go to the trouble of changing.

Christie fought against asking, but she lost the battle within five minutes.

'Dawn, can I ask – are you all right? You look so low, love.'

'Oh, I'm fine,' said Dawn, pinning on a smile. 'I just have so much to organize it's wearing me down a bit, to be honest.'

'Aren't you getting any help from anyone?'

'Oh yes, loads,' said Dawn as chirpily as she could manage. That was partly the trouble. Hardly any of Dawn's plans for her wedding had escaped from being Muriel-ized. Anyway, it wasn't the wedding that was getting Dawn down the most. She had tried to put the eBay guitar thing to bed, but it refused to sleep. What if she hadn't spotted it? Would Calum have sold her guitar? Was that the sort of man she wanted to marry? Every day seemed to bring up another reason why she and Calum shouldn't be walking down that aisle, and she was less and less able to pretend that everything would be all right when she got his ring on her finger. And how would she feel getting that ring on her finger at the same time as Al Holly was packing up the tour bus and leaving her life for good? Why was that Canadian Cowboy even in the equation? Maybe she shouldn't go to the pub this Friday. But still she knew she would.

'Daft question, I suspect, but is there anything we can do to help?' said Anna.

'Thanks,' said Dawn, shaking her head. 'I'll be fine. In a month I'll be Mrs Crooke and all the pressure will be off.'

'Where's the honeymoon?'

'Still not sorted anything,' said Dawn. 'Maybe we won't bother.' Her dream of a romantic fortnight in the sun alone with her new husband wasn't going to happen, she knew that. He'd already taken a thousand of Aunt Charlotte's money to buy some more dodgy DVDs so he could 'make a big profit and that way they might get their honeymoon.' She knew as soon as she handed over the cash that it wouldn't go back in the wedding fund and that she had seen the last of it. She was trying so hard to fight against second thoughts about the wedding – especially as so much was organized and paid for. She was on a conveyor belt and heading for the aisle however many bodily parts of hers might be protesting about it. Damn Al Holly and his bloody Strat!

'Anyway, enough about me, how are you, Grace?' said Dawn, deflecting attention away from herself. 'Just because I haven't asked this week, it doesn't mean I haven't thought about you. You must be fed up of answering that same question though and you know what I'm like, always putting my foot in it.'

'I'm fine, pet,' said Grace with a lovely smile. 'I just have a lot of things to think about. The house will have to be sold and I can't imagine that Gordon is going to be very flexible on that front. I'm taking it all in bite-sized pieces.'

'I think that's very wise,' said Raychel. She was involving herself more in their conversations recently, rather than hanging back. Part of her was really freeing itself up. And it felt so good. 'Pub tomorrow after work as norm?'

'I think I can safely plan that far ahead, yes,' said Grace.

'You as well, Dawn?' asked Raychel.

Dawn smiled for the first time since last Friday.

Chapter 62

'That guitarist can't keep his eyes off you!' said Anna, nudging Dawn.

'He can so!' protested Dawn.

'He's very handsome,' said Grace.

'He looks very sexy with that floppy Elvis hair,' said Christie.

'And the guitar makes him even sexier, if that's possible,' added Anna. 'Imagine him playing you like that.'

'Oh, wow!' said Dawn dreamily, forgetting temporarily to play it cool.

'I told you, you fancied him!' came a merry chorus, pointing fingers at Dawn and poking her.

'I don't fancy him,' she laughed, 'but I do think he's nice. How could I not? We like the same music.'

'So you're making beautiful music together,' teased Christie.

'I didn't say that!' said Dawn. 'But he is a really lovely bloke. If I weren't getting married, I might let myself fancy him.' Then, for the benefit of Anna, she added quickly, 'But I am, so I'm not allowed.' It wouldn't have seemed right confessing that she had a bit of a crush on Al Holly when Anna's man was bonking another woman. She remembered how she had flown at Christie that one time for saying something about taking a married lover. She didn't want any of them to think ill of her.

'Ah, don't panic. We're only having you on,' said Anna, hoping that she hadn't frightened Dawn into refuting that she liked the guitarist because of her fit in the pub about mistresses.

'So what are we all up to this weekend?' asked Christie. 'Anna, how's the filming going?'

'I'm getting into my stride,' Anna winked, 'though half of me thinks I must be mad. I'm going to have no control about what footage they use. There's a bit of a difference in an experienced film crew seeing my bad underwear and the rest of England – including all the pervs. Like Malcolm, for instance.'

'Bet he tapes it so he can see you on a continuous loop,' grinned Dawn.

'Stop, you'll make me vomit!'

She almost told them about Tony and his presents, but she jammed her mouth shut just before the first word came out. It wasn't as if there was anything to tell at the moment and she didn't want to jinx anything by blabbing yet.

'I've got my bridesmaids' dresses fitting tomorrow,' volunteered Dawn.

'What colour are you going for again?' asked Raychel.

'Peach,' came the answer. 'The same colour, actually, that's on the ribbon on the wedding invites. I've got all the favours to wrap up in the same colour tissue paper, and I've also got to ring up about the cake and the flowers, so it's going to be a wedding-heavy weekend.'

'You sound a bit chirpier today than you have all week,' said Anna.

'I'm gradually getting less stressed and more excited,' she lied.

'Maybe it's that guitarist who's cheering you up,' said Raychel.

'Oh, don't you start!' said Dawn. She didn't deny it though, because when Al Holly was nearby she couldn't stop that smile rising up from within her and spreading across her face. She virtually sunbathed in his presence.

They all stayed for an extra drink so Dawn missed Al's break. She was twitching to get to him but couldn't exactly leave the company so she stayed after the others had gone until the end of that night's gig. It wasn't a hardship. She sat at the bar and just watched him. She started to imagine, as Anna had said, that he was playing her like she was a guitar and then had to thrash those thoughts down with a mental sledgehammer.

'Ah, Dawny Sole,' said Al, coming straight over to her after resting his guitar on the stand. 'And how are you this evening?'

'I'm good, and you?'

'I'm good too. Drink?'

'Er . . . please. What are you having?'

'I've finished work so I'm having a beer.'

'I'll just have a Diet Coke, thank you. A small one.'

Al paid for the drinks.

'Time is surely flying. We've only got three more Friday nights to play here now.'

'Only three?' said Dawn. Of course there were only three. But it sounded such a little number. It yanked her spirits right down.

'Come and sit outside,' said Al, picking up the drinks and leading her to the back of the pub where there was a beer garden. There was a free bench and table in the corner by the boundary hedge and that was where Al Holly headed. They sat opposite each other, their beers and a night-light candle between them, their hands sitting dangerously close on the surface of the table.

'What a lovely evening,' said Dawn, trying not to look at Al Holly's unblinking eyes. The candlelight was dancing in them. 'What's the weather like in summer where you live?'

'Ah, the weather question again!' he said playfully.

'Oh, be quiet and answer me.'

'OK, it makes this look like the Arctic.'

'Really?'

He nodded. 'Well, a little exaggeration there, but nice and hot in summer and mild in the winter. Just the way I like it.'

'Me too,' said Dawn. 'This is the first decent summer we've had for ages. It's been absolutely sogging wet for the past couple of years.'

'We have ski hills though. We've kind of got everything. Except the Kiss Me Quick hats.' He grinned and his eyes crinkled up at the corners and something inside Dawn leaped and put her breathing out of sync. She shouldn't be looking at this man and feeling these feelings. He was a constant feature in her head and being near him every Friday was like recharging a battery in her heart. He was supplanting every thought she had of Calum and he had no place to. Tomorrow she was getting her bridesmaids sorted and on Sunday she was wrapping up chocolates in peach tissue and ribbon in preparation for her wedding. She took a long sip of her drink that cooled her throat but did bugger all to still the palpitations.

'Are you going straight home when you leave here? To Canada?'

'Well, we have a few days in London, then we head off for home,' said Al Holly. 'Got a month relaxing by a lake fishing in the sun, then we set off for America on tour. You ever been?'

'Me? Naw,' said Dawn. 'My foreign experience is limited to one Greek island and France as a schoolgirl. I don't know why I bother even having a passport.' She had renewed it for her honeymoon. Why?

Al took a long drink of beer and Dawn watched his throat. He had a strong neck that smoothed down to big shoulders. She wondered what he would look like without his shirt. His leg brushed accidentally against hers under the table as he shifted position. *Jesus Christ, she was going to leap on him in a minute and rip his clothes off.*

'Is this your first trip to England?' she asked instead.

He shook his head. 'No, I've been before. Not to Yorkshire though. It's been fun. Got some nice, happy memories to take back with me.'

He didn't say what those memories were. As if he too was aware of the intensity between them, he dragged his eyes away from her and up to the sky where an aeroplane was ploughing across the heavens leaving a puffy trail behind it.

Dawn studied Al's profile unwatched and suddenly wanted to drag her hands through his hair. He was gorgeous, he was beautiful. Too beautiful to bear this.

'Al, I have to go,' said Dawn, suddenly panicked by the surge of her feelings.

He didn't protest. He didn't point out that she had hardly touched her drink.

'I understand,' he said, staring thoughtfully at his beer.

How can you? thought Dawn. *How can you understand that when I look at you my whole life seems to fall apart in the background?*

She stood up and looped her bag over her shoulder. Al Holly scratched his head and sighed.

'Hear me out, Dawny. I am not in the habit of making a play for other men's girls, I just felt I had to say that. I like you a lot. I think we have that kindred spirit thing going on and I really look forward to seeing you for this little time on Fridays. But I'm not trying to complicate things for you and if I have, I'm really sorry. I hope you'll be here next Friday and not stay away.'

'Next Friday, erm . . .' She would have had time to compose herself by then. She should say 'no'. She should tell the others she couldn't go to the pub again after work for a few weeks, then she wouldn't be drawn close to this man like a moth to a flame. It could only end with third-degree burns to her wings. No, tell him no, end it now.

'Yes, I'll be here,' she said.

*

As Anna rounded the corner to her house, she could see that there was another parcel peeping out from behind her wheely bin. She couldn't wait until she got inside to open it. She ripped the paper off to find a heart-shaped box of Ferrero Rocher. She looked around to see if she could see Tony peeping out from a hiding place where he was stationed to watch her reaction. Surely he was going to make a move soon? First a photo-plate, then a rose and now this: a third week of presents with no follow-up. Anna caught a fleeting glimpse of Butterfly slipping through the widow's fence as if he too was teasing her with a hint of his presence but not a chance of full-show.

Yet.

Tony Parker, what the hell are you up to?

Chapter 63

By the time Dawn got home, Calum was already there with a Chinese meal keeping warm in the oven.

'Makes a change, I know what you're going to say!' he laughed. 'Thought I'd give you a nice surprise.'

'Lovely,' she said, pasting on a smile, but in truth she felt nothing. And when he hinted at an early night and raised his eyebrows suggestively, she lied and said she had just started a period, which would keep him at a safe distance, she knew.

She was up the next morning, not bright but early after a restless night's sleep. Her head was like a washing machine full of different coloured items. She was a mess of contradictions and duty was a struggle. *Why did I go off early last night?* Why did she cut short the precious time she had with Al Holly in the beer garden? It wasn't as if she had loads of it with him left to waste. And all night her imagination had seemed hell-bent on finishing off the evening for her, had she stayed. What if she had leaped on him and kissed him? Calum would have been in waiting for her with a Chinese meal and she would have been snogging another man. She felt as guilty as if she had actually done it. She took a couple of Nurofen with her morning toast because a stress headache was just threatening at her temple.

She was at Muriel's for 10 a.m. and for once Demi was up and dressed. It appeared she had a brand-new boyfriend – Liam – on the scene and he had obviously injected a bit of life into her. As well as other bodily fluids.

Denise didn't seem impressed with him.

'He's another dicksplash,' she confided in Dawn. 'She'll be dumped this time next week, you mark my words. Plus I'm sure he has a girlfriend already so she's heading for a thump. Anyway, what are we doing for your hen night? Where do you fancy? Blackpool? Too far maybe . . . hmm, let me think.'

'Oh, I wasn't going to bother,' said Dawn. It wasn't as if she had hordes of mates to invite. And she couldn't exactly see Christie and Grace dancing on tables in a gay bar in Blackie.

She watched Denise's face suddenly form into something quite unpleasant.

'God, you can be a miserable beggar, Dawn!' she said. 'Well, you're having one whether you like it or not. *We* want one if we're going through all this bridesmaid crap for you.' And she huffed impatiently and turned and muttered something about going to the loo before they went across the road to Bette's house. Her reaction shocked Dawn. She had thought Denise was more on her side than that. Her wedding, which she had thought would bring her completely into the bosom of the family, was doing the opposite – turning it all into a Bride versus *Us* competition.

Across the road, big Bette sipped delicately from a china cup and beamed as the bridesmaids modelled her creations.

The dresses were bright orange and Demi's neckline was so low she could have been wearing it and still appeared on the centre pages of *Playboy*. She adjusted her boobs so they stuck out of the top in big squashy semi-circles.

'I got Bette to lower my neckline a bit as well,' Denise said, adjusting her much smaller bosom inside her dress. 'Might as well give the vicar a flash and cheer up his day. Hope you don't mind.'

'No, 'course not,' said Dawn, hating herself because what she wanted to say was, 'Yes, I bloody well do mind. And if that is peach, then I'm Cheryl Cole!' Plus the fabric smelled of cigarette smoke. How could it not, being stored in the fug of this house?

'Chuffing hell, I feel like a space hopper,' said Demi, voicing some of what was in Dawn's head. 'Thought it was supposed to be peach!'

'Well, they didn't have that exact shade of peach in the warehouse so I went for the next best thing. Plus this was a lot cheaper. You don't want to be spending a fortune for one day, do you?' Bette explained, dunking a digestive into her cup. 'I ran it past Mu first.'

'There's not that much difference,' said Mu, confirming with a nod what Bette had said.

'You two haven't been to Specsavers recently, have you?' smirked Demi.

Why didn't you run it past ME – I'm the bride! screamed Dawn inside. But she wouldn't have dared risk the wrath of the Crooke women by saying as much.

'Itches like fuck,' said Demi.

It looked as if it did too. The material was cheap and tacky and didn't lie in soft folds but stuck out stiffly and made even the slim Denise appear thick-waisted.

'Oh, you pair of moaners! You can change straight after the wedding, you don't have to wear it all day. Eeh, it's a bonny colour though, isn't it, Dawn? Nice and bright for summer,' Muriel enthused.

Dawn took a deep breath and sucked back the comment that Pumpkin Orange was much more suitable for Hallowe'en. And she didn't want the bridesmaids changing straight after the wedding. She would have liked them to wear the dresses all day so they were in them for any evening photos. Rage was bubbling in her and she was scared to unleash it fully, so it seeped out through pinholes.

'I'd bought all the peach ribbon to match for the favours and the invitations!'

'No one notices stuff like that!' said Muriel, waving it off as another one of Dawn's pernicketies.

'I do,' said Dawn, getting about as shirty as she could.

'Ooh, you want to save your "I do's" for the big day,' laughed Bette, sending her five chins into vibration.

'Oy, Mam, talking of "do's", she don't want a hen do,' mocked Demi, thumbing at Dawn.

So her future sister-in-laws had been gossiping about her. Again. That made Dawn feel extra fine and dandy.

'It's just that I don't have anyone to invite,' Dawn tried to explain.

'You've got us and Bette,' said Muriel. 'And I daresay Demi and Denise have some mates that'll want to come and beef up the crowd.'

'Calum's having his stag do on the Saturday before the wedding,' said Demi.

'Is he?' It was the first Dawn had heard of it.

'Oh, didn't he tell you?' gloated Demi. 'Mind you, if you're as miserable with him as you were about not wanting a hen night, there's no wonder.'

Ouch! Dawn felt suddenly outlawed by them all. Blood in this family was about twelve million times thicker than water. She was wishing more with every passing hour that she'd never started this whole wedding process. She had liked the family much more before their relationship got smothered by cakes and karaokes.

'Well, it would be nice to have a hen do, I suppose,' said Dawn, caving in because she didn't want to cause more bitching behind her back. *What would be the point in marrying Calum if his family hated her?* However much she didn't want to admit it to herself, belonging to a loving family again had influenced her decision to be Calum's wife. Of course it had.

'Good, you can leave all the arrangements to us then,' said Denise, her face returning to her usual cheeky, cheerful look. 'I promise you, we'll have a night to remember.'

Dawn suspected it would be more a night to forget.

Chapter 64

In the kitchen of West House, Grace was making dinner for her temporary landlord and landlady. She was happy in a kitchen, especially one of that size which had comforting, family vibes. She felt she wanted to thank these two lovely, kind people who were caring for her and sharing their home most selflessly with her, so she pulled out all the culinary stops.

'Can I help?' asked Niki, putting his head around the door. 'I'm the best potato peeler this side of Leeds.'

'I'm not doing potatoes, so go away and let me cook for you,' said Grace with a smile. *Not cooking potatoes!* That was rebellious in itself. For years she had boiled potatoes every Saturday night to accompany Gordon's pork chops. Even when they were on holiday self-catering. That single thought of Gordon brought a grim cloud with it, drying up her smile. An over-soft part of her would worry about him coping on his own if she let it. Sarah had watered that particular seed with her 'Who's going to look after Dad when he comes home?' questions. Gordon was, she had reminded her daughter, only fifty-nine, not eighty-nine. He would just have to learn how to stuff his washing in the machine and iron it afterwards. But still, being indifferent and self-protective didn't come naturally to her.

'Let me pour you a glass of wine,' said Niki. He and Christie were sitting out on the patio in the back garden, enjoying the balmy late afternoon.

'Well, if you insist.'

'I do,' Niki said. 'A lovely chilled pink Pinotage Rosé for madam.' He handed her a glass with a long, fragile stem.

'Thank you, Niki.'

He stared at her long after he had handed over the wine, which disconcerted her. Then he suddenly realized that he was embarrassing her and apologized.

'Sorry, Grace, forgive me. I was just thinking about what you've been through. No one could ever tell from looking at you. You're so remarkably . . . together. I don't know how you do it.'

'Inside I'm not, Niki, trust me,' said Grace, grating some gruyère cheese into her white wine sauce. 'I can't stop thinking about that weekend and a whole host of "what ifs". What if no one had come for me? What if I'd never been chosen to work with your sister and I didn't have her to sound the alarm when she did? When I don't take a tablet, the "what ifs" keep me awake at night and when I do fall asleep, I sometimes dream that I'm back living with Gordon and I wake up in a panic.'

She dropped the grater and Niki came to pick it up at the same time as she bent to it. Their heads bumped and Niki reached out to Grace, rubbing her head soothingly.

'Oh God, Grace, I am SO sorry. Are you all right?'

'I'm fine,' said Grace, laughing despite a second or two of sickening pain. 'You have a very hard head, you know.'

'Russian genes,' said Niki. 'Our ancestors grew thick skulls when they were slaves, pre-emancipation.'

His soothing fingers left her scalp but he didn't move away.

'Grace . . .' he began in that beautiful, deep, fruity voice. 'Grace, I think you're wonderful. That's all I wanted to say.'

There was a sudden intensity between them that Niki sensed Grace was not ready for, so he stepped back from her and lightened up. 'And I'm sorry I nearly smashed in your cranium.'

'I'll live,' said Grace, feeling hot and shaken and confused but hiding it. 'I just hope I remember the recipe through the concussion.'

'If you don't, there's the Oriental Dragon less than five minutes away. Best spring rolls in this hemisphere. Anyway, – *Na zdorov'ya,* as we Russians say!' He raised his glass to Grace. 'To your health. Especially to the skull part of your health. I pray to my gods for its quick recovery.'

'Cheers, Niki,' said Grace, raising her glass in his direction. In his kind, smiling, handsome direction.

Vladimir was waiting outside Darq House, a tall, unsmiling figure with strange, beautiful eyes scanning the drive for her. Anna gulped as he opened the car door and presented his hand to help her out. It was the heart-touching hand.

'Our last shoot, Anna,' he said. 'Are you ready?'

'As I'll ever be,' she said, thinking how cool his skin was, despite the lovely warm air of the evening.

'Hiya, babe,' called Bruce. Mark blew her a kiss, Chas waved, Flip had a coffee waiting for her, Leonid nodded courteously at her to acknowledge her presence, Jane gave her a big hug and Maria pushed her down onto a chair and started cleansing her face. Anna felt her eyes watering and coughed the tears back before Maria slapped her legs.

She was made up to the 'natural look' for the first part of the evening. Out of the corner of her eye, she saw Mark setting up the laptop.

'No, not again!' groaned Anna.

'Oh shush,' laughed Jane. 'You'll love this one.'

They had projected two images of her this time on the side of that Leeds building. The left one, the same as last time where she was wearing her rubbish underwear, and on the right, the picture that Leonid had taken of her last week in 'The Darqone' bodyshaper. No one was more surprised than Anna to admit that she didn't look half bad. There was certainly a big difference between the two pictures. She looked thinner and younger on the right one, as if she'd been Photoshopped.

Are these before and after surgery pictures? said one passer-by.

Is it the same woman?

This woman has a nice figure but the one on the right has an amazing figure.

Absolutely gorgeous. The one on the right is the younger sister, isn't she?

I'd say she was about thirty-six, thirty-seven tops.

'What do you think of those reactions, Anna?' asked Jane.

'I'm amazed but I'm thrilled to bits,' smiled Anna, in shock. 'I felt so much better about myself when the second pictures were taken and it must show. Vladimir's underwear really does make me feel confident and womanly. I wouldn't have believed it.'

'Cut!' called Mark. 'Bloody fantastic. This will be magic. Anna, we're going to be turning this one around fast as a special to pilot the new series, so be in front of the TV on Thursday the nineteenth.'

'Which month?'

'This month.'

'So soon!' croaked Anna.

'Full make-up time and your grand finale photoshoot time!' smiled Jane, pointing Anna to Maria's chair and gently shoving her forward.

As Maria brushed and dabbed, Anna listened to Leonid and Vladimir conversing in very fast Romanian. It sounded like a record being played backwards containing subliminal messages about the Anti-Christ. God, she would miss these manic evenings. She'd even miss the untalkative Maria who was now lifting up her hair and twirling it around, dropping it and re-arranging it. Anna loved having her hair played with. She found herself drifting off, her eyes closing, and then she felt a sharp jab in her shoulder.

'Don't go to sleep,' barked Vladimir, making her jump to attention.

'I wasn't!' she protested.

For once, there was a screen to allow Anna to strip off completely and put on the highest price point lingerie set which Vladimir had made. Professional models might not have minded about photographers and make-up artists seeing their bum, but Anna certainly did. She went behind and slipped off her clothes and into the velvety pants he had made which caressed her bottom cheeks and promised not to crawl up. They actually pushed her stomach in flat while allowing her to breathe and bend. Never mind 'higher price point', these things were price*less*. Then she called for him to assist her with the corset, a beautiful red one that made her feel very queenly. 'The Darqone' was an amazing creation and would transform the figures of thousands of women, but his premier collection was *so* worth saving up for. His fingers worked slowly and carefully on the hooks and she felt his cool breath blow against her neck and she shivered. There were strangely no mirrors around that evening so the only reflection she was holding was one in her mind. She hoped when she did see the mirror that it wouldn't shatter the illusion she was holding of herself: small-waisted, busty, long-legged, lips a sex-slash of scarlet.

He held up a pair of stockings. Black and sheer and sparkly, she had never seen hosiery as gorgeous. To her horror, he bent to help her put them on.

'No, I'm fine, I can do it!' she rushed, feeling the heat in her cheeks again as her brain presented her with a mini-play of Vladimir smoothing the stockings onto her legs, clipping the deep lace at her thigh. The ferocity of her imagination shocked her and by the time he had straightened up, the colour in her face would have matched 'boiled lobster' on a Dulux paint chart. He did a double-take of it and shouted over the screen,

'*Maria, Şi-a dat cu prea mult fard de obraz*! She has too much blusher on!'

No one needed to know any Romanian to work out that what Maria screamed in return intimated that she wasn't too fond of his criticism. Anna madly fanned at her face, trying to cool the blood vessels and persuade them to retreat.

Vladimir helped Anna into the dress he had made for the photoshoot, red velvet with a fishtail skirt. It was very plain and very gorgeous. He was silent as he zipped her up and smoothed the material over her back. She tried to rein in her imagination before her cheeks started cooking again. Then Vladimir held up the highest pair of blood-red shoes she had ever seen in her life. She would need oxygen after getting into them. Luckily she didn't have to walk far in them, just stand there and look like a woman worth shagging for the camera. *Yeah, easy.* Actually, she did feel worth shagging in these clothes. Her legs felt about six feet long in these shoes.

'Anna, how do you feel?' Vladimir asked her.

'Nice,' she replied in a breathy voice.

'Nice?' he growled. '*Nice?*'

'OK, I feel fantastic,' said Anna, clicking her tongue at his indignation. 'Can I see myself now?'

'*Nu*,' replied Vlad firmly. 'Anna, I want you to remember how you feel.'

'Oh ho, that sounds suspiciously like I don't look as good as I feel,' sighed Anna with disappointment.

'Let me show you your mirror for today,' he said. He beckoned her out from behind the screen and she did her best to walk gracefully in the stilt heels.

The jolly banter going on between the film crew dried up immediately. Maria and Leonid raised their heads to see her and their eyes widened so much their eyeballs nearly dropped out. Leonid dropped his camera and swore in his native tongue. '*La dracu!*' Which was mirrored in English when Bruce said

'Fucking 'ell!' Maria was shaking her head now in total and utter disbelief – and then she actually smiled. It wasn't much of one, admittedly, but then Maria didn't look as if she would crack her face if she was being tickled by three feather-duster-bearing octopuses.

'Well, well, well,' said Mark. 'Anna, you look . . . look . . . what's the word I'm searching for?'

'I'm not sure there is one,' smiled Jane. 'We might have to make one up. Marvefanwondertastic. Gorgemazing.'

Anna puffed out her cheeks. She was faced with so much evidence that she actually might look rather tasty that it battered through the barrier of her poor self-image and a pleasant warmth spread inside her.

Leonid greedily captured her image with the lens and even Maria seemed under her spell, moving in to pat shines away from Anna's face when needed. Then it was necessary for Anna to lose the gown and stand there in some very moody shots in Vladimir's fabulous, luxurious underwear.

'Oh wow, Anna Brightside!' smiled Jane, hands in prayer position by her lips. 'You look totally gorgeous.'

Anna pouted and posed like a pro. She lapped up the feeling that she was sexy and curvy and womanly. She felt as if she could have pulled Johnny Depp if he'd been in the room. She was so spent at the end she needed a cigarette. Everyone broke into rapturous applause when Mark called it a wrap.

Vladimir handed her a goblet of wine.

'Rest and enjoy,' he said.

'Let me get out of this corset, I don't want to spill anything on it,' returned Anna.

'No, sit, please,' insisted Vladimir, so Anna sank into a chair and Vladimir took the one opposite her, his large arms resting on his thighs. There was a light dancing in his eyes and the faintest hint of a smile playing on his soft, generous lips.

'So, do you think it went all right then?' she asked.

Vladimir stared hard at her, his brow creased in the middle. Then, when he realized she wasn't joking, he threw back his head and laughed. He relayed in Romanian what she had said to him to Maria and Leonid and their laughter joined his.

'*M-a întrebat dacă este destul de bună!*' Then Vladimir turned back to her. '*Tu glumeşti?* You joke? It was fantastic. You were fantastic, Anna, a queen. *O regină!* I was right to wait until I had found you. I know this for sure.'

'Blimey,' said Anna, taking a big glug of wine. Her system was thrown into shock by this lifetime's worth of compliments in one breath.

Soon the camera crew were all packed up and were almost ready to leave. Back-to-normal-life-land was just around the corner now for Anna. Back to being ignored by her own supercilious moggie and waiting for a boyfriend to finally make his mind up who had the superior tits – his fiancée or his teenage concubine.

Anna tipped the last of the wine into her mouth and then slipped into her ordinary clothes behind the screen. Bruce was waiting for her at the other side of it when she emerged.

'I never said thank you for giving Jane an injection of sense,' he said. 'You saved her job and probably some of ours too.' He gave her a fat kiss on her cheek. And then Mark appeared with the world's biggest bouquet. 'From us all,' he said. 'Some flowers for a woman who has totally blossomed before our eyes.'

Anna burst into tears for all sorts of different reasons. She was totally overwhelmed by the gift, but also she would miss these Saturdays so much. The thought of never again hearing fierce Romanian conversations and wondering what they were all about hurt her like a physical pain. But all that paled into nothing when she thought of never again feeling Vladimir Darq's hands on her shoulders, his breath on her skin.

'You're going to love the show,' smiled Jane as she climbed into the crew van. 'We've got *surprises!*'

'That sounds ominous,' Anna replied with a grimace.

'Trust us,' said Jane. 'You've been wonderful. Stay gorgeous.' And they drove away with waves and smiles and blown kisses and Anna wiped at her leaky eyes and waved back until her arm was sore. Then Leonid and Maria kissed her, three cheeks each, and vigorously shook her hand. She would even miss Maria pulling her this way and that and arguing with Vladimir. *Vladimir.*

The car pulled up to take her home. She didn't want to go. She had to go. It was all over now. Vladimir lifted up a smart black case.

'As promised,' he said. 'An exclusive set of Vladimir Darq lingerie designed for you.'

'Thank you. I shall treasure them,' replied Anna, hoping her voice wouldn't embarrass her by crumbling. She daren't look up at his pale blue eyes flecked with gold and ringed with black. She wasn't sure she would hold it together if she did.

'Anna, I will be in touch,' he said, opening the door for her. *Yeah, 'course you will,* she thought. He bent and put a kiss on her cheek. His lips were soft and cool but the place where they touched her burned all the way home.

Grace and Niki and Christie ate their meal outside. The evening was warm enough but Niki had lit the huge chiminea in the garden which kicked out a lot of heat in their direction when the air started to cool. Citronella candles kept the insects away from the king prawn and avocado salad starter, the gruyère and mushroom chicken and the summer pudding and clotted cream. After devouring Grace's homemade chocolate mint ice-cream truffles, Niki left his sister and Grace together in the garden with a cognac each while he apologized for being a typical bloke because he wanted to check up on the sports results on the TV.

'He likes you very much,' said Christie, as soon as her brother was out of earshot. She was a lot further down her glass of those very large cognacs than Grace was.

'I like him too,' said Grace.

'No, I mean he *likes* you.'

'Christie Somers, listen to yourself. You sound as if you're at school, matchmaking.'

'He sparkles when you're around. Of course he wouldn't dream of making a move on you while you're a guest in our house, he's far too gallant,' Christie trilled. 'Gentlemen are such a mixed blessing in that respect.'

'*Tut.* You're imagining things.'

'I'm my father's daughter and I know my psychology, Ms Beamish! I think he's scared a lot of women off by being too good-looking and too nice. They can't quite believe he could be real. Funny creatures, aren't we, women? Even if we find what we want, we're too scared to believe it and run from it.'

'Yes, aren't we?' said Grace.

'Except I was the exception to the rule and didn't,' said Christie. 'I ran to love with my arms open wide and it was wonderful. I can see you two together quite easily, you know.'

'Christie, stop it.'

'Did you ever love Gordon, Grace?' Christie asked, suddenly serious.

'No,' Grace admitted after a long and thoughtful pause. 'I wanted to. I think I could have, given the chance.'

'What do you mean?'

'I thought we'd be like an arranged marriage couple; you know, that we'd grow close together. But he had . . . problems . . . sexually. Right from the beginning. With me anyway.' Grace knew her tongue was loosened by the wine and the brandy but she didn't care. It felt so cathartic to talk about things she had kept bottled up inside her for so long. 'He managed it just the once, but it was difficult. He said it must be my fault because he'd managed to give Rita three children and for a long time I thought he must be right.'

'Oh, Grace, how cruel.' Christie touched her arm.

'I once got some leaflets from the doctor about impotence and he went mad. I wasn't allowed to ever speak about it again. He never tried to touch me after the first few attempts, he just moved into the bedroom opposite.'

Christie shifted forward in her seat. 'But wasn't he tender with you at all? Didn't you try other things?'

'I don't know if he had a low sex drive or if he'd stamped down on it so hard because he wanted to kill it and spare himself the indignity, but no, there was nothing like that. No embraces, no kisses. Obviously I never got to find out what his love life was like with Rita. I tried to ask but, as you might imagine, I didn't get very far into the first sentence. Piecing things together though, I don't think sex was high on his agenda with either of us. I presume he saw it only as part of his manly duty and with three children to show to the world, he'd proved himself to be "a true male". Gordon was very good at not acknowledging things that threatened to dent his ego.'

'Grace, how could you have stood it?' Christie shook her head, unable to comprehend such a dry desert of a marriage.

'I would never have left Gordon and risked not seeing the children again. I know he would have ripped them away from me had we ever split up.'

'What about when they were old enough to make their own minds up though?'

Grace gently rotated the brandy in the glass and looked into it as if she were staring into a crystal ball, but one that could decipher her past rather than her future.

'I don't know. I was acclimatized after so long. I just stayed; the desire to up and go occasionally visited but I never had the guts to see it through. It's a poor answer, I know.'

'What an incredibly sad story. All that unborn love.'

Grace swallowed hard. 'I wanted to love him, so much. I was grateful to him for the children but also I wanted to have a real marriage and be a proper family. He was a very attractive-looking man when he was younger, serious and aloof and *grown-up*, and he intrigued me. We used to work for the same company – he in another department. I felt sorry when the office gossip reached me that he'd lost his wife and had young children. I couldn't have children of my own, you see. I was only a young woman when I had to have a hysterectomy. And one day he bumped into me, literally, in a corridor and we began talking and he asked me out for a meal. He was very correct, respectful – or so I thought.' Grace gave a bitter little laugh. 'After the second date, I met his children and his mother and I fell in love with them all on sight. He needed a wife and companionship and I desperately wanted a family and so we married and sealed the deal. I thought I could make everything all right.'

'Were you a virgin, Grace?'

'No,' said Grace. 'I had one lover before I married. A good, caring man. Maybe it would have been better if I had been a virgin. Then I wouldn't know what I was missing.'

'You poor thing,' said Christie softly.

'Please, Christie, that isn't the whole of the story. The children were worth everything. I love them so much.'

Christie sighed. 'I thought I'd been so short-changed when Peter died. You make me realize that I wasn't after all,' she said eventually.

'Do you think you'd ever marry again?'

Christie shrugged. 'Who knows what the future brings? But Peter Somers is a hell of a hard act to follow. I sometimes curse him for that.'

'Were you very happy?'

Christie smiled, her eyes glassy with affection. 'He was the most wonderful man: kind, passionate, funny. He was my heart. Funnily enough, I met Peter at work too. He was my married boss, older than me. He was living in a sexless, childless, unhappy marriage and I loved him away from his wife. Grace, do you remember that day in the pub when Anna said something about women who mess around with married men deserving all they got? For a long time I thought I was cursed because I broke up his marriage. But I would have done it all again to have him. And in a way I'm lucky because some people never find the love of their life but at least I can say I did. For a while. My punishment is that I'll never find anyone like him again and I wouldn't want to take a lesser man to my bed. We all pay for our sins in the end.'

'Could you have children?'

'I presume so, but I don't know for sure. We thought we had all the time in the world. We planned to have them late on when we'd got our travelling bugs out of our system, but he died before then. We missed our chance.'

'Oh, Christie.'

'Life makes no guarantees – I accept that, I've had to. There are certain things, like children and longevity, that are privileges, not rights. All we can do is play the hand we are dealt. Another cognac, Grace?' was Christie's reply to that. 'Let's toast our health and our future happiness and a Malcolm-free existence in the office. My God, I know it's evil but I hope the lazy bastard gets kicked out soon.'

Grace accepted the turn of conversation and poured them both another cognac which they drank together in comfortable silence. The way only good friends, close friends, can do.

Chapter 65

Dawn burst into the office on Monday morning with the force of someone who has been rehearsing a speech for hours and cannot hang on to it any longer.

'OK,' she started her announcement to everyone. 'I'm having a hen night but, and don't take this the wrong way, I don't want to look rude by not inviting you but I know it's going to be awful and I wish I could get out of it but it's my future sisters-in-law who are organizing it and they've got really rough mates and the big fat woman who's making the brides-maids' dresses is going as well and it's all going to be really awful and embarrassing and I don't want—'

'Will you chill!' said Anna. 'And you'd better take a few breaths because you're turning blue around the gills.'

Dawn collapsed into her chair and her head fell into her hands. 'They've organized it for a week on Saturday. Please tell me you've all got something on. If I'm going to have a hen night at all with you there, I'd prefer it just to be like Anna's birthday – all of us having a meal at the Setting Sun together.'

'Then we will, it's sorted, so don't get upset,' said Christie, preparing to gee her up. 'How did the bridesmaids' fitting go?'

Dawn burst into tears and her work-mates immediately swarmed around her, which made her feel even more pathetic.

'I'm so sorry,' she said, preparing to lie as Raychel thrust the office box of tissues under her nose. 'I don't know why I'm crying. They were fine; she'd done a good job.'

'Oh well, that's lovely then,' said Grace. She noticed they were all exchanging worried glances above Dawn's head. 'Everything will come together soon, just you see.' *You must miss your parents so much at a time like this*, she thought, but didn't say because she knew it would probably upset Dawn even more.

Dawn nodded, biting her top lip hard to stem the stupid tears. She was thinking about her parents too. What on earth would they have said, seeing her in this state about what was supposed to be the happiest day of her life?

She wasn't the only one with a glum Monday-morning face. Anna was very quiet and her thoughts so preoccupied that Grace had to ask her four times if she wanted a coffee.

'Earth calling Anna, can you read me?' said Grace.

'Sorry, yes, er, what did you say?'

'Do you want a coffee? It's my turn to get them.'

'Yes – yes, please. Sorry.'

'What's up with you this morning?' asked Christie. 'You look as if you've come back to us after an out-of-body experience.'

They watched as Anna wrestled with something in her head that she obviously wasn't sure if she should tell them or not. Then it flooded out of her.

'I wasn't going to say anything, but I'm confused. A couple of weeks ago it would have been mine and Tony's anniversary, I think I mentioned it when I blew up that day in the pub, well, not a real anniversary 'cos we aren't married, as I said, but when I got home from work I found a plate on my doorstep. One of those with a picture on it, do you know what I mean? A photo of me and Tony and underneath it just said, *Together.*

And last week there was a red rose on the doorstep and this week a heart-shaped box of Ferrero Rocher.'

There was a silence as they waited for her to go on.

'No, that's it,' said Anna. 'Three presents over three weeks and nothing else. No phone calls, no guest appearance, nothing.'

'Crikey, it's like one of those Czechoslovakian fairy stories I used to watch on the box,' said Christie. '*Three Gifts for Cinderella*, I think it was called.'

'Aye, well, this Cinderella can't work out what Prince Charming is up to. Am I supposed to drop my chuffing shoe outside the barber's?' Anna grunted.

'What's he playing at?' asked Raychel.

'You tell me. But there he was as normal as you like with *her* in his shop on Saturday morning when I did a sneaky drive past. Groping her arse. I can't think what to make of it, I really can't.'

Dawn stopped herself from saying that she would have bagged up the presents, burst into his shop with them and told the other woman to keep his lead on. But it was easy to advise on other people's relationships, not so easy to take that advice and apply it to your own.

'And how does it make you feel? Are you upset? Angry?' asked Christie.

Anna made an attempt to self-analyze.

'I don't know. I suppose I felt all excited at first – full of anticipation. Now I just feel pissed off because I don't know what's happening.' She didn't say that Vladimir Darq's tender hand on her heart had shifted something within her and made her rip off the rose-coloured specs about this so-called exciting development in her and Tony's relationship.

'It sounds to me as if he's trying to assert his presence in your life again, just in case you had forgotten him,' said Christie. 'I could be wrong, but it's very much as if he's warming you up for his return.'

'What, you mean he's really thinking of coming back?' said Anna. 'And he's not just mucking my head about?'

'Be careful,' warned Christie. 'He's sending you quite blatant love tokens. He's definitely up to something.'

'Would you have him back though?' said Grace. 'After all he's done to you?'

'You've come so far,' said Dawn softly. 'You're a different person to the one you were when you collapsed in the toilets and were sick on Christie's skirt. Would you really have him back?'

'Would I hell,' said Anna. But her voice had a definite waver in it.

Strangely enough, Anna's mobile rang at lunchtime, interrupting her thoughts about Tony and his hand on Lynette Bottom's bottom as she absently chewed on a beef and onion sandwich in the canteen. It was Vladimir Darq. Her hands were shaking as she answered it.

'Anna, my car will call for you at eight p.m. on Saturday,' he said. 'I have something that I want to give you – it won't take very long.' Then he added pointedly, 'It isn't a plate.' He put the phone down before she could say a single word in answer.

If that wasn't enough mystery for one day, Christie was acting very oddly that afternoon as well.

'Yes, I'll make sure,' she was saying quietly on the phone. 'Secret squirrel.' Then, when she saw Anna walk into the department, she switched to a bright and breezy voice. 'Yes, absolutely, *Beryl*. We'll be here,' before slamming the phone down quickly.

'Nice lunch?' Christie asked.

'Er . . . yeah . . . I suppose so,' replied Anna.

'Good, good.' Christie's mind appeared to be chewing on something. Anna could virtually hear her cogs turning. 'Anna, you couldn't do me a favour, could you? I wouldn't ask but I'm a bit busy myself.'

'Yeah, 'course, what is it?' Anna presumed she was going to ask her to put the kettle on.

'Will you call into Boots on your way home tonight and get me . . . get me a Boots magazine. I want to . . . look at their food offering. Sandwiches. You can leave an hour earlier so you don't miss your train.'

'I don't need to leave an hour earlier—'

'Yes, that's fine. An hour earlier. I insist,' said Christie definitely.

'OK,' said Anna, very puzzled. She accepted it, but felt that Christie wanted a Boots mag about as much as she wanted a Malcolm-type spray tan.

Dawn had a fitting at 'White Wedding' at seven o'clock that evening. She put the dress on and found that it gave her no thrill to do so. And Freya was reprimanding her because it appeared Dawn had lost quite a bit of weight.

'If you keep this up, this dress will slip off you down the aisle,' said Freya, pinning some alterations. 'You need some shape at least to carry this design off.'

'Will you take a picture of me in it?' asked Dawn. 'My fiancé has an old auntie in a home and I promised to show her my dress. She won't be able to come to the wedding itself.'

'Oh, that's a shame,' said Freya.

'I hope she remembers me. She's not been well the past couple of weeks apparently. I didn't want to confuse her even more, seeing as I've only met her once and she might not recognize me. But I did promise to show her a picture.'

'You should always keep those sorts of promises,' said Freya. 'My goodness, you've lost inches!'

'Shame dresses aren't magic, isn't it? Shame they can't alter themselves to your shape and choose you instead of the other way round.'

'All my dresses are magic,' said Freya. 'I guarantee that wearing this dress will lead you to the happiest of lives.'

'I wish you really could guarantee it,' said Dawn.

'Oh, I can,' said Freya unequivocally, resting her hand on her heart and smiling a warm, strange smile. 'I can most definitely promise a bride the happiest of wedding days when she wears one of my dresses. Especially this one.'

Dawn so wanted to trust Freya in that. She looked at the reflection of herself in the mirror, with the dress pinned to fit her exactly. It really was beautiful and she willed that she would feel wonderful in it, swishing down the aisle. Everyone would love her in this dress and all the niggling and nit-picking of the wedding arrangements would be over and she and the Crookes would be united in happiness. Everyone would enjoy the food and the karaoke, and the horrible orange dresses were something they would laugh about one day. The most important thing was that she and Calum would be joined in holy matrimony and have a solid foundation to build their future happiness on. And Al Holly would be gone and unable to cause any more upset to her feelings. His image would fade and she would think of him as just a nice guy who once crossed her path, a pleasant memory.

It was a little more difficult to be positive when she got home that night though, to find that Calum had moved all the chocolate favours that Dawn had so painstakingly wrapped up next to the radiator, where they had melted.

'Sorry we're late, I got held up at work,' Raychel apologized as soon as the door opened.

'No matter, just glad you could make it. Come in, come in.'

Elizabeth Silkstone warmly greeted Raychel and Ben, pulling them into her house and then escorting them out into the lovely garden at the back where John and a large, thick-set bloke with a smiley face were cooking meat on a barbecue. John instantly came over and gave Raychel a big hug.

'Hello, Flower,' he said. 'George, Janey,' he called to the big man and a buxom red-haired woman standing nearby. 'This is Raychel.'

'It's so nice to meet you, love,' said the big-bosomed Janey, bending to give Raychel a kiss on her cheek. 'Elizabeth and I and Fatso over there have known each other since school. We were forced to do Latin together. I'm still having therapy.'

'Don't forget me,' said a slim, pretty blonde with a pronounced bump, cutting in between Janey and George. 'I'm Helen, or Fatso as they've no doubt called me. I'm the third member of the Latin triumvirate.'

'She's just got married,' said Janey, pointing a thumb at her friend's swollen stomach. 'The brazen tart! Him a partner in a firm of solicitors as well. What is the world coming to?'

'Come and get a drink,' said Elizabeth, linking her arm through Raychel's and leading her away. 'We're so glad you're here.' Ben was now standing with John and George by the barbecue. 'I have been dying for my friends to meet you.'

'Do they know?' asked Raychel.

'They know you are Bev's daughter,' said Elizabeth. 'They're so happy for me that I found you. Now, how are you settling into that lovely apartment of yours? Have you got it as you want it yet?'

'No, that'll take a while,' said Raychel, cutting to the chase. 'Elizabeth, I had a letter forwarded on to me this morning from our old address. From my mother.'

'Do you have it with you?'

'Yes,' said Raychel, foraging in her handbag.

'Let's go inside,' said Elizabeth. The irony wasn't lost on her that she had drawn a total blank trying to trace her sister for years and here was Bev's letter finding Raychel relatively easily.

In John's office down the hallway, Raychel handed over the envelope.

*

'Dear Lorraine/Rachel,

Have I found you? Please let me no. I'm at my wits end wandering if you are alright. I want to see you again. I do'nt want anything from you but I have something imporant I need to tell you. Can I come and see you or you can come and see me.

Best wishes
Your mother.'

As old as she was now, Raychel had read the letter with a shake in her hands. It acted like a key to a door in her head which held back all those memories of her childhood: the scruffy house, the strangers buying drugs, Nathan Lunn and his cruelty and her mother, too spaced out to stop him when he went on his smashing, hitting, violent rampages. But finding Elizabeth had strengthened her. She no longer felt as if she and Ben were alone in the world. John was looking after Ben like a son and she could feel Elizabeth's strength and love radiate out towards her. She felt safer than she had ever done in her whole life within the confines of her new family circle.

'I don't want to see her but I feel that I have to. She can tell me what she has to and then she can leave me alone. What should I do?'

Elizabeth gripped Raychel's hands in her own.

'Would you like me to go to her?'

'I can't ask that of you.'

'Yes, you can. Leave it with me.' Elizabeth took in a deep breath as she made the decision to commit herself to this. 'I'll deal with it. I'll see what she wants.'

The time was long overdue. Elizabeth *needed* to see her sister. She had things of her own to sort out with her.

Chapter 66

At West House, things had fallen into a routine as if they had always been so. Niki was chopping up vegetables in the kitchen when Grace got home. He had opened a bottle of wine and three glasses stood waiting impatiently at the side of it.

'Ah, good evening, Gracie,' said Niki. 'Where's my sister?'

'Christie's nipped into town. She needs shoes.'

'No, she doesn't, she *wants* shoes,' said Niki with a big, booming and infectious laugh that Grace couldn't help smiling at. How different this house felt to her old one. Despite the age of the walls, it was young and alive with no atmosphere sliding down towards a grave. Niki had Lily Allen playing out of his iPod station. Gordon would have had, at best, some morbid radio programme on that sounded as if it was being broadcast through the war. She wondered where Gordon was and what was going through his head at this moment. Then she cut off the thought as Niki pushed a generous glass of Chablis into her hand.

'Try this,' he invited. 'I think it's divine, personally.'

'Anything I can do to help?' asked Grace.

'Nope,' said Niki. 'Cooking unwinds me. And I had the patient of all nervous patients in today. Fifty-eight-year-old company director and terrified of needles like you wouldn't imagine.'

'How do you calm down someone like that?' said Grace.

'Acupuncture,' said Niki.

'No!' said Grace.

'Joke,' replied Niki, clicking his tongue. 'Gotcha, Grace!' Their eyes met and locked and Grace knew that Christie hadn't been exaggerating at all when she intimated that her brother was growing fond of her. His next words confirmed it.

'I . . . we both like having you here so much,' he said in his lovely deep bear of a voice.

'Thank you, Niki. I'm so grateful to you both. I shall try not to outstay my welcome.'

'You couldn't possibly do that, Gracie,' said Niki. Then he notched up the humour by singing a falsetto opera song about his scallops because, as his sister so rightly said, he would not want to compromise Grace as a guest, not after what she had been through recently. He knew her thoughts would be a jumble and the last thing she would want was some bachelor-dentist declaring an ever-growing batch of undeniable feelings.

She was, however, a woman worth waiting for. And Nikita Koslov thought he might just have been waiting his whole life for her.

Chapter 67

'Can't believe we are at the end of another week!' said Christie, pouring the bottle of chilled Zinfandel into five glasses. 'Anyone doing anything exciting this weekend? It only seems like two minutes since I was asking that question last Friday.'

'I'm off to see Calum's old auntie in a retirement home,' said Dawn.

'Bloody hell, I can't compete with that much excitement,' said Anna.

'Aw, don't be rotten,' laughed Dawn. 'She wants to see my dress so I had a picture taken. She's too frail to come to the church.'

'Christie and I are off to the theatre,' said Grace.

'And my brother is coming as well,' said Christie. 'He has rather a crush on Grace.'

'Get in there, Gracie,' said Anna, which mirrored exactly what Paul and Laura had said. It was, apparently, obvious to them also that Niki rather liked their mother. He was always fizzily cheerful around her and, though Grace had told her children that he was like that around everyone because it was his natural disposition, they didn't believe her at all. Did she like Niki enough to say 'yes' if he invited her out to dinner? Paul had asked her. The thought terrified Grace, to be honest. The idea of starting a new, *normal* relationship, with all that it entailed, was scary stuff. Especially with a fifty-five-year-old body, although it was still in fantastic shape, thanks to years of yoga. But then Niki was fifty too. Did men feel the same insecurity about their bodies with new partners?

'What are you going to do now that filming is over? Won't you feel lost?' Raychel asked Anna.

'Well,' Anna leaned forward to impart her information. 'Mr Darq is sending a car for me tomorrow night. Says he's got something for me.'

'What?' asked Dawn, her eyes lit up with excitement.

'Haven't a clue. I won't be there long apparently, so he says.' She sighed rather heavily at the thought of having to say a second goodbye to him.

'Ooh, how exciting,' Christie grinned. 'Wonder what it could be. Can you wait?'

Anna downplayed the thrill that tripped along her nerve-endings at the thought of seeing him again. 'I'll have to, won't I?' She had thought of his hand on her heart more times than she cared to count that past week. She'd even dreamed about him one night, wild and saturnine and threatening to eat her. Although the dream had ended before he had fulfilled his promise and she never did get to find out if he meant literally or metaphorically. She wondered if she could look him in the face after the sexual tension that her night-brain had created. *Vladimir Darq.* He was taking up more and more of her thought space, which concerned her. There was no point in forming an attachment with someone like him. But she was aware that was exactly what was happening.

'And I'm going shopping with my aunt,' said Raychel after taking a deep breath.

She cut through most of the story and told them that she had been contacted by an estranged aunt who was, by fantastic coincidence, living in the area.

'What an amazing story,' said Christie. 'I didn't think things happened like that in real life. You must be delighted.'

'It's a long, complicated story,' said Raychel. 'I gave you the abridged version.'

'And the happy ending,' said Dawn. 'So that'll do nicely.'

On Raychel's face was a great big wide arc of a smile. She had so wanted to tell her work-mates some of her story: the nice parts. They had made it so easy for her to be friends with them. Accepting her without wanting to know all the ins and outs of her past life. She felt like she had a big, cosy blanket around her. She was content, despite the niggle about her mother's reappearance in her life. But she had Elizabeth on her side and that made her feel protected in a way that not even her lovely Ben could manage.

After the others had left, Dawn sat at the bar and watched the band.

'Are you going to sing again?' asked the barman when she gave him a drinks order. 'You were fab.'

'It was a one-off,' said Dawn, secretly glowing.

'The manager wanted to see you. Think he was on about offering you the odd singing job.'

'Oh?' said Dawn. She was flattered but she didn't relish the thought of standing on that stage alone. Al would have gone back to Canada then and singing solo had never been part of her plans. 'Tell him thanks but I don't think I dare,' she said. 'But it was nice of him to say so.'

'Shame,' said the barman. 'But then you fitted in so well with that band. Maybe you should ask them to take you with them when they go.'

Dawn laughed politely, but the barman's words were too close to the bone for comfort. They brought pictures in her head of her touring on a bus with the boys, setting up the stage with them, jamming together outside with a backdrop of Canadian mountains and warm, orangey sunsets.

Al Holly's arm circled her waist. The contact lasted barely a second but it was enough to send fireworks rocketing up towards her brain and then onwards to the moon.

'You looked lost in thought,' he said. 'Anything interesting?'

'Sort of,' said Dawn. 'How are you? Have you had a good week?'

'Yes, good,' he smiled, his eyes as twinkly as polished rhinestones. 'And how are you, Dawny Sole? I was going to invite you on stage to sing with us again tonight but you were talking with your friends. I didn't see you even look up at me once.'

Dawn felt her cheeks grow hot. He had such a dreamy voice. He had a head start on anyone else she could ever meet for giving her palpitations. George Clooney included.

'Every time I looked up, you were looking down,' replied Dawn. 'Seems we didn't have our eyes coordinated.'

'I looked at you quite a lot,' said Al. 'Not sure how I'm going to spend my Fridays not seeing you out there at the back of the room.'

'Bet you say that to all the girls,' said Dawn, her smile shaky on her lips.

'No, Dawny,' said Al, 'I don't. I ain't no womanizer. My music is my woman. But if . . .'

The room melted into a big blur behind Dawn. There was nothing but her and lovely Al Holly and she was desperate for him to finish his sentence. But he didn't. He said, 'So, Coke or beer?'

Dawn could have battered him. But she wasn't free to be flirted with. There was no point in complicating anything. *Yeah, right, like it wasn't already complicated!* A huge part of her didn't want to be right and honourable and decent. It wanted Al Holly to lean into her and kiss her hard on the lips and show her what he tasted like. She wanted to do things with him that would make Paris Hilton's love life look like Mother Teresa's.

'Diet Coke, please. A small one.'

'Two small Diet Cokes, please,' Al told the barman before turning back to Dawn and asking, 'Anyhow, how are your wedding plans coming along?'

Dawn didn't want to talk about her wedding plans. She ignored his question and gave him one of her own.

'Do you write your own songs?'

'We write some. I've been writing one this week, as a matter of fact.'

'What's it called?'

'Haven't finished it yet. Hope to have it ready for next week,' he said. 'We . . . er . . . have a private party to play for this evening. I can only stay for five minutes.'

'Oh sure,' said Dawn.

'You could come, the guys wouldn't mind. We could pass you off as a roadie if I lent you my hat.'

'Thank you,' smiled Dawn. 'But I'd better not, I should go home.'

'I'd prefer not to go to the party and sit here with you and talk about music and guitars or whatever you wanted to talk about and drink beer.'

'I couldn't anyway, I'm driving.'

'I might take your car keys away from you.'

'How would I get home then?'

The question hung in the thick silence between them and they both knew what his answer would have been, had he spoken.

Dawn felt so hot her brain was in danger of blowing up.

'Where's the party?' she asked.

'Somewhere called Maltstone Lodge. Do you know it?'

'Yes, it's not far away.' Dawn took a long drink and noticed that Al had already finished his.

'You have to go,' she said.

'Yep, I do.' But he didn't move. And neither did Dawn.

'I—'

'Dawn—' They both started to speak simultaneously. Al's hand twitched upwards. Then dropped back to his side. Then it made a smooth arc to her face. His fingers had barely touched her cheek when a man's voice called across the bar.

'Al. We're ready to go, man. Oh, hi there, Dawny. How are you?'

Al sighed. 'Samuel's timing was never all that good.'

'Maybe his timing is too good,' said Dawn. Samuel had saved them from God knows what, because if she had kissed Al Holly then, she didn't know what bombs it would set off inside her. She was clinging onto every reserve she had to resist him and it wasn't working.

Al dipped his hand into the back pocket of his jeans and pulled out a piece of paper.

'This is my mobile number. Just in case you want it. Just in case you want to talk. As friends.'

Dawn took it from him. She wouldn't ring, she couldn't ring, but it was nice to have.

'I know you won't ring,' he said, as if he could read her thoughts. 'But I want to hope that you might.'

'Thank you. And if I don't ring, will you be here next week?'

'Of course I will.'

'Bye.'

'Bye.'

He touched the tip of her nose. Just one little touch with his finger and those bombs detonated inside her, each one setting off another in a different part of her body.

Bugger – she was falling hook, line and sinker for a country boy and she wished that before he left her forever, she could taste his lips upon her own. Just once.

*

When Anna reached home, she found a small packet on the doorstep. She huffed and ripped it open to find it contained a tiny black thong. She opened the door and threw it on the hall-side table.

Chapter 68

To say that Anna was nervous that Saturday evening as she waited for her car was the equivalent of saying that the 'sun was a bit hot.' What the heck did he have to give her? Whatever it was was secondary to the fact that she was going to see him again. The anticipation was killing her. She had paced a furrow in the hall carpet by the time she heard the car pull smoothly up outside her front door.

She dropped her house keys twice while she was locking up, and attempting to laugh off her butter-fingers to the Romanian driver with the sense of humour bypass didn't help her confidence levels.

Vladimir was waiting for her outside his house, his legs astride, his arms folded over a Nehru-collared long, open jacket that made him look sexily authoritarian. She gulped as he presented his hand to help her out of the car. It was the heart-touching hand.

'Anna, how nice to see you again,' he said. God, he was so gallant. The most gallant thing Tony had ever done was tell her that he wouldn't climb over her to get to Angelina Jolie if they were all in bed together. Then he had spoiled even that by asking her if she thought she might fancy a threesome in the future. Anna said that quite categorically she didn't. Besides, the way Tony's brain worked, she wondered if given the chance, he'd pick two other birds and leave her standing outside.

They went inside Darq House. Anna was thrilled to see it again. Luno came stalking over, his tail whirring like a helicopter blade, and pushed his muzzle into Anna's hand.

'Hi, boy, I've missed you,' she whispered to him. Luno stayed for a pat, then returned to his basket, slumping down but keeping his eyes on his master who was pouring two goblets of wine, one of which he handed over to Anna.

'*Noroc!*' he said, which she took to mean 'Cheers!' and repeated the word back to him before taking a sip. It was very nice for virgin's blood. No wonder vampires were always thirsty.

'Anna, next week it is the *Balul Lună Plină*.'

'The what?'

'A Full Moon Ball. I hold it here in Darq House.'

'A ball?'

'Yes.'

'Here?'

'Right. You will be coming, of course.'

'Me?'

'Yes, Anna.'

'A ball?'

'Yes. I want you to come.'

A thought crossed Anna's brain, carrying a long dark shadow with it.

'It's not one of those surprise things, is it? Jane's not going to turn up and ask me to model naked up a specially-built catwalk?'

Vladimir smiled. Just out of one side of his mouth. His eyes twinkled. They were *so* not contact lenses, as she had once suspected. 'No, no tricks, you will be in a dress as a guest. An honoured guest of mine.'

'Oh God, I haven't got a dress posh enough for anything like that. What sort? Long, short?'

He held up one finger to silence her, got up from his seat, disappeared for less than a minute and returned with a long, soft, silver case over his arms. He unzipped and opened it and held up the most beautiful long gown in a shade of blue reminiscent of a late-night sky. Anna's jaw fell open so wide it almost got lost in her cleavage.

'I told you I had something for you,' he said.

'Well, you were right, it's not a plate!' gasped Anna. 'That can't be for me, can it?'

'Yes, of course,' said Vlad. 'Don't worry, it will fit. You don't need to try it on before. Trust me. Put it on next Saturday only. I will send the underwear to you before then, but I need to work some more upon it first. The car will pick you up at nine o'clock.'

'Do I bring a bottle?'

Vladmir gave her a disapproving look. She guessed the answer was a no then.

'Thank you, Vladimir, it's gorgeous. I've never had a dress like it.'

'Of course, it's a Vladimir Darq. How could you?'

Anna smiled and lifted her eyes to the man in front of her with the black hair and the full red lips, and had to pull them away again fast. He was too gorgeous. How could she go back to ordinary Saturday nights watching Ant and Dec and eating a sad fart ready meal for one? Anna felt suddenly empty inside and tearful and gulped at her red wine.

'You know that the show is going to be broadcast on Thursday night at nine p.m., Anna? The lingerie will be in the shops the next day – so the timing is perfect.'

'Yes, I know.' Only five days to find out if she'd made the biggest chump of herself and wrecked Vladimir Darq's career single-handedly. Oh God, how could she dare to go into work the day after? And why nine p.m.? After the watershed? She daren't ask. She wasn't sure she wanted to know the answer. There was nothing she could do now but wait for it, watch it and die of shame afterwards.

Anna put her goblet down. She didn't want to outstay her welcome.

'Well, thank you for this beautiful dress.'

'My car will pick you up at quarter to nine next Saturday evening.' He kissed her hand. She cradled that hand all the way home. Not even the sight of Tony's thong gift could pull her back down to reality. She'd be back there soon enough. *But please God, just give me one more week to enjoy being up on this number nine cloud!*

Chapter 69

Dawn was glad that no one wanted to come with her to the old people's home to see Aunt Charlotte on Sunday afternoon. Her obligation to show the old lady the photograph of her wedding dress gave her the perfect excuse to miss out on eating a big lamb roast dinner with her soon-to-be in-laws and enduring scary hints as to what was in store for the dreaded hen night. Denise had turned up with some huge inflatable willies the day before and Demi was getting some T-shirts printed.

'I'm getting them cheap from Empty Head,' she declared proudly. 'They're only costing you forty quid, Dawn.' Dawn noted the *you*.

Dawn didn't want to pay forty pounds for T-shirts for a bunch of strangers with, no doubt, something crude and embarrassing printed on them. Then again, she envisaged Demi's face if she said as much – a look that would spread to Denise's and Muriel's faces as quickly as nits hopped. She opened up her purse and handed over two twenty-pound notes.

'Bit of a bloody cheek asking her to pay when you've ordered them,' said Denise.

'Well, they're only coming out of that money Auntie Charlotte gave her, aren't they?' retorted Demi as if Dawn wasn't there.

'Yeah, I suppose,' said Denise with a hopeful raised-eyebrow look at Dawn.

'Er, do I owe you anything, Denise? For the inflatable er . . . things,' she asked, hating herself, hating her weakness, hating the fact that the closer she became to the Crookes, the further away she drifted.

'Forty quid will cover it all,' said Denise.

'Can I owe you ten? I've only got thirty left in my purse.'

' 'Course,' said Denise with the beaming smile of someone who had just made a healthy profit.

At the old people's home, Dawn approached Reception and asked the woman behind the desk if she could see Charlotte Sadler. The woman's face dropped into a sorry kind of smile when Dawn explained who she was and why she was there.

'She's very fragile and confused at the moment,' she said. 'It'll be one-way traffic, I'm afraid.'

'But she was so fit and well the last time I came,' said Dawn.

'That's how some of them go, love. It can happen so quick.' She came out from behind the desk and beckoned Dawn to follow her to Charlotte's room.

'I shan't keep her long,' promised Dawn, following her down the carpeted corridor, 'but I told her I'd come.'

There was a drastic change in the old lady since Dawn's last visit. She was half-sitting up, propped by lots of fat pillows, her long hair now lying about her shoulders in ghostly white tendrils and she was decidedly thinner. Her bones looked as fragile as those of a baby bird and she was reposing, mouth open, devoid of teeth, which sucked her cheeks down into dark holes.

'Charlotte, love,' said the woman quietly and rubbed her hand. 'Charlotte, you've got a visitor.'

The old lady's eyes flickered open. There was no recognition in them at all. They moved over Dawn as if she were just part of the furniture of the room.

'Sit with her for a bit,' said the woman, moving to the door. 'Can I get you a coffee or a tea?'

'I'd love a coffee, please,' said Dawn, taking the seat at Charlotte's bedside. 'Milk, half a sugar if it's not too much trouble.'

'Not too much trouble at all, love,' said the woman. 'Kettle's always on here!'

Dawn studied the old lady. Her breathing seemed laboured and she looked so much older than she had appeared last time.

'Hello, Aunt Charlotte,' said Dawn softly. 'Do you remember me? I'm Dawn. I'm going to marry Calum, your great-nephew. We came to see you a few weeks back. You wanted to see a picture of my wedding dress. I had one taken at my last fitting for you, so you can see what I'll look like.'

Charlotte's eyes roved back to Dawn and she gave the slightest nod. Dawn opened her handbag and pulled out the photograph.

'It's so pretty,' Dawn carried on. 'It's ivory with tiny peach roses at the neck and a V at the waist and a big full skirt. Would you like to see?' She held up the photograph in front of Charlotte and kept it there. To Dawn's delight, the old lady's eyes locked on it and then her hands came up and reached for it.

'I didn't want to let you down after I'd promis—'

'You look very happy,' Charlotte said in a scratchy, toothless voice. 'I like your boots.'

What a shame, thought Dawn. She couldn't really see it.

'Who's that man?'

'What man, love?' asked Dawn.

'That man in the hat.'

'Oh, er . . .' There was no man there, of course. Dawn made something up on the spot so as not to confuse the old lady even more.

'He's the man who owns the dress shop,' she said.

Aunt Charlotte dropped the photo. As Dawn reached to pick it up, Charlotte said in a voice that was steady and weighty with tears, 'Oh, Dee Dee, what are you doing? We just want you to be happy.' The old lady's left hand fell on top of Dawn's and squeezed it with a strength that seemed impossible for a woman of her fragility. Then the brightness seemed to fade from her eyes and she closed them with a tired sigh. She had drifted off again by the time the woman returned with the coffee.

'Did you manage to get her to see it then?' she asked.

'Sort of,' said Dawn, thoughts and memories bombarding her head. *I must have misheard. She called me Dee Dee?* 'She told me that she wanted me to be happy.'

'She didn't speak, surely?' said the woman with a gently disbelieving tone. 'She hasn't spoken for a while now.'

'It was the oddest thing . . . she called me Dee Dee' – *Mum and Dad used to call me Dee Dee* – 'Then she gripped my hand . . .'

Dawn's voice faded away. It was obvious the woman thought she was nuts.

'Well, if she did, then that's lovely,' she said sympathetically though. Some people saw what they wanted to, she had seen that so much, in this place especially.

Dawn cleared her coffee in two gulps. It was luke-warm from the amount of milk in it. She laid a soft kiss on Aunt Charlotte's cheek. Her breath was so shallow in her barely rising chest as she slept that Dawn wondered if she would see the old lady alive again. She was so glad she had come as promised, but what Charlotte had said made her feel so shaky she had to fill up her lungs a few times with fresh air before she dared to start driving home. How she wished she could have seen that photograph as Charlotte had seen it! *And Dee Dee? How very strange.*

Chapter 70

'So, any more presents left on your doorstep then?' Christie greeted Anna first thing on Monday morning.

'A thong,' replied Anna flatly.

'What is that man up to?' said Grace. Relationships! Did anyone have a happy story to tell, apart from young Raychel who was obviously love's young dream with Ben.

'What does he mean by leaving you a thong?' asked Raychel.

'Fuck knows,' said Anna. 'Can't understand why anyone would wear a thong like that anyway. It covers nothing.'

'I think that's the idea,' smiled Christie. 'How overtly sexual!'

'What do you reckon he'll leave next week?' asked Dawn. 'Himself maybe? Naked on the doormat?'

'Don't know,' said Anna. 'He's obviously still with scrawny arse, but if he *does* turn up next weekend in person he'll find I'm too busy to be impressed.'

'Why's that then?' asked Grace.

'Well,' began Anna, 'if I haven't fled the country because the show is being broadcast on Thursday, I'll be at Vladimir Darq's house at a Full Moon Ball. Beat that for an action-packed rollercoaster of a week.' Then she filled them in on the dress he had made for her.

'Wow!' said Dawn. 'Imagine getting that sort of attention from a man.'

'Why do you get that sort of attention from a man when you aren't going out with him and will never see him again after next weekend, but get bugger all from one you're supposed to be living with? How does that work out?' Anna grumbled.

'Because you're with the wrong man, that's why,' said Christie. 'My husband treated me like a queen. I felt blessed every day that I had him.'

Is that how I'll feel about Calum one day? thought Dawn. *Can I really see my eyes mist over like that for him?* She knew the answer already, otherwise why was she carrying that scrap of paper with a guitarist's telephone number around with her wherever she went? She volunteered to go for the coffees before her head bombarded her with any more questions and drove her potty.

That afternoon, Christie sat in a meeting with the heads of department. James McAskill was present and picked his seat next to Christie. Across the table, Malcolm noted how his eyes lit up when he talked to her. He saw Christie's hand touch his as she spoke privately to him before the meeting started. And when it did commence, he listened to James McAskill telling them all how proud he was of his flagship scheme and how well it was doing under the jurisdiction of Mrs Somers. He listened to Christie's presentation on how the scheme was growing as she cited examples of some of the most useful ideas that she had received – one in particular about a new programme to process sales figures which a manager from the Rothwell branch had devised himself. She impressed everyone with her delivery and enthusiasm. Then it was Malcolm's turn to deliver a limp speech about the state of Cheese, trying to smooth over the disappointing figures and doing his best to ignore a few barely-covered yawns. Then he had to withstand being questioned aggressively by McAskill while he stumbled and bluffed by way of answer. McAskill made him look a fool. Everyone around that table seemed to be delighted that he was getting a well overdue bollocking. He hated McAskill. He hated *her.* If they weren't having an affair, then he was Tom Cruise. Maybe it was time that *Mrs* McAskill knew what was going on behind her back. He'd blow the pair of bastards out of the water and see if they were so touchy-feely with each other then!

Chapter 71

The next day at home-time, just as Anna logged off, a thought crossed her mind and jetted from her mouth with the speed – and volume – of Concorde.

'Shite, I've no shoes!'

'Are you aware you said that out loud?' said Dawn.

'I've no shoes for Saturday! I've got the frock but no shoes! Oh God! How could I forget I need to buy shoes?'

'What size are you?' asked Christie.

'Five. Oh flaming hell! Where am I going to get shoes to match? It's a dark blue dress! I've only got black high heels!'

'No one will see them, surely, if it's a long dress?' said Raychel.

'There will be all sorts of posh people going, there's bound to be. They'll notice. Vladimir will notice. I'll notice! You can't imagine how gorgeous that dress is, so I don't want to wear shoes that don't match. I want to feel fab from the feet up and I *don't* want to let him down! Oh hell fire! I'll have to go to Meadowhall but I know I won't find anything because you never do when you're desperate!'

Christie, calm as a cucumber, fished her keys out of her handbag.

'I'm a size five too. Why don't you come to my house and I'll fix you up. I've got every colour of shoe known to man. In fact . . .' She thought for a moment, then nodded at herself. 'Yes, in fact why don't we all have a nice girly evening at mine. We can watch the show with you, Anna.'

'Ooh, that sounds lovely,' said Raychel, looking forward to it already.

'I'm not sure I dare watch it with anyone I know.' Anna covered her face up with her hands and muttered a series of expletives to herself.

'Don't be so silly.' Grace gave her a playful slap on the arm. 'We can't wait to see it.'

'I'd better go to Meadowhall straight from work,' sighed Anna. 'Thanks for the shoe offer, Christie, but I can't risk leaving it to chance.'

'You worry too much,' replied Christie.

'Oh God, I'm stuffed, I know I am!' groaned Anna.

'Think of me as your fairy godmother,' smiled Christie. 'Trust me.'

Raychel opened the door to Elizabeth, John and Ellis and warmly invited them in. Ben had so taken to the little boy, he was wonderful with children. Raychel loved being called 'Auntie Ray.' She tried not to think that she would never have children of her own.

'I'm just warning you, you may get another letter from your mother,' said Elizabeth, stepping into the kitchen behind Raychel, leaving Ben already crawling on the floor making neighing noises with Ellis perched on his back. 'It's fine, it's nothing to worry about,' Elizabeth reassured her. 'I wrote her a letter. I wrote it as if it had come from you. I asked if I – *you* – could come and visit her next Sunday at twelve. That's all I wrote and signed it *Lorraine*. If a reply comes, give it straight to me.'

'Thank you,' was all Raychel said, and all she needed to say.

*

Mr Williamson, Anna's neighbour with the yellowy cataracts, delivered a parcel for her five minutes after she had got back from Meadowhall. As she suspected would happen, she had walked the length and breadth of the Mall and found bugger all in *any* shade of blue. It was the 'out' colour, it seemed. Until designers like Vladimir Darq made it the new black.

'A gentleman dropped it off earlier on,' he said. 'I said I'd give it to you.'

Tony? Anna presumed it was another of his gestures which, frankly, were becoming annoying. But as soon as Mr Williamson produced it from his old-man shopping bag, she knew it couldn't possibly be from anyone else but Vladimir Darq. Wrapped exquisitely in silver tissue paper was the most beautiful boned corset in the same blue as her dress, plus matching pants and the sheerest blue stockings. The corset was encrusted with tiny blue beads, each one hand-stitched on. Why had he gone to that amount of trouble when no one would see it? More work had gone into that corset than the dress – and a *lot* of work had gone into the dress. Her heart began to thump in a way that it hadn't done for Tony's rose, or his plate or his Ferrero Rochers.

Chapter 72

Malcolm had been buzzing all week with vicious anticipation and was finding it very difficult to keep a lid on it. It wasn't until Thursday morning though that the dish which he had started to cook, with his anonymous letter to Diana McAskill, looked set to reach boiling point. He could barely breathe for excitement when he saw the stately, elegant figure of the boss's wife marching down the office past his desk and making a bee-line for where that bitch Christie Somers was sitting. He watched as Christie raised her eyes to see the woman she was so obviously cuckolding and he waited for Diana McAskill to slap the sanctimonious smile off her face. But, alas, that didn't happen. Diana merely dipped her head and said something to Christie, who then rose to her feet and followed Mrs McAskill silently into one of the meeting rooms. Then again, he considered, Diana Mac was too classy for a cat-fight. She would verbally slaughter Somers in private.

He gave it a few minutes before he grabbed a clutch of papers and wandered purposefully down the office, pretending to look for Christie. What he saw through the glass of the meeting-room window was disappointing, to say the least. Diana McAskill was visibly distressed and Christie was comforting her. He cheered up though when the thought visited him that Christie might be confessing the affair she was having with Big McAskill and that was why his poor wife was crying.

'Can I help you?' said Grace, pulling his attention away from the activities behind the glass.

'Oh, er, I just came to deliver this to Christie.'

'I can see that she gets it,' said Grace, her hands coming out for it. Malcolm tightened his grip on the papers. He hadn't even a clue what he had picked up.

'Oh, it's fine, I'll come back later.'

He stole a last sneaky look. Christie was handing Mrs McAskill a handkerchief. He couldn't wait to see the fallout from this one. He could barely sit still at his desk for itching to find out what was going on.

But ten minutes later, Mrs McAskill, restored to her composed, serene self, walked past his desk with Christie. There was no hostility between them; in fact they were chatting softly, if seriously, to each other as they made their way to the lift.

Of course it was an act. There was only one reason why Diana Mac could have been crying and that was because she had found out that her husband was poking a mistress under her nose. Somers was just being a hard-faced cow, enjoying her last moments of composure before her dirty secret leaked out like pus.

Malcolm was so deep in smiling contemplation as he envisaged the gossip machine cranking up and spreading the muck like shit on a field that he never saw Christie's approach until she had leaned right over his desk and stuck her face too far into his personal space for comfort.

'Apparently you were looking for me to give me some papers,' she said tartly.

'Oh . . . er . . . it's all right, I don't need to see you about it any more,' he said, caught on the back foot.

Christie didn't move. She continued to lean dominantly over him and then a grim smile spread across her lips.

'Now, I can't prove that you're the phantom letter writer,' she began slowly with menace, 'but we both know you are. We *all* know you are.'

Deny, deny, deny, thought Malcolm. *She can't prove a thing.* But it perturbed him that he could be so easily highlighted as the instigator, and more so, that she would say something to McAskill on those lines. *But she doesn't* know, *she only suspects.*

'I don't know what you're talking—'

'Oh, cut the crap, Malcolm,' snarled Christie. 'You have *so* crossed the line this time. You have no idea what you've done.'

'I haven't done anything,' said Malcolm, coughing away the belying tremor in his voice, but she had started walking away from him on the second word. Her unshaken demeanour was in stark contrast to his. He felt sure they could hear his palpitations down in the London regional office.

'What the heck was all that about?' said Dawn. 'Are you all right, Christie?'

'I'm perfectly fine,' said Christie with stiff control. 'But it seems that Diana McAskill has received an anonymous letter alleging that I'm having an affair with her husband.'

'Malcolm?' said Grace.

'Funny how everyone jumps to his name first, isn't it?' said Christie. 'His body language was screaming to me that he was involved. All the signs were there and there were many of them. God, I'd love to hook him up to a polygraph.'

'He came down for a nosey when you were both in the office,' said Dawn. 'His eyes were out on stalks to see what was going on.'

'Why would he do such a horrible thing?' said Raychel.

'Because he's Malcolm and an arsehole?' suggested Anna.

It was a reason that no one disputed, although only Christie knew just how much of an arsehole he had been on this occasion. He had as good as signed his own death warrant by putting that letter in the post to Diana.

Chapter 73

'You've got a gorgeous house, Christie,' said Dawn that evening as she spooned the last of her pasta into her mouth. 'I don't mean to be nosey and look around as much as I am doing, but I can't keep my eyes off your things.'

'Dad was lucky that the previous owners didn't rip all the original cornices and ceiling roses out. So many old houses lost their original features through the fads of the day.'

'You lived here long then?'

'Most of my life,' said Christie. 'Niki and I grew up here. Of course, I moved out when I got married, only to move back in when I was widowed.'

'It's nice you get on so well with your brother,' said Anna. 'My sister's nuts. I don't feel connected with her in any way at all. She thinks hedgehogs are gods and smokes "herbs".'

'Niki gets on with everyone,' said Christie fondly. 'He's the most laidback, patient man I've ever known. He even put my husband to shame and Peter was calm as a mill pond.'

'He can't half cook as well!' said Anna, eyeing up his culinary contribution to the evening which sat in a big bowl waiting to be served up. He had made them all a 'Bad Girl's Trifle' for dessert. It was very boozy, very chocolatey and very full of calories.

'Shall we have coffee in a little while? After I've sorted Anna out?' Christie suggested with a twinkly smile. 'She's looking jumpy. She doesn't trust my claims that I can complete her outfit.'

'I've tried Barnsley and the whole of Meadowhall and I still can't find a single pair to match, can you believe?' Anna huffed.

'Come on, o ye of little faith,' Christie said, rising from her chair and heading off upstairs.

Anna followed quickly. She was desperate to see what Christie had for her, although she doubted they would find a match. Anna just wasn't that lucky.

The others came up behind, after Christie beckoned them, and went into Christie's bedroom which was like a miniature country house room with its oak panels on the wall and a large, heavy four-poster with velvet drapes tied at the corners. Christie went over to a door at the side of a huge wardrobe and pulled it open to reveal another cavernous room filled with banks of clothes – modern and vintage – in every colour of the rainbow and then some more. There were cabinets full of bags and purses, pashminas and stoles, and racks and racks of shoes.

'Chuffing hell, where's Mr Benn?' said Anna.

Christie laughed. 'I've always loved clothes. I inherited quite a few from an aunt of mine who had a shop. I've been collecting the rest of them for years.'

'Good grief,' said Grace, looking at a shimmering silver evening dress behind glass. 'Do you wear any of them?'

'I used to,' said Christie. 'When Peter was alive. We went to a lot of parties and did a lot of cruising around the world. Something I intend to start doing again when I'm ready.' *When I'm ready?* wondered Grace. What a great hole Peter Somers must have left, for her to take so long to recover.

'Good God, I don't believe it!' said Anna, honing in on a pair of long, slim blue shoes from a rack with at least twelve other pairs in dark blue. 'They can't be the same colour, that would just be too spooky.' She pulled out a small square of material that Vladimir had included with the dress, presumably for the purpose of accessorizing, and placed it against the shoe.

'It's a match. I don't believe it!'

'It's not quite,' said Christie. 'But you'd need to be lit with a thousand-watt bulb to notice the subtle difference.'

'That was just too easy to be true. Pinch me, Raychel,' said Anna, still shaking her head. She let loose a near-hysterical laugh. 'You're magic, Christie Somers. Pure bloody magic.'

'But do they fit?' asked Christie.

'Who gives a fart!' said Anna. 'I'll either cut my toes off or bung bog paper in the bottom. They'll fit.'

'Try one on,' said Raychel, who was holding her breath more than Anna.

Anna threw off her shoe and put the blue stiletto on. It slipped beautifully onto her foot.

'No, that just cannot be,' Anna gasped. 'Can I borrow them, Christie?'

'Say no, Christie. That would be really funny,' giggled Dawn.

'Of course you can borrow them, silly. There's a bag to match somewhere. I never bought shoes without getting hold of the bag to match. Ah, here it is.'

'Here's another!' said Raychel, finding a second in that shade buried deep on one of many shelves full of purses and folded wraps. It was, like the shoes, darkest blue, jewelled with blue sparkling stones studded along the heavy clasp. It was slightly dusty, so she rubbed it against her knee.

Anna's hands greedily came out for it. She held it reverently, then thumbed open the clasp. 'Christie, are you sure? It's never been used. Look, there's the price label still on. Oh no, hang on, it's not the price – it says—' Her voice cut off.

Christie reached slowly for the bag and read the handwritten label.

For you, my darling girl.

'Christie, are you all right?' said Grace, seeing the lightning change on her features.

'Yes, I—' Christie crumbled against the wall behind her and Grace leaped forward.

'Good grief, love, what is it?'

'Nothing, I'm fine.'

'You're not!' said Anna, coming to the other side of her for support. 'Dawn, get that chair!'

Dawn pushed the chair behind Christie only a split second before she fell backwards onto it. She struggled for composure, looking blankly up at the four women who were watching her with concerned confusion, and then she burst into tears.

They closed around her like flower petals protecting their precious centre. Then Anna ran to Christie's en-suite and grabbed enough toilet roll to satisfy a pack of Labrador puppies with a tissue fetish; Raychel raced to get a glass of water; Dawn hunted down a flannel to soak with warm water – she didn't know why. Grace remained with her arms around the woman who had given her comfort in the same way through her recent dark times, as Christie sobbed into her shoulder. Then, like a summer shower darkens a blue sky and ceases as quickly as it started, Christie recovered. She raised her head to see these four dear women she had become so fond of in such a short time.

'Forgive me,' said Christie. 'He used to give me so many presents. I'm sorry, it was the shock of it after all this time. I never knew he'd bought that for me. I've never seen it before.'

'What a lovely thing to do,' Dawn said softly. 'He sounds a really great bloke.'

'I miss him so much. It's taken me years to move on just a few steps. I will never find another man like him. Even though a lot of people think that James McAskill is warming my bed.'

'Then they're stupid,' said Dawn decisively. 'None of us think that.' She knew she spoke for them all. 'Although it's obvious he likes you. That's what people are picking up on and twisting.'

'James McAskill and I go back forty years. He was the proverbial boy next door,' began Christie, pointing left. 'I never met people as cold as his parents were: so negative, so critical. If he got an A at school, they'd ask him why he didn't get an A plus. He used to play with Niki and myself when we were small. He found a lot of love and warmth with my family in this house. He was, is and always will be, one of my dearest friends. He *and* Diana, of course, who I love as a sister. The truth is as simple as that. They are the most wonderful people. When Peter died, it was James and Diana – and Niki, of course – who stopped me following him. But I want you to know that it's only since I started working with you all that I've truly felt part of the real world again.'

Grace looked around her at all these hundreds of clothes. She wondered if Christie Somers hoped to block up the holes of loss inside her with shopping expeditions. This amount of clothes and accessories seemed less like a hobby and more like an obsession.

'I know what you're thinking, Grace. Yes, I was almost mad with grief. Looking at this room, I don't think I entirely escaped.'

'I don't think you're mad at all,' said Raychel. She sounded wise beyond her years as she went on, 'You do what you have to do to stay strong and go on.'

Christie nodded slowly in agreement. 'I'd always hoped Peter would send me a sign to say he was OK, but it never happened. I was convinced it would, to give me some hope that his spirit had moved on. That would have helped.'

'I know. I felt the same. But I believe life goes on. I—' began Dawn, then she cut off.

'Go on, love, you were saying?' said Christie.

Dawn wondered if she should shrug it off and not continue.

Then she looked at the four women around her and knew that what she was about to tell them wouldn't be ridiculed or dissed. However clumsily she explained it.

'I didn't tell you all this 'cos you'd think I was even more doolally than usual,' Dawn began. 'But when I went to see Calum's Auntie Charlotte in the old people's home, she suddenly grabbed my hand and said, "We want you to be happy, Dee Dee," and it didn't sound like her voice at all. And it knocked me for six because, you see . . . you see, my mum and dad always used to call me Dee Dee. It was their pet name for me. I know it sounds crackers, but it was like they were sending me a message. I can't explain it, but I *knew* it was them.'

'That must have been so comforting,' Christie said with a lovely wide arc of a smile.

Dawn nodded, even though she didn't tell them that the voice that came out of Aunt Charlotte also said, *What are you doing?*

'I've never believed that death was the end of everything. I don't have proof. I just believe it. I believe my mum and dad got their ranch in heaven and Dad is playing his Strat and Mum's got her piano and one day I'll be there with them both again.' Dawn poked the tears back into her eyes. 'Maybe finding that bag is the sign you've been waiting for, Christie.'

'You're all lovely,' said Christie. 'Thank you for being so kind. The bond I have with the McAskills is unbreakable and precious. That's why the likes of Malcolm Spatchcock can't even put a dent in it. What he did to try and sully our relationship was unforgivable.'

'Orange-faced bastard,' snarled Anna.

'Diana never believed it for a moment, of course. She came to warn me there was tittle-tattle. She thought if the gossips saw us together, united, it would put a sudden stop to it. But of course there is no real proof it was Malcolm who sent the letter so James can't sack him for hearsay. He's far too fair a man for that.'

'He'll get his comeuppance, I bet,' said Dawn.

'Alas, life doesn't work like that,' said Grace. 'If only it did.'

Christie made a huge cafetière of coffee and all five women sat in her lounge, marking off the seconds to the programme starting. Anna was clutching a bag with the purse and shoes in it as if it would give her some support.

'Nervous?' asked Dawn.

'I should be sitting on a commode, not a sofa,' replied Anna, as a commercial came on saying that, '*Jane's Dames* was sponsored by Treffé chocolates.'

Dawn grabbed Anna's right hand, Grace her left one as she screamed, 'Oh my GOD!'

'*Hi, I'm Jane Cleve-Jones with* Jane's Dames *and tonight I'm going to sunny Barnsley in South Yorkshire to meet forty-year-old Bakery Administrator, Anna Brightside, who thinks her reflection is an enemy. We've got five weeks to locate her inner Mojo and capture it in photographic form to prove to her it exists!*'

A picture of a smiling Anna in her frumpy, comfy, round-necked jersey jumped out of the screen. That was *so* going in the bin when she got home.

'*Anna isn't just forty — she's a string of other F-words too because she's feeling fat, frumpy and forgotten. Can international designer of underwear, Vladimir Darq, make our Anna feel flighty, fabulous and fantastic instead?*'

'I can't look!' screamed Anna.

'Yes, you can; open your eyes, you big coward!' Grace demanded.

'Oh my Lord, I didn't realize I was being filmed then!' Anna would have covered up her eyes but her hands were being too tightly held, for there she was sitting in a robe talking to Jane while Maria was taking all her make-up off. She had thought they were off-camera!

'*When my partner left me, I just fell to bits. I feel so old and blobby and I can't find the energy to do anything about it. Sorry.*' And then Anna burst into tears on screen. She felt her hands being sympathetically squeezed by her co-workers.

Then it switched to a mini-biography of Vladimir and a very moody shot of him in his house, surrounded by his underwear collection.

'*Anna is a classic case of a damsel in distress and I am here to rescue her and women all around like her. When will women learn they should be at their most confident and beautiful at forty? They hide themselves away in stupid clothes and the ultimate in fashion disasters – minimizer bras! But with the right underwear on, a woman can be amazing!*'

There flashed an image of Anna on screen in the red velvet dress.

'Wow!' came a chorus from either side of her.

'*But first, let's see what Anna finds so bad about herself.*'

'Aargh!' Anna shrieked as she watched herself strip down to her undies and stand in front of the mirror and go through a list that her boobs were too wide, stomach not flat enough, hips too big, legs not long enough, blah–di–blah . . .

'Are you looking at a different body to the rest of us?' Christie tutted.

Anna studied herself and surprisingly, even though the camera was supposed to add half a stone, she didn't look quite as bad as she thought she would. Give or take the awful underwear which, on screen, Vladimir was ripping to bits (not literally – alas, she thought).

'*This bra is too tight and not supportive at all.*'

'*It's comfortable,*' Anna retorted.

'*How can it be?*' replied Vladimir sternly. '*It's gouging grooves into your shoulders. And these pants!* La Naiba! *Take these off and throw them away! Good underwear can do more for a figure than extreme surgery.'*

Then there was Anna clad in some of her awful clothes in her bedroom and Vladimir Darq's voice-over.

'Anna is a beautiful, sensuous woman and I wish she could see herself through my eyes.'

Four sets of eyebrows raised in Anna's direction.

'Women with no self-worth are too concerned with what other people think about them. I want Anna to feel sexy because she is sexy. Look at her beautiful clear skin, her eyes, her hair, her cheekbones, her fantastic breasts – and all she can see is her stomach. She thinks all she is is one big stomach – ach!'

Just before it cut to a break, it showed Vladimir trying to get Anna to stand up straight. He was barking at her in Romanian. Every time he let her go, she was slouching back. He looked as if he was going to smash his head against the wall in frustration.

Then the adverts came on. Christie put a brandy in Anna's shaking hands when Grace and Dawn released their grip.

'Thank you, I need this,' she said, taking a gulp and feeling the burn at the back of her throat.

'I don't know why, you look fab even in awful underwear and no make-up on,' said Dawn. 'I'd ditch the wardrobe though. Can't wait to see you in that red dress again.'

'That's nothing to the blue one he's made me.' Anna threw the last of the brandy down her throat. 'How the heck I'll have my hands steady enough to do my own make-up on Saturday is anyone's guess.'

'Shhh, it's back on!' Dawn settled back on the big squashy cushions. She was loving this.

'What Anna doesn't know is that we projected a sixty-foot picture of her onto a building in Leeds and asked the locals what they thought about our girl.'

'Look at that bloke walking towards the camera – it looks like Gok Wan,' Raychel pointed.

'*And, surprise surprise, a certain gentleman filming up the road here just happens to be passing.*'

'Bloody hell, it *is* Gok Wan!' gasped Anna. They'd kept that one quiet!

'*So, Gok, what do you think about our lovely Yorkshire rose?*'

'*She is fan-tas-tic – look at that womanly figure and that hair! I have to say, Vladimir Darq is one of my favourite ever designers and, if anyone, he's the man to make that gorgeous girl feel like the gorgeous girl she is.*'

Anna was in raptures as Gok Wan blew her a kiss from the TV screen.

Then Anna was back in Vladimir's house and he was trying to do up a front-fastening corset. Anna tried to take over and he slapped her hand away.

'You look like an old married couple,' sniggered Dawn.

I wish, thought Anna. She wondered what being wed to someone such as Vladimir Darq would be like. How did celebs like him spend their days? Did they do ironing and watch *Coronation Street* and eat Penguins like ordinary people? Or was it just all hopping from New York Fashion Week to the Venice Film Festival, after refreshment at Caffe Florian? Not a life she could ever imagine fitting into. Not that someone like Vladimir Darq would ever seriously look at someone like her *in that way*.

'*Anna's friends, Christie, Grace, Dawn and Raychel are also hoping Vladimir can work his magic.*'

Anna froze. There on the TV screen were her co-workers.

'*Anna is totally blind to how lovely she is,*' Christie was saying. '*She's a gorgeous woman who is not making the best of herself.*'

'*We think Anna is brill and we want to see her confidence levels running on full,*' Raychel nodded at the camera.

'*She needs to realize that she is only forty years old – she's still a baby!*' smiled Grace.

'When the bloody hell did that happen?' Anna's jaw had dropped past sea level.

'Ooh, one day after work,' Christie beamed.

'While I was looking for Boots magazines, by any chance?'

'Possibly,' winked Christie.

Vladimir was now standing with Anna, who was dressed in 'The Darqone'. The screen was split, showing her both in that and in her old rubbishy undies. Then she was wearing a simple V-neck T-shirt above the good and bad sets of underwear.

'*Quite a difference.*'

Vladimir and Jane were now discussing the availability and price points of his designs whilst Maria was expertly dabbing at Anna's face.

'Who's that? She looks scary.' Raychel pointed to the little snow-haired woman with the angry expression.

'Maria, the Romanian make-up lady. She is absolutely terrifying, but Vlad swears by her. He insisted the programme makers use her rather than their own people.'

Then Anna was having her hair done and Vlad suddenly poked Anna in the shoulder, telling her not to go to sleep. Dawn giggled.

'This is so funny, Anna. Wonder if your Tony's watching?'

Christie elbowed her sharply.

Then Anna was standing, hand on hip, in the most beautiful red corset and stockings. The picture segued into one of her in the red gown looking like a 1950s starlet with that most amazing hourglass figure. Leonid was snapping madly at her and Anna Brightside was beaming from the inside out.

'Oh wow, Anna!' Raychel clasped her hands together as if in prayer. 'You look amazing.'

Anna didn't say anything. Vladimir had not let her see herself. She hadn't had a clue she looked like that. It wasn't her, it couldn't be her. That woman was sex on legs. That woman *was someone to sew hundreds of tiny beads onto a blue corset for.*

'*Darq Side Lingerie will be available in the High Street from the nineteenth of June. Finally, Vladimir, do you have anything to say to Anna and the self-proclaimed "forgotten women" out there?*'

Vladimir Darq smiled at the camera, the tiniest hint of fangs showing.

'*There are no forgotten women out there because Vladimir Darq has remembered you. And, Anna, I hope you are sitting with friends and a glass of sanguine wine and saying to yourself, "Darq was right, I am sexy after all".*'

Cue the music.

Anna let out a big breath. It felt like the first time she had breathed since the programme began.

'That was so brilliant, lady!' Christie gave her a big hug.

'I can't believe you did that behind my back!' said Anna. She was genuinely moved. Were they really that fond of her? Her eyes felt suddenly watery but Dawn made her laugh on cue.

'I said loads,' said Dawn. 'I expect they cut all my bits out though!'

'Wonder why!' Christie nudged her again, affectionately this time.

'Dare I venture out tomorrow?' asked Anna, accepting the offer of a nightcap coffee with a nip of brandy in it.

'With your head held high, *girlfriend*,' grinned Christie.

Chapter 74

The next morning Anna walked onto the train station platform and felt as if she had been rubbed over by a fluorescent high-lighter. Was it always so busy? Did that fellow commuter with the big boobs and the black coat really take a long second look at her? She felt her cheeks flaring with colour. Trust the damn train to be late. Should she put on the big Jackie O sunglasses she'd brought with her in order to remain anonymous or would that just draw more attention her way?

She picked up a free *Metro* newspaper, opened it and pushed her face into it.

'Excuse me,' asked Black Coat. 'Were you on *Jane's Dames* last night?'

She could have said it a bit more quietly, thought Anna. A few people turned to take in a prolonged glance or twelve.

'Er . . . yep, that was me,' smiled Anna bashfully.

Black Coat's mouth stretched into a wide smile. 'I thought it was you. I recognized you straight away. I just want to say, I thought you were marvellous. I'm going out at lunchtime to buy one of those Darq bodyshapers. You really sold it to me.'

'Thank you. Thank you so much,' said a stunned Anna. She felt a couple of people staring but Anna Brightside fought the old urge to curve into herself. She imagined Vladimir Darq behind her, pushing her shoulders out. She stuck out her chest, lifted her chin and smiled.

'So, are you looking forward to your hen night then?' asked Raychel later in the Rising Sun, although it was perfectly obvious that Dawn wasn't from the look of horror on her face after being reminded what was happening the following night.

So no one quite believed her when she said, 'Yes, I've come around to the idea now. It will be fun.'

'Where are you going for it again?'

'Blegthorpe-on-Sea. Have you ever been?'

No one had except Grace. She shook her head along with everyone else though. It would have been very hard to try and convince Dawn she was going to have a marvellous night in that godforsaken hole.

'I see Mr Guitarist is staring over a lot, as usual,' Christie noted, pouring out the wine.

Dawn felt herself colouring.

'We're just friends.'

'Yeah, and I'm Basil Brush,' said Anna. 'Are you going to snog him before he goes home?'

'Anna!' said Dawn, with virginal affront. 'I didn't think you'd be saying anything like that!'

Neither did Anna, but she was in less of a position to get on her soapbox these days with a head split between a possibly returning boyfriend and a possibly vampiric underwear designer who was giving her erotic dreams. She worried about Dawn. It couldn't be more obvious to her that Calum wasn't her Mr Right. Some days, when Dawn came into work, she looked as if she had the weight of the world on her shoulders, not at all like an excited bride-to-be should behave. But come Friday she was a different person, badgering them out of the door in the direction of the pub with a smile on her face. And it wasn't because she was dying of thirst for a Shiraz.

'Dawn, the sexual tension between you two couldn't be cut with a Texas Chainsaw,' said Christie. 'We've all seen it building for weeks. You staring at him, him staring at you. What's going on with you both?'

'Nothing. Honest. I couldn't,' Dawn shrugged. 'It wouldn't be right however much—' She cut off. She sounded so sad that no one jumped in to tease her about the unfinished sentence.

'Ben's a lovely kisser,' put in Raychel at last.

'I haven't been kissed in a long time,' said Grace with a gentle laugh.

'Maybe it's about time you were then?' said Christie, her eyes mischievously widening. Grace narrowed her eyes at her friend and shook her head in exasperation.

Anna exhaled loudly. 'It's supposed to be very nice and romantic, but I've never really thought it was all that wonderful a thing to do – snog. Tony isn't a snogger.' He might have used a snog as an introduction to open proceedings but after that he wasn't interested.

'Well, I'm a big believer in a kiss being able to tell you more than anything,' said Christie. 'You'- she turned to Anna – 'have obviously been kissing the wrong men. And you' – she pointed a finger at Dawn – 'you need to listen to what your heart is telling you. That's all I shall say on the subject.'

After the others had gone, Dawn waited at the bar, watching the band. Al Holly raised his head and smiled at her and it was as if the sun had shone his full beam on her and almost melted her to the ground. She thought of Al Holly's lips pressing down onto hers and, wrong as it was, she didn't fight the fantasy. What was that Christie said about listening to her heart? She couldn't help but listen to it, because it was shouting at her and scaring her.

He made his usual bee-line over to her when they had finished.

'Howdy,' he said.

'Hello there, pardner,' said Dawn. *He will be gone next week. You will be Calum's 'pardner', the respectable Mrs Crooke, and there will be another band on this stage.* The words hit her hard from left field.

'Have you had a good week then?' he asked.

'Yes, it was OK. What about you?'

'I was wondering if you would ring me.'

'And say what?'

'"Hello," maybe.' His eyes were bright and soft greeny-brown. They were looking at her as if they liked what they saw so much. It was almost painful to meet them.

'It wouldn't be right, would it? Me phoning you when . . .' *I'm getting married to someone else next week.* She didn't want to say the words.

'Dawny, can you come with me for a moment? There's something I need to show you,' he said, suddenly urgent.

' 'Course,' said Dawn, following him as he marched purposefully through the standing drinkers and out of the door. She could barely keep up, his stride was so long. He beckoned her on behind his shoulder as he strode down the beer garden, past the benches filled with groups and couples and on to where the lighting stopped and the grass began to slope down to the wood behind the pub.

'Look!' he said.

'What?' said Dawn, seeing nothing but a load of trees and a grass bank.

'The moon,' he said.

Dawn looked up. She knew it was one day off being full because Anna was going to the Full Moon Ball tomorrow, but it looked as near full as damn it. It was huge, like a perfect hole in the sky, a portal to another world where things were brilliantly lit and clear and uncomplicated. But there were big moons every month and Al was acting like he'd been in a cupboard for thirty-odd years and had never seen one before.

'It's lovely,' she said, feeling the need to say something because he was looking so expectantly at her. 'You like moons, I presume?'

'Dawny.' He seemed to be having some internal battle with himself from the way he was shaking his head and puffing the air out of his cheeks as if he was in labour. Then he steeled himself and plunged headfirst into an obviously unprepared speech.

'I shouldn't do this, I know. I didn't bring you out here to see the moon. I brought you out here to kiss you underneath it. Just once. '

Flaming heck! 'Oh, did you?'

'Yes I did, ma'am,' said Al Holly, and though every nerve in Dawn Sole's body was telling her to back up because she was in danger of having portals opened inside her that made the moon look like a pinprick, she stood unmoving and let Al Holly slide his arms around her, tilt her head back and slowly, slowly press his sweet lips against her own. And it was every bit as good as the fantasy.

When he stopped for breath, she came up for air with every intention of pushing him away, but instead she filled her lungs up with oxygen and let him do it again. His body was so warm and strong against her, his arms tight about her but gentle as if he were holding something precious and delicate. She drank in the smell of him, spicy aftershave and skin and a hint of peppermint. And when the kiss came to a soft end, the words that came from his mouth made her gulp more than a salmon which had just jumped from a river onto a dry concrete block.

'Dawny Sole, you and I both know that you shouldn't be marrying anyone but me.'

'Don't say that.'

'But I am saying it.' Al's tender hands came up to her face and forced her to look at him. 'I can't get you out of my mind.

The week just can't pass fast enough until I see you again. I want to take you home with me and love you.'

'Al—'

'I wanted to kiss you once to see if you felt the same, and you do. I know you do.'

Dawn's knees were in danger of folding beneath her.

'Al, I think you're wonderful, truly I do,' she began, having to throttle back hard on the words that could have so easily pumped out from her vocal cords: *I love you too, I've tried so hard not to, but I do . . .* 'But let's not get carried away. This is like a holiday romance for you. You'll have forgotten me as soon as you get to the airport—'

'The hell I will!'

'Please.' She placed her finger on his lips. God, they were flushed with blood. 'We barely know each other.'

'Then come with me and let me find out all about you.'

'I can't give up everything I have,' said Dawn.

'What do you have? You're marrying a man you don't love, who doesn't like your music, who doesn't put a smile on your face, and all because you want to belong to a family. I know you an awful lot better than you think I do, Dawny Sole. You're filling up my heart, girl. I've never felt like this about anyone. It's knocked me off my feet and I've tried to ignore it but I can't and I don't want to.'

Dawn's breath snagged in her throat. *I do love Calum.* She had been saying it to herself like a mantra these past few weeks. She felt she had to.

Al Holly put his strong hands on Dawn's shoulders and squared her in front of him.

'You don't think you're anything special, do you?' he said. 'I see it in your eyes. You think you're not capable of making someone feel so strongly about you.'

'I'm not special at all,' said Dawn. 'I open my mouth in all the wrong places, I don't stand up for myself, I don't know any general knowledge . . .' *Dawn Sole, your wheel is still spinning, but alas the hamster has died* . . . She thought of the unforgotten words a teacher once said to her at school.

'Bet your mom and dad thought you were special.'

'Yeah, well, they aren't here any more, are they?' said Dawn with a shrug of bravado.

'Wherever they are, they want you to be happy.'

He was too close to the truth for comfort. Again.

'Don't say any more, please.' She was hurting, but her feet were rooted to the spot and wouldn't move.

'One final thing, then I'll go,' he said. 'You think on what I've said. And let me tell you that you *are* one special woman. You are beautiful and you're funny and you have the voice of one smokin' angel. And I've been fighting against this but I can't do it any more without telling you what my heart is crying out for me to say. I want you, Dawny Sole, more than I've ever wanted anyone in my life.'

Dawn tore her eyes away from him. If only she was free, things would be so different. But she wasn't. This was so wrong. *But why does his body feel so right against me?*

Al stepped back. His hands left her shoulders.

'You have seven and a half days until I leave for London. You have seven and a half days to pack your suitcase, grab your guitar and come with me to live a life you know you want. Hell, it won't be a life of luxury, but you'll be singing and you'll be happy and you'll be loved more than you ever would be if you stayed.'

'Al—'

'Seven and a half days,' he cut in. 'I've said all I should say. It's not what I do, Dawny. I'm a decent man but I'm in love with you and if you don't come, then that will be my punishment for moving in on another man's woman.'

Then he leaned in and kissed her full on the mouth under the big moon, and afterwards Big Al Holly walked away, leaving Dawn trembling like a leaf in a tornado.

Chapter 75

Anna was woken up at seven thirty the next morning by a big leather-clad bloke on a motorbike. A courier, who had a small square package for her. She knew this one wasn't from Tony because it had the Corona Productions logo on the top. Intrigued, she opened it hurriedly to find a disk case and a folded-up note.

Dear Anna, Here are some out-takes especially for you. Enjoy!
With love, Jane, Bruce, Flip, Chas and Mark xxx

Out-takes? She slipped the disk into her DVD player and waited for it to begin.

After the official Corona Productions logo, Vladimir Darq's body filled the screen and she felt herself begin to melt, even though he was striding up and down saying, 'She drives me crazy!'

Then the camera panned onto him and he was sewing blue beads onto *that* corset.

'This,' he explained, 'is a goodbye present for Anna.'

'It's very intricate,' came the disembodied voice of Jane.

'*Desigur*. Of course. She is worth it.'

Then Vladimir was back to his passionate self, talking Romanian to Leonid, and then Leonid faced the camera and asked Bruce, in English, if he was filming. *What did they send me this bit for?* thought Anna. *My Romanian extends no further than a 'no', and 'of course' and a few choice swear words, thanks to Maria.*

Then Flip was saying to Jane, 'I thought we'd got a dead seed here but we've got a flower, haven't we?'

'A fucking big perfumed one,' Jane replied with a delighted smile. 'It's absolute magic. And I really like her too, so I want her to look gorgeous.'

Then Flip was doing some practise filming on the handheld camera, spying on Bruce and Mark talking.

'Do you think he really is a vampire?' Mark was whispering.

'Before I came, I would have said, "Don't be so fucking stupid", but now I'm not so sure.' This from Bruce. 'Have you seen his eyes? Scar-ee!'

'Those fangs are real as well.'

Bruce secretly slipped in a pair of huge false fangs, threw himself on Mark with a growl and scared him to death. The pair of them descended into giggles like two naughty school-boys.

Then Vladimir was fastening Anna into a corset from the back and his eyes were transfixed on Anna's neck. He was inhaling the scent from her skin, wetting his lips with his tongue. He looked as if he might devour her at any minute.

Then Vladimir was ranting at Mark.

'I would like to get all women like Anna Brightside in a group and bang all their heads together. She drives me crazy!'

Then the action switched to Leonid, smiling fondly as he watched Anna and Jane be interviewed in the distance. He was talking quietly to Bruce.

'Vlad could have found no one more perfect to model for him. She is wonderful. She will drive this campaign to the stars. Perfect.'

That was the end.

Anna had an idiot smile on her face. That was so sweet of Leonid, especially because he didn't know he was being filmed. And the way Vladimir looked at her neck! It was scary and thrilling and something to remember always, that he had once really desired her – even for a few minutes. Even as a meal.

Anna put the disk back in the case and the note with it. It was then she noticed there was writing on both sides. She turned over to the unread side.

> PS. One of our location managers is Romanian, so here is a translation of that Leonid/Vladimir conversation. Go, girl!
> Leonid: My friend, why are you in such a hideous mood?
> Vladimir: I don't know, it's crazy. She drives me crazy.
> Leonid: Yes, I wondered if that was the problem.
> Vladimir: I am sending her home to a man who buys her plates! Week after week, I have seen her becoming more beautiful and all for him – Plate Man!
> Leonid: (laughs) Maybe at the beginning. Not now. Haven't you seen the way she looks at you, you fool?
> Vladimir: Ignore me, Leonid. I've said too much. Now about the core selection of colours for 'The Darqone' . . .

Anna's hands were shaking. She took in a deep breath and steadied herself. *OK, let's get some perspective on this*, she told herself. Actors were always falling for each other on projects, weren't they? They got the edges between real life and scripts blurred. It wasn't real; they got infatuated and as soon as the film was in the can they split up. She needed to keep remembering what he had said about that corset: it was a goodbye gift. The key word was 'goodbye'. She had to get a grip on her excitement before it ran away with her. Although, to be honest, it was already halfway down the M1. Vladimir Darq was grateful to her, that was all. By his own admission, she drove him crazy. By tomorrow morning, she would be merely a memory for him. In a few weeks' time, maybe not even that.

At 5 p.m. that evening, Anna carefully laid the corset out on her bed. It was stunning. She had hardly been able to stop looking at it since she received it. It was all the intricacies which intrigued her: the hundreds of glittery dark beads, individually applied. Why? Now, after watching that DVD she knew. *She is worth it,* said that voice inside her head: a deep, East European voice with an impatient edge. She shivered with desire for him. But after tonight, who knew if she would ever see him again? But still, she couldn't get those little beads out of her head.

There was a bing bong at her door. It only ever rang at this time of night because the gormless local pizza delivery service mixed up her house number 2 with 2A next door. She ripped the door open, prepared to tell them yet again that the house they needed to deliver the Supremo with extra mozzarella to was, in fact, the next one along.

But she was wrong. She opened the door to find the *pièce de résistance* present from Tony. Tony himself. Beaming, with his arms wide open and bearing a red rose in his mouth.

'Babe!' he said through clenched teeth. He whisked the rose into his hand and then under Anna's nose. She stood in stunned silence.

Over the past months, she had imagined many times what she would do at this point, and that was to throw herself gratefully into Tony's arms and cover his lying, cheating face with kisses of forgiveness whilst dragging him over her threshold. But now the moment was here, she didn't do anything of that sort at all and no one was more surprised than her. She stood there, a stunned statue, while he continued to stick his rose uncomfortably close to her left nostril.

When she did eventually speak, because it was getting a bit ridiculous standing there like a tableau for the benefit of the pizza-eating and the cat-nicking neighbours, it was merely to say his name.

'Tony.'

'Yep, that's me, babe. Oh, I. Have. Missed you so much.'

His arms came about her and she almost staggered backwards with the force of his embrace. His familiar aftershave enveloped her, the aftershave that had once made her go as slushy as a Solero after a minute in a microwave. It certainly wasn't travelling up her olfactory passages and making her knees knock now though. He'd applied rather a lot of it recently, by the whiff of it, and she could feel a big sneeze building up. He was cooing in her hair like an amorous pigeon. Then he pulled back from her and looked at her as if she had returned from a long absence: back-packing in Australia, perhaps, and he was relieved to see her home again and in one piece.

'Wow, you look great, babe,' he said. 'What have you done to yourself? Had some work done or something?'

'No, of course I haven't had any surgery,' said Anna, still in shock.

'I've come back, babe. I've been an idiot. Let's go inside.'

He tried to push her backwards through the door.

'Whoa, Tony, slow down,' she said, extricating herself, not giving a toss about any would-be curtain twitchers now. If Tony got inside the house, she wouldn't get him out again. And she had her evening to think about. This was Vladimir's big night. She couldn't let him down. Tony might have had the gift of the gab, but his timing was crap.

Tony's eyebrows knotted in confusion. It was obvious he thought that five seconds after ringing her bell, they'd be in bed where he would continue to try and ring her bell. And, a few weeks ago, maybe they would have been. She had cried and drunk herself to sleep playing out the scenario of his coming back all hugs and kisses and open arms so many times and now she had him on her doorstep doing those things, all she could feel was totally detached. No, she wasn't going to fall back into his arms so easily. She was now a woman worth sewing small beads on corsets for. Tony would need to appreciate that.

'I'm sorry but I'm going out tonight.'

'You're going out? Who with?'

'A friend.'

'You're joking,' he said, lip curling over with churlish disappointment. 'Cancel it. Life's just not been the same without you, babe.'

Her wounded ego had a smug moment. *He wants me more than Lynette Bottom*. But it was quickly overridden by the stronger desire to see Vladimir Darq again.

Tony pushed once more and moved in for a snog and she stopped him with a hard hand on his chest.

'No, I can't,' she said.

'Yes, you can.'

'OK then, I won't.'

Tony stopped trying to kiss her.

'What "friend" is this then that's so important?' he asked suspiciously.

'A designer friend. I've been modelling for him. He's having a party tonight.'

The expression on Tony's face showed that he didn't know whether to believe her or not.

'Modelling? You?' he said eventually.

'Yes, me,' said Anna with a huff. 'And I'll tell you something else, Tony Parker, I'm not bad at it either.'

'What, like nude modelling? For artists?'

'Nope,' she said, bristling and thinking, *typical*. She didn't want to give him details. Whatever she said, he wouldn't take her seriously. Or believe that she was the face of 'Every Woman has a Darq Side'.

'I've missed you so much, babe,' he said. 'Did you get my presents?'

'Yes, I got them,' said Anna. 'I was beginning to wonder what you were playing at after so long!'

Tony smiled that lopsided, cheeky grin of his. 'I figured that if I didn't find them smashed up where I put them that you might still want me.'

Ah, so it *was* a softener. Christie was right. That made sense. He *was* hedging his bets.

Anna rubbed her forehead.

'Tony, I can't think about this right now.'

'I'll come back later, shall I? After your little do?'

Little do?

'That is, if you want me to . . . ' he added in such a way that intimated he was backing off already.

'Yes,' said Anna, her voice coming from a last vestige of the old-deserted-lonely Anna place within, but she didn't know if she truly wanted him to or if it was just some automatic kick-back response.

'OK, I will then,' he replied, the grin flooding his face again.

She would sort all this out later, but now she needed to get ready. She wanted to take a long time getting ready too, to be perfect for Vladimir.

'I don't know what time I'll be back,' she said.

'I'll be here at midnight. If you aren't here by then, I'll wait.'

Anna looked at him. He was staring at her like he used to do, as if his heart was full of her. He was always so good at the 'look of love'. She had to avert her eyes, otherwise she might have given way to a basic urge, pulled him into the house and salved her savaged ego.

'I'll go then,' he said, turning slowly away from her, giving her maximum chance to change her mind.

'I'll see you later,' said Anna.

'Cinderella is going to get her prince back at midnight,' he said, grinning.

Anna closed the door and thought, *You've won, girl! Tony is coming home*.

So why wasn't every part of her body singing about it?

Half an hour later, she was staring at herself in the mirror and uttering expletives.

She looked like she'd put her make-up on in a bumper car. Maria had applied it so easily, but Anna appeared at best as if a big lad had given her two shiners. And it didn't help that her hand was trembling so much that when she applied her eye-liner she might have been preparing to go to a fancy dress party as a panda with a Goth fixation. She sighed, grabbed the cotton wool and eye make-up remover in order to start again. Why the sodding hell did Tony have to come stirring up her life – today of all bloody days?

The door bell sounded just as she was about to have another go at the eye-liner and her heart nearly stopped with shock. *Please let it not be him. Please make it be another misdelivered pizza.*

She opened it to four grinning and wonderfully familiar faces bearing cases and bags.

'We thought you might need some help getting ready,' said Christie. 'And looking at the state of your eyes, I think we were right.'

Dawn was all dolled up herself. She could only stay about an hour because she was setting off on her hen night, and helping Anna get ready was infinitely better than sitting at home waiting to be whisked off to Blegthorpe. It had been her idea to turn up at Anna's and if she didn't need their help, at least they'd see her in *that frock*. And they were all dying to see Anna done up like a princess.

Dawn, firmly back in her hairdressing mode, curled and pinned Anna's hair into the most beautiful tower, leaving loose tendrils around her face. She made it look so easy, even easier than Maria actually. They didn't know that Dawn was glad of something to concentrate on that didn't involve weddings or guitars or giant inflatable penises. To be fully focused on Anna's hair was exactly what she needed.

'I was all fingers and thumbs to start with, then Tony turned up and made my nerves even worse!' said Anna. She had filled them in on the details of her recent visitor.

'Have you decided what you're going to do about him?' asked Raychel.

'I'm trying not to even think about it,' said Anna. 'I need to concentrate on Vladimir's ball first. Then when I come home I'll give Tony some head space.'

'You're very wise,' said Grace. 'This is an important evening for you and you deserve a wonderful time.'

While Grace popped the kettle on, Christie set to work on Anna's face. Raychel took over when it came to her eyes. She had the very steady hand needed for the dramatic wings she was going to give Anna. When she was finished, she stood back and beamed.

'Wow!' she approved proudly.

'Let me have a look then,' pleaded Anna.

'Wait, impatient Mary,' said Raychel. 'Lips first.'

'I've got five minutes left,' said Dawn when Raychel had sealed Anna's scarlet lipstick. 'Please put the frock on and let me see.'

'Have you tried it on already?' asked Christie.

'He said I hadn't to. He said it would fit.' Anna dropped her voice as if Vladimir was in earshot. 'I know it sounds daft, but I thought he'd be able to tell if I did.'

'Right, well, fingers crossed, everyone,' said Christie. Grace brought the dress in. It really was the most beautiful shade of blue. Like a twilight sky in the heat of summer.

'Your hooks and eyes are all skew-whiff,' said Christie, as Anna slipped off her robe to reveal the corset Vlad had made for her. 'How the heck did you think you'd manage on your own?'

'I know, I'm useless,' said Anna.

'No, you're not. You're just nervous,' said Dawn. 'I would be as well, everyone looking me up and down all night, no doubt. I bet there will be loads of professional models sticking their noses up at you.'

'Dawn, please shut up,' said Raychel.

'There, you're sorted!' said Christie with a triumphant note in her voice. 'My goodness, how long did it take him to stitch all those beads on?' She smiled at Anna and Anna beamed. Christie knew why he had worked so hard on that corset too.

'It's *so* Cinderella, isn't it?' said Raychel, clasping her hands excitedly.

'I don't know,' huffed Anna. 'If it is, it's a bit of a twisted version. Christie and Vladimir are both fairy godmothers and there's no Prince Charming. Well, there is but he's run off with the teenage Ugly Sister with the tiny arse.'

They all laughed because it was impossible not to, the way Anna had said it. Then she stepped into the dress which Grace and Christie lifted upwards. It skimmed over her hips and rested perfectly on her bust as she threaded her arms into the sleeves.

'Bloody hell,' said Dawn, her eyes as wide as the full moon hanging outside the window. 'I take it back. Those models won't be sticking their noses up at you, they'll be too busy turning lime-green with envy.'

A taxi beeped outside and Dawn's delighted smile dropped. She stood to go. 'That's got to be mine. I ordered one to take me down to the bus station. Can I leave my gear here?'

'Yes, of course you can. Go and have a great time,' said Anna.

'You'll have a better one,' she replied. 'You look gorgeous, Anna. Like a totally different woman to the one you were before your birthday. You're like a little bud in a vase that's suddenly become the biggest bloom of the bunch.'

'Good grief,' said Christie, making them all laugh. 'You've managed to say something right for once!'

Dawn gave Anna a small peck on the cheek. It was a sad little kiss, Anna thought.

'Now we'll let you see yourself in the mirror!' said Grace.

But Anna surprised them all. Tempting as it was, she was remembering the last photoshoot in Darq House, when Leonid and Maria started dropping things.

'No, I don't want to see myself,' she said.

'But you look gorgeous, Anna,' said Grace.

'You *feel* gorgeous, don't you?' said Christie with a knowing smile, handing her the blue bag that was a present from her beloved husband when his heart was still strong and beating. 'And you're savouring that feeling, aren't you?'

'Yes, Christie,' nodded Anna. 'I couldn't possibly look as good as I feel at this moment.' It was so wonderful to be understood. By friends.

'Here are your shoes,' said Raychel, guiding Anna's toes into them. 'You are so stunning, Anna. Dawn's right. You've blossomed before our eyes.'

For once, Anna didn't bat back the compliment; she accepted it wholeheartedly and said thank you. She didn't feel like Anna, the ordinary Barnsley sparrow. She felt like a golden, gorgeous Phoenix, rising from the ashes of her former rubbish self-worth.

'Chuffing hell, I'm scared!'

'Don't be saying that tonight in illustrious company,' said Christie, packing her make-up away. Their job was done and now it was time to leave Anna to be picked up by her pumpkin coach.

'I hope I don't cock anything up,' said Anna, grabbing Grace's warm, steady hand.

'You won't, don't worry,' said Grace. 'Remember, you were chosen to show off your inner siren. So let her out, girl. Oh, and, obviously, we want to know every last detail on Monday.'

'We will hold an emergency meeting in the canteen,' said Christie. 'Let Malcolm try and report us. James is baying for his blood as it is. Goodnight, darling Anna. Have a ball.'

Chapter 76

The car arrived, and when Anna stepped out into the night she saw the usually impassive chauffeur take in a second and a third glance as he opened the door to let her in. It empowered her to think she might have cracked Mr Impenetrable and she grinned to herself. She saw him taking a couple of extra glances in the rear view mirror too. He didn't smile at her, obviously. That would have been just too freaky.

Her new-found confidence bobbed temporarily right down to her bowel and made it spasm as they turned into the drive at Darq House, for there in front of them was a line of posh cars, Rolls Royces, Porsches, Bentleys, Limos . . . She half expected to see a helicopter landing.

As the Merc came up to the designated dropping-off point, Anna looked at all the stick-thin women emerging from the cars with their creations on. They almost disappeared when they turned sideways. But they wore the most gorgeous, beautiful dresses, although she couldn't have recognized the designers in a million years from one glance at a button like they did on the telly. A small part of her almost wanted to tell the chauffeur to keep driving and take her home. It was suddenly all very serious. Then she saw Vladimir wearing the most exquisite black suit and a moon-white shirt with an extravagantly tied white cravat at the neck. His hair was loose, a magnificent midnight mane which made him look more vampiric and untamed and romantic than ever before. Was he waiting for her? She didn't know. But then he made it plain that he was as he came forward to open the door for her and he presented his hand for her to take. She pictured it on her breast, above her heart.

'Anna,' he said, 'good evening. You look . . . beautiful.'

Do I? she was about to say, until a stern voice stopped the words coming out of her throat. *Ah ha – yes, you do. Don't insult the man by inferring that his creation makes you look any less than fantastic.* 'I feel wonderful,' she said. 'It all fits like a glove.'

'Of course,' he said with haughty surprise. 'How could you expect anything less from me? You found a purse, I see.'

'And shoes,' said Anna. 'I didn't think I would, but I did.'

'But you cared enough about yourself to try,' he said, nodding, with an amused smile playing on his lips. 'I hoped you might.'

He led her inside as if he were a crown prince and she were his chosen bride. She was aware of being watched and stared at and talked about, and she tried to stop blushing in case it melted her foundation. Then, as she entered, she realized why she was drawing so much attention, for, as well as being escorted in by the man himself, there – hanging from the gallery – was a *huge* poster of herself in a grainy film-noir type shot. It was black and white, the corset picked out in red, and underneath the words: *Every Woman has a Darq Side.* It was amazing.

'What do you think?' said Vladimir.

'I . . . er . . . I'm stunned,' said Anna quietly.

'That's because it is stunning,' he said. He turned to her, his gold-flecked eyes directed on her like million-watt light bulbs. '*Eşti ameţitoare! You* are stunning, Anna.'

Leonid wafted over with two glasses of champagne and pecked Anna on both cheeks.

'*Eşti o regină!* My God, you are a Queen!' he said, which was funny coming from him.

Someone grabbed Vladimir's attention and he clicked his heels in that military way of his to be excused.

'So, do you like the poster?' said Leonid.

'I think it's . . . it's . . .' Anna struggled for the word. Would it be too big-headed if she said what the first word was that came to her? *Sod it.* She went with it. 'It's gorgeous, Leonid.'

'Vladimir – he wants to show you off. Like Pygmalion.'

'Well, he's done that all right.'

Anna looked around. There was a woman in a gold dress who must have weighed less than Anna's left earlobe. Everyone looked fabulous and beautiful. And she was amazed to feel one of them.

'Anna Brightside,' began Leonid, with a kind softness to his voice she hadn't heard before, 'you make me so proud. You are a real woman. A lady. Vladimir will owe the success of The Darqone to you.'

'I hope it is successful for him,' smiled Anna. 'But the success will be down to his design alone. It's miraculous.'

'Yes, his order books are very full. I think he is not worrying. But you underplay your part.'

Anna's attention was diverted by the back of a woman whose shoulder blades jutted out further than her bum did. She waved away the tray of canapés being proffered. There was probably her whole week's intake of calories in one tiny bruschetta. Tony didn't like ultra-thin women. He said real men might lust after them in magazines but where was the fun in feeling tits that were flatter than his own? *Tony.* In less than three hours he would be sitting outside her flat, waiting for her to let him in. And she would take off this dress, wipe off her make-up and her cloud nine would let her down to earth again where she would do her best to fit into normal life. Although she felt her new normal life might be slightly different from the old one – with or without Tony's inclusion in it.

A wisp of a woman in the tallest heels Anna had ever seen in her life gushed at Leonid and did a left, right and left again cheek kiss. Anna recognized her immediately from magazines although she couldn't quite put a name to her.

'Leonid, how majorly marvellous to see you,' said Sticky-Thin Woman, smiling with a set of white teeth that would have made a crocodile pig-sick with envy.

'This is Oona Quince,' introduced Leonid.

'Yes, I know,' said Anna. 'Wow!'

The Supermodel nodded as if it was normal to hear such flattering exclamations attributed to her. Which it probably was. Anna felt obliged to say how beautiful she looked, which again seemed expected.

'Excuse me, please,' said Leonid, waving at someone and then disappearing. Anna watched him head towards a man wearing a silver tuxedo and greeting people very flamboyantly. When she turned around to Oona, it was to see a much colder-faced woman than the one who had been draped around Leonid not two minutes ago.

'So you're Vlad's little pet project,' said Oona spikily, taking a swill from her champagne glass. Obviously not her first of the evening.

'I beg your pardon?' said Anna, smiling politely still. She wasn't sure if Oona had put that clumsily or was being an out-right cow. She would give her the benefit of the doubt. She needn't have bothered being so kind. *Moo.*

'You're Vlad's temporary fixation. His *plat du jour*.'

'Am I?' Anna answered, trying not to rise to the bait. If Oona carried on bitching, she'd give her one good push and send her careering off her shoes. Funny, she looked gorgeous in photographs. Close up, her face had more spots under all that make-up than a teenage Dalmatian.

'Enjoy it while you can,' Oona said, her eyes glittering with malice. 'He'll suck you dry and then discard you like a used diaper. You'll be back to your cleaning job in no time.'

And with that, Oona expertly turned on her killer heels, switched on her charming barracuda smile and went off crying 'dahling' at someone across the room.

Anna closed her agape mouth and started to giggle. Wow, she really must be getting up some noses! Fancy, Oona Quince bitching about her! How good was that? Anna took another sip of her champagne. She would need to take it slow. She suspected there would be a lot of drunks at this party shortly and she owed it to Vladimir to stay sober and dignified. Plus she could observe so much more that way. This was surely *the* place for people watching.

The room next to the great open reception hall was booming out disco music. A live band was playing at eleven million decibels. Leonid was heavily involved in conversation with Silver Jacket Man and Vladimir was chatting merrily to some people. She saw him glance over at her and wave. He made some tiny gesture that she knew meant, 'Are you OK?' and she nodded heartily back. She grabbed a canapé for something to do with her hands and ate and looked around. She spotted a few celebrity people, some of whom she could name and some of whom she couldn't. There were lots of tall, stunning women, who looked as if they had just stepped off glossy mag covers, and men with stretched, Botoxy faces and hair dyed too dark for their skin tone. Plus a few orange people who made Malcolm look like an albino. There were also a lot of drop dead gorgeous hunks too, with classical aquiline noses and Kirk Douglas chins. But none of them had the effect on Anna's knees that Vladimir Darq did when she caught sight of him in the crowd. She had so much difficulty keeping her eyes from searching him out that she wondered if she'd been glamoured.

Oona had snatched another champagne flute and was hanging

around Vladimir now and trying not to sway. She appeared to be trying to monopolize his attention and he rather expertly wasn't allowing that to happen. Her lower lip was petulantly pouting out five inches in front of her cleavage because he clearly wasn't one of the 'isn't-Oona-amaaazing' brigade. That explained a few things, Anna thought with a wry smile.

By the time Dawn alighted from the minibus at Blegthorpe in her 'Last chance to shag me – I'm the Bride' T-shirt which she was pressured into putting on over her new dress, she was the only one of the thirteen sober. Demi, Denise and their group of friends were all in various stages between half-blasted and completely blotto. It was the wedding rehearsal tomorrow at 1 p.m. She dreaded to see the state of her future sisters-in-law then.

Demi's best mate, Sherideen, was the worst hit so far and had already vomited on her 'Little Hen Seeks Big Cock' T-shirt. Luckily, there were some spares on the bus that Demi had brought just in case anyone was sick on themselves – how well she knew her crowd. Sherideen slurringly explained to Dawn that she'd been drinking on an empty stomach and went straight off the bus to the nearest chip shop to put a lining on her tum before hitting the bars of Blegthorpe. Dawn checked her watch. Given the choice between this evening and root canal surgery without anaesthetic and a blind dentist, the latter would have won easily.

They weren't the only hen or stag party there. The town was heaving with groups of women bearing L plates and veils seemingly made out of net curtains. Dawn tried to look jolly only because she didn't want Denise or Demi scoffing at her for being miserable, but she could think of better ways of enjoying herself than carrying a giant inflatable knob around with her in a place she didn't like, with people she didn't know.

Bette and Muriel were wearing big summer frocks that showed off their bingo wings to best effect. Apparently Empty

Head didn't have T-shirts large enough for them. Dawn didn't even want to think what Bette would look like in a white T-shirt. There would have been avalanche warnings as she walked down the hill to the pubs. Bette couldn't stand up for very long, given her bulk, so she and Muriel found a cosy corner to sit in with their pints of lager and lime. Luckily, most of the party were too far gone to even remember Dawn's existence, something at least for which she was grateful. Dawn pushed herself into the background and watched her 'hens' dancing on tables and flirting with 'cocks'. She pressed her fingernail hard into the inflatable willy and heard the air sigh out of it. There was a cheer to the side of her and she turned to see that Demi had taken her T-shirt off and was jumping up and down with her bare breasts bobbling. The bouncer came over and told her to put her top back on, but he was very slow in pushing through the crowd, considering what a huge, flabby bloke he was.

Two of the women were virtually unconscious by 2.30 a.m. and Denise asked Dawn if she would mind ringing for the bus driver to pick them up now instead of 5 a.m. Dawn didn't mind at all; in fact she was ecstatic, but she made a lot of 'Aw!' sounds for effect. She clambered on the bus with them all and did a convincing job of saying what a fantastic night she'd had and feigned being well tipsy. Even Bette and Muriel were too drunk to notice that Dawn was stone cold sober and play-acting her little heart out.

Demi fell asleep halfway through her kebab on the bus. The meat hung from her lips, giving the impression that she had just ripped it from the back of an animal. Dawn was scared of Demi, if the truth be told. She thought of the years to come pussy-footing around her, fearful to upset her at family gatherings. Then Al Holly and his proposal pushed through to the front of her thoughts. But how could she just up and leave her whole life to chase a dream? What if it all soured? She could never come home because she would always be looking over her shoulder for a scary Crooke sister. It would be something always to keep in the treasure box section of her head, but people like her didn't up and cross the Atlantic with just a guitar and a few pairs of clean pants with a man they barely knew on the strength of a few conversations about Gibsons and Stratocasters. They did nine-to-five jobs and married men who never put their dirty washing in the laundry bin and worried about the bills and had a perfunctory bonk on Saturday nights and dreamed of lives they weren't ever brave enough to chase.

Dawn wished she had got drunk after all. Madly and totally drunk, so that a hangover drove all thoughts of guitars and weddings and dresses and old hallucinating ladies from her head. She was so tired, so very, very tired.

Anna also was stone-cold sober. A few times she had seen Vladimir about to come over to her, only to be snatched back by someone. He was a victim of his own success, tonight more than ever. At least she had the big dog, Luno, for company. He had wandered over when she flashed a miniature Yorkshire pudding canapé at him. Surprisingly, he had stayed hanging around her when he had eaten it, settling at her side with his big head on his shaggy paws.

Anna's portrait seemed to be attracting attention, but she herself was superfluous. She was a mere extension of Vladimir and the man himself was in this room, so why would anyone want her – the mere clothes horse?

'You're the girl on the poster, aren't you?' boomed a raucous voice in her ear. She turned around to see a presenter from the *Morning Coffee* breakfast show. Someone they used as a stand-in when Drusilla Durham and her husband, Gerald 'The Man' Mandelton, were off gallivanting. *What the hell was his name again?*

'Tony Barrett,' he offered, right on cue, holding out a big

meaty hand. Of course: *Tony*. How could she forget? 'I had to
come over. I think you look absolutely fantastic.'

'Oh, thank you,' said Anna, relieved to be talking to someone, even for a few minutes.

'And you're even nicer in the flesh!'

He was sniffing a lot. And his eyes looked glassy, she noticed
on closer inspection.

'I don't think Vlad could have picked anyone more perfect,'
said Tony, leaning in a bit too close and looking down her top.
It seemed he had the same charm offensive as the other Tony.
He'd probably cut to the chase and ask her for a shag with his
next breath.

'Well, that's very kind of you to say so,' said Anna, pulling
back to give herself some personal space.

'I'd like to have you on the show. Are you up for that?'

'Sounds great!' smiled Anna, as he fell forwards onto her and
knocked the remainder of her drink down her dress. Luckily
there wasn't much in her glass and it was stain-free champagne,
but it gave Tony the excuse to wipe his hand down her front
apologetically. It felt like the unadulterated grope it was. Anna
stepped away from his hand politely.

'It's fine,' she said. 'Don't worry.'

'Come and have a dance,' said Tony, gripping her arm.

'Maybe later,' said Anna, her smile tighter now.

'No, come on, we can talk about the show. I've got a lot of
power, you know. I can get you a big slot.' She didn't like the
way he said 'big slot' – he gave it a very sexual tone.

'Anna, come, I need you,' said a welcome voice at her side.
Leonid. 'Tony, go away. She has no time to dance, she has to
come with me.'

Tony shrugged his shoulders and moved off, knocking into
the lady with the canapé tray and sending a couple of mini-
quiches Luno's way.

'He's been on the sniffy-sniffy stuff,' said Leonid. 'I had to rescue you. He's a horrible man. He tries to get anything into bed.'

'Flattering!' tutted Anna.

'Vladimir sent me to say he's so sorry you are on your own so much. You are such a great success.'

'No, he's the success,' said Anna. 'I'm just the shop-floor dummy.'

'He will be with you shortly,' said Leonid, tutting at her self-denigration and giving her a gentle slap on the bottom. 'Don't move.'

He replaced the empty glass in her hand with a full one, deftly swept from the tray of a passing waiter, and then he moved off himself.

She looked at her watch. It was eleven o'clock. Tony would be at her house in an hour. She thought of how much she had wanted him back, but now she felt nothing at the prospect of his return. Was that because she was anaesthetized by the shock that it was actually going to happen at last?

She looked across at Vladimir in his gorgeous suit and starched white shirt again and something definitely happened to her heart that wasn't supposed to happen. It seemed to flood with warmth and smiles and sighs. He was engaged in conversation with a rotund older actress from *Emmerdale*. He was so charming and at ease with his crowd. But this was his world, after all, and not hers. He was glitz and glamour and chauffeur-driven Mercs. She was a Barnsley woman whose idea of exciting fashion before she met Vladimir Darq had been a sale on in Dorothy Perkins. She was his *fait accompli*. The words of that vermicelli-thin Oona woman thumped back into her head. Bitchy, but true. Yes, Vladimir had made her feel beautiful, as he swore he would. He delivered to her a corset covered in tiny beads that her body was so proud to wear for him. She, Anna Brightside, aged forty from Courtyard Lane, was *worth the effort, worth the time, worth the trouble*. And women all over the world would soon be in touch with their own Darq sides because this inspiring man thought they should be valued as much, if not more, than his A-list clients.

Her work here was done. She belonged in Ordinary World and she needed to get back to it sooner rather than later because complications were already setting in. She was in mortal danger of falling in love with his tender ways and reverence for her, and could only get hurt. Yes, he had awoken her inner siren. The trouble was, that siren wanted him. He had lifted her so high she wasn't sure if normal life was possible any more.

It was time to go home and face Tony. She would listen to what he had to say and then decide what she wanted. What *she* wanted.

She took a last look at the beautiful room decorated with giant moons and stars against black velvet drapes and buzzing with music, chatter and stunning people. She raised her glass in Vladimir Darq's direction and took a long sip of champagne.

Good luck, Vladimir. I wish you everything that makes you happy.

Anna patted Luno's big head, then slid out through the front door where the complimentary taxis were waiting. She thought no one noticed she had gone.

The taxi driver took a wrong turning. He tapped his Satnav fiercely and gave the excuse that he had only been doing the job a week. He didn't take much of a detour but, as they rounded the corner for Courtyard Lane, Anna saw that Vladimir Darq was standing by her front door, so pale in the moonlight that he looked like a visitor from another world.

'How . . . how did you get here so fast?' was her first breathless question to him when she had got out of the taxi and waved goodbye to the driver, followed by the second: 'Why are you holding a blue stiletto?'

He held the shoe out to her.

'You dropped this, running away from my ball, Cinderella. Didn't you?'

Anna lifted her dress up so Vladimir could see her feet, both with a shoe on them.

'No, I didn't,' she said.

'Oh goodness,' he said, rubbing his forehead. 'I found it outside by the cars. I presumed . . . Someone is going to be rather angry with me then.'

'Hopping mad,' said Anna with a smile. 'Plus it's massive!'

It wouldn't have looked out of place on the Norfolk Broads.

'Why did you go, Anna?' He pronounced her name as always, more Ah-na, than Anna. Like a sigh.

'Oh Vladimir, why do you think?' said Anna, with a loaded sigh of her own. 'Look at me. Look at where I live!' She pointed backwards at the small house. 'It's a terrace in the middle of Barnsley. I work in an office. I don't jet off to Milan. I don't have friends who are pop stars. You've made me feel wonderful. Now I have to be wonderful in my own world.' *If I can, after the way you've rocked my world so much that I don't know where the hell I belong any more, you vampire swine.*

'You could go to Milan and mix with pop stars.'

'Yeah, course I cou— Mw!'

She had no chance to finish her sentence because Vladimir Darq cleared the distance between them in a nano-second, seized her roughly in his arms and stifled her words with his lips.

Good God, her brain said on behalf of her mouth, which was otherwise engaged. His arm was around her waist, his other pulling her hair back and stretching out her throat to him. They looked like a Mills and Boon cover. One entitled: *Yours to Devour.*

Chuff, he's going to kill me! she thought. Quickly followed by, *And I don't care!* His lips smudged along her jugular, setting off dormant fireworks on her nerve endings. Those big ones with multi-heads that kept firing into the sky and made whole towns go, 'Wow!'

She could see his black hair, taste him on her lips, smell the wonderful alpha-male cologne he wore, hear him breathe, feel his strong body pressing against hers . . . She only wished she had a load more senses that could experience him because five didn't seem enough. She had wondered, more often than she cared to admit, what kissing him would be like, but never in her wildest dreams did she imagine it would be as good as this. It was an experience bettered only by his voice vibrating against her neck and saying, 'Anna, you drove me crazy when I first met you and you drive me crazy now for very different reasons. I want you so much. You do belong to my world. You belong to me.'

This couldn't be happening, of course. She'd had too much champagne and was hallucinating. Could you hallucinate on two glasses though? Maybe someone had spiked her drink with 'sniffy-sniffy'? In reality, Vladimir was back at Darq House, chatting up that long, skinny, bitchy bird and she was here alone in the moonlight, having the best daydream of her life. But she wasn't hallucinating, this *was* happening, Vladimir *was* saying those things and she *was* making gaspy noises because his mouth was moving up and down her throat as if he was playing slow blues on a harmonica.

Then he straightened her up and held her in front of him and looked deep into her eyes.

'I have guests. I have to go back. Tomorrow, at eleven in the morning, I will come for you. I will show you the true world of Vladimir Darq.' He lifted her hand and kissed the back of it, then once again he planted a long, sensuous kiss on her lips. He drew apart from her slowly, torturously, leaving Anna bathing in the aftershock, afraid to open her eyes and see him go.

When she opened them, he was no longer there. She felt as if she had just done ten rounds with an amorous Rocky Marciano. She was so light-headed she was sure she would have risen up to that big full moon like a helium balloon, if she had let go of her weighty clutch bag.

She leaned against the door for support, stretching out her neck and presenting it to an imaginary Vladimir for more of the same. What did he mean by 'his true world'? she mused. Was he going to show off the his-and-hers coffins in the basement? The bottles of maidens' blood in his cellars? The moon beamed down on her with its soft, silver light. Stars studded the sky. They were like tiny beads stitched on velvet cloth.

She stood there sighing like something out of a Hollywood musical, thinking she would never sleep tonight, not in a million years, when she heard the low rumble of an approaching car which, within the minute, swung into the lane. *Tony.* She'd forgotten about him. She'd actually forgotten about him. Half an hour ago, she'd been ready to listen to his excuses, but after that kiss there was no way on this planet that was going to happen. He was grinning assuredly at her as he pulled up, then his brow furrowed in confusion, then that smile came back wider than ever.

'Anna! Wow! I didn't recognize you for a minute there. I thought you must be someone else. You look amazing – like a model. Is it really you? Wow!'

He jumped out of the car and she immediately noticed the suitcases on the back seat.

'I'm early, babe,' he said. 'And so are you. Couldn't wait, huh? Me neither. That dress is fantastic on you. I can't wait to see it on the bedroom floor. Come here, I have missed you so much.' He came forward, arms open wide to enclose her, but she held up an arresting palm and said his name firmly.

'Tony.' She couldn't think of anything else to say then but, 'No.'

He froze, arms still open. 'No?' he said eventually. 'What do you mean – *no*?'

'I've been thinking. I don't want you back.'

'Oh, come on,' he said, still hanging on to that smile. 'You know you do. That's why you told me to come back at midnight.'

'I didn't tell you. You volunteered,' Anna corrected him.

'Same difference.'

'Tony, about earlier . . . you caught me on the hop. I was mixed up. But I'm not now.'

'You're kidding me,' he said. Still smiling and now, apparently, enlightened. 'Ah – I see. You're playing hard to ge-et!'

'No, I'm not. You'll have to go back to Lynette.'

'I can't,' he said. 'I mean, I don't want to. I want you, not her.'

'Tony, I don't want you.'

'You do. How many times have you passed my shop to look at me?'

The cheeky chuff, thought Anna. He'd seen her. No doubt it had thrilled him, made him believe that her door was open to him whenever he deigned to return.

'Let's go in and talk about it,' he said.

'No,' said Anna, holding up that palm again. 'I don't want you to come inside. I don't want you, Tony. It's over.'

He was still smiling as if he didn't believe her. That was until a moment later when the sound of a second car's screeching tyres cut through the night air and a rusted pink Fiat Punto ground to a halt about a gnat's leg's length away from Tony's bumper. His smile dropped like a brick then.

'I knew you'd be here, you two-timing twat,' said a very angry, scarlet-faced Lynette Bottom, leaping out onto the pavement. A curtain twitched in the upstairs bedroom of the cat-stealer's window. Then Lynette looked at the glamorous woman in blue velvet and her face creased up with confusion and embarrassment. Then she did a double-take and realized it *was* Tony's ex-girlfriend after all. Blimey! She pulled her cardigan around her, feeling very dull and scruffy by comparison.

'Well, you can have him,' said Lynette through hot, angry tears. 'He's bloody useless at anything that doesn't involve a pair of scissors and a comb. Like – in bed!'

'Oy,' said Tony.

'He's got the words "quality" and "quantity" mixed up just a bit!' Lynette went on waspishly. 'He thinks if he does it three times, you'll not notice he's crap!'

'Lynette—'

'Did he tell you I thought I was pregnant last month?'

Tony was covering his eyes with his hand. Maybe he was doing that thing kids did where they thought if they closed their eyes, no one could see them either.

Anna's breath caught in her throat. 'No, he didn't.'

'You're not pregnant,' said Tony, peeping out from behind his fingers.

'No, but I thought I was and I told you I might be,' said Lynette, twisting round to him. 'And where were you while I was sat in the doctor's? Sniffing back round here, weren't you, you . . . you . . . arsehole.' She stabbed a finger at Anna, then dropped it because this woman in the long dress was making her feel a bit common. 'Well, you're welcome to him. The bastard left me a note saying, "I need a break" and "there's no one else" and then he crept out, thinking I wouldn't notice. But I saw him loading his suitcases into the car because his leaving technique is as shite as his foreplay. And I just knew he'd slither back here! Have him, he's yours!'

'Thank you for your generous offer, Lynette, but sadly, I must decline,' said Anna, in more control than she could have thought possible. 'Goodnight to you both. Tony, we'll be in touch about splitting the assets.' Although from the scream she heard after unlocking the door and shutting it behind her, she thought Lynette might have started splitting Tony's assets already.

Shortly afterwards, Anna heard one car drive off with tyres

squealing and then the other, much more slowly, as if it had its tail between its legs. She didn't know if they were going in the same direction. Nor, she realized with some delight, did she care.

There was a disgruntled screech at her feet when she walked into the darkened kitchen to put the kettle on and stood on something soft. It appeared that Butterfly had picked this night to come home too. In typical male fashion, with his tail between his legs.

Chapter 77

Elizabeth held in her hand the letter that her sister had written to Raychel saying that she was thrilled she had agreed to come and giving her directions to the hostel where she was staying. Elizabeth was trying to remain calm but it was so very difficult. Thank goodness John was driving. He was, clichéd as it was, her rock. He always had been. She was so glad her niece had a rock in Ben too.

Young Ellis was at his 'Auntie' Janey's house. Her husband George was as daft as a brush and, no doubt, the little boy would be having a ball playing with Janey's son Robert and their new hulking great St Bernard puppy, Jimbo. This journey was no place for a child.

The drive to Newcastle was two hours long. Elizabeth's nerves started to rev up even more when they passed the Angel of the North on the right. She closed her eyes and asked it to instil some strength in her because she wasn't sure what she would feel when she saw Bev. The monster who had both beaten her own child and stood aside whilst her boyfriend did the same was also the little girl she had heard crying in her bedroom when they were kids because their dad was an abuser. She didn't know which Bev she would see when Bev opened her door.

The Satnav announced that when they turned around this

corner they would have reached their destination. John drove slowly on, trying to find a sign for the hostel where Bev lived and where she was presently expecting a grand reconciliation with her daughter.

'I'll come in with you,' said John.

'No, wait here,' said Elizabeth. 'It's not exactly the sort of area you'd want to leave a nice car anyway.'

'It's not exactly the sort of building I want my wife walking in by herself,' said John adamantly. 'I'll at least see you to Bev's door.'

Elizabeth didn't protest. John would want to see she was safely in. And her nerve was slipping by the second.

The entrance area was reminiscent of a Chinese takeaway in a rough district. All cheap wood panelling and a quarter-hearted stab at cheering up the walls with some tacky pictures hanging up in plastic frames. There was a serving hatch in the wall, presumably 'Reception'. Through it, Elizabeth could see a woman sitting with her back to the hole, listening to an iPod and watching a portable TV at the same time.

'Hello,' John called through it, getting her attention when his voice didn't work by hammering on the hatch frame. 'We've come to see Marilyn Hunt.'

'Top floor, room eight,' said the woman, giving him her briefest attention before turning back to the TV again.

'Obviously a very secure hostel,' said John in a whisper.

'You go back to the car,' said Elizabeth.

'Like I said, I'll see you up first.' John was insistent.

They walked up a very bare, narrow, twirly staircase three floors up till they got to the top. A cobwebby, scruffy skylight let in a bit of grey light to make the place look even more depressing. The landing carpet was crusty, and hanging Magic Tree air fresheners didn't quite mask the fustiness.

Elizabeth's heart was racing as her hand rose to knock, but she snatched it back at the last second and took a moment to collect her thoughts. She had no idea what she would find when that door opened and no way of preparing for it. *Come on, Elizabeth,* she geed herself up, lifted her knuckles and rapped hard. There was the sound of some activity behind the door, then it opened and there stood the sister she hadn't seen since she was a child, the sister she had cried buckets' worth of tears for, searched for, prayed for. It took her breath away to see the woman version of the girl she had last seen all those years ago. She would not have recognized the bloated bleach-blonde who looked so much older than her years. Only in her grey eyes was a hint of the Bev she once knew.

The two women stood staring at each other, unable to move. It was Bev who eventually broke the silence with one breathless word.

'Elizabeth?'

'Yes, it's me.'

'God. I didn't expect this. Where's Lorraine?'

'Let's go inside,' replied Elizabeth. 'John, you can go now, I'm OK. John!' She had to waken him out of a reverie. Some unpleasant one from the look on his face. He nodded at her and went slowly back down the stairs.

Bev moved aside to let Elizabeth into her room.

'It's a dump, I know, but it's only a temporary place,' Bev said, gesturing towards the room with some embarrassment.

'It doesn't matter. I didn't come to see where you live.'

It was a functional basic space but it was immaculately clean. There was a double bed standing along the left wall, and a table, chair and old sofa tarted up with a red throw under a sloping Velux window. To the right, an old walnut wardrobe, bashed pine drawers, a shoe rack with male and female shoes on it, and a run of three kitchen cupboards, two drawers and a small, shiny steel sink. There was a thick Chinese rug over a gaudy patterned carpet and the smell of Citrus Shake 'n Vac in the air. Two cups and a plate of chocolate Hob Nobs sat waiting at the side of a kettle. The door was still open and Bev was looking out of it.

'Is she here? Will she be coming up in a bit?' Bev said. Her accent was pure Geordie now. Another degree of separation between the sisters, if there could be another one.

'She isn't, no,' said Elizabeth. 'So you can close the door.'

'Why isn't she coming? She said she would.'

'Talk to me first. Shut the door.'

Bev shut it and then went over to switch the kettle on.

'Can I get you a drink?'

'Not for me, thanks,' said Elizabeth just as Bev was about to ask her the 'tea or coffee' question. Bev spooned some coffee into a cup and Elizabeth watched her, trying to associate this stranger in front of her with the sister she had grieved so long and hard for, and failing.

'It's strange to see you, Elizabeth. It's been a long time, hasn't it?' said Bev awkwardly. She was shivering as if she was cold and pulled her cardigan tighter and defensively around her. 'How did Lorraine find you? Is she well?'

'She's well,' was all Elizabeth could manage to respond. She had planned for days what she was going to say to Bev, but the script had been torn up and left back there by the Angel of the North. Elizabeth could no longer predict how she would react in front of 'Marilyn'.

Calmly, Bev tipped some sugar into her cup from a bag and stirred it daintily with her little finger sticking out, an action at odds with the clumsy-looking bulk of her. It was obviously for something to do because she didn't drink from the cup afterwards, just continued to stir.

'I don't know what to say to you,' she said quietly.

'Me neither,' said Elizabeth, in a much colder voice.

'I really need to talk to my daughter though,' said Bev. 'I need to see her.'

'Talk to me instead. She doesn't want to see you, Bev.'

'She wrote and—'

'I wrote the letter – with her permission, of course. I wasn't sure you'd agree to see me.'

'Oh.'

'She told me everything and I can't say that I blame her for not wanting to come.'

Bev placed her spoon into the sink. 'I'd hoped she would see me, just one time. I know she wouldn't want to see me any more than once. I don't blame her for that. I wanted to say I'm sorry. For everything I've done to her.'

'You could say that by letter and spare her the face-to-face ordeal,' replied Elizabeth.

'I was doing it for her. I thought she might . . . might want . . .' Bev stumbled. She took a big breath. 'I thought she might want to pay me back.'

'What – you wanted her to come here and slap you?'

Bev shrugged. 'Or shout or scream at me. Whatever she needed to do.'

'She's not a vengeful person. She's a wonderful, kind-hearted girl.'

'I made so many mistakes with her.'

Marriage and motherhood had softened Elizabeth but at that moment she felt once again like the feral teenager she used to be. 'Mistakes? That's putting it finely, isn't it? How could you? How could you let all those things happen? To your own child?'

'Do you know what happened to *me* as a child? No, you don't!' Bev returned, the hint of a sob present in her voice. 'You haven't a clue what I went through.'

'Yes, I do,' said Elizabeth, matching her for volume. 'I know what you went through because Dad started on me when you'd gone!'

Bev's mouth opened into a long O. 'I'm sorry about that,' she said at last. 'I didn't know.'

Elizabeth laughed without the slightest bit of humour. 'Well, you wouldn't, would you? Because you left me to it. Didn't it cross your mind he would try and do to me what he'd done to you? You could have told someone about him when you left, just in case, but you didn't.'

Elizabeth thought back to the pale-faced, big, moody sister whom she used to tease, not knowing that their father was abusing her. For years, she had punished herself for not realizing, for being too young to help until John Silkstone had come into her life and loved her and forced her to face the fact that she was worthy of being loved.

'I can't turn the clock back and there's too much I can't make up for, but I wish more than anything I could. I used to take a lot of drink and drugs,' said Bev, not meeting her sister's eyes, 'and I'm not trying to use that as an excuse.'

'It isn't an excuse,' Elizabeth butted in.

'No, it isn't. Everything was my fault. I'm clean now. I got myself sorted when I came out of prison. It's taken me a few years, mind. I'm leaving here next week. I've got a little council flat.'

'That's good,' said Elizabeth quietly, because she couldn't think of what else to say.

'I should never have been a mother, I know. I should have had her adopted. I can't ever make up for what . . . what I let happen to her. And the other one. The drugs killed her. I couldn't stop taking them. I've had to face that I killed my own child, did Lorraine tell you?'

'Yes, I know,' said Elizabeth.

Bev sank onto the sofa and twiddled nervously with her necklace. 'I've been so scared of meeting Lorraine again. I . . . I felt I had to though. But I didn't know how to say it.'

'I'll tell her that you're sorry,' said Elizabeth. She wanted to hate this pathetic woman but she couldn't quite manage to. Pity, revulsion, anger whirled inside her – but not hate.

'It's not just that.' Bev coughed away the rasp in her voice. 'There's more.'

'What?' asked Elizabeth, as Bev's face dropped into her hands and she sighed 'Oh God,' over and over.

'It's . . . I'm not one hundred per cent sure . . .'

Elizabeth had presumed Bev only wanted to apologize. What else could there be? 'Not sure about what?'

'Do you remember the Siddalls at school? I think they had a girl in every year. Charlene Siddall was in my class. She had a twin brother who went to the all boys' school: Michael.'

'I remember them,' replied Elizabeth, not sure at all where this was going, but yes, she knew of the Siddalls: a rough, large family. The name still cropped up a few times in the *Barnsley Chronicle*, connected usually with drugs and fights and shoplifting.

'I had sex with Michael Siddall,' Bev went on.

Elizabeth was confused now. 'What's this got to do with Ra . . . Lorraine?'

Bev took in a long fortifying breath, but the cruel secret she had kept for over twenty-eight years came out with a whisper.

'He could be Lorraine's dad. I don't know for sure, but I think he may be.'

'What?'

'When she was a baby, she had the look of him. Tell her I'm sorry, I'm so sorry.'

Bev began to cry softly into her hands as Elizabeth tried to process that information: that Raychel might not be a child of an illicit union, that she might be able to have children of her own after all.

'Jesus Christ. Why didn't you tell her that before?' Elizabeth couldn't get to grips with this at all. Why would Bev have kept something like that to herself? Why would she have told her daughter that she was born out of an incestuous relationship when the likelihood was that she hadn't been?

'I was a very different person then. I was hurt and I wanted to hurt back.'

Then Elizabeth knew. Bev had wanted to hate and punish her daughter for what she herself had gone through. It was so twisted it made her feel physically sick.

Bev continued to twiddle with her necklace and when Elizabeth noticed it was a crucifix, she nearly lost it totally. She covered the distance between them in two strides and, lifting Bev by the edges of her tatty cardigan, she crashed her back into the wall.

'You told a little bairn that her father was her granddad when you didn't know for sure? What kind of an animal are you?'

Bev shrieked but she didn't try to defend herself. 'I know, I know, I'm sorry. I'm sorry I did that. I'm sorry I left you too. I'm sorry I ran off and didn't tell anyone for you.' She was flinching, waiting for the slap that didn't come. But Elizabeth released her grip. There was nothing to be had from more violence. She had seen enough of that. Bev remained curled against the wall.

'I'll tell her what you've said,' said Elizabeth, calming herself. She wanted to go home now and work out how she was going to put this all to Raychel. There was just one more thing she had to do: the reason why Elizabeth had come to face her sister. She reached inside her bag and pulled out a cheque which she forced into Bev's hand.

'When Dad died, I sold his house. I put the money in an account for you in case I ever found you. I never touched a penny of it. It's yours by right.'

Bev looked at her cheque blankly. Then, slowly, her hand extended towards Elizabeth. 'It's Bev Collier's money,' she said. 'There's no Bev Collier here.'

'It doesn't say "Bev Collier". I left the payee line blank. I didn't know what name to write,' said Elizabeth.

'Whatever name you write, it's still Bev Collier's money and there is no such person any more.'

'It's yours anyway.'

Bev's hand was still stretched out. 'I don't want it.'

'You have read that cheque correctly, haven't you? There's over forty thousand pounds in that account and it's all yours.'

'I can read. But I don't want it. Take it back.'

'You're turning it down?' asked Elizabeth disbelievingly. 'No one turns that sort of money down.'

'You obviously did. You would have used it otherwise,' said Bev.

'I'll leave it with you,' said Elizabeth, moving towards the door. She had done what she came for. But the sound of tearing paper halted her step.

'It isn't mine,' said Bev, still holding the cheque, which was now in eight pieces. 'I don't want that sort of money. I live simply and without any complications. It's taken me a long time to get to this stage.'

Elizabeth still didn't look convinced.

'Please, Elizabeth,' implored Bev. 'It would change things for me and I don't want that. I can't cope with it. Give it to Lorraine. Just don't tell her it came from *him*. Tell her something else, something nice,' Bev went on. 'Don't tell her I gave it to her. That would tie us together and we don't belong together. She needs to be free of me. Please. That's why I wanted to see her today. One last time.'

Elizabeth saw then that Bev meant every word.

'I'll do as you ask.' Elizabeth opened the door to go. She had to get out of this room.

'Elizabeth.' Bev's voice came small and cracked. It was the long-ago voice Elizabeth remembered of her sister. It dragged her back to the past, to being two girls doing a jigsaw together. Before. Tears stabbed behind Elizabeth's eyes.

'Just tell me, she is happy, isn't she?'

'Yes,' nodded Elizabeth. 'She's happy.'

'I'm glad. Goodbye, Elizabeth.'

'Goodbye, B— Marilyn. Good luck.'

'You too.'

Elizabeth closed the door behind her, walked down a flight of stairs, stood on the landing and wept the last tears she would ever shed for her sister. Then she dried her eyes and composed herself before going on, so John wouldn't see she'd been crying. She strode into the street towards the car. Never did fresh air feel so good in her lungs.

Chapter 78

Vladimir Darq was a man who considered himself blessed. He was born in Tiresti, a small village at the foot of the Transylvanian Mountains by the side of the beautiful Mureş River, to kind and loving parents. But something had always set the Darq family apart from the rest of the village. Stories circulated that they were descended from an ancient bloodline of night-dwelling creatures to be revered, feared and, above all, respected. Indeed, the sensitivity to bright sunlight that had plagued generations of the male line of Darq men, and their elongated canine teeth that grew naturally added credence to the stories. Nevertheless, the community was warm and protective over its mysterious family and Vladimir Senior wanted more than a lifetime in the mines for the son who had an amazing artistic talent and who loved to stitch with his seamstress mother. Alas, his parents had not lived to see their son catapulted to the A-list of the fashion world by both his amazing accomplishments and his mysterious vampiric allure.

The people in the Yorkshire village where he now lived were kind, accepting, straight-talking – the English version of the Romanian villagers he had grown up with. They were even becoming proud of him, the more they knew of him and his accomplishments. He had houses in Italy, Paris and London too. But Darq House was truly his home.

Vladimir was the dark darling of designers. The paparazzi adored him, reporters courted him, models tried to bed him and the young Vladimir had woken up many a morning with a beautiful woman stretched at the side of him. To the outside world, Vladimir Darq had everything. Almost. For in his heart he was still a simple boy from Romania, craving the love and family warmth sadly lacking from his dynamic career.

Seeing Anna at the train station that night had lit something within him. He couldn't explain why the sight of the sad woman with the long chestnut hair had the effect on him that it did. He saw her potential as *the* model for his intended project. But it was more than that for him. Something primal within recognized a connected soul. A fellow being who needed love and to love. Her vulnerability called out to him and his heart answered.

Week by week, he watched Anna bloom, and the smell of her creamy skin almost drove him mad with lust. It took every reserve of strength to keep his lips away from it.

And at the Full Moon Ball, he had wanted the crowds to disperse early and for there to be only he and Anna left. He had planned to lead her out onto his balcony and dance with her in the moonlight. He wanted it to be romantic and lovely for her. He wanted to tell her as they waltzed under the stars that he had fallen in love with her. He wanted her to tell him she felt the same.

He had flown to her house when he discovered she had left. He could no more have stopped that kiss happening than he could have held back the River Mureş when it burst its banks one summer when he was a child. But was it just a kiss for her?

He was actually shaking with nerves as he got in the car to pick her up the next morning as he had promised he would.

The wedding rehearsal went ahead after the morning's Sunday church service. There was a slight hold-up while both bridesmaids were sick in the graveyard and the best man had to go and buy some paracetamol and Red Bull from the nearby shop. The groom had only one eyebrow. The other had been shaved off when he was tied naked to a lamppost in Wakefield town centre. He was exceedingly quiet and well-behaved during the rehearsal and didn't join in any chance to make fun of the vicar's lisp as the best man would have liked.

As he looked at his future bride by his side, Calum Crooke realized what a good lass he had in Dawn. He had woken up that morning next to Mandy Clamp – his final fling, as arranged by Killer and Empty Head. But now he felt like a dieter who had just wolfed down a whole Black Forest gâteau – ashamed, regretful, nauseous and aware that the anticipation of such a treat far outweighed the reality of it. Mandy Clamp was a total slapper and not worth risking losing Dawn for. The realization had hit him hard that morning when Mandy had made it perfectly plain that a wedding ring made no difference to her and he was welcome to more of what she had on offer whenever – and wherever. He'd always been out with slappers with their boundaries blurred, and even though Dawn wasn't one and would never have done to him what he'd done to her last night, he'd been treating her with as little respect as he did the Mandy Clamps of this world. He looked at Dawn, smart in a summer frock, her long red hair tied behind her and her face all nicely made up, and compared her to his sisters, zombie-white and swaying in jeans and knock-off designer tops. His mother, in her omnipresent flip-flops, was pushing them into position and swearing at them in a whisper that really was anything but, and he thought that it was no wonder he went for Clampesque women, because it was all he'd ever known, until Dawn came into his life. Demi and Denise had slagged off every woman he'd ever been with, behind their back of course, which was a cheek because they were as bad, especially in Demi's case because all his mates'd had her. But recently, when they'd been laughing at Dawn for getting above herself wanting matching ribbons on her little chocolates, he'd got quietly annoyed. The next time they made fun of her, he'd say something back and shut them up. She'd worked so hard and he'd been less than helpful. He'd borrowed Auntie Charlotte's money with no intention of putting it back or financing a honeymoon with it. And standing in church then, he felt true shame that he was the sort of man who'd thought it was big and clever to deceive her. When they were married, he was going to make sure he tried very hard to keep it in his trousers.

Vladimir looked very grim-faced and stern as he pulled up outside her house and Anna half-expected he was going to tell her that he was a bit drunk last night and hadn't meant to kiss her. Well, if he did, he could go and sod off. She'd seen one weak-willied bloke off in the past twenty-four hours, and she would do it again if she had to. She stiffened her spine in readiness for a confrontation, then Vladimir got out of the car, crushed her violently in his arms and planted such a kiss on her lips that she thought if his fangs sank to her throat she would happily bleed to death there in front of the neighbours.

'It's daylight,' she said, with the little bit of breath that he spared her. 'Won't you turn to dust?'

'God save us from fiction story writers,' said Vladimir. 'Get in the car.'

She gladly did as she was told and was driven to Darq House, which an army of cleaners had miraculously restored to its magnificently neat and gothic glory. He showed Anna around his home, his world. He introduced her to the extravagantly sized kitchen fridge which had a Marks & Spencer's minced beef pie and a jar of Hellman's mayonnaise in it as well as Cristal champagne and Italian white truffles. He took her into the cavernous sitting room with a massive TV, a thousand DVDs and CDs lining the shelves on the wall, and the biggest, squashiest sofa ever. He showed her the bathrooms, his office, a storage cupboard full of dog food and rooms stacked high with material and sewing machines. There were no coffins, no bottles of virgins' blood, no Black Mass altars.

Then Vladimir Darq took Anna Brightside upstairs to his ornately carved gothic bedroom, where he threw her down on his four-poster, pinned her there in the shape of a crucifix and did all manner of unholy things to her.

Chapter 79

'Bloody hell, have you had plastic surgery?' said Dawn to Anna as she swaggered in like Mae West the next day. 'You look about twenty years younger than you did on Saturday when we left you – and you only looked about nineteen then! Was it really one of those Botox parties you went to?'

Everyone turned to the phenomenon that was Anna with her fresh face and sparkling eyes. Even her hair seemed more alive, falling in chestnut curls around her and bobbing when she moved, as if she were straight out of an old Harmony Hairspray advert.

'I don't know what you mean,' said Anna with a grin so smug that Cheshire cats worldwide would soon be ringing her for tips.

'Emergency meeting, I think,' said Christie, switching her phone to voicemail and leading the way down to the canteen.

'Did you see Spatchcock's face as we walked past his desk?' said Raychel, who felt considerably lighter this Monday morning than she had done for years. Her aunt was wonderful, she loved her so much. She felt truly content with her lot.

'Sod him,' said Christie. 'I don't care what that little twerp thinks of me or any of us.'

'I hate him,' said Dawn. 'I never liked him before, but after what he tried to do to you and to Grace, I doubly hate him. Trebly even.'

Anna was last to the table with her cappuccino. The others were waiting for her to begin and so she teasingly said in a very slow voice, 'Once upon a time . . .'

'You are so dead if you don't hurry up,' said Dawn.

'Well, I was standing by myself for most of the evening, to be honest, sharing canapés with the dog—'

'Tell us about that bit later,' said Christie, rolling her hand as if to fast forward to the juicy bits.

'—So I came home early but Vladimir followed me and kissed me goodnight and then he collected me from my house yesterday morning and I spent most of the day with him.'

'Doing what?'

'We watched a film, he cooked me dinner—'

'And? You witch!' said Dawn.

'We listened to music, then—'

'Anna!'

'—Then Vlad impaled me—'

'Hallelujah!' said Grace and they all gave Anna a round of applause.

'Did Tony come back?' asked Dawn.

'Oh, yes.'

'I hope you told him what to do.'

'More or less,' said Anna. 'And, you'll never guess – the bloody cat came back to me as well.'

'We'll let you keep the cat,' said Grace. 'Seeing as he's got no balls.'

'Have any of them?' said Raychel, making a rare risqué joke.

'I know one that has,' said Anna dreamily. 'Although they won't be quite as full this morning.'

'Anna Brightside, you dirty girl!' laughed Grace.

'And how did your hen night go?' said Christie, turning to Dawn. She worried about Dawn.

'Awful,' said Dawn. 'But we had the wedding rehearsal yesterday and Calum was . . . like a new bloke. It was so odd. He didn't go out to the pub or drag me to his mother's for lunch. He wanted it to be just me and him.' *He was like he was at the beginning*, she added to herself.

'He'll be getting into wedding mode,' said Grace. She had been including Dawn in her nightly prayers. *Please God, make her be getting married for all the right reasons.* 'When do you pick up your dress?'

'Tonight, after work.'

'So the countdown begins?' said Anna.

'Yes, it most certainly does,' said Dawn. She tried to smile in the same way that Anna was, but the truth was Calum would never be able to light her from the inside the way that Vladimir Darq was doing for her grinning co-worker. Calum had been as nice as pie all day yesterday and it made no difference because every thought was still bending back to Al Holly. She had silently cried herself to sleep and it had taken hours because, yes, the countdown clock to her wedding was ticking loudly now, but the one that was tocking for Al Holly boarding a bus with his suitcases was so much louder.

Chapter 80

Dawn was gazing at herself in the mirror. She looked pretty, even if she did say so herself. How could she not in a dress like that? But she wasn't smiling at her reflection one bit.

'What a perfect fit,' said Freya. 'You must be feeling very excited now.'

'Yes, yes, I am,' said Dawn, making a breezy attempt at pulling the corners of her mouth up. But she could do nothing about the clouds of tears gathering in her eyes. They spilled over and down her cheeks faster than she could wipe them away.

'You'd be surprised at how many brides I've seen sobbing,' said Freya, handing over a well-timed tissue from a ready supply behind her.

'Really?' said Dawn, not quite believing her. Brides were supposed to be skippy and laughing and sunshiney, weren't they? Brides didn't walk down aisles with their heads full of guitarists leaving on jet planes.

'I cried,' said Freya. 'I cried so much that my father said to me at the church door, "Now, Freya, if you don't want to go in there, then we'll turn around and go home. Don't think about letting anyone down, just concentrate on what you want".'

'And did you go in?'

'Yes, I went in,' said Freya. 'But I lied to myself. I didn't want to let anyone down. So much money had been invested, the church was full, guests had travelled from far away and bought presents; I couldn't bear the thought that people would talk about me if I called it off at the last minute – so I went through with it.'

She started to unzip Dawn's dress and help her out of it.

Dawn hardly dared ask.

'And did everything work out fine and dandy in the end?'

'No,' came the reply from behind her. 'It did not. Not in that marriage anyway.'

'Oh blimey,' said Dawn. That really wasn't what she wanted to hear.

'But then I met the love of my life,' smiled Freya. 'And I became the lucky bride who first wore this dress.'

'It was yours?' said Dawn.

'Yes,' Freya admitted. 'It was mine. And when I tasted the true happiness that love can bring, I was determined never to see another unhappy bride.'

You failed then.

'Love is the best magic of all,' said Freya, beginning to fold the dress fondly into leaves of tissue at the table. She didn't look up as she packed it into its box. 'You can do anything when you're in love. Nothing fazes you. Be brave and let love make you strong. Once you let it into your heart, you could fly to the other side of the world, don't you think?'

Chapter 81

Dawn had to make an obligatory trip to her future in-laws on Thursday to finalize the times of the cars arriving. When did coming here become a chore? she thought as she walked up the path, narrowly avoiding a dried-up greyhound turd. Life had been so much less complicated when she had felt part of them all and craved their love. Why the hell had she to go and cement the arrangement in wedding cake? In saying that, Calum had been uncharacteristically tender since his stag do. Maybe getting tied to a lamppost had sent some blood rushing to the parts in his brain that dealt with demonstrations of affection.

'I know I've been a bit of a twat in the past, Dawn,' he'd said in bed that night. 'But I do love you. And I know you wanted to get married more than me and I went along with things, but now I do want to get married. Just think, in less than forty-eight hours now, we'll be man and wife.'

This new nice Calum made Dawn feel even more duty bound to go down that aisle. She almost wished he would slap her again – really hard this time – and give her an excuse to rise up and run, but he didn't. Instead, they had sex and she kept her eyes shut and faked her pleasure with tears trapped under her eyelids.

Chapter 82

'Are we all ready then?' said Christie.

'Yes, as we'll ever be,' said Grace.

'Well, to the pub we go then for our bride-to-be's hen night!' said Christie. She started striding down the office. They all heard the loud tut Malcolm made when Christie was level with the man himself, standing by his desk, arms folded, exuding resentment out of every pore.

She turned slowly to him. 'Is there anything you wish to say to my face, Mr Spatchcock?' she asked. 'Or maybe you'd prefer to mail it anonymously?'

Malcolm's eyebrows rose in two innocent, bushy arches. He hated the woman standing in front of him. He'd been in a meeting with McAskill that afternoon and the man had vetoed and pulled down his every proposal. He knew it was because he suspected he'd written the letter to his wife. There was no proof though, but he felt the venom towards him coming off McAskill in waves. He shouldn't have sent the letter, he realized, but he'd been driven to it by *her*. And now she was standing there like Lady Muck, making accusatory comments.

'No,' said Malcolm with a plastic smile. 'Do you have anything for me?'

'No,' said Christie.

'I have though,' said Anna. She cleared the two strides

between them and crushed Malcolm's testicles in one grinding upwards swoop of her knee. The action was fuelled from the mix of powerful, feminine, oestrogen-driven emotions flying around her system – all lumped together in one mighty leg arc of adrenalin.

'I think that says it all for us,' she said, slapping her hands together to signal a job well done as Malcolm crumpled into two, fell to the floor and groaned in soprano agony.

'Quick, move,' said Christie, gathering her troops and pushing them physically out of the door. 'Oh, Anna, what the heck did you do that for? He'll report you for sure.'

'After all you lot have done for me in the past couple of months, I owe you,' said Anna, making a note to wash her knee with some strong soap in the Setting Sun toilets.

They ate a Thai banquet as they had that night for Anna's birthday and had a second good chortle at the names of the dishes. And they raised a glass of champagne to Dawn, each wishing with all their hearts that she knew what she was doing. For once, Dawn was trying awfully hard to bubble about her wedding, saying how lovely her dress was and that her bridesmaids had promised to stay sober, at least through the ceremony. She looked unnaturally cheerful.

'Did you manage to get a honeymoon sorted out at the eleventh hour then?' said Grace, pouring the last of the champagne into Dawn's glass.

'No,' said Dawn. Alas, this new attentive Calum had been born too late to organize one, and half of Aunt Charlotte's money had gone now. Plus Muriel had been going mad and inviting the world and its bingo crowd to the reception, which would put paid to the rest tomorrow when she settled the final bill. Dawn hadn't volunteered her horse-race winnings which she had only just nibbled into. She would use that after the wedding to get some plastering done on those dangerous loose wires in the house. How thrilling. For now, it sat safely in her bank account with the half of Aunt Charlotte's money that Calum hadn't got his mitts on so far.

'Calum says he's going to take some time off next month and we'll see about getting a weekend away in Butlins or something,' she chirped on.

'Have you said goodbye to your cowboy?' said Anna.

That did it.

Dawn's head fell into her hands and she broke into an agonized sob.

'Oh, Dawny,' said Anna.

That made it worse. *He* called her Dawny. And he was going tomorrow. For good. Out of her life.

Christie's hand gripped hers. 'You know, if you're at that church door tomorrow and you don't want to go through with the wedding, we'll all be there to support you. You don't have to be afraid.'

Dawn's thoughts flicked to Freya. Even after what she had told her, Dawn knew she would walk down that aisle the following day, however many doubts she had. She knew she was pathetic.

'I'm sorry,' said Dawn, recovering and attempting to stick a smile back on, but it had lost its glue and it wasn't happening. She lied about the reason for her tears and fooled no one. 'It's just with Mum and Dad not being there. They so wanted me to have the big white wedding.'

'Darling, I'm sure your mum and dad would just want you to be happy, with or without a meringue frock,' said Grace. She above all knew how hard a loveless marriage could be.

'I will be happy,' Dawn said. 'I promise.' Freya at 'White Wedding' had said she would. And Dawn so badly needed something to hang her faith on.

Al Holly was having a drink at the bar when Dawn went in

later. Their gig was over, thank goodness, because she didn't think she could bear hearing their music and Samuel saying the words: 'Well, thanks for being so kind to us, folks. You've made us so welcome in Barnsley and we'll take your kindness back with us to British Columbia.'

Al Holly's back was broad and long and she wanted to press her cheek against it and feel its warmth through his black shirt.

He sensed her presence, turned around and gave her a smile. Not the usual cheerful, lazy smile that lit up his whole face but a reserved, gentle one.

'Dawny Sole, you came,' he said. 'I didn't see you out there, I thought maybe—'

'I came. To say goodbye,' she said, the words sticking to her throat on their exit as if they were barbed and hooked. 'I wouldn't have not come.' *I had to see you.*

'You missed my song,' he said. 'I played it as our last piece tonight. It's about a man who loves a woman he can't have.'

Dawn's lip trembled. What if she had heard him sing it? She would have crumbled, she knew. Fate had stepped in and put her on the straight and narrow by making the waitress lose the bill and keeping them all in the restaurant a quarter of an hour longer. But a huge part of her wanted to hear that song, she wanted to crumble and give in to what her heart was telling her to do.

'I'm sorry I missed that.'

'The bus leaves here at three p.m. tomorrow. You got' – he looked at his watch –'eighteen hours to change your mind and come with us. Girl, I would love you so much—'

'Don't say it, Al.'

His lips dropped to her ear.

'I love you, Dawny Sole. And you love me too because I kissed you and I felt your heart against mine and I *know*. Come home with me.'

'I can't.'

He kissed her cheek. A slow, soft kiss that ignited every cell, every nerve, every atom in her body. She would always remember that kiss as the saddest and most beautiful one she ever had.

'Goodbye, dear, lovely, sweet Al Holly. Be happy and safe always,' she said and turned, not looking back once, for then he would have seen the tears streaming down her face.

Chapter 83

'You look nice,' said Niki as Grace made an entrance into the kitchen in a navy suit that made her hair look like moonlight silver.

'Oh, thank you,' said Grace bashfully. She was fiddling with a necklace, unable to get the clasp to fasten.

'Here, let me,' he said.

She relinquished the necklace to his outstretched hand. She wanted to shiver as his finger lightly touched the back of her neck. He fastened it too quickly, she thought.

'There, you're perfect,' he said, looking at her square on.

'I wouldn't go that far.'

'Oh yes, Grace, you really are perfect,' he repeated, with deeper meaning.

Grace felt her cheeks heating. Niki was getting bolder with his compliments. She knew he would never take advantage of his house guest, he was far too much of a gentleman. But something dormant was being awoken within her every time he said her name. Grace found that the prospect of Nikita Koslov taking things one stage further was not an unwelcome one.

'Come here, you scruff. You've fastened up your buttons all wrong,' said Ben, pulling Raychel none too gently in front of him and re-doing the top two buttons of her new shirt. She had bought a bigger size than usual for she had put on half a stone over the past couple of months. Ben loved that she looked so much more womanly for it. He could have kissed those women she worked with for beefing her up a bit. And Elizabeth and John, with all those garden barbecues.

'Good job I have you,' Raychel laughed. While she was at the wedding, he was helping John put up a playhouse in the garden for young Ellis. She suspected John could have easily done it by himself, but he obviously wanted the young man's company. It was wonderful being part of such a lovely family. And having friends like the women she worked with. And she'd had a huge recent surprise when Elizabeth handed her a cheque for forty-two thousand pounds, apparently her share in some old forgotten family matured bonds that had been recently discovered. She had protested, but Elizabeth had insisted the money was hers by rights and forced her to take it. There was a lot of sunlight in her life now and just the one cloud left to clear – the identity of her true father. But today that thought was pushed into second place. Today was Dawn's Day.

'*Vino înapoi, în pat!* Come back to bed, my Anna!'

'Will you let me get up!' said Anna as Vladimir pulled her backwards into a bed that was full of rose petals and rolled on top of her to hold her down. She had once mistaken Tony's rampant sex drive for love and romance. It paled into insignificance beside this man who fed on her lips and did things to her body that would have seen her excommunicated from the Catholic Church if she'd given them up in confession. He was passionate and yet gentle and the quality was so good, any more than once a night and her brain would have blown out of her ears.

'Why are you leaving me? It's the weekend,' he said.

'Because a) I've got to feed the cat and b) I've got a wedding to get ready for and I'm already late because you insisted we have a chocolate breakfast in bed.'

'How can you leave a man who gives you truffles in the morning?'

'Because my friend is getting married,' said Anna. 'And my cat needs to eat.'

'I need to eat.' Vladimir started to feast on her neck. Anna groaned. Anything less than Dawn's wedding would have seen her resistance crumble.

'Stop that. I have to go. Oh God, please stop before I die!' said Anna, trying to struggle, but it was so very, very difficult.

'All right, I give in on this occasion,' he said, letting her go regretfully. 'I shall cook tonight for you. A traditional Romanian dish.'

'What's that then? Rare-roasted sacrificial victim?'

'My darling, never mock *Vampiri*,' he said, baring his teeth. 'They will kill you for less.'

'And what's their preferred method?' smiled Anna playfully.

'Death by a thousand nibbles,' said Vladimir, drawing his finger down her breast.

'Oooh – I'll hold you to that,' said Anna, sparkling.

Chapter 84

'Flaming heck, it's like a holding pen for *The Jeremy Kyle Show* in here,' said Anna as they sat in church, alone on the bride's side except for an old lady right at the back who kept coughing. They took her to be one of the distant aunts whom Dawn said might turn up.

But she wasn't. She was Mavis Marple, a regular feature at church 'specials', and her grey, unprepossessing appearance earned her natural acceptance in grieving or celebratory throngs. Mavis enjoyed the buzz of being a temporary guest of parties, blagging a lift to the venue of the post-service food and then hoovering up the buffet with seasoned aplomb. She even brought her own enormous serviette to transport some of the booty home.

The four women were all watching in amazement as the groom's side of the pews began to fill up with big women in gaudy dresses and scrawny teenagers, a few in smart trousers, most in jeans and trainers and even a few in hooded tops.

'Shh, Anna,' said Christie. 'The sound carries in these places.'

'Imagine if Anna had kneed Malc in the spuds in here,' said Raychel. 'You'd have heard the echo in Aberdeen.'

'He was long overdue for getting his cock spatched,' replied Anna.

That set them off giggling.

'Did you remember the money, Christie?' asked Raychel. They'd had a collection for Dawn instead of buying her a present.

'It's here in my handbag,' said Christie, patting her bright yellow bag. She was dressed from head to foot in lemon and looked like a walking sunshine. Which, coincidentally, was how the others saw her: a warm, wonderful force. Their centre.

Grace let her eye rove around the church. It was a beautiful building. She would be sitting here again within the year, watching Charles and Laura walk down the same aisle. They, and Paul, had come over on Thursday to break the wonderful news. Christie had opened a bottle of champagne and the women had sat on the patio watching Charles and Paul and Niki playing football with Joe. Like Christie, warmth seemed to ooze out of Niki's soul. It had been one of the smiliest evenings she could remember. It wasn't even sullied by the sad news that Sarah had decided to cut herself off from them, siding with her father. But then she didn't need them any more for babysitting duties, it seemed, as Hugo had invested in an au pair from the Eastern bloc. Very young, cheap to employ and pretty no doubt. Paul said that he could see trouble brewing already. Grace hoped Sarah would come round and had written her a letter. Maybe the new baby would help to heal the rift when it arrived. And Gordon would be out of hospital within the week too apparently, Paul carefully informed her. Grace had found she wasn't as nervous about that as she thought she might have been. But then she felt truly safe now, especially in the presence of solid, kind Nikita Koslov and his wonderful sister.

'Are you thinking what I'm thinking?' Christie nudged her as a very loud 'Fucking hell, shurrup will ya' travelled down from an usher at the back. Female as well.

'Probably,' said Grace with a sigh.

'Good grief!' said Anna as what could only be the groom's

mother marched to the front of the church in huge pink trousers, an ill-matching pink jacket and a black hat that looked like an overthrow from a funeral. There had been an attempt at coordination with black shoes and a black handbag, though it didn't quite work as an ensemble. She was wearing the sort of pink lipstick that made her lips look as though they had sustained third degree burns. All that and a spray-on tan that made her appear as if she'd been standing too close to a barbecue. She resembled an extra on *Shameless* who had just been dropped for being too rough.

The groom was easy to spot with his one eyebrow. He had a smart penguin suit on with a peach cravat. He looked designer-untidy and good-looking but not at all like any of them had imagined as a match for Dawn.

'That's never him, is it? Calum?' asked Anna, eyebrows raised to the max.

'I think it must be,' whispered Grace.

'I want to hijack Dawn at the door and run off with her,' said Anna. Sweet, daft, pretty, ethereal Dawn didn't belong with this lot. Surely?

'We may all be wrong, of course, and she'll be blissfully happy with him,' said Grace.

'Yeah, and the moon is made of Red Leicester,' said Anna.

The church settled. Five minutes ran over the allotted time, then a tinny 'Here Comes the Bride' made everyone's nerves ping, but it was only the best man's mobile phone going off.

He stood up and turned to everyone, throwing his stick-thin arms wide. 'Sorry folks,' he said, and turned the phone off. 'Killer, you pillock,' shouted someone from the middle, causing a low rumble of laughter.

Raychel wasn't sure if she should have been praying for Dawn to come to her senses and run off with that Canadian guitarist, but she did anyway in the silence.

Then the organ music started full pelt and with hearts full of all sorts of mixed emotions, the four friends stood and turned to see a veiled Dawn, a beautiful, tall Dawn in an exquisite gown and carrying a teardrop bouquet of peach flowers, walk slowly down the aisle. Tears bombarded their eyes. They tried not to look at the two bridesmaids in satsuma orange behind her, one with her cleavage pushed so up and out that it almost got to the altar before the bride.

They saw Dawn smile at them through the veil. It was the smile of a woman saying, 'Thanks for coming,' not a smile that said: 'This is the happiest day of my life.'

As she got to the altar, Dawn smiled back at Calum but inside she was screaming. She wished she had been brave enough to blurt out the truth to her friends last night when she had started crying into her jasmine rice. Why didn't she beg for them to help her while she had the chance? There was nothing for it now but to go ahead and get married because if she hadn't been brave enough or big enough to halt proceedings before, she wasn't going to be able to do it at this stage. If only someone else would do it for her. *Pleeease!*

'If anyone here prethent knowth why thethe two thould not be joined in holy matrimony, thpeak now or forever hold your peath,' lisped the vicar.

There were a few humorous coughs from the groom's side. The vicar scowled as Calum turned around to them and flicked the Vs, before remembering where he was and apologizing.

Had Dawn's four friends looked down, they would have seen that all of them had their fingers crossed. Each one was wishing or praying or calling to cosmic forces that if this wedding was going to be happy, let it go ahead. And if not, *please God,* let something stop it in its tracks.

In that prolonged silence, Dawn waited for Al Holly to throw open the door, stride down the aisle, pick her up and run out. But he didn't. The vicar began to speak again. Calum and

Dawn knelt at the altar. Someone had written 'SH' on Calum's left sole and 'IT!' on his right which set a lot of shoulders shaking. But Dawn wasn't laughing. She had switched onto automatic pilot, reciting vows that no longer meant anything to her, and was way past the point of caring that she would be damned for it. Her dress wasn't magical after all. How could she have believed that tripe Freya had spouted?

The bride and groom exchanged the rings they had picked from the Argos catalogue and the church erupted as Calum and Dawn were declared man and wife. Her four friends exchanged dry glances. That was that then. Dawn was married. For better or worse. It was done. As the bride and groom went to sign the register with the tangerine twosome trotting behind, the music began for the hymn, 'Guide Me, Oh Thou Great Redeemer.'

Grace's lovely voice cut through the out-of-tune cacophony as clear as a nightingale's. It was her favourite hymn. Privately Christian, Grace prayed every night and never doubted that He had pulled her through her darkest hours. She only hoped He would do the same for young Dawn. Anna's throat was full of tears and she had to mime her singing. It didn't help that Dawn emerged emulsion-white from the vestry door as the hymn ended on a dodgy descant from some cocky Crookes. She couldn't have been wearing a more fake smile if she'd tried.

The Crookes piled out of the church for the photographs, a huge percentage of them lighting up fags as soon as they got into the grounds. Anna saw the massive mamma in baby pink nudge the bride hard and tell her to, 'Cheer up, it's your bleeding wedding day!' No one suggested a picture of Dawn and her friends. It seemed the bridesmaids were directing the formations.

Christie drove in convoy with the others to the reception. The pub car park was full and she had to pull in on the road, but at least it would be easier to get out.

'I think there must be more people here than there were at Princess Di's wedding!' Grace commented.

'I think there must be more people here than there were at Princess Di's funeral,' said Anna.

'Yes, and I wonder how many of them Dawn actually knows,' replied Christie, accepting a small sherry from a waitress but passing on the 'canapés', a selection of Rubik's cube-sized pork scratchings, foot-long sausage rolls, potted beef sandwiches on quartered oven-bottom cakes and sizzling-hot roast potatoes that took the fingerprints off anyone who happened to pick one up.

The diners were squashed at the tables. Grace didn't verbally comment on the meal, but the eyes she raised to Christie as she lifted up the plastic slice of meat on her fork before putting it back down again didn't need accompanying words. Anna noticed the line of furry dust on the skirting boards behind her. Not the cleanest of holes, this place. Her eyes found Dawn and saw that her meal was virtually untouched. Calum was hooking up a piece of her meat onto his fork and she was telling him to go ahead. She looked like a Degas dancer on a Lowry background: totally and utterly out of place.

After the meal, when tar-strength coffee was served up, Calum said that he 'wasn't one for speeches so he was just going to toast the bride' and that was it. The best man more than made up for it with embarrassingly near-the-knuckle stories of Calum's past love-life that were meant to reassure the bride that Calum would never stray, but ended up doing quite the opposite, much to the amusement of the, by now, loud and swaying Crooke family and entourage.

People started to move into the main bar, Dawn included. She needed some air.

'Where are you off to?' said Muriel to the bride. 'I've got some aunties and uncles that want to meet you.'

'I'm off to the toilet,' said Dawn. 'I'll be back soon.'

'All right,' said Muriel, holding her glass up for Ronnie to fill. She was ticking off the minutes now to the karaoke.

On the wall, outside the toilet, there was a full-length mirror. Dawn passed it, then doubled-back and stared at herself. What looked back at her was the most miserable bride in the world, a truly unhappy woman. She would have no sweet memories attached to this dress. She could bag it up and return it tomorrow to Freya and not think twice about it. And she was sure Freya must have got her measurements wrong, because she could hardly breathe in it, it felt so tight around her body. *Be brave,* Freya had said. She hadn't been brave at all; she had been stupidly and idiotically weak. As in the words of that last hymn: *I am weak but Thou art mighty*. She might as well have been singing that line to the entire Crooke clan. She had been pushed and shoved and cowed and controlled by them all because she wanted their love and their acceptance, enough to lie down like a sacrificial lamb. And all she had really earned was their resentment for being such a walkover. She looked again in the mirror and her eyes sprang open. She was going barmy. Her reflection was dressed in white and the colour wasn't draining her at all because she looked tanned and healthy. She had a simpler affair on, ballerina length, cowboy boots, a Stetson and a waistcoat studded with rhinestones. Behind her was Al Holly, also in white. The smiles were bursting out of their faces because the couple in that mirror were in love. No woman should wear a wedding dress for a man she wasn't in love with and she knew she would never feel the way about Calum Crooke that she had grown to feel about Al Holly. *What am I doing?*

Oh, Dee Dee, what are you doing?

Dawn's eyes blurred over with tears and when she dabbed them dry with her fingertips the image had gone and she was Dawn in a floor-length ivory gown again, alone, crying.

Dawn didn't really need the toilet, she just wanted to escape a long line of Crooke second cousins three times removed. She did, however, desperately need to *breathe*. She felt as if all the oxygen had been sucked out of the whole building and replaced with something heavy and cloying.

Who's that man? The man in the hat?

Charlotte's words bounced into her head and suddenly Dawn understood what she had seen in that photograph.

We just want you to be happy.

'Oh God, can I? Dare I?' she asked the bride in the mirror. The bride nodded.

Dawn slipped out of the fire exit at the side of the toilet door and into the bright sunshine of the day.

Inside the toilet, Denise was reapplying her lipstick at the mirror, while Demi was squirting perfume down her cleavage.

'Killer looks well in his suit, doesn't he?' she said. 'I might have a go at him later when Liam isn't looking. Did you hear him coughing when they said "Anyone here know why these two shouldn't be wed"?'

'I half-expected Clampy to turn up at that moment.'

'I wouldn't have put it past her. Did our Calum 'fess up to Dawn in the end about him shagging her on his stag night?'

'I doubt it. He's never 'fessed up before, has he? Stupid git, he was cutting it too near the bone there.'

They both froze as they heard the flush in the end cubicle, which neither of them had noticed was occupied. Bending to take a fearful look under the gap at the bottom of the toilet door, they saw a flash of white material touching the floor.

'Shit!' mouthed Demi. 'It's Dawn. Out!'

She and Denise teetered outside, giggling nervously. Despite their promise to stay sober, they'd both had at least one bottle of Lambrini each since leaving the church.

*

At the other side of the car park, Dawn saw the welcome sight of Anna, Grace and Raychel clustered around Christie who was having a cigarette. Christie was trying to cut down and didn't smoke much these days, only when she felt the need to have a few calming puffs in her lungs. This was one of those days.

'Hello, love,' said Grace as the beautiful bride strode out towards them. 'Are you having a lovely day?'

'No,' said Dawn, desperately clutching at Grace's hands. 'Oh, girls, I've made the most dreadful mistake. Can you help me?'

'Are you serious?' said Christie.

'I've been pathetic, I know I have. I've married Calum because I was too scared to back out but I don't love him. I love Al Holly and he's asked me to go to Canada with him and I said no but I want to more than anything and I have to because he's the one in the photo and I've been ignoring my own feelings and what Aunt Charlotte said and what she saw and what my mum and dad were trying to tell me . . . I know none of this makes sense to you but it does to me because I've seen myself in the mirror and I know where I should be.' She took in a well-needed breath. 'Yes, I've never been more serious in my life. Help me!'

Christie dropped her lit cigarette to the floor and killed it with her yellow heel.

'Right,' she said. 'We'd best get cracking then, hadn't we?'

Chapter 85

They sprang into action like a well-oiled military elite force trained from birth for such manoeuvres.

'Get in the car,' said Christie, fishing out her keys from her yellow handbag. 'Quick.'

They moved as one into Christie's BMW, Grace in the front, the other three squashed up in the back with Dawn's frock, which was so big it almost constituted another person. They did a totally synchronized belt-up and Christie slammed the automatic gear lever into drive.

'Where am I going? Direct me!' she said, looking in her rear-view mirror at the pub. Their exit hadn't been spotted, despite the squeal of her wheels as she took the corner like James Bond.

'Is that the right time?' said Dawn, pointing to the clock on the dashboard.

'To the minute.'

'Oh Jesus. I'm going home first. Turn left here and follow. I'm picking up a suitcase, then I'm catching a bus.'

'Would this be a tour bus full of cowboys?' asked Raychel.

'Yes, it would.'

'Marvellous!' said Anna. 'What time does it leave?'

'I've got half an hour. Oh God, what will Calum's family say?'

They noticed she was more worried about his family than the man himself.

'Sod his bloody family. This is the time to think about your-self for once.' This from Anna.

'Am I doing the right thing?'

'God knows!' said Grace. 'But you're young enough to take a chance, love. And anyone looking at your face over the past few weeks could tell you were doing the wrong thing.'

'I should have stopped this wedding months ago!' said Dawn, dropping her head into her hands.

'Well, that's as may be,' said Grace. 'But you've stopped it now. We'd all be a lot wiser if we could visit our past selves.' As she knew only too well.

'I bet there's a hold-up,' said Dawn, because the traffic stream seemed to thicken as they hit town. But there wasn't. As if by magic, every traffic light either stayed on or turned to green at their approach. Christie broke the speed limit but reckoned the risk of a fine would be worth it.

'Right, stop at the second to the last house on your right!' commanded Dawn.

Christie screeched up to Dawn's front door. Raychel pulled Dawn out of the car because her frock was making it impossible for her to get out unaided. She was shaking too much to get the key in the lock so Grace snatched it from her and did the honours.

Led by Dawn, they flew up the stairs. Grace pulled two suitcases down from the top of the wardrobe. Anna emptied underwear drawers into them and threw hangers of clothes on top. Raychel was gathering shoes. Dawn's dress, by now, felt as poisonous on her as Hercules's shirt but there was no time to change.

'Where's your mobile and charger? Bank books? Make-up? Jewellery?' Grace said, thinking back to the important things she had needed to take from her own house.

Dawn opened a drawer and gathered up everything in it.

'It's all here!' she said.

'Is your passport in there?'

'Yep. Everything.'

'You are so beautifully, wonderfully, fantastically anal!' said Anna with a face-splitting grin. She gave Dawn a big smacking kiss on the mouth. God, she loved women! They were magnificent in a crisis.

'I just wish my thoughts were anything like as organized,' said Dawn. She grabbed her two guitars from the side of her bed and said, 'That's it. I've got everything I need. Let's go.'

She didn't even give the house a backward glance as they set off like a rocket in the direction of the Rising Sun.

Chapter 86

'Where's the bleeding bride?' said Muriel. 'Your Uncle Walter and Auntie Enid are ready for off and I've looked everywhere for her.'

'Dunno,' said Calum, who suddenly realized he hadn't seen her himself for a while. The bar had rather held his attention and all the back-slapping chat with his mates.

'Have you two seen her?' said Muriel to her much subdued daughters.

'Er, no,' said Demi, exchanging glances with her sister.

'What's up?' said Muriel. She'd never seen her daughters so quiet before.

'Nowt!' said Denise.

'What's up?' said Calum, suspiciously looking from sister to mother.

'Come on, out with it!' said Muriel, hands on her large, pink-clad hips. She carried on asking until one of them started to talk.

'It might be nothing, right,' began Denise hesitantly. 'But you know earlier when we came out of the toilet and asked you where Dawn was and you said she'd gone to the toilet—'

'Ye-es,' said Muriel, preparing herself. She couldn't tell where this was going yet, but it didn't sound too good so far.

'Well, we all must have been in the toilet at the same time—'

'Fucking wow,' said Calum, about to turn back to his mates. He hoped his sister never decided to write crime novels.

'Carry on,' said Muriel. Now her arms were folding which signified that she wasn't happy by a long chalk.

'Well, we didn't realize anyone was in with us—'

'Go on,' said Calum, all ears now. 'GO ON.'

'And we . . . we . . .' Demi was nearly crying now.

'We started talking about our Calum and Mandy Clamp on his stag night,' Denise ended the sentence for her sister.

'We aren't sure if it was her in there though,' Demi put in.

'Although whoever was in there had a long white frock on,' added Denise.

'Didn't you go back and check?' said Muriel, rubbing her forehead in disbelief.

'Er . . . no. We didn't think to.'

Calum swung around, clutching his hair.

'You didn't think to! Who else would have a long white frock on here? Some gate-crashing angel? Aarrrghh!' He flew at his sister but was dragged off before his hands made contact by Denise's bloke, Dave, who thumped the groom right in the jaw and sent him flying over the table.

'I don't care if it is your wedding day, mate, you don't fucking hit women.'

'They aren't women,' screamed Calum. 'They're thick, blabber-mouthed, idiot, marriage-wrecking tarts with shit for brains.'

'You're the one with shit for brains, you cocky twat! There's only the bride that didn't know you'd shagged Clampy on your stag do, so how long do you think it would have taken her to find out anyway?' Denise roared at him.

'No there wasn't, but they do know now don't they, you stupid cow!' said Calum, looking at the gob-smacked faces around him.

'Well, you should have kept it in your trousers, then there would have been nothing to tell, shouldn't you, wanker?'

Suddenly all hell was let loose. Denise lunged forward with her false nails in claw mode. Empty Head came to Calum's rescue and, by mistake, lamped Demi. Then Demi's new boyfriend, Liam, waded in with fists raised for anyone that moved before he was promptly flattened by Muriel's handbag. Then someone threw the top tier of the cake and Bette, trying to escape, slipped in it. The last sight Calum saw before he woke up in hospital with concussion was Bette's giant buttocks descending on his head.

No one noticed Mavis Marple and her big white serviette full of nibbles slip away. She had rested it on the floor, the food tied up safely inside, when she went to the toilet and heard those women talking about the groom and his stag night. Despite the plentiful supply of sausage rolls still available, this was one wedding that was just too rough for her.

Chapter 87

'So you're really going mad and doing it then?' said Raychel.

'Do you think I am mad?' said Dawn.

'I think this is the most sane you've been since I met you,' said Anna. 'Follow your heart, kiddo. Be brave.'

Be brave. That's what Freya had said. Was that the magic in her dress after all? Is that why it felt so tight and uncomfortable? As if it didn't want to be worn for an unhappy occasion? Anyway, if it was, it had worked. She couldn't wait to get it off, beautiful as it was. She would send it back to Freya with her compliments and hope that a future bride wore it for the right man. All that money wasted. And she didn't give a flying fart.

'Oh, and before we forget, here's your wedding present.' Christie fished in her pocket and dropped an envelope of cash into Dawn's lap. Then more fell on top of it as the girls emptied their purses onto her.

'No, I couldn't possibly—'

'Yes, you can, you'll need it,' said Grace.

'But it's a wedding present and I'm not really married.'

'It's for the next wedding.'

Dawn smiled a big wide arc that took up most of her face. Her whole heart seemed to swell up at the thought of getting married in cowboy boots. She knew she would. She'd seen it. She felt her mum and dad relaxing in heaven. They just wanted her to be happy and she jolly well was going to be. For all of them.

'Am I legally married now?'

'Yes,' said Christie. 'But I think you'll find it's voidable. Let a solicitor sort all that out for you. You just concentrate on being love's crazy cowboy young dream.'

'My head feels like a tumble-drier,' said Dawn, rubbing her temples. 'I'll never be able to thank you all for this. I can't believe I'm doing it.'

'Better late than never,' put in Grace.

'We all want signed CDs when you record those albums,' said Raychel, pressing her hand on Dawn's shoulder. Her touch felt so comforting that the tears rose to Dawn's eyes and she let them flow out because these were happy, sweet tears and they felt warm and welcome on her cheeks.

'I absolutely love you all to bits,' said Dawn. 'You've been like mothers and sisters to me. I'll miss you like hell.'

'We will miss you too,' said Anna. 'How will we cope without that mouth of yours and learning all about women who have sex with sheds? Oh God, now I'm filling up.'

'Hang onto your hats,' said Christie, stealing a look at the clock. It was showing 3 p.m. exactly and there was the tour bus in front, about to nudge out of the car park into the road.

Christie stamped her foot down on the accelerator, honking her horn like a mad woman, then she braced herself, hit the brake and her posh car skidded to a perfect stop alongside the bus.

'Oh hellfire, I'm stuck!' shrieked Dawn. The car door handle was lost somewhere in the folds of her dress and her very big handbag.

Raychel had to jump out and open Dawn's door from the outside. Anna applied leverage and pushed Dawn and her giant frock out of the car. She would have been wedged on the back seat for eternity without help.

Al Holly came bounding down the bus steps and froze as his feet hit the ground. His face bore all the signs of a man who thought he was hallucinating and if he moved the vision would disappear. Dawny Sole had thought she would fly into his arms but the opposite was true. She moved slowly towards him, her eyes locked on his. *How could I ever have thought I could live without him?* she asked herself.

'You're here,' he said in a croaky whisper. 'Is this a second goodbye?'

'No,' smiled Dawn. 'This is a great big fat hello.'

'Oh, Dawny.' His eyes glistened with emotion as his hand reached out to take hers, shyly, like a little boy and a little girl in the playground. 'I will make you so happy.'

'You better had,' said Anna from behind him, lugging one of Dawn's suitcases. 'Dawn, couldn't you get suitcases with wheels on like normal people?'

'I'm not normal,' grinned Dawn.

'You're telling us,' laughed Raychel, struggling with the other case.

Samuel hopped out of the bus and jokingly muttered about women really being the weaker sex as he lifted the cases effortlessly on board.

'Take good care of her,' said Christie to Al. 'Despite the fact that she's a nightmare and our nerves are in shreds and we will all need stress counselling after today, take really good care of her.'

'Yes, ma'am, I promise you that I will,' said Al Holly, wearing the sloppiest grin a mouth could form into. He put his arm around Dawn and squeezed her into his side. They fitted perfectly together and between them they were giving out vibes that could have fried a passing egg.

Then Dawn leaped forward and hugged each one of her friends in turn. Big squashy hugs full of happy strength. She saved the biggest one for Christie.

'You've been wonderful,' she said. 'I'll never forget all you've done.'

'Be happy, my darling girl,' said Christie. 'Go and be loved and enjoy every minute of it.'

'Take care, I'll miss you so much,' Dawn beamed, blowing them all a big kiss. 'I love you all. I'll be in touch, I promise.'

'You better had be,' said Anna. 'You barmy cow.'

Al Holly took Dawn's hand and pulled her gently onto the bus and they saw Dawn's grinning face framed in one of the windows as the bus engine started up. The four women stood and watched it drive away and grow smaller as it travelled down the road. Their arms were sore from waving by the time it had disappeared.

'Whoever said that life was dull in Barnsley ought to come and live here for a bit,' said Raychel.

'What now? Shall we go back to the Dog and Duck and get some cake?' said Anna with innocently raised eyebrows.

'Well, I don't know about you three, but I think a glass of champagne might be in order.'

'I've got no money,' said Anna. 'I've just tipped my purse into Dawn's hand.'

Christie smoothly produced a Visa card from her sunny bag.

'Who needs cash these days?' she said.

Epilogue

27 June – The following year

Anna stood in the walled garden behind Darq House in a sumptuous black gown and closed her eyes. She pulled the fragrance from the red, red flowers that she carried into her lungs and sighed with contentment.

'You all right, love?' said Christie, dressed also in black, a much shorter ensemble with fancy ruffs at the sleeves and neck. Her own inimitable style. Even in black she looked colourful.

'Ohhh, yes,' said Anna.

'Such a beautiful day too,' said Christie, tipping her head upwards. The sun was gently lowering, its edges melting into the blue of the sky. The Pennines stood misty in the distance.

Grace wended her way towards them, carrying a bottle of Dom Perignon. Behind her, Raychel followed with four glasses. Both of them were in stylish black suits too.

'Do you remember this date last year, we were drinking champagne then too?' said Christie as Grace poured her a glass.

'When Dawny became Mrs Crooke.'

'And now she's Mrs Holly and singing her little heart out.'

They kept in regular touch and, thanks to the wonders of webcam, they could see that smile still bursting out at them from the screen. It was a smile that they suspected was like the sun and never went out.

'Beautiful ceremony,' said Grace, sipping the cool, sparkly champagne.

'Absolutely!' said Raychel. 'And you look gorgeous, Anna.'

'Thank you,' smiled Anna. She felt gorgeous too. She was *only* in her forties and she was going to look back on this decade some day with the sure and certain knowledge that she had sucked it dry.

'Hear hear,' added Grace.

'There were some fantastic black dresses in the congregation,' said Anna.

'Oh, hark at her! She's gone all fashiony already. She's only been Mrs Darq for two hours and she's turned into Zandra Rhodes.'

'Great idea having a black wedding,' said Raychel.

'Aye well, that's what happens when you marry one of the undead.'

'Is he undead, really?' asked Raychel.

'Some parts of him are very much alive,' said Anna with a cheeky smirk.

To the rest of the world, Vladimir Darq was an enigma, a mystery and a businessman par excellence, thanks to his amazingly successful lingerie range. The Darqone creation alone was judged to be a wardrobe basic for over one-fifth of the female population in Britain, and it had taken America by storm since its Christmas launch.

Anna alone owned the man who liked to watch Harry Potter films with home-made popcorn and waltz with her in the garden. Still, there were plenty of 'darq' things about him to keep even Anna intrigued. His skills in the bedroom were out of *this* world, that was for sure.

Anna patted the bump at the front of her dress, where her baby was snug and warm and growing.

'Christie, come round for dinner next week while Grace and Niki are away. I'm obviously not going anywhere in this state. Don't be lonely.'

'I will do that,' said Christie. She winked at Grace. Grace who was going to be cruising around the Mediterranean for a fortnight with her brother. Nikita Koslov was ready to make up for a lot of lost time. Grace was both nervous and giddy about the impending trip. Shopping for fancy underwear for the first time at fifty-six had been a revelation. Especially when you took your son and his new partner along to help you choose it. But Grace had learned from young Dawn that when a chance at happiness came, to grab onto it with both hands.

The money from her divorce was finally through and a lavish spending spree for cruise clothes did her good. Gordon had been, as expected, hideously uncooperative in their divorce in the beginning. Unexpectedly, it had been Sarah who had convinced him to let go and be reasonable. His first act as a divorcé was to move permanently into his Blegthorpe caravan.

'What date have they given you for the baby?' asked Raychel.

'October the thirty-first,' sighed Anna. 'As if it could be anything else. What about you?'

'Feb fourteenth. As if it could be anything else!' Raychel grinned back. She felt positively euphoric today because this had been the first day she hadn't been sick. She hadn't realized morning sickness lasted all day, but she didn't really care because she was having the baby she never thought she and Ben would dare to conceive. The Siddalls were a big and sprawling family and loads of them were living in Barnsley. Thanks to Elizabeth's persuasion, Michael's twin sister had been willing to provide some DNA to test, once they had assurances they wouldn't be sued by the CSA, and yes, there was a match. That meant that Raychel was not a child of incest as she had believed all her life. Michael wasn't exactly perfect dad material, being in prison for armed robbery, but Raychel had no intention of building relationships with strangers. She had all the family she wanted in Elizabeth, John, Ellis, Ben and the women now surrounding her.

'I'm going to have to have a big reorganization in my depart-ment,' tutted Christie. 'Everyone will think I'm a boss from hell because my staff are leaving me in droves!'

'Give over, there's a queue of applicants to work with you,' smiled Raychel. 'And I hope you don't replace me because I'll be coming back after my maternity leave. Least I won't have Malcolm staring as my boobs get bigger and bigger.'

Malcolm was long gone. He'd tried to report Anna for crushing his conkers, but as James McAskill said, with a totally exposed sparkle of *Schadenfreude*, 'There was no proof.' Malcolm wasn't about to leave things there, but there *was* proof, however, that he'd squeezed a young typist's bum. What her father did to Malcolm made Anna's knee work to his knackers look like foreplay.

Anna topped up her glass. 'I think I'm allowed this. The baby won't object, will he?' She smoothed her hand over the front of the wedding gown that her husband had designed for her. Underneath it, she was wearing a loose but incredibly sexy pregnancy corset. Vladimir had made it very easily rippable-off at the back.

'A toast,' said Christie. 'To Anna and her new husband and all the lovely babies to come.'

'And to us,' added Anna. 'To women, because we're bloody marvellous.'

'To friends,' said Raychel.

'Both here and absent ones busy playing guitars,' added Grace.

They all raised their glasses to each other. Then to the West. To Canada. To the Sun.

Acknowledgements

A big warm thank you to the following.

To my agent Darley Anderson and his Angels, my editors Suzanne Baboneau and Libby Yevtushenko and my publicist Nigel Stoneman, whom I drive insane on a regular basis, but I appreciate more than I can say.

To my old mucker 'Super'-intendent Pat Casserly for patiently filling me in on police technicalities and procedures – all mistakes are mine!

To my greetings card buddies – Alec Sillifant, Paul Sear, Fraz Worth and Pete Allwright for support and well-needed chuckles during the 'Robert de Niro' weeks. And Freya Halvorsen for her essential music at *myspace.com/freyahalvorsen* which soothes the most savage of beasts (i.e. me, according to the kids!).

To my pals – Cath Marklew, Maggie Birkin, Tracy Harwood, Rae Hobson and Judy Sedgewick – I'm so lucky to have you. And to master photographer and substitute brother Chris Sedgewick at *www.untitledphotography.co.uk* for taking the only pictures of me that don't make me want to open a vein.

To Mr Gary 'Jaws' Tiplady at *www.garytiplady.co.uk* for being a giant in every sense of the word and giving my family such fun Bond memories to treasure – plus a stockpile of material.

To the *Barnsley Chronicle*, the *Yorkshire Post*, the *Sheffield Star*, the *Barnsley Eye*, Sadie Nicholas, and the very dashing Darryl Smith at the *Sunday Post* for the amazing press support. And to the *bellissima* Franca Martella, Gareth Evans and all the BBC Radio Sheffield crew – who are like my family after all this time (you poor buggers!).

To Dr Peter O'Dwyer who knows I'm mental but has always made me feel more like a tortured genius. You've been a total brick over the years – love, good luck and much happiness to you.

To Camelia Popescu and Jaiken Struck of Kwintessential for being a brilliant translation service. Thanks to you I can now swear in Romanian as well as seduce any passing vampires. And to the super Heidi Sheeran at TalkbackThames for helping me with film-crew details in record time before little Anna arrived.

To my writer mates, Sue 'Dalai Lama' Welfare, Louise Douglas, Tara Hyland, Jane Elmor, Katie Fforde, the world's best poet James Nash and the beautiful Lucie Whitehouse for not only being my friends but writers that I'm truly in awe of. As are my New Romantic buddies – Lucy Diamond, Sarah Duncan, Matt Dunn, Kate Harrison and JoJo Moyes. Thank you for letting me into your gang *www.thenewromantics.org*. I'm honoured to be in such illustrious company.

To Stu Gibbins who is the best designer of websites I have ever met, but I don't tell him that in case he puts his prices up. His address is *sg@sn4s.com* and he's a smasher.

To Lynsey Thompson at Toni & Guy because I can't live without her magic scissors!

To 'my fellow Gateway Plaza owner' Martin Brook and Matthew Stephenson of The Brook Group. Richard Ward and Dean Cook of Bapp Industrial Supplies, David Sinclair of the Civic, Jill Craven of the Library, Louise Weigold of the Lamproom Theatre and 'Mrs Barnsley' Mel Dyke for being truly supportive Patrons of the Arts in our town. We have so much talent here and thanks to them, people are starting to realize we are more than flat caps and whippets – at long last!

To Emma Bruce and Wayne Smith at Morrisons and Mike Bowket and Celia Chappell at Reedmoor Distribution for giving me the sort of backing that authors usually only dream of.

To my P&O mates, Liz, Elle and Wayne 'Mr Bump' Baister, who own the most essential clothes shops on land – *www.bertie.co.uk* – and, at sea, supply me with so many laughs that I could write a book every day in their wonderful company.

To my absolutely wonderful *Come Dine With Me* fellow chefs for the most rock 'n' roll week I've ever spent, Phil Davies, Paul Hoyle, Verene Farrell and Christian Whiteley-Mason. And to the crew lovelies, Natalie Watts, Nicole taylor, Nicola Cornick, Laura Harding, Hugh Lambert, Martyn 'The Bear' Brake, Russell Scoltock and Steve Grealey. And to my fabulous florist friend Gail Lawrence. You've all given me yet another book to write.

And last, but by no means least, to my family: my lovely mam and dad – Jenny and Terry Hubbard, who are always there for me. And my cheeky, funny, fast-growing sons, Terence and George, who make me smile, drive me nuts and fill up my heart with sunbeams.

I think you're all ace.

**POCKET
BOOKS**

If you enjoyed *A Summer Fling*, you'll love these other
fabulous novels from Milly Johnson. These books and
other **Pocket Books** titles are available from your local
bookshop or can be ordered direct from the publisher.

978-1-84739-282-4   A Spring Affair   £6.99

978-1-41652-591-2   The Birds and the Bees   £6.99

978-1-41652-590-5   The Yorkshire Pudding Club £6.99

Free post and packing within the UK
Overseas customers please add £2 per paperback
Telephone Simon & Schuster Cash Sales at Bookpost
on 01624 677237 with your credit or debit card number
or send a cheque payable to Simon & Schuster Cash Sales to
PO Box 29, Douglas Isle of Man, IM99 1BQ
Fax: 01624 670923
Email: bookshop@enterprise.net
www.bookpost.co.uk

Please allow 14 days for delivery. Prices and availability
are subject to change without notice.